MW01106163

SLUMBERSCYTHE

Vance Bastian

Slumberscythe

A Novel of the Outré War

Book One

Rogue Ravens
Publishing

Published in the United States by Rogue Ravens Publishing.
www.rogueravens.com

Rogue Ravens Logo designed by Cloo Stevenson
Author photo by Alexandra Schaefer Karvala

First Edition
2 4 6 8 10 9 7 5 3 1

ISBN: 978-0-9912806-7-4
eISBN: 978-0-9912806-9-8

Library of Congress Control Number: 2014920582

This story is dedicated to Jason for providing support in every way imaginable... even when I was too proud to ask for it.

CHAPTER ONE
1972 – SOMEWHERE IN AMERICA

I'm a woman this time. That's a first. She's a young adult, and I can feel that she's good at what she does... which is to say I think she sleeps with men to gather information for her... what? Her Country? Her Company? Her Family? The context of "for whom" is muddled in this particular dream.

The car, I'm pretty sure it's hers, is rocketing along. I suddenly know she's going to meet with the head of her agency... family... whatever. She checks her makeup in the mirror. It's perfect. She's going for the right combination of professional woman and groovy go-go dancer. She tilts the mirror to double-check that her blouse is unbuttoned just enough to show the upper curve of cleavage. Satisfied, she looks back at the mirror. Looking directly into her own brown eyes, she says, "Remember," and pushes an emotional spike of energy out with the word. In that instant, everything comes sharply into focus, colors brighten, and any vestige of dream fuzziness vanishes completely. Satisfied again, she returns her attention to the road. She is leaving the city, though I can't tell which one. Traffic is moderate, but moving normally. About twenty minutes later, she has her sapphire Chevelle on the open highway. She kicks off the toe-pinching heels and pushes down on the accelerator, thrilled at the feeling of the engine's vibration on her bare foot through the silky nylons.

Somewhere in the country, she turns at a gold and red barn and shoots down an unmarked country road. Snaking between several copses of trees, she comes upon a gate with a guardhouse. Within the context of this dream, she brings to mind one of her own recent dreams and mentally pushes it at the guard. A small glowing light zips from her forehead towards him. Against all logic, he catches it in his hand. He inspects it, then gives her the thumbs-up as he opens the gate and waves her through. While I try to puzzle out what that dream exchange had to do with a security checkpoint, she blows him a kiss and guns the engine.

A couple miles deeper in, she comes to the complex. It had once been a large farm, and many of the original buildings are still intact and in service. However, a two-story office building has been added behind the barn. It feels more out-of-place due to the attempt to hide it than it would have been if it'd just been along the road. Driving into the barn, she puts her heels back on and checks her makeup again while the floor beneath her car slowly descends to an underground parking facility. Pulling into a spot I knew to be hers, she quickly grabs her briefcase and heads for a tunnel that will take her to the area of the complex beneath the house.

Several checkpoints later, she's telling a receptionist, "I'm here to see Section Chief Morpheus." I can't tell if I laughed in the real world, but I should have. Though she utters the name without a glimmer of humor, I can't help but be amused at the triteness of it. I feel myself almost waking, though I somehow know there is more to see here. I focus back in on the dream and try to ignore my personal reactions.

She is ushered into a paneled office. Again, it's all very stereotypical of the seventies, but I feel her acceptance of it as a very stylish and sumptuous room. The man seated behind the desk would never have stood out in any era. Brown hair in a short cut, he has no glasses, no dominating emotion or expression, and wears only a plain blue suit. "Agent Sopora," he addresses her, "thank you for coming."

As with other aspects of her life, I somehow know she couldn't have turned down his request to meet, but he often insists on politeness from his agents. "Of course, Chief." Everything I've seen so far hints at this agency being more espionage than military.

"Your unique talent, it seems, has you in high demand. Now it's my turn to put it to good use," her chief continues.

I have the feeling she knows what unique talent he's referring to. Unlike other aspects of her life, knowledge of this talent does not come to me. She only nods that he continue.

He pulls a tied bundle of stuffed-full manila folders out of a drawer and pushes it all across the desk toward her. "I trust you're fully briefed on current political events? One of our more reliable dream oracles at Tivoli has seen that most of the political murders in Africa have a connection, a strong one."

Dream oracle? Again, within the dream she isn't fazed by that part of the statement, but my interest is piqued by the mention of oracles and Africa. A man named Morpheus talking about a dream oracle may be utterly normal to this Agent Sopora, but come on… I nearly wake up again because of the humor in it.

"Annoyingly, we don't have much more information," he continues, "but then oracles aren't known for helpful specifics.

We'd like you to familiarize yourself with these files. Your mission is to ascertain any possible Outré involvement. Once you have confirmed or denied that possibility, you are to contact your handler. Further action will be determined based on your findings."

Outré? Confusion over that word hovers in my semi-consciousness. Back in the dream, she pulls the bundle of folders closer, "What's my cover?"

The chief lets out a long sigh. "You will be in and out of regions that are unfriendly to women. Your usual cover won't get you far. Foreign business women aren't taken seriously. However, wealthy traveling women are somewhat respected as the wives of wealthy husbands. So you get a posh stay at the region's finest tourist palaces, an expensive ring for your finger, and invitations to several of the most elite venues. You will ingratiate yourself to the people in those files, and you will keep your aura hidden while you search for the possible involvement of Outré. If you find a lead, you will sleep with them and extract the information you need to complete the mission as defined. Make note of any clues and oddities regarding suspect individuals, but take no further action without your handler's knowledge. Do you have any questions?"

"No Chief. I'll read these on the flight tonight and be prepared when the plane touches down."

"Do us proud, Sopora."

She flashes a dazzling smile as an answer. I get a sense that smile is part of her arsenal. She then leaves with the folders. As she walks down a corridor, she starts rehearsing the mannerisms and personality of a wealthy wife traveling alone to see the wonders of the world. She makes her way through several halls and past another checkpoint. The décor is an odd fusion of successful seventies corporation and functional starkness.

Arriving at the lounge that's been her destination, she absentmindedly waves at the other occupant while she starts looking through the files. All had been leaders in Africa in the past several years, and all had been assassinated in 1969. Eduardo Mondlane murdered in Tanzania, Tom Mboya murdered in Kenya, Abdirashid Ali Shermarke murdered in Somalia, and Mutesa II of Buganda murdered in London. The last one grabs Sopora's attention as the only killing that didn't take place in Africa. It was also the last of the four chronologically.

Something snags Sopora's attention. She lifts her eyes, and therefore my thoughts, up out of the file with its newspaper clippings and mimeograph copies of various reports. The other man in the lounge is looking at her thoughtfully.

"Agent Bruadair?"

He smiles thinly, "You're being sent on something really important, aren't you, Sopora?"

"You know we're not supposed talk about it. How have you been?"

He looks at her deliberately thoughtful, "Doesn't it seem odd that we can't talk about our missions with each other? We're not the government, we're not holding national secrets, and given the ethereal nature of our abilities we might even have useful insight for one another."

I feel her nodding at the familiarity of this, "You know I agree with you. I'm just not going to break the rules."

"I know you're not, but I am going to continue to try. As for how I am? I'm glad you asked... I get to go sleep with a Nobody who may have seen a Somebody do a big Something.

The Nobody refuses to tell the authorities what she knows, so I'm being loaned out to retrieve the information from her after I find a way to get her to sleep in my presence. You know what that makes me?"

His vehemence hits her hard, and I suspect that Sopora may have had a relationship with him at one point. She just steels herself so her voice won't shake and says, "It makes you a Sandman agent, Bruadair. You know very well that if I couch my mission in your vague terms that's exactly what I've been assigned to do as well."

"We're perfect for each other," came his bitter reply. "No, correction. You're too good for me. YOU can hide your aura, so that makes YOU the favorite agent around here. So YOU get all the special training. And YOU get all the high profile assignments."

She begins gathering up her files. I sense that his extremely negative emotions probably won't let her focus on the tasks at hand. As she stands, she tries one last time to soften his mood, "You know we're not prisoners. If it really bothers you so much, you can leave. You'll receive a stipend in exchange for your silence about all things Outré. I'm staying because deep down I believe that when we find something useful, it's turned over to authorities who in turn try to make the world a better place." She pauses looking for the next thing to say. "Best success on your mission should you choose to undertake it."

He doesn't reply, and she doesn't feel as though she expects him to. Instead she offers one last smile and makes her way to the door. "I need to visit Anoushka and put together my travel items."

The negative feelings of Bruadair's emotion fade as she gets closer to the Fulfillment Department. I sense Sopora's genuine excitement at seeing Anoushka, and can't help but look forward to it myself. When she arrives, the first male secretary I've seen in the Agency tells her to "Go in, she expects you."

Sopora opens the door and walks in smiling. Her emotions are so strong that in the real world, I realize that I am also looking forward to meeting Anoushka. She is tall, calm to the point of serene, and completely comfortable her black zip-up bodysuit that looks like something right out of a 1960s spy show, right down to the heeled boots. Her features and lustrous black hair look like they are mostly Hindi, but there is a touch of something else I can't identify in them.

She is the only point of serenity in the room, which is saying something. It looks as though several costume trucks collided behind and around her. The chaotic disaster of un-categorized stuff threatened to engulf the small warehouse. There is a table near the door, and a few items have already been gathered there. In Sopora's quick glance I pick out a nice purse, a couple of evening gowns, a wallet, and a small packet of white pills.

"Anoushka!" Sopora moves forward and offers her friend a hug. Anoushka lowers her clipboard and returns the greeting warmly.

"Sopora, you did not sit idle for long. Already I get word that you are leaving and we've not even been to the coffee shop for some of those scones." Her voice is warm and musical. She doesn't have a noticeable accent, but her voice is very comforting. I know Sopora hears her voice often, but I swear I've heard it too. I can't place it, but I'm immediately comforted by it.

"And I fear I shall be gone even longer this time. Two continents this time, while looking for something people want to keep hidden. I'll bring something back for you."

Anoushka makes pouty lips, but then breaks into a wide smile, "Well you'd better not use Agency funds on buying gifts. They have annoying ways of finding out."

"I'll be good. I promise. You received the usual briefing?"

She holds up her clipboard, "You mean the usual vague and useless write-up that is utterly lacking in any detail that would help me outfit you for your cover? Then yes, it's right here."

"I'll be a wealthy American wife traveling alone. One target in England, three targets in Africa."

"Have you decided what your husband does to make this money? It would affect some of your belongings."

"Not yet, do you have any thoughts?"

"Your southern accent is terrible, so I'm ruling out oil baron."

The worse southern belle imitation rolled out of Sopora's mouth, "Oh, come on sugar, it ain't that bad."

Anoushka cringed theatrically. "Yes, it is. You would never be able to sustain it. Most foreigners assume American East Coast money comes from newspapers. But anyone with secrets will shy away from people tied to newspapers. Likewise, West Coast money is assumed to be from Hollywood. If you claim he is an actor you had better be ready to talk about his roles and movies. A famous director, an auteur, would be respected but not known overseas, though you still might have to talk about his movies. Midwest money is perceived to come from department stores. Personally, I would choose this one. You and I both love a good shopping trip, it is reasonable he had to stay home to manage the opening of a new store, and it's unlikely any of your targets will have the curiosity and desire to ask you about an American department store that isn't Macy's."

I don't know why I'm impressed with Anoushka's insight, but it shows she has a quick mind for thinking these things up. Sopora, it seems, agrees with me, "While there are a lot more avenues to American money, you're right. I need them talking about themselves and not asking me questions about my famous husband. A boring merchant he is!"

Making some notes on her clipboard, Anoushka turns to the chaos behind her and takes it all in for a minute. She then motions that Sopora follow her into the pandemonium down one of the aisles. She doesn't say much, but it doesn't feel like Sopora expects her to. Sopora just carries the items her friend hands her. When her arms are full, she delivers the items to the table and returns for more. I have a strange sensation that Sopora loves this exercise, as though it is a surrogate for shopping. Ironically, I hate shopping in real life and my feelings threaten another emotional disconnect that nearly wakes me from the dream.

After the table holds enough expensive-looking outfits for several weeks' worth of travel Anoushka turns and says, "I have the appropriate amount of cash in the wallet, along with two credit cards. Knowing you would be American, I took the liberty of starting the documentation for your identity as Deborah Gardner. I will finish it today with the rest of the information we have created here."

Bam! Hearing my own last name as Sopora's cover identity's last name is a punch to the gut. Once again, I nearly snap out of the dream. Only the strength of my sudden curiosity cements me to what's unfolding.

"Since we're creating a husband out of thin air, can we name him Clint?" Sopora asks, not filling in any blanks for me at all.

Anoushka shakes her head, "That will stand out. Besides, it does not convey the image of a boring merchant. I was going to suggest Gerald."

Sopora scrunches her face in dislike. "Please, Anoushka, please, please, please do not betroth me to a Gerald." She immediately needles her friend, "If you do, sugar, Ah swear Ah'll simply have to burn mah'self in protest!"

Anoushka merely raises one eyebrow. I try to mentally will her to return to the name Gardner, but my role as an observer prohibits me from changing what transpires.

Unaware that I need to know more Sopora continues her threat, "Ah mean it! Ah'll pretayend Ah was born in Georgia an' mah daddy done wed me off to some Yankee for a big'ol hunka caysh!"

Her serene countenance finally cracks and Anoushka laughs. "Fine, no Gerald. But no Clint either. You must choose a third name somewhere between the two."

Sopora thinks it over a while and blurts out, "Charles."

Anoushka approves and writes it onto her clipboard. "I'll make sure Charles Gardner, the founder of a Midwest department stores stands up to scrutiny as well as just being the source of all your money. What about weapons?" Every time one of them says Gardner I take another punch to the gut. She doesn't need weapons, Anoushka. My own last name is killing me. I can feel my anxiety ratcheting up.

"I don't think I should carry one. Deborah wouldn't have one, and I'm not to engage without further orders. If I need one, I'll find one in the field.

More notes on the clipboard. "First target?"

"Get me to London, and a room at the Dorchester. I've always wanted to stay there, and it'll solidify Deborah's apparent wealth. I'll hire transport from there as fits Deborah's plans."

"That should be enough for me to complete your Legend. I will have everything dropped to you via courier. Remember, when you return from this you owe me two scones and two cups of coffee."

"I don't forget these things."

"Neither do I."

They hug again and Sopora leaves Anoushka to do her job.

Knowing there is nothing left for her to do on the farm, Sopora makes the decision to leave and wait for the courier.

Back in her Chevelle, she drives onto the car lift to wait for it to rise. In her side mirror, she notices Agent Bruadair hurry into the garage and look around. He sees her car and starts towards her at the same time the lift began to ascend. She could probably move the car slightly and the lift's safety measures would sense it and return down. Instead, she pretends she hasn't seen him and continues the ride up. Above ground, she drives quickly to put as much distance as she can between herself and Bruadair's negativity, and she's out of the complex in no time.

At the gold and red barn on the highway, she turns away from the city and travels another mile or so, pulling up to what looks like a family-style restaurant. The sign shows the profile of a small red deer and announces the name The One-Eyed Roe. Instead of parking in the lot, she drives around back and parks her little car in the carport of a trailer home quietly snuggled behind the diner. She covers her car with a tarp, making sure no part can be seen from the stretch of road that is visible.

Heading inside, she seats herself in one of the smaller booths, pours herself a glass of water from the silver pitcher on the table, and waves familiarly at the woman behind the cash register. The lady is on the far side of middle age, with the look and demeanor of a friendly matron. Her brown and steel colored hair is piled in large curls high on her head, and her fingers and teeth are both stained from a lifetime of smoking. She sets her cigarette in an ashtray next to the register, goes to the far side of the counter where she pours a mug of black coffee from a percolator. She reaches into the bakery case and pulls out a scone, puts it on a plate, and brings the food and drink over.

"I saw it last night in my dreams. They're sending you on a four-stop trip," she says with such familiarity I wondered if she's merely continuing a conversation.

"They are, Margaret, and I think it's the most globally important assignment they've given me yet."

The older woman slides into the booth across from her and takes her hands. "Dear, it is and it isn't. The motivation isn't global at its roots, though what you uncover will ultimately help the world. The desires I sensed last night were personal. Oh, I wish I could be more specific, honey. But I didn't get more detail than that. I just want you to be careful that you don't get caught in a crossfire that has nothing to do with you."

She looks into Margaret's kind green eyes and sees concern and hope.

Sopora breaks off a piece of the scone and lets the buttery goodness sit on her tongue a second, focusing on remembering that flavor. I feel another emotional shift, and the dream's clarity changes. I suddenly somehow know that Margaret has spent her life hiding from the Sandmen, and that she is the one who helped Sopora learn to hide her aura. I realize Sopora specifically wants me to know about that. Looking into the older woman's eyes, she is intentionally forcing me to share her memories of day after day meetings in the kitchen of this diner. Day after day of Margaret saying, "Your power leaks from your pores like a vapor, honey. You've got to swirl those vapors around you and breathe them back in so nobody else senses them. Take a drink of cold water and try again."

To punctuate these memories, Sopora braces herself and takes a large gulp of ice cold water. I feel a strange, ethereal energy swirling around her being pulled in tight. I somehow know that what frustrated her was Margaret's command to 'breathe it back in.' That imagery didn't work for her, so she cast about for one that did.

Still looking into Margaret's eyes, Sopora forces me to see the memory of the day it finally worked. The day she didn't so much breathe it back in, as swirl it around her in a small vapor storm of power and then pull it back into her pores, locking the power down with a skin-tight layer of pure willpower.

Margaret's eyebrows shoot up, as though she suddenly realized what Sopora is remembering and it surprises her. Where most people would have asked, Margaret instead looks around sharply. Not seeing anything alarming, she looks like she's letting herself lose visual focus, but her eyes move back and forth even though they're not seeing anything in the physical world.

"Someone's watching?" Margaret declares somewhere between a question and a statement.

"Yes, Margaret, but it's someone I invited." She is keeping me from Margaret. But I'm aware that she's keeping something from me too. There is something she is locking down, some piece of information that is so important she can't let either of us know it. The knowledge, whatever it is, rests in the strongest mental lockbox she can create.

Margaret looks at her a moment longer. Her gaze is neither critical nor demanding. I don't realize she's still holding Sopora's hands until she lets go and pats the backs of them lovingly. She may not have all the information, but she understands and supports it. And that's enough.

Sopora lowers her eyes for a moment, looking into the steam coming off the coffee. "Thank you."

"Of course, honey. When you're ready for my help, you have only to ask. You know that."

"I know, and I am most grateful for that as well."

She senses the older woman lean on the table to stand up. Looking up, she offers a half smile. It's returned with a warm, beaming smile. I have a brief moment where I wish Margaret had been my mother, but I can't tell if it's an echo of Sopora's wishes, or my own yearning for the birth parents I'd never been able to find. I realized that all those feelings came rushing back when Anoushka had given Sopora my last name.

A brief second later, Margaret's eyes snap up and scan the parking lot. "That man is pulling up. He comes here looking for you a lot, you know."

"I'm not surprised. He tried to get under my skin at the complex today. Do you think you can hold his attention for a few minutes while I slip away?"

"Of course, honey. If he's nice to me, I might even diffuse some of that anger for him."

"It appears my debt to you keeps growing."

"Just you shoo. We can finish catching up later."

Sopora throws the scone into her purse and decides to leave the coffee untouched. Keeping low, she scoots around the counter and out the back through the kitchen. She pauses, making sure to time the opening of the kitchen door with the diner's front bell, and the closing of the kitchen door with the closing of the front door. Quickly uncovering her car, she speeds out of there as fast as she can without loudly gunning the engine. In her last view of the diner she glimpses Margaret hold a menu up to Bruadair and point out one of the options.

CHAPTER TWO
2012 – MILWAUKEE, WISCONSIN

"JAMES!"

My head snapped up at the sharpness in my boss's voice. Six people were staring at me around the conference table. I'd fallen asleep in a meeting right after eating part of a buttery scone. Dammit, why now? Her cover name had been Deborah Gardner. I was raised in the foster system. I didn't think I had parents. Pleased to meet you, I'm James Michael Gardner.

When I wake from someone else's dreams, I always feel like I should have a massive headache or a feeling of disorientation. I never do. This time, knowing my co-workers saw me sleeping, I tried unsuccessfully to fight off a growing feeling of massive dread.

"I'm sorry Cal, I..."

"Save it." He cut me off. "Just give us your update and then go sit in my office until I'm done here."

That clinched it. I was going to get seriously chewed out. All of the spit in my mouth disappeared. I looked down blankly at the reports I'd brought. "Social media marketing has been predictably slow, but still heading forward. My team has adapted to the changing popularity of the various apps, and we're steadily increasing our 'likes' within our targeted groups of parents and surprisingly even grandparents. The actual numbers are detailed in this summary." I passed out the sheets that were my contribution to the overall report my boss would put together and send up the corporate chain.

Nobody even glanced at them. Nobody ever does. All that hard work to compile the information and they'd rather stare at the freak who fell asleep at the meeting. I had probably talked in my sleep. Scratch that. The way Jeni-who-uses-a-heart-over-the-i was staring at me, I know I'd been talking. I just don't know what she'd heard. Her thumbs were twitching, a clear sign she was anxious to get to her social media and post about it. She posts every time someone sneezes, drops a pen, or farts. I couldn't wait to read what she had to say about me today.

Now that he had my report, Cal dismissed me. I gathered my stuff and made the long walk to his office. Everything had a surreal tint to it, though nobody seemed to notice until they saw me sitting alone next to his desk. One-by-one my coworkers tried ever so casually to peer around cubicle walls as though they could see me in such a way that I couldn't see them. Middle management offices were mini-fishbowls bordering the edges of the cube farm. The floorplan defied secrets. Rumor said the founder's daughter used to have closed-door escapades in the old downtown building on a regular basis. When the company grew into a larger space in the Milwaukee suburbs, the founder made sure the floor plan was completely open. Thanks to Melinda's afternoon adventures, my reprimand would be visible to everyone. At least Cal could close his door so nobody would hear it.

I only waited ten minutes while they finished the meeting, but it was enough time for my attention to ping back and

forth between dreading my current predicament and tearing
myself up over why I'd had such a powerful dream from the
perspective of a female agent who'd been given my last name
as a cover identity for a high-profile mission.

I hate these powerful dreams. As with Sopora they feel
more like memories, though today was the first time I'd ever
had one from a woman's perspective. More incredibly, this
was the first time the subject of the dream wasn't sleeping
nearby.

My foster parents had signed me up for therapy because
of these dreams. My child therapist had never been able to
talk me out of the idea that I'd been seeing my foster father's
memories at night. As an adult I've learned to not say anything, but my lovers eventually can't handle that I just seem
to know things about them. Experiencing a lover's dreams,
the ones that include you as well as all the ones that don't, is a
very quick way to find yourself feeling distrustful and suspi-
cious. It's also the fast road to becoming single.

Everyone else just thinks I'm a narcoleptic weirdo. Jeni
has called me those exact words in her posts when I've fallen
asleep at my desk. She even tried tagging me in one, as if
'narcoleptic weirdo' was a title I wanted to announce to the
world. That's when I stopped "heart"-ing Jeni.

By the time Cal stormed in, I'd managed to work myself
into a nice, cold, sticky sweat. He closed his door and looked
at me for a moment, trying to figure out where to start. I
tried to fill the uncomfortable silence.

"Cal, I'm sorry..."

"Save it James." He shut me down. I snapped my mouth
shut.

I waited him out, perspiration rolling down my side

over my love handles. Dammit, I managed to get MORE self-conscious thanks to roving beads of sweat reminding me I need to lose weight.

"Do you have a medical diagnosis?"

His question caught me off guard. "What? For what?"

"Your narcolepsy, or chronic fatigue, or whatever-the-hell keeps putting you to sleep at work."

I blinked stupidly back at him, "Uh, no... I..."

"I'm going to level with you so we're on the same page." I hate his reliance on corporate catch phrases, but held my tongue. He powered on, "I can overlook nodding off at your desk once in a while. You're a good worker. But this time you did it in a meeting. Maybe you think update meetings are boring, but they are necessary for keeping this company's wheels spinning. Yet you fell asleep in front of people. I can't overlook that. They're going to talk. Which eventually means I'm going to have to answer to Melinda. She's been itching to fire you since the holiday party incident. The only way I can head that off at the pass is if you have a medical reason for falling asleep in an update meeting."

"But..."

"No buts. Take the afternoon off, go to the doctor, come back with something diagnosable and I'll handle Melinda."

I nodded submissively. "Ok. Thanks Cal."

Turning to leave, I saw Jeni staring into Cal's fishbowl office from her cube. Jeni who had maliciously posted that Melinda made a fool of herself drunkenly hitting on the gay narcoleptic weirdo at the holiday party. Jeni who was salivating to post about the weirdo being sent home after a closed door meeting with the boss. Jeni who deserved to be beat upside the head repeatedly with a rotary phone. Jeni who was pulling out her smart phone as I walked past. I hated Jeni with all my heart.

DOCTOR'S OFFICE

Where Jeni pays too much attention to my life, my doctor hasn't clued in to the fact that I'm a real person. When I have to talk to my friends about him, I simply call him The Quack. It shouldn't bother me that he never knows who I am. I'm sure he sees a lot of people. I just don't believe a healthcare professional should make me feel like I'm always interrupting his golf game. I pass my wait time dreaming of ways to stand up to him and point out that I'm the reason he can afford golf clubs. Maybe one day I will. You know, if he ever deigns to examine me himself. Today, like most visits, I've been relegated to a student doing her residency.

She came in and made a big show of reading the notes the nurse had made on the clipboard. She moved to the sink for the ritual hand-washing and said, "Why don't you tell me in your words what brings you here today."

"Obviously, there's something wrong with me." I was shooting for sarcasm, but halfway through I realized I believed it. "I keep falling asleep at work. I usually get caught in a vivid dream I can't wake up from until one of my co-workers shakes me or says my name. I probably haven't cornered the market on feeling anxious, but I'd say I have a lot of stock in it."

She pondered that for a minute. "You told the receptionist you were probably narcoleptic, have you been tested?"

"No, there's a test? Is it possible that's what's wrong with me?"

She nodded, angling her eyes up like she was thinking back to class notes, "You indicate sleep at inappropriate times and entering dream stage quickly. Those are the signs I was taught to look for. I'm going to refer you to our sleep clinic. I just need to get the doctor to sign off on it. The receptionist can help you set up your first appointment. Do you have any questions?"

"Yeah... Can you give me a written diagnosis or something I can take back so I don't lose my job?"

She smiled softly, "let me see what I can do."

The Quack must have been in the building, because he signed off on the referral quickly enough. He never bothered to look in on me though. Thankfully, the receptionist was very helpful. When we were done I had a stapled packet of reading material about narcolepsy, an official looking explanation of the diagnosis and subsequent referral, and an appointment for next week.

I felt like progress was being made. Pulling into traffic I realized I almost never had free time during daylight hours. I hurried home, packed workout clothes into my gym bag, and headed to the shiny gym I've been paying for. I didn't ever want to feel sweat on my love handles again.

THE GYM

I am always surprised when I genuinely enjoy a workout. People fling demands at me all day long. I spend most of my waking hours grinding myself down to meet their deadlines, complete their reports, and address their needs. It's easy to set aside an activity that has no person squawking about it. Too easy. Yet here I was, enjoying how it feels to push myself to get stronger and leaner for nobody but me. It felt decadent. It felt great.

Of course as soon as I came to that conclusion, reality took a step sideways. A black shadow flitted across the gym floor. It was almost impossible to see against the black rubber flooring. It only stood out because unlike the floor it didn't reflect light on any visible wavelength. It was black because it was the true absence of all light. As it moved from point to point, I realized nobody else was reacting to it. It went right under a woman's shoe, but she didn't pull away. She didn't respond in the slightest. Nobody did.

Tracking its progress, I pretended to take a swig from my water bottle. The blackness came to rest under a huge bodybuilder named Gregory. Oblivious like everyone else, Gregory stacked plates onto a squat bar so he could grunt and swear and throw it around loudly. You know, just in case there was somebody in southeast Wisconsin or northern Illinois who didn't know how much he was lifting. Gregory grabbed his chalk thingy and started psyching himself up with his ritual "C'mon! C'Mon! You 'kin do this! C'MON!" The blackness expanded, sending creepy tendrils up Gregory's leg. I started uncontrollably shaking and sweating with a case of the chills. Gregory still hadn't noticed, nor had anyone else. The blackness expanded outward into a huge, shadowy leech. You never feel leeches while they're sucking all your blood out. I had to do something. Though I was still shaking, I got up to try to help get whatever it was off of Gregory.

I had barely started moving as he came around the rack and positioned himself under the bar. The black tendrils were gone. I didn't see them on either the floor or Gregory. I hesitated, looking around for where they might be lurking. Gregory started his set normally and nothing weird happened. I felt like an idiot standing there. I didn't want to interrupt, and I would have felt really foolish trying to explain creepy black leech-like tendrils to a man who could tear the roof off a city bus with his teeth. Failing to see anything, I turned to head back to my spot.

Seconds later, there was a flicker out of the corner of my eye. The blackness was inside Gregory! It was in his core, wrapped around his spine like vaporous tendrils that sucked in all light and gave back nothing. Ignoring the unspoken rule about not staring at another guy at the gym, I looked directly at him. When I did, there was nothing unusual about his workout at all.

At that point, I rationalized to myself that I was seeing things. That the dream I'd had at work was affecting my vision, and that it would be best for everyone involved if I went home and laid down.

I didn't leave, though. Instead I went back to my spot and halfheartedly finished my set. And the next one. And then I moved on to the next exercise. A continued sense of dread made me feel like I needed to keep Gregory in sight. He just kept adding weight to his squat bar, chugging his pre-workout drink, and joking loudly with a couple of the other big guys. Twenty minutes and two exercises later I hadn't seen the blackness again. I'd come down off of my chills, and it really was time to wrap things up. I hit the locker room to shower.

My shower was blessedly normal, but I heard some commotion out by the lockers. By the time I finished and got out there, I was alone. An eerie foreboding came over me. I hurriedly dressed and went out into the weight area, my hair dripping wet. When I saw what was going on, my vision tunneled and I felt my pulse in my head. Everyone was clustered as close as the EMTs would allow. Gregory was strapped to one of the hard carry-stretchers. He had an oxygen mask on his face, and it looked like there was a brace around his neck.

Someone bumped into me. "What happened?" I managed to ask.

"He kept adding weight and bragging to his buddies," said an older man's voice. "Then we all heard the crack and saw him collapse under the weight."

I couldn't focus. I concentrated on breathing, fearful I'd black out. Something was still terribly wrong. Gregory's body came into focus sharply, and I saw the black tendrils separate from his spine, pulling an afterimage of Gregory with them. His ghost looked around bewildered. Nobody else was reacting. Nobody was whispering, blinking, or breathing, or moving. They weren't being still out of respect or shock, they were frozen. The only sound I heard at first was my own heartbeat still pounding in my head. I actually heard the rushing of blood in my veins, cyclical somehow, yet strong.

Gregory's spirit focused on me. "Bro, you can see me... what happened?" His voice was flat, thin, and forced. He sounded like someone trying to speak without air.

"I don't know," I replied, still in shock. Even in shock my voice was a vibrant and rich in contrast to his, I sounded full and strong and powerful. I sounded alive. "They say your spine snapped under the weights."

The tendrils kept pulling at his edges, almost sucking on him. "I'm dead then?" He sounded almost relieved, as though having that answer would solve everything for him.

I half shrugged, "I think so... maybe."

At my answer he gave up the fight and let the tendrils pull him. He just sort of vanished from this existence. Somewhere deep inside me I felt like he'd connected to someplace else. It was peaceful. The sound of my pulse slackened for a split second, and motion returned to everyone around me. The EMTs realized they'd lost him, and they made everyone get out of the way so they could rush him out.

It was too late.

I had seen a man die and his spirit pass on.

I thrust my hands into my pocket and moved away. I had to get out of there. I couldn't be near people. I needed time to gather myself after that macabre incident. What was most horrible, to me at any rate, was his spirit's calm acceptance that he had died. I didn't know how to handle that. I like to think I would have fought for all I was worth, but he'd just given up.

And I'd seen it.

THE LIBRARY

After emptying my gym bag, I wandered from room to room in my townhouse. As soon as I fired up my computer, I had the urge to do the dishes. As soon as the sink was full of soapy water, I wanted to do a load of laundry instead. Grabbing the basket, I saw my gym clothes and the whole ordeal replayed itself in my mind. I suddenly couldn't be alone with my thoughts. I locked the house and headed for the only place I felt I could be surrounded by people and yet withdrawn while I researched some of the crap that had just happened to me – the Milwaukee Public Library.

The main lobby is pretty impressive. There are an awful lot of signs pointing this way for one subject, that way for another. As usual, none of the myriad of signs said anything useful like "this way for secret agents using your name" or "that way for real answers regarding black tendrils and after-death experiences." Or maybe what I needed was just cleverly obfuscated in terms I didn't recognize. At this point, I was willing to believe a lot.

Exercising what I felt was remarkable focus, I talked myself into starting with something tangible. Feeling good about that decision, I tried the information desk where a young college girl displaying T'Angilique on her name badge was studiously ignoring me with the help of her smartphone.

I politely waited.

She politely fired wingless birds at increasingly large fortresses guarded by angry swine.

"Excuse me..."

She mashed her thumb onto the screen, "Jus' a minnit."

I looked around, but there was nobody else who could help me. Don't get me wrong, I'm a fan of video games in general. I usually try really hard to avoid being a jackass. So I tried to speed things along by encouraging her. I blame my failure on the fact that I was keyed up about my day and a little out of sorts. "Teach those imperial swine not to mess with your nest of rebels!" I encouraged sarcastically.

Instantly annoyed with me, she shot a red bird into something that exploded satisfactorily, and she made a show of pausing her game. "Yeah, what?"

Fine, I didn't want to talk about your stupid game anyway. "I need to find the location for a business whose name I just heard in a conversation."

She looked me over. Not seeing my phone, she held up her own, "Di' you try the innernet?"

"Yes," I lied. "It's apparently a restaurant from the seventies before there was an internet."

She just pointed down a wing that looked darker and more ominous than the others. I turned to head that way, and she came around the counter and started walking with me. I raised an eyebrow in question.

She shrugged, "We're s'posed to walk ya to where ya need ta be."

"Oh." I would have said something more meaningful to at least try to make the walk worth her time, but her phone snapped up and she continued her epic space battles against the swinetroopers.

She didn't look away from her phone as she pointed me to the Research Desk. I thanked her, but I'm pretty sure I was already forgotten.

In contrast, Justin-the-research-desk-guy was very eager to help.

"This is going to sound odd, but I'm looking for more information on a restaurant that was in operation back in the seventies." T'Angelique's derision was still fresh on my mind so I added, "I didn't find much on the internet."

His smile reached his eyes as he pulled out a note pad and pen. "Let's start by looking at business registrations through the government's trade name database. What was it called?"

"The One-Eyed Roe. Roe spelled R-O-E. I guess it's a kind of deer."

"That's unique enough." He wrote it down and led me to a terminal where he started the search. "Do you know what state it was in?"

"Er..." dammit I'm no good at this. "Not really. I saw it in a family picture from before my time. I was hoping to determine its significance, but the scrapbook pictures didn't have a convenient year written on them."

"Well, that'll just give us more time together while we look into this!" I swear he smiled a huge smile at my chest.

I am usually clueless when someone's hitting on me. I'm pretty average looking, and certainly not in shape, so it doesn't happen often. But every once in a while someone comes along making it really, really difficult to act like I don't know what they're doing. Since I was already on edge and completely freaked out by everything that had happened it's possible I was misreading the situation. I chose to play stupid just in case.

He clicked open a couple windows. "These are all connected to several of the largest national information databases. Think tanks keep scanning data in, so most of it goes back pretty far. Let's see what we can find."

He moved in behind me like he was going to reach around me. I was immediately self-conscious, so I scooted to the side to give him access to the keyboard and mouse. If I was reading his interest all wrong, then he was just encouraging me to do my own damned search. But if I was right, he was putting himself in the perfect position for me to just make a public idiot of myself.

While he typed at the computer, I allowed my inner monologue to try sending telepathic messages. *Not today, Justin. I've just had my first 'I'm a woman' dream memories, then saw a dying man's soul leave his body. I'm really damned confused. Today's a bad day for flirting.*

There was neither a glimmer nor a flinch from him. Which meant I probably couldn't add telepathy to my list of crazy events for the day. Part of me was glad, part of me was sad. Mostly I just felt a little sheepish for trying.

"Hmmm..." he said after several minutes. "I'm not finding

anything at all. Is it possible you have the wrong year range or name?"

"Maybe the year, I'm just making a guess based on people's clothes in the pictures. Oh, and a car in the background. But the name of the business was clear on the sign, One-Eyed Roe."

He tried a couple more searches and came up with nothing. "I'm sorry. I don't think any business with that name was registered in the United States after 1960."

I felt a little deflated. "I didn't realize it would be such a long shot. Can you think of anywhere else I can search?"

He shook his head, "Not really. As paper records are scanned, they're sent away for long-term archiving. So if they don't appear in the online search they would take weeks to get in hard copy, and even then we'd have to ask for something fairly specific."

"Thanks Justin..." I wanted to thank him for being interested in me too. It made me feel a little better, but I didn't know how to not sound weird about it. Instead, I put my hand on his forearm and just said, "... and thank you." I even remembered to smile.

Justin's face brightened a bit, but then I lost track of him. Over his shoulder was a man who looked so familiar my vision tunneled. He wasn't complaining about his career or ordering the special of the day, but negativity still emanated off him in waves. He was older than I had seen him in the Agent Sopora dream, but his narrow, angry eyes were instantly recognizable... and they were staring right at me. He was speaking into a mobile phone, and I clearly heard him say, "The Oracle was right, it's him. Mobilize."

My heart froze. A feeling of pure dread lanced into my gut.

Justin was asking something, "... dinner or drinks some time?"

"Yes, I'd like that..." I had to get away. What the hell was going on? Morpheus had mentioned Oracles to Sopora.

Agent Bruadair put the phone into his pocket and pretended to read his newspaper. Logically I should have wanted to go over and ask him questions. But logic was gone. I was afraid. Terrified.

I turned back to Justin, "Let's go to your desk and I'll give you my number."

His face lit right up. If it suddenly hadn't felt like the hounds of hell were closing in around me, his smile would have been cute in a very, normal, guy-meets-guy sort of way. Instead, it was extremely surreal. "I didn't think you were interested at first," he was saying.

Bruadair glanced at his watch.

Justin put a pen and slip of paper into my shaking hands. I scrawled down my number.

"Is this mobile? I can text you mine?"

"Yes, that'd be great."

"I should know this, what's your name?"

"Oh, I'm James. Sorry. I..." I glanced back at Bruadair. He hadn't turned the page of the paper at all. His eyes weren't even scanning the text. He was waiting. Forcing all of my focus back on Justin, I tried to pick the conversation back up, "I got yours from your nametag."

Justin laughed and covered his nametag with his hand. Again, it would've been cute, but it just added to the increasingly surreal nature of everything going on. I had to get out of there. Now. I had an idea. I wrote a couple scribbles onto another piece of paper. Turned to Justin and said, "Thank you again. I'm looking forward to it."

I then made a show of looking at the paper, glancing around, and heading to the far side of a kiosk where I hoped neither Justin nor Agent Bruadair would be able to see me. Once I was there, I tried walking backwards in a straight line until I got to the hall. It was stupid. I realized halfway through that I had no reason to expect this escape would work. At the entrance to the hall, I saw him stand up, step to the side of the kiosk, and check his watch again. I saw Bruadair as clearly as he saw me. He set down the paper and started towards me. I noticed Justin's confused look as I was turning to bolt, but I couldn't do anything about it.

Running down the hall, I flew through the lobby towards the front door. I stopped when I saw two men in expensive suits standing not quite so casually near the exit. I angled my run and scooted up the other wing, already out of breath. I looked for an emergency exit. I'd have to break the law. I had heard horror stories about ink packs exploding when you open emergency doors. I'll never understand why that fact occurred to me while running for my life, but I almost fell over trying to come to a stop. Looking around, I grabbed a chair and holding it out in front of me the long way, I pushed on the door's mechanism. Predictably, the alarm rang through the building, but no ink pack exploded. Not wanting to add grand theft furniture to my record, I dropped the chair and bolted out the door.

People were beginning the mad rush to get out of the building. I ran along the wall to a full bike rack and ducked down. A suited woman was standing near the van scanning the crowd.

Scanning people?

Dammit. Did I have an aura? What was Margaret's lesson? Pull my personal vapor in tight? Cold water? Right, I looked over the bikes, wasting precious seconds. There, one had what I hoped was a water bottle. I grabbed it and took a swig. It wasn't super cold, but thankfully it was actually water. There was an added benefit to concentrating in that I had to calm down or choke on it. I tried to imagine what my aura vapors looked like. I visualized them swirling in close to my skin, trapped. Since Sopora made a point to remember pulling the vapor back into her pores, I tried that too. One of the suited men came out of the front of the building and turned my way. I assumed his partner was going around the corner the opposite direction.

My phone chimed. A text? Now? "This is Justin's number. Call me." The agent was getting closer and I stopped to look at a text? What the hell is wrong with me? No time...

Aura. I tried to pull everything inward. I took another swig and focused on the fluidity of the water in my mouth. The man was getting nearer. I was sweating like mad. He looked me over and I felt his thoughts reach out to me. I almost screamed. I tried to smile instead, but he just gave a small shake of his head and moved on.

The bikes. Did he think I was sweating because I'd just been biking? Sirens were fast approaching. I spied an unlocked red BikeShare bicycle, hopped on, and pedaled across the street and around a corner. I almost tore out of there, when a thought hit me and I slammed on the brakes. The van would have a license plate! It may have been a rental, but it was something traceable. I spun around and peeked around the corner. The female was talking with Bruadair while he climbed up into the passenger seat. She trotted around to the driver's side and hopped in, bringing the engine to life and pulling forward in a fluid motion. As she pulled away, I caught the words "Ocean State" on the plates.

If it was a rental, I probably had nothing. But if it was theirs, then I had a shot at this. I pulled out my phone to search that state motto while the van circled the library once. I saw them pick up one of the front door agents. I assume they picked up the other before they disappeared into downtown traffic.

Rhode Island?

My phone was showing me the color and design I had seen on the van. I knew nothing about the state really. Just that it was small. But I guess its proximity to Washington D.C. made it a good location for a quasi-official espionage group. I didn't know what to think. If they were looking for me, did they want to buy me a cup of tea and scone and train me to use my abilities? I doubted it given the intense fear that had come over me. If Margaret's warning to Sopora had been any indication, then this group had an agenda that had very little to do with the happiness of its agents.

Did the Oracles think I belonged with the Agency? Did experiencing Sopora's dream somehow trigger their attention? Why else would they be looking for me at the Library? Even if I was on one of their watch lists, this wasn't one of my usual spots. But Bruadair had clearly identified me and mobilized his team.

Sopora had obviously gone to Margaret for unsanctioned training. Was her dream trying to tell me to seek out Margaret so she could be my sensei? I didn't know what to think.

Would I be safe at home? Morpheus had said Oracles weren't good on specific information. I decided I should hurry home and pack a bag in case I had to disappear for a while. If they were coming to kidnap me... well... I'd jump out the back window or something. But if I was dead wrong and Bruadair was actually here to offer me a friendly job with the Agency, I would need a bag packed to leave with them for training or something. Ugh... that didn't feel right at all. For my own sanity, I had to figure out what was going on with me. The only person from that dream I trusted right now was Margaret. And I could only think of two ways to connect to her. I could either ask Bruadair for the location of the One-Eyed Roe, or I could keep trying to track down the restaurant through normal means. The first option guaranteed exposing Margaret. The second was a risk if I got sloppy and someone noticed.

Chapter Three
1972 – London

In spite of my dread, or secret insane hope, that Bruadair and his team were coming for me, they didn't. I packed up everything I felt I would need in order to run. Then made time to take a shower, which I needed again. I sat on the edge of my bed and had a moment of identity confusion when I realized I didn't have my usual spare tire. I had breasts.

It took a second to realize I must have fallen asleep when I sat down. I was in one of Sopora's shared dreams, again. She was pretty obviously in London during the tail end of the go-go era. People looked pretty groovy, and I suddenly knew she had seen hippies out and about earlier in the day. She was wearing a silky white blouse that buttoned up the front with some frill, and a floor-length black skirt. I felt the knee-high boots pinching her toes already. She was in a bathroom, at the hotel I think, checking her makeup. She looked directly into her own eyes and said, "Remember."

Everything became crystal clear.

She was going out looking for a government official of some sort. An inspector or general I think. The sky was dark out the windows, but I didn't immediately see a clock. She gathered up a few things for a night on the town, and headed out.

Downstairs in the lobby she told the concierge she needed a car. "I think I'd like to go to Annabel's. Please see to it that I'm on the list."

She slipped the concierge a tip I recognized as both generous and a guarantee of getting into the club. One of the staff came by with drinks on a tray, and she helped herself to a flute of champagne. She pretended to take a sip, and smiled at the staff giddily. She had to stay sharp, and I knew she was going to be pretending to drink all night.

When the cabbie arrived, he was everything she hoped he would be. Charming, chatty, cockney, and more than eager to think he was actually helping her by driving a little extra out of the way so he could keep telling his stories about famous people who had been in his cab. I didn't recognize any of their names, but Sopora did and she tittered meaninglessly about them to keep the cabby talking.

Eventually he lit upon the death of Billy Murcia. It apparently happened quite recently here in London. "Dun 'imsef in wif drugs'n booze, 'e did!"

"That's terrible!"

"Did you know'im? Bein' from America an' all?"

"Oh, no. I didn't. I think he was from New York. I'm from Chicago. That would be like you knowing someone from Glasgow."

"Right! Cor' tragedy too."

"Is that a common way to go in London? Drugs and booze, that is?"

"Wha? Blimey no! Wot makes ya fink that?"

"Well, isn't that just how that African prince died too?"

"That's th'official line, tha'is! If y'ask me, I b'lieve 'e wos murd'rd, 'e wos. They say 'is cronies from Africa broke in, see, an' forced vodka right in'im!"

"Dreadful!"

"Right, 'here you are then!" The ride came to an inconvenient end.

We had stopped next to an unassuming side entrance on a large brick building. She tipped the cabby so well he did a double-take. Before he could even pretend he wasn't considering shortchanging her, she told him to keep it. Regally, she turned and walked up to the doorman. "Deborah Gardner, I should be on the list?" Hearing my name again sent a jolt of emotion through me.

The doorman stepped back and spoke into a receiver. After a quick conversation, he returned. "You are indeed, Miss. We sincerely hope you enjoy your evening at Annabel's and please consider joining our club as a member."

I was surprised at how many doors were open to a wealthy American in her era. I've never been wealthy, not even for pretend, so all I'd experienced was the lingering distaste much of the world has for us.

She beamed her smile at the doorman. "If the food and dancing are as good as your reputation," she assured him, "I'm sure I will!" He opened the door allowing her inside.

Opulence is opulence, no matter what time period. I personally knew nothing of the club's reputation. It appeared to be underneath the rest of the building, but it was undoubtedly a place for the wealthy and social elite to relax. Just beyond the threshold, the bar had to be worth more than my apartment building. A closer look made me realize it wasn't throwing wealth in anyone's face. This was just how it was. This was a nice place. This was a place where someone could escape the rigors of being a public figure, and enjoy a fine drink at a fine bar. Sopora asked the bartender for a white wine, whatever he recommended, and she glanced over the crowd. Apparently, she didn't see who she was looking for.

Wine in hand, she approached the host and asked for a table in the restaurant.

"Will you be dining alone, mum?"

"Sadly, yes."

"A table shall be made ready at once. Would you care to wait at the bar but a moment longer?"

"That'll be lovely! Thank you for taking such good care of me!" she sparkled a smile at him. His stuffy demeanor cracked a little as the edge of his mouth came up in his version of a return smile.

Sopora took a seat that allowed her to look deeper into the room.

The ceiling was an appealing collection of arches. Dining tables were situated around a floor that looked like it might be open to dancing later. There were also areas with couches and chairs for sitting and socializing. The place was maybe half full. I sensed that she aimed to keep watching, though she hadn't seen what she'd been looking for.

Later, well into her salad course, a man came in with a woman on each arm. He looked African, the women most certainly did not. One of them must have said something clever, for he was laughing a deep and booming laugh. The host showed them to a table, and a waiter appeared with wine and glasses. The man took no notice of the server, but absently went through the motions of approving the wine while listening to his clever companion.

Miss Not-So-Clever was trying to interject herself into the conversation, but the other two ignored her. Finally, she stood up in a show of frustration and walked into the bar area. The other two barely registered her departure.

Based on her attention, and the vague feeling of excitement, I'm pretty sure this man was Sopora's target. It was a little frustrating not having control of her head and eyes, and I had a fleeting sensation of being a puppet. She didn't actually watch the couple directly, though she remained aware of their location at all times. It wasn't until after the main course, which she barely ate, that I realized what Sopora was doing. She had positioned silvered items to catch reflections. The clean knife leaning up against the butter tray was the best because it didn't distort the image in a curve. She was watching the ignored woman in the bar a little more intently. Miss Not-So-Clever, it seems, was talking to any man who would listen. She kept casting glances back at the African to see if he noticed her, but if she expected a jealous outburst, she only set herself up for disappointment. He showed no interest in anyone other than Miss Clever.

Palming a familiar white pill from her purse, Sopora made her way to the bar. She ordered two amaretto sours, counting on the strong flavor to mask the pill she dropped into one. She swirled it quite a few times to get rid of traces of the enhanced sleeping pill. She then casually approached the increasingly agitated Miss Not-So-Clever.

"Hi. I couldn't help but notice how your man treats you. Mine sent me to London so I wouldn't catch him with his mistress." I felt Sopora accentuate those words with mental push that carried a vision of a handsome business man wining and dining a busty red-head. I imagined I saw the hallucinatory thoughts as they left Sopora's mind and floated toward the woman. "Here, a drink to bolster us against uncaring men."

It first looked like Miss Not-So-Clever was going to tell Sopora to pound sand, but a change came over her when the vision reached her mind. Her features softened as the phantasm pulled her in. "I rather dislike men tonight!" She reached out for the drink, raised it once in something of a salute, and downed it in a single long swallow.

Knowing it would take a bit of time before the full effects of the pill hit her, Sopora asked, "I've finished my dinner, but haven't had dessert yet. Would you like to join me?"

I could tell food was the last thing on Miss Not-So-Clever's mind, but she was still under the effects of the dream vision just enough to consider it. Then, quick as that, she shrugged off the influence and shook her head, "No. I'm going to find myself another man. Thank you for the drink."

Sopora nodded in complete understanding. She gave an encouraging smile, then returned to her table. The staff had cleared the dishes during her time at the bar. A moment later the waiter came by to inquire about dessert and coffee. "Yes, to both. Thank you."

Catching her own eyes in the dessert spoon, Sopora told me to, "Remember," lightly under her breath. She was reinforcing my participation in the dream! As if she was giving me an espionage lesson she followed up with, "One down, but she was an agitated lone target which made it easier."

A clarity and sharpness of vision I didn't even realize had started to fuzz out returned. I had a strong suspicion she knew exactly who I was and she wanted me to see all of this. If she was purposefully sending these dreams somehow, I couldn't hear her actual thoughts. I only ever heard her spoken words and received some knowledge about things she knew to be true. I think I was feeling some of her stronger emotions as well, but it was tougher to separate those from my own emotional reactions to what she experienced.

She was also correct. Miss Clever wouldn't be so easy. She and the African were deep in their conversation, largely ignoring their drinks and food. Sopora strained to eavesdrop, but couldn't make anything out. The club was just loud enough to cover quiet table conversations. In a place like this, such privacy was probably deliberate. Sopora wasn't feeling any stress about it, though. So I relaxed to see how things would play out.

In time, people finished dining and started dancing. I hadn't seen Miss Not-So-Clever in a while, but the club atmosphere seemed to bring people out of the woodwork and it was getting harder to keep an eye on all three of them. Sopora eventually got up and put herself on the dance floor where she could move around and make seemingly normal, if short, glances around.

Several songs into this routine, the Miss Not-So-Clever finally passed out on a couch near the bar. One of the hosts, no doubt worried about the establishment's reputation, made a discreet stop at the African's table. Miss Clever sighed. The African laughed and shrugged. He mimed taking drink after drink and then theatrically passed out back in his chair. Miss Clever didn't pretend to look anything but annoyed and resigned. She excused herself and left to go tend to her unconscious friend.

Sopora knew her opening had arrived. She created an image of herself dancing and alone, laced it with an emotional need for companionship, and pushed that emotional construct towards the African. Much like his companion at the bar, his features softened when it hit him. He glanced at Sopora, as though seeing her for the first time. He motioned her over.

She danced his way, and when she reached him tried to pull him up, "Come dance with me!"

He shook his head and stayed firmly seated, though he didn't let go, "No, I do not dance in public." Instead, he motioned for her to sit.

She thought about it for a minute, but finally claimed the vacated seat. "Why don't you dance?" she inquired, trying to keep it light and conversational.

"A man in my position can no longer afford to even be close to such spectacle. Too many people depend on..."

"Ah!" she cut him off. "For one night, let's not talk about who we are or who expects things of us. For one night, let's only talk about the positions of two bodies when dancing or making love."

He mulled that over, and I wondered if his usual pickup routine included talking about how important he was. I felt another wave of loneliness push out of Sopora and into him. That seemed to do the trick. He smiled broadly at Sopora. "Very well. Tonight you are the moon and I am the night sky, and together we will not talk about the day."

"I'd like that, very much."

At that he took her hand and stood up. Instead of the dance floor, he led Sopora to the exit. He instructed the host to put it all on his tab, including anything Sopora had ordered, and then asked the valet to summon his car. "Where do you live?"

"I'm staying at the Dorchester."

"Perfect, I know it well."

He deduced she had recently arrived in London, and she didn't disabuse him of the notion. He used the short ride to describe some of London's sites she really ought to see while she was here. "I will write them down with the concierge for you."

"Such a perfect gentleman."

He preened at the compliment. I was right about his ego.

"Have you been in London long? It sounds like you know all the best places!" she asked. She wasn't being completely breathy, though I half expected it of her. He laughed. There really didn't seem to be a reason to pretend he wasn't coming up to her room, and nobody tried.

In her room, she turned on the radio, found a station with danceable music. He took the cue and they danced in private. I'm a bit jealous that it was so easy for Sopora. I probably should try something like this with Justin, you know, some day when I'm lean and muscled, and not seeing people die, and not being chased by a shadowy organization. I felt the dream slipping as my real life started to intrude on my thoughts. Sopora pulled back from the African, "I need to check my makeup and make a drink. What would you like?"

"I have discovered a fondness for fine Scotch."

Sopora did a quick pass of a mirror, looked deep into her own eyes and said commandingly, "Remember!" Sheesh. Once again, everything sharpened and I was pulled back into the dream. She poured the drinks, reached for her purse, but hesitated and ultimately decided to not drop a pill into his Scotch. I probably would have for safety's sake.

Instead, she entertained him through a few drinks. With each drink their dancing and innuendo was more suggestive, until at last they were pulling each other's clothes off and falling onto the bed. Interestingly, he never kissed her. She tried once, but he gently shook his head no, and she left it at that.

When a great deal of their naked skin was touching, I felt her reach deep inside herself. This may sound overly poetic, but it felt like she drew from a universal world-weary tiredness we've all felt deep in our bones. She brought that fatigue to the surface of her skin and pushed it into her lover through his skin. I remembered how she used her pores to hide her aura. Suddenly the feeling of pushing tiredness out through her pores and into the African's became even clearer and stronger.

He tried to fight through the onset of fatigue. I don't blame him. He was in bed with a new lover and was fired up and ready for making love. Instead of forcibly pushing himself into Sopora, though, he slowly lowered himself down onto her. As his breathing deepened, he rolled off her to the side. She used his momentum to make sure he rolled all the way onto his back. She then positioned herself so she was half laying on him with her head on his chest. From the outside, it probably looked like a heartwarming, post-lovemaking moment.

Unseen, though, Sopora was willing her consciousness out of her body and into his mind. Though I'd never done this intentionally, I knew this feeling. I've accidentally entered the dreams of my own lovers in the past. I've just never considered doing it on purpose.

I knew where Sopora was taking us. We were headed for his dreams. In all my accidental shared dream experiences, nothing had ever indicated I could have tried to exert Sopora's level of control. Frankly, I didn't know these dream visits could be controlled. Yet she flew deftly past things that looked like islands of thoughts and memories. She held my consciousness close, as though she practiced bringing visitors into other minds all the time. Based on her conversation with Bruadair, this was probably exactly what she did for a living. I briefly tried to wrap my brain around the fact that I was in a dream within a dream. I heard Sopora laugh and say, "Just remember."

This time clarity didn't sharpen. Nothing was particularly out of focus, but I sensed that this part of reality didn't have a focus knob. Sopora flew from island to island along the stream of the African's thoughts. Most of the islands we initially passed had women on them. Sopora wasn't interested in those, though as we flew by I couldn't help but notice more than one had a scene of domesticity. I wondered if he had multiple wives. Most of what I saw indicated that might be the case. Other island scenes clearly showed that domesticity was a convenience for this man, only to be indulged when the mood suited him. When home bored him, he took an exciting new lover. Or lovers. One of the first islands showed the fantasy he'd had in store for his original companions this evening. Miss Not-So-Clever would have enjoyed the attention.

Past all the islands of women, Sopora stopped. I looked ahead and the stream connected to what looked like an ocean upon which hundreds, if not thousands, of dreams floated. I heard Sopora start chanting, "Mutesa... Mutesa... Mutesa..." We were still tethered together, but I had the feeling we were more separate here than we had been in her body. She relinquished control and allowed the winds to carry her along a swirling path.

There were dreams from childhood, and dreams of pure fantasy. She ignored all of these. There were dreams where our African was playing with his own children in a comfortable house. She kind of ignored those too. Every time we passed one I sensed a bit of irritation from her.

Finally, deeper in, we saw a dream island with an African

man being sworn in as President in two languages. Thankfully one was English. They were calling the man Obote. I didn't know if that was a first or last name. We saw another island where Obote was talking with a group of men who felt like advisors. Sopora appeared interested in one of the advisors and shot off that way. The advisor had been to England, college I think. We saw islands where Obote and the advisor worked together to free the Ugandan federation from British rule. We stopped long enough at one point to hear the advisor addressed as Mutesa, King of Buganda.

Satisfied we were on the right trail, Sopora continued to follow the trail of dreams the African remembered about Mutesa. After helping oust the British, he was appointed the first President of Uganda, serving under Obote who became the Prime Minister of the federation. Several dream islands later, Mutesa and Obote had a disagreement over legislation that took land away from Buganda. The dream islands then showed greater conflict, ending with Mutesa's exile to England.

Years later, our African was sent to find Mutesa. His whereabouts were not a huge secret, and our African waited outside in a car while Mutesa was interviewed by a reporter. While the African waited, a man walked by bundled against London's November chill. It only stood out in the dream because the African noted that the man stopped and looked right up at Mutesa's front window. But then he walked on, and though our African kept an eye out for him, he did not return. This island's memory play held Sopora's attention and she stopped to watch it unfold.

After the reporter left, our African waited a while longer to make sure no other guests were coming to call. When none did, he went up to the flat.

Our African was shocked to see the poverty that the once-king of Buganda was living in. The conversation between the men was tense, but Mutesa allowed him to stay. At one point, he even offered a shot of vodka. Our African turned it down but suggested Mutesa take one to calm his nerves. A short while later, he observed Mutesa was still nervous, and this time pretended to drink as well. The charade went on for a few more shots. Then Mutesa made a disparaging comment about those still ruling Uganda. Our African got angry, but knew his orders required that he keep a clear head. As long as Mutesa lived, there would be Ugandans who wanted him to return.

Overpowering the once-king and sitting on him, our African poured vodka down his throat and held his nose shut. Mutesa fought for his life, but he was a scholar, not a warrior. Pouring and pinching, our African kept it up until Mutesa passed out. When he was no longer consciously able to drink, our African began forcing vodka down his throat, saying that drowning was as good as poisoning. It was a brutal killing, steeped in political upheaval. When our African left, he took one empty bottle with him, leaving only one other empty on the floor next to Mutesa.

Reflexively checking out the window, he saw the bundled man standing in the street staring right up at him. Pulling his gun, the African rushed down to remove the potential witness, but by the time he reached the street, the other man was nowhere to be seen.

Our African checked through alleys and tenement entrances, but he couldn't find any sign of the other man. Frustrated, more than a little nervous, and knowing he had to make a phone call, he finally got in his car and drove away.

Sopora pulled away from that island and floated above the ocean of dreams for a minute. She was deep in thought, though whether committing it all to memory or undertaking some other mental task, I couldn't tell.

Finally, she rocketed back the way we had arrived. It felt easier because we weren't hunting for something relatively unknown. That is, until I noticed the islands had shifted on the currents of dream and fantasy. Even Sopora, who appeared an expert in these matters, had to stop and orient a few times before we neared the point where we entered.

She stopped, hovering over a new island where our African and Sopora were in a fantastically large bed. Distorted by drink and desire, it was larger than any real bed. The African was dreaming of the many ways he'd like to make love to this American woman. Sopora picked one that was far tamer than most. Motioning like a conductor, she pulled that dream to the fore of the island. I felt power stream out of her to fuel that dream scene. "This will be your memory of last night," she whispered to the African. Then she stayed and made minor corrections in the lovemaking any time it strayed too far from actions that were physically possible for people. Her ability to craft the dream into a more tangible memory was pure art.

When the actors in his dream's scene were both spent and sleeping, Sopora pulled me to the exit. We seeped out of the African's pores and back into Sopora's body. She stood up off of the man and took a long look at him. I was kind of surprised to see dawn's light sneak through a crack in the curtains and highlight his skin. She shook her head and walked into the bathroom, closing the door. Instead of turning on the bright lights, she pulled back a curtain just enough to let real light in. Turning to the mirror she looked right at where I was riding behind her eyes. "If you can avoid it, stay out of the dreams of killers."

The dream ended as she reached to turn the shower on, and I was back in my own body on my own bed.

Chapter Four
2012 – Milwaukee, Wisconsin

Gah! I didn't have time to sleep! I certainly had not meant to see that side of Sopora. Or any side. The last time I'd seen a naked woman in one of my dreams was never, and I didn't really appreciate my mind being taken hostage like that. Next time just give me the facts without the skin, thank you very much. I didn't need the booty show to learn there's an organization of people with my talent, and they have a mission and a purpose.

That was unfair. Though her methods were not Rated-G, it looked like Sopora was trying to do something good for the world. She was trying to find a possible supernatural link behind a string of political murders. I really could get into that. If the Agency's motives were that altruistic, I might actually want to be a part of that.

Bruadair's van had displayed a Rhode Island license plate.

Why not? I had banked some vacation time. I could head to Rhode Island and try finding Margaret through some leg work. In the worst case, I could always try to find the Agency and ask some questions. Sopora had told Bruadair he could get out by signing what amounted to a confidentiality contract. In all my favorite movies, the secret organization, school for gifted youngsters, or Jedi academy always had to seek out trainees, explain things to them, and then test them for eligibility. Maybe the Oracles had a giant spherical room where they went to sense where in the world people with dream abilities might be. Maybe Bruadair had my letter of acceptance? Maybe the overwhelming fear I'd felt was just a natural human reaction to this kind of change? I doubted it, but I wanted answers before things went farther.

That left one big huge problem. How in the hell would my friends believe that I wanted to suddenly vacation in Rhode Island? They were the family I'd built here. The years have added up, and we've gotten each other through a lot. They knew me better than anyone else. Which means they knew damned well I wanted to visit Maccu Picchu, Italy, London, Scotland, Portland, Seattle, and Australia. Rhode Island was conspicuously missing from any conversation we'd ever had.

I'd have to explain it as something they'd believe. If I didn't find anything and came home empty handed, it'd have to be something that would foster a good discussion while we shared the latest hip local wine.

Where should I begin? What did I know about finding people like me? We had auras. Sopora was highly valued because she could hide hers. It stands to reason, then, that not all four of the agents I saw at the library were able to hide theirs. I wonder if the auras leave a trail. Can they be followed mystically? Psychically? Supernaturally? I didn't even know how to classify it.

Sopora had very deftly insinuated herself into a man's dreams. Could the same sort of finesse be used to track an aura? I looked around my narrow townhouse. If auras did linger, then mine should be all over this place. It would be pointless to try to track myself, but I'd at least know if there was any sort of residue to trace in all this.

I thought back to the old New Age books I had packed away in storage so nobody would see that I had them. They all extolled the many virtues of that one thing I could never successfully do. Meditate. The couple times I tried I conked out within seconds. In hindsight my inability to meditate should have been an early warning sign of my latent narcoleptic awesomeness.

I closed my eyes and started the recommended breathing exercise. I wanted to be all Zen master about it, but ended up using more of a Darth Vader breathing groove. I tried to quiet my mind like they always suggest, but I was worried I'd drift off. You have failed me for the last time, James.

Besides, my thoughts were buzzing. I've never been one for stillness, and it showed. I also spent my childhood dreaming of having super powers. I admit it. I was geeking out a little. Screw meditation, I had tests to run! First, I tried the obvious. Flight. I was not so obvious as to tie a cape around my neck. Though if this was a type of mystic ability, I might need a focus. Wait, wouldn't that mean Sopora's focus was her pores? That's a poor choice for a focus. I mean, what if they were clogged? Okay, no focus for the moment. Not surprisingly, I failed to float across my apartment. Gravity still had me in its cruel grasp. Damn. Okay, back to what I knew.

Auras.

I tried squinting. I'm really good at relaxing and crossing my eyes to see those pictures in mall kiosks where thousands of tiny images make one large, three-dimensional image. Those images had always seemed like some sort of photo-sorcery, so I tried that. No aura. I tried running in place and getting my heart rate and breathing rate really high. It didn't take much. Then I casually glanced around. Nothing. I felt stupid.

The strangeness I'd been experiencing lately was so real. I was convinced I was just missing something. I kept at it. I tried meditating again. I managed to slow my racing heartbeat. I just couldn't bring myself to say, "Om." That crossed the line into ridiculous. There was no way my subconscious would accept "Om" as a symbolic metaphor for anything but a rockabilly-powered precursor to OM-paw-paw-maw-maw. I needed to try something else.

Sopora had modified the African's memories. That was probably a type of dream telepathy. Justin had proven I didn't have waking telepathy. Besides, mind powers were too difficult to test without a partner. Her example was worth filing away for later. I wonder how one went about finding experimental subjects for those tests? "Oh, hello. Wanna sleep with me so I can practice messing with your memories?" I can't imagine that pickup line going over well.

Everything I had seen occurred in the seventies. What if she wasn't necessarily "showing" me anything? What if I was seeing the past with my own kind of postcognition? I suppose it's possible, but she did start each vision with a command to remember. Plus, her ex Bruadair had suddenly appeared in my life. Add in my own history experiencing some of my lovers' dreams and precognition seemed unlikely. Besides, there was no way to test it in my own apartment where I knew the history of almost all of the items, and couldn't verify the ones I didn't.

Moving on.

I wasn't about to stab myself to test for resistance to harm or regeneration. I just had to hope my life would never depend on possessing those powers.

It wasn't until I was straining desperately to move a glass with my mind that I broke a blood vessel in my nose. I gave up on testing for other psychic powers. It seemed like a dead end.

Dead.

Gregory.

As morbid as it sounds, my inner monologue piped up with, "You could call yourself Captain Deathvision! Get a black costume with some silver mirrorshades!" I can count on my inner monologue for inappropriate comments at the weirdest of times. It shouldn't have been funny, but my sudden chuckle highlighted the stresses this whole situation was putting me through. I certainly didn't want to say I saw a specter of death stalking Gregory. But maybe it was some sort of premonition of his pending death. If that's the case, I wonder if I could have stopped it. Oh lord I was giving myself a headache. I sat down on the couch and put my head back.

Just as I was closing my eyes to protect myself from seeing more death, I saw a thin mist all over my house.

I kept very still.

Somehow I knew I was seeing faint traces of aura residue and that it had flavors of me all over it. I looked toward the stairs up to the bedroom where I'd just had Sopora's dream, and it was much stronger there. There were barely perceptible imprints that made me think they were hints at my dream islands. I wanted to go explore them, but Sopora's hunt through the African's dream islands had taken her all night. What if temporal distortion was common when exploring the dreams? I did not want to be locked away in my own dreamland if agents came to the door with holsters full of unhappy crap for me.

I tentatively stood up, fighting to keep relaxed so the aura would not go away. I walked slowly up to my bedroom. I saw an afterimage of me napping on the bed, vaporous and insubstantial, but I was there. Hovering over me, barely more visible than wind, was the Sopora I had just seen dressed up for a night out in London.

"Ok, Sopora, what can I do with this?"

She didn't answer, so I started playing around. I tried sucking wispy aura vapors in through my pores. I didn't feel anything at first. A faint pin and needle feeling started in various places where my skin was exposed to air. Slowly, inexorably, I started pulling the vapor into me. It was really happening. I pulled harder. Bits of aura residue near the bed responded as well, and got caught in my vacuum stream. Vacuum stream? Great, now I'm Captain Suck. Like that didn't have any bad connotations. As my mind wandered towards this new, and dumb, heroic identity the vapor in the air around me began returning to its previous strength. Dammit. Can't let my mind wander. I started pulling it back in through my pores.

It was slow going, but after many minutes, I started to get a feel for how it responded to my thoughts. It really wasn't like dust or fog. The auric residue was a lot more like energy in cloud form. Once I thought of it in those terms, it got easier to manipulate. I found I couldn't affect auric residue farther than an arm's length away. I hoped I'd get stronger at it with practice, but that also meant I had to stand up in order to completely cleanse the room.

I took it slow and steady. Several times I almost lost the

visual link to what I was doing. Each time, I'd stop and allow my eyes to lose focus. As long as I took it slow, I was able to keep at it. I later confirmed it had taken me just over a half-hour to remove my aura's entire residue from my townhouse's upstairs rooms. I imagined Cal spouting one of his damned witticisms, "Practice makes perfect."

Sighing, I worked my way downstairs. Would you believe different rooms gather their own entirely unique set of emotions? I'd never considered it. But, it made sense. You pray for very different results from a kitchen than you do a bathroom.

Also unsurprisingly, the energy in the bedroom had been the strongest. I'd have to say it's probably because my abilities seem to be tied to dreams and subconscious perceptions. The energy signatures of the aura residue in the bedroom were all over the emotion spectrum. Where else do we allow ourselves to feel love and loneliness, hope and despair? Where else do we dwell on these things and more but our bedrooms?

I continued to experience the aura residue as a nebula cloud of light and energy. It was easy to see how someone would misconstrue it as a vapor. Then again, if this was all based on the subconscious, then maybe each mind developed its own symbolism for defining how it perceives the stuff. I needed to talk to experts, or at least the quasi-experienced. A few times Sopora had reacted in such a way that made me think she was aware of me. Maybe I could reach out to her in the next dream and see if we had a breakthrough.

As a bonus, my apartment was cleansed of all emotional residue.

LATER

I wasn't ready to go to bed. Not so soon after the trauma of Gregory's death. I still had too many questions and couldn't allow myself to conk out again. If Sopora had been able to use her abilities to investigate political assassinations, I figured there had to be a way to use mine to track down those agents and determine whether they were friend or foe. I should have recognized that as the first of my many dumb, dumb, dumb decisions.

The trip back to the library was uneventful. There were no black vans parked conveniently outside. I'd been a little hopeful they'd have left an agent to see if I returned. Of course, they may have and the van wasn't conveniently parked out front. I'm going to have to step up my game if I'm going to think like a conspiracy theorist. I decided to use myself as bait and walked right up to the front doors.

Nothing. No agent stepped forward to ask me a few questions. No poison dart stabbed into the back of my neck. No bag dropped over my head. I didn't even get so much as a grumpy, "Move it" from a passerby.

I made an obvious show of looking up and down Wisconsin Avenue while I tried to turn on the Captain Suck-O-Vision. I hate my inner monologue. Thankfully, I'd spent so much time using the ability in my townhouse that it came pretty easily. A lot of people had passed by here, but most of their trails were less powerful than a day-old wind ripple. Most. I found the spot where the agent had walked by the bike rack. His residue was still strong. It felt like a shackled dream. It felt like a child full of imagination had tried to tell a brilliant tale to an adult who had simply said, "that's not possible" and shut the child's imagination off completely.

Now the child was walking through life as a rigidly bottled up tightwad. But the tightwad had a strong aura.

Buried under the rigid control was his connection to the full power of the dream world. It hadn't been banished, it was just behind very solid walls. But at its core it was like my aura. I just hadn't realized our auras were so powerful compared to normal ones. Surely there had to have been more people walking past this bike rack since this afternoon, yet the agent's aura trail was easily the strongest here.

That meant a couple things. First, I was excited to confirm mine wasn't detectable. So either I was no more powerful than the next person or I'd managed to actually hide mine in all the excitement. Second, the agent was a very powerful psychic-wizard-spy-whatever. Third, he didn't hide his aura, and likely couldn't. Finally, and probably most importantly, I thought I could follow it.

I dropped all pretense of going back into the library. I stayed on the sidewalk and walked along towards where the van had been. I had to be kind of spaced out to see the aura trails and I didn't want to risk a driving accident while I was all tuned in to my apprentice-level powers. For the safety of the citizens around me, I elected to walk. If I needed to, I could catch a bus back here.

The path went around the library. I hadn't seen where the van went after it circled the library, so I dutifully followed it. For the most part, I didn't want to miss anything. On the far side, I picked up the other agent's aura trail. It also felt shackled, though not quite as powerful as the first. That was something. I wondered if power levels were trained or innate.

The shell of the van muted them a little bit, but they were still detectable by the proximity of multiple shackled auras if nothing else. Slowly my creeped-out-o-meter was ratcheting up. Either the woman or Bruadair had something else in their aura. I couldn't identify what it was or to whom it belonged. Only that it felt unnatural and somehow fabricated. Like a car's tire. You don't really like to touch them for very long because they collect all the dirt on the roads of the world and somewhere in the back of your brain you know they're fabricated from the worst dregs of the petroleum process. The more I tried to pin it down, the more I was sure it was Bruadair's.

Not for the first time I wondered if I should stay away from these people instead of head toward them? No guy likes to admit it when he feels pure terror. So I wasn't about to admit that I felt a return of the sheer panicky terror from earlier in the library when I realized Bruadair was watching me. However, just because I wouldn't admit to something so irrational and unmanly does not mean I maybe sort of kind of didn't really feel something a bit like it. Maybe.

Fortunately for people everywhere our brains can rationalize anything. Then the brain's worst conspirator, the Ghost of You're-All-Alone-In-The-World, murmured lies about finding where I came from and being trained for an exciting job by people like me. Thanks to my dumb brain, I followed the trail of a man who had the foul auric residue of old tires.

The other stupid thing about us masculine types is we have a hard time admitting our "brilliant" ideas might have a flaw or, heaven forbid, several flaws. I decided it was time to own up to my stupidity. I wasn't going to just march up to these agents, introduce myself, and expect them to buy me a coffee, take me in, train me up, and let me solve the shadowy crimes of the world. Instead, I formed a new brilliant plan to go spy on them to see if they were the type of agents I wanted to walk up and introduce myself to. We may not like old tires, but dammit, they've got a purpose.

See, I'm not a Judgy McJudgerpants.

The aura trails looped around the library back to Wisconsin Avenue. They drove past the Domino's Pizza, past the Dunkin' Donuts, and pulled into the Hilton's parking ramp. Three blocks. They had driven three blocks.

I walked the perimeter of the ramp and concluded the auras had not left the ramp at ground level. Looking up, I saw a skywalk leaving the ramp crossing to the hotel. I went up to the skywalk level. My guess was confirmed, they'd walked across the skywalk to the hotel. Multiple times. Over the course of multiple days. Dammit. It seemed like the Oracle had known where, but not when.

I tracked the aura trails from the skywalk back through the ramp. Two of the stopping points did not have vans any longer, and I doubted these agents drove either a rusty Pontiac or a Subaru. The third trail lead to an empty spot. The remaining trails were old and faint and indicated they always parked within one slope up or down from the skywalk.

I returned to the skywalk and hurried across. Again, there was some confusion. Older, fainter versions of the trails went down the main stairs to the lobby. I guessed that was check-in or coffee or lunch runs, and therefore irrelevant. Annoyingly, the more recent trails went to the elevators. Double damn. Now what? Superpowers are dumb sometimes.

I could see two options. I could ride up and down checking at every floor. Not only would that annoy anyone who got on with me, but it would conveniently trap me in a suspended metal box. The other option was to take the stairs and poke out on each floor to see where their trail exited the elevator. I ultimately chose that option because they were not using the stairs, so I had less fear of bumping into them accidentally. On the plus side, experts say to take the stairs instead of the elevator if you want to lose weight, right?

I decided to start working my way up instead of down. If I didn't find anything, I'd come back down to the lobby and figure something else out. I was kind of worried that if I shut off my Suck-O-Vision I would have a difficult time turning it back on. However, the stairs were more treacherous when out of focus than the street had been. My own safety won out. I let my vision return to normal.

One floor up, it was fairly easy to check for the aura trails, so I relaxed about turning it off and on. I hit a lucky break on the fifth floor. Their four auras had a regular path into and out of the elevator. I hesitated. It's stupid that I felt safe in a hotel stairwell, but the hallway felt too wide open and exposed.

Somewhere down the hall, a door closed and my heart froze with dread.

I let the stairwell door close quietly. Dammit, I had been walking around with my aura hanging out all over the place. I focused on pulling my own nebulous energy in tight. I then went up to the landing between fifth and sixth. I could just barely see across the fifth floor hallway to the elevator bay, but not much else. A shadow crossed in front of the window a split second before the stairwell door opened. It gave me just enough warning to duck back around the corner. If the stalker came up the stairs, I was caught. I held my breath and my aura and tried not to shiver.

From the doorway, I heard Bruadair's voice. "He's not here,

but I know I felt him. You two, down the stairs to the lobby. You said you thought he might have been the man at the bike rack by the library? Check outside around the hotel's perimeter. You, with me. We'll take the parking ramp. He's untrained, so he can't know her tricks yet. Remember, Morpheus needs him alive, but not necessarily conscious. Move!"

Two sets of feet sprinted down the concrete stairs. The stairwell door on five slammed shut. My heart was jackhammering in my chest, but I stayed completely still. I heard the elevator beep. The pair of feet finally reached the bottom, and I heard the lobby door open and slam shut. My fear kept me frozen in place. It felt like hours were ticking by, though it was probably only a few distorted seconds. I almost moved to look around the stairwell when I heard Bruadair make an angry hmph sound. The door to five opened again and then slammed shut, again.

I almost pissed myself.

He did not sound like he wanted to offer me a cup of coffee.

The elevator binged again.

I waited. Fuck his little mindgame traps. I didn't have anywhere to be, I could wait for hours if I needed to. He was an old man, eventually his bladder would give out before mine. Or he'd fart. I could wait.

Dammit.

Was he still there waiting?

I held out as long as I could. I even tried to be clever and sense for his aura, but either I didn't have omnidirectional Suck-O-Vision, or he was gone. I'm guessing Suck-O-Vision was still tied to what my eyes could see. I could wait.

I am pretty sure I made it another couple minutes. I finally caved and peeked ever so slowly around the corner. My heart was pounding in my chest, and I was dripping more sweat than I ever had in the past. I fully expected Bruadair to be inches away, waiting to be all sinister and say, "Boo."

He wasn't.

The stairwell was empty.

I let out the breath I didn't realize I was holding, and I sat down on the stair behind me.

I still had to get out of here. And I definitely had to get out of town.

I pulled out my phone and called my closest friend. "Nate, I need a favor. Are you available? I need you to pick me up by the convention center. I can wait across the street at the Capital Grille.

"What's up?" he asked.

"It's a really long story, but my car's not starting and it looks like it's going to rain."

At that precise moment, the skies opened up and the sound of rain pounding the roof echoed through the stairwell.

"Damn, dude, that was practically psychic."

I would have laughed if he hadn't hit so close to home with that one. "Uh, it's a new app."

"Uh-huh. Sure, I can be there in about ten minutes."

"Thanks, I owe you."

"Oh, I know you do."

The hotel connected to the convention center across another skywalk. The restaurant was through the convention center and across a side street. If the agents were scouring the street and the parking ramp, it seemed like a safe pickup spot. I'd have to cross the upper lobby, but it was at the top of the escalators and far enough back that I should be able to stay out of sight.

The stairs were clear. My luck held as I made my way slowly down. There was some business convention spilling out across the upper lobby. I was able to move through the crowd at a normal pace and not draw attention. Even though it was busy, reaching the convention center felt like making it to the safe zone in a deadly game of tag. I wove through the crowds, keeping my aura tight. I regularly checked my Suck-O-Vision looking for auras that were more powerful than normal. Nothing jumped out at me.

True to his word, Nate pulled up and I jogged the twelve feet in the rain to his car. "Thank you so much again." I'd heard of people giving "fierce" hugs, but I had never given one myself until that moment. I didn't even care that it was awkward to lean over the armrests in his car to do so.

"Hey, you're wet!"

"I'm not that wet. And I think you just saved me a long, wet walk."

"You have got to learn how taxis work. I'm meeting someone for a dinner, so let's save the drama for some other time."

"Okay, but promise me we can talk after dinner tonight. I think I need to leave town, and I want to know if you'll look after a few things while I'm gone?"

"One, I hope to be busy after dinner and into the wee hours of the morning. Two, you have no money, how are you leaving town?"

"I have some money. You'll know when I have no money because I'll have to shack up with you. Anyway," I was thinking really quickly, "it's a job interview, but it's in Rhode Island. I'm willing to dip into funds to give this one a shot."

There was a long pause while he processed all the implications behind what I'd just said.

"You're leaving?"

"I'm investigating the option."

He didn't look happy. "Well it'd better be a good job. Because if you move to Rhode Island you're going to have to afford to come back and visit a lot."

The friendly banter continued as we navigated traffic back to my car.

LEAVING HOME

I was pretty sure the Sandmen would be staking out my townhouse once they finished searching the hotel. By the time Nate dropped me at home I had talked myself out of staying there. I grabbed my bag, unplugged everything except a living room lamp, locked up and got out of there.

In spite of his teasing, I did know how taxis worked. But if I was going to head to Rhode Island without much of a plan, I'd need to be frugal. I swallowed my pride and took a bus back downtown. I spent the majority of the trip practicing keeping my aura in tight. Watching a cute little kid pick her cute little nose and paint the bus window with it was just the sort of bonus entertainment that made you want to levitate and bathe yourself in hand sanitizer.

From the library, I took a circuitous route to Nate's house. My inexperienced paranoia didn't detect anyone tailing me. I even tried to pay attention at least three cars back. When I was safely in his driveway, I called him to let him know I was making dinner at his place. He didn't answer, so I left the message. I even promised I'd hide out in the back bedroom in case his post-date activities came back here.

I had a love-hate relationship with Nate's house. I loved

that it was his and he could do things like add a deck or plant a garden. I hated that he could also tear down a wall to "open up the space" only to discover the wall had been hiding a crucial support beam. I'd spent three days pulling insulating fiberglass micro-splinters out of my skin after helping him re-support the ceiling and clean up the mess from that one. Don't get me started on the bathroom plumbing incident.

I found leftover beef roast and vegetables in his fridge, along with lettuce that wasn't too wilted. I debated opening a bottle of his wine, but decided against it. I stuck it in the fridge to chill in case I changed my mind.

Nate's dinner date must not have ended well, he was home alone before the news came on.

He had already processed my car on the unused side of his driveway, so he barely raised an eyebrow my way. He went to the fridge, reached for a beer, but stopped when he noticed the wine.

"I've told you before to not to try getting me drunk. The way my night went you just might get lucky, then it'd get awkward, and we'd have to try to pretend nothing happened. And I don't think you're ready for that."

I smirked. "In your dreams."

"Those would be my nightmares." He ignored the beer, "Open the wine anyway."

I did and I poured him a healthy serving. If those agents were on my trail, I wanted to be able to think clearly.

"So," he took a healthy swallow, "Tell me about this job."

I'd had most of the evening to think through my answer. "The initial interview is with a headhunting firm, but they are specifically looking to place people in a corporation that funds international research. They're currently focused on dream research."

"What, like a think tank? Those are all over the east coast."

"You could say that, though they don't classify themselves that way."

"Does this mystery company have a name you could look up online?"

"The headhunting firm does, and they're reputable. They have not given out the name of the research company yet, though I assume I'll get it in the interview. If not, I'll be far more skeptical."

"You have skepticism? Where?" He helped himself to another gulp of wine while he thought it through. "Just don't get caught in something weird."

"What, like dream-o-naut experimentation where we're blasted into people's skulls while they sleep?"

"You know what I mean."

I did, and I nodded sheepishly for his sake.

He rallied for another argument against my bad idea, "What does a social media marketing manager know about dream research?"

I'd expected that. "Apparently my skill with market research translated into something that got me an interview. Plus, you know my track record with weird dream things. I'm curious."

"Jesus James… You're not signing on as one of the guinea pigs, are you?"

"Nope. Just an employee so I can be near the results when they're written up."

He mulled it over for a while. "I don't like it. I'm also being selfish. I don't want you to go."

"Nate, I'm …"

"I know, I know. I see how unhappy you are here. I just

don't want my best friend to move away."

I could only nod. It wouldn't have been manly to get choked up. But when you've grown up in the foster system, having a solid friendship really means something. I'm sure it means something to everyone, but in my own head, it meant an awful lot to me, dammit. I still wasn't going to get all gooey.

We switched to talking about the details of him checking my mail and looking in on my place while I was gone. By the time the wine was empty, nearly everything was settled.

Nearly. "I have one more favor to ask…"

"What's that?" He was pretty buzzed and usually a happy drunk, but my decisions had him skeptical.

"Can I borrow your old Jeep?"

That caught him off guard and he stared at me confused.

"It's my chance to be the dude driving halfway across the country in a Jeep with the top down. Call it a stupid bucket-list thing, but I've dreamed of it for a while. I even kind of want to document it online or make a story of it or something."

"You think that old thing will get you to Rhode Island, and then back?"

"I hope so, it'd be awesome."

He pondered for a few minutes. "Dessert would make this decision easier for me."

"Would you like some ice cream?" I grinned, feeling hopeful.

"That sounds delicious." While I was at the counter scooping it up he said, "Okay fine, but any repairs are yours to pay for. As are gas and tolls."

"Deal! Thank you!!" I gave him extra scoops.

CHAPTER FIVE
1972 – SOMALIA

Sopora was in Somalia, though I have no way of explaining why I knew that. She was covered in a jilbāb and some sort of head wrap. She stared deep into her own darkly-lined eyes reflecting back to her from a dirty puddle on the ground under a flickering street lamp. She had just commanded, "Remember." This was familiar enough that I accepted she had something, or several things, I needed to see. I was supposed to remember to ask her something from my own wakefulness, but it wouldn't come to me.

She was already breathing heavily. Without looking around, she took off at a run down an alley between a chaotic jumble of shack-like houses. I heard footsteps somewhere behind her, it sounded like a single person headed this way. She didn't turn to look. She didn't want to waste the precious time she could use to distance herself from her pursuer.

As she ran, she held her hands out to her sides, fingers clawed as though she was raking the night air. Suddenly, a dim mote of light no larger than a pencil's eraser phased through a wall and disappeared into her palm with a small flare of light. A few houses later, another flew into her palm as though drawn by a powerful magnet. Another followed, and then another. She was harvesting them.

She held up one hand so I could see through her eyes, and I no longer doubted that she was doing this for my benefit. She was showing me something important. The motes floated and swirled slowly in a dim cloud just under the skin of her palm, but each retained its individuality. They were a little mesmerizing in their beauty. She insistently pushed her hand closer and I realized what she was showing me. Those motes were dreams she's been harvesting from sleepers as we passed by their houses. Within each mote was a dream island. She was gathering them.

I wanted to ask if the dreamers lost them forever, but the footsteps had gained on us while she'd been trying to get me to understand what she was collecting. She dropped her hand back down to collect more dreams and ran faster.

The chase continued for the better part of a neighborhood. She used corners and parallel alleys to both throw around the sound of her movement and pass by as many dreamers as she could. Not every house yielded a dream mote, but many did.

In a particularly dark part of the neighborhood, she rounded a quick succession of corners, stopping after the third one. Spinning to face the archway, she brought her hands up. Using her palms like putty knives, she made a few passes across the empty space of the corner she'd just turned. Where her hand moved through the air a swath of a dirty, stucco wall appeared. As her slapdash creation took on more size and appearance I saw that she was painting an illusionary wall. I could feel the dream energy flowing off her hands. She was burning through the dream motes to power the illusion. Though it probably would not withstand careful scrutiny, she was running out of time.

She must have known about or somehow felt the dream energy as well, because she quickly absorbed the residual energy like she did with her own aura. Satisfied with her quick work, she moved away from the phantasmal wall quietly so her footsteps wouldn't betray her. I felt her draw her aura in tight.

Heartbeats later, I heard her pursuer's footsteps pass by the dream barrier and keep going without a break in rhythm. Seemingly satisfied, she moved away from her hunter's path picking up speed the farther she went. Her hands were once again open, collecting dreams as we passed homes with dreamers.

She moved quietly and confidently through the dark alleys. I sensed she knew where she was going, though as usual I was clueless. When her hands were filled with dreams, she pulled them up into the sleeves of her jilbāb so the glow wouldn't give her away. She deftly avoided areas where it looked like people might be out and about. As we moved deeper into the city, houses became nicer and there were more and more spaces between them, but fewer and fewer alleys.

She was still choosing her path carefully, but her walk had become less stealthy and more hunched over and almost beaten down. It was heartbreaking to understand why she had to camouflage herself, but I'm not naïve enough to believe she could risk strolling around like a proud woman.

By the time houses had become estates, she was checking addresses. When she found the one she wanted, she took a deep breath and looked the property over. The outer wall was made of recently re-painted brick, and was high enough to keep out spying eyes from the street. I estimated she could pretty easily pull herself to the top with a running leap. I wondered what would happen to the dream motes in her hands if she tried.

She didn't though. She walked around the back checking exits. There was a gate in the wall back there, with a narrow drive. It looked locked and unattended. The front had a mechanized gate and gatehouse with a lone guard.

From her vantage in the shadows at the corner, she pulled out her right hand, keeping her sleeve to the guard. She mentally willed one mote, one entire dream island, up to the top of her hand. From there, she blew on it lightly and I watched it bob and weave its way toward the guard. When it neared him, she made it flare like a firefly. It caught his attention and he watched it curiously. Sopora pulled a handful of shimmering dust out of her robe as she snuck up behind him. She clucked her tongue. He spun, and she blew the dust into his face. His features relaxed when it hit him, and it looked like he was slipping into a light daydream. She pulled out another handful and blew it his way to bolster the first one.

Back in the Agency, Sopora had told Bruadair his missions marked him as a Sandman agent. What she was showing me now was undoubtedly the reason for the name. It was the iconic trick associated with the Sandman in all the childhood bedtime stories. The way she did it looked exactly like I would have imagined it to look if someone had told me a Sandman was putting someone to sleep.

The second mote was all it took to send the guard to dreamland. His head drooped for a moment, his shoulders relaxed, and he just sort of drifted off. Sopora wasted no time. She hustled along the wall to the gate and looked over the controls in front of the sleeping man. I didn't recognize the language, but Sopora must have because she made a fairly quick choice and the gate slid open enough to allow her entrance.

Once inside, she adopted the hunched over walk again, slow and deferential to the world as a whole. With her head bent, she looked around. The estate had a large house, a long garage with an upstairs, and a pool with a few assorted maintenance buildings. She shuffled toward the garage.

When she tried the side door of the garage, it was unlocked. Behind it was a tight staircase heading up. Not looking around, she entered and quietly closed the door behind her. The upper hallway had a row of doors, but nothing convenient like name plates or a directory.

Undaunted, Sopora moved to the first one. As with the houses we'd run past, she held out her hand and summoned the occupant's dream to her. This time, though, she lifted her hand and focused in on the dream she'd acquired. The island turned over to show a young man with a really nice, classic, Rolls Royce. The young man was directing or motioning something, but Sopora stopped. It wasn't what she wanted.

Working her way down the hallway methodically, Sopora repeated the dream test when she could draw out a mote. Not every room yielded up a dream. However, with only four doors to go, Sopora found her target.

The man in this dream was white, and not native. Other than that, his dream seemed incoherent, an old woman, a purple tree, a talking horse. Sopora looked at the door, and didn't see a keyhole or any method of locking, or unlocking it. She transferred all the motes from her right hand into her left. Slowly and quietly she turned the knob and let herself inside.

As far as servant rooms went, it wasn't bad. It was almost as large as my living room and kitchenette area. He had comfortable furniture, a fan, a floor heater, and what looked like a hotplate. The man's guard uniform and gun belt were draped over a chair within easy reach of the bed. Sopora blew three motes at him before she risked any noise closing the door. His breathing deepened, but that was the only clue that confirmed he'd fallen into a deeper sleep. It seemed enough for Sopora, and she shut the door.

She looked around the room in more detail. Stopping at the gun, she deftly emptied the rounds and chamber, and placed it back in the holster. As an afterthought, she kicked the bullets under the chair. Pulling her right sleeve up to her shoulder, she sat down next to the guard. Without hesitating she laid her bare forearm over his.

I felt the sensation of her consciousness flowing out of her pores and into his. Tethered as I was to Sopora, she pulled me into the man's inner dream realm. Only... this man's dreams were weird. And that's saying something. The first couple islands were fused to each other at odd angles. They were rotating on a skewed axis, showing bits and pieces from each one, but never the full tale from any of the three at once. When one finally rotated to show a young man with a Rolls Royce, I understood. These dreams right at the front of his mind were the motes Sopora had just blown at the guard to put him to sleep. They weren't integrated into his mind, so they were just parked here keeping his sleeping mind busy.

She didn't stop to look, so I was pulled past them. She flew deeper in. His dreams were still a chaotic jumble, though the islands were no longer fused together. Unlike the last man, this one didn't have recognizable streams of thought with tenuous themes like family and mistresses. This man's dream-scape was a wide open sea with islands haphazardly placed for reasons I couldn't discern. My guess was Sopora couldn't really find a pattern either, but I also had the feeling she'd dealt with minds like this before.

She tried a bit longer, spying on island after island. Each one we reached appeared unrelated to its neighbors.

Lifting her left hand, she coaxed a mote forward with her right hand. She whispered to it and released it. The mote started zipping from island to island far faster than she could move. Sopora continued to float along while the mote covered all the islands in a wide radius around her. Occasionally it would flit back as though checking in. She whispered to it again and it took off to check on the next batch of islands. Time ticked on, but I couldn't effectively tell how much.

Far deeper into the ocean, the mote glowed brightly over an island and then popped out of existence. I wondered again if that meant the original dreamer would never have that dream again, or if it had just been borrowed to become Sopora's seeker mote? She gave no indication she was aware of my question. She pulled closer and hovered just off the periphery of the island.

In the island's memory scene, he wasn't dressed as a guard. He wore some sort of military garb. I didn't recognize the country of origin. He stood with his squad. His commanding officer was giving some sort of orders. The men spread out, covering different angles of the street. The one furthest away pulled an African shawl over his uniform, and they all tried to affect poses of casual readiness. As cars came toward them, the disguised soldier peered into them. It wasn't too long before he saw what they were looking for and he signaled to the others.

The squad tensed and readied. Our sleeping guard had the best angle. From his belt he unhooked a grenade, and in one swift movement pulled the pin and rolled it toward the car.

It exploded just before rolling under the car, blasting the side but not blowing it up. The squad dispersed, but the leader shot our guard a dirty look before the dream ended.

Sopora looked puzzled for a brief second. She strained to see the events playing out on nearby dream islands, but must not have seen anything relevant. She lifted her hand and coaxed forward another mote. She whispered to it like she had the last one. Like the last one, it zipped off and searched islands in a wide radius. Once again, she floated along behind it at a slower pace.

The mote zipped back and forth. It diligently sought out the information Sopora had been sent by the Agency to acquire. The dreams were getting darker. Island after island showed the guard living out his desire to kill. He carried in his heart a vicious, violent hatred for all black men, but in his dreams he only seemed to vent it on those with money or power. He spent his nights inventing ways to kill those better off than he was. It was revolting. In my own life I'd had late night, after-movie talks with friends about what kind of darkness lived in the mind of a killer. Actually seeing a killer's dreamscape was something else entirely, and now I wanted nothing more than to un-see it.

The mote found something and she zeroed in on it. A Somalian cavalcade was pulling up to a rented estate much like the one Sopora had just broken into. Security men stepped out of their cars and began checking the property. Our guard was part of the security detail. They found no dangers, and the captain made a call. It was obvious they didn't realize the worst danger was among them, eating at their table and sharing their duties.

In the dream, several days of politicking and coming and going passed by. A routine started to develop, and the guard set the stage to make his move.

Though I didn't understand the language they spoke, Sopora did. She listened to them intently. The guard motioned a well-dressed African to follow him. The African pointed to his watch, but assented after a minute. Neither man's posture was tense. The African official was willing to trust his security detail. Reaching the guest house, the guard walked around the corner mere steps ahead of the African. He picked up an automatic rifle and had it braced by the time the official rounded the corner. The surprised man had no opportunity to speak or call for help. The guard fired immediately. As his target lay dying in the grass, the guard sprinted toward the fence. He had prepared for his escape, and a convenient gardener's cart gave him all the boost he needed to get up and over the wall.

Landing on the other side, the fleeing guard froze and swore loudly. A man in a black trench coat stood there, watching everything, waiting. Sopora moved quickly to watch the confrontation. The murderous guard drew his revolver, intending to shoot the witness. In a flash, the man pulled a black baton out of his trench coat. The guard sneered at the baton and squeezed the trigger.

The baton moved faster than Sopora's eyes could track. All I saw was a trail of black tendrils that reflected no light. The tendrils rippled as they caught the bullet. In the time it took for us to realize what had just happened, the man in the black coat was ready and waiting for the guard to make another move.

The guard stared wide-eyed at the tendrils, which were still lightly rippling in the shape of a crescent blade. Then she felt the man in the trench coat unleash something. Sopora looked around curiously, but didn't immediately recognize the phenomenon. The guard's reaction gave it away. The man in the trench coat had projected an intense beam of pure fear at his attacker. The guard's ego wasn't equipped to deal with it, and he ran off in terror.

The man in the trench coat didn't give chase. He just stood there and watched the murderer run. Sopora spun around so she could see the man's face. It was the man who'd been bundled against the London chill in the previous dream. He turned to the estate's fence and walked right through it towards the dead African. Then the dream island re-set the scene and started to replay it.

I had forgotten we were in the guard's dream of this memory and he hadn't seen any more of the man in the trench coat than that. Sopora glanced down at the empty sea where the island was replaying the scene. She was deep in thought. Shaking it off, she called up another mote. She whispered a request to it and it zipped around a bit, then shot off in a straight line. Sopora followed it out.

Leaving his dreamscape, her hand was still on his forearm but something had changed. There was an intensity in the air. Sopora checked the motes in her left hand. She was a few down but she still had a handful.

She heard the unmistakable sound of the door to the room next to ours opening. There were a few moments of silence as though someone was just looking into a room, and she heard the door close quietly. Somebody in the hallway was checking rooms.

Sopora stood up, distributing the motes evenly between her hands. She started using her hands like a potter uses clay, sculpting the dream motes into another illusion. Instead of a wall this time, she sculpted the phantasm of herself lying on top of the guard. She made certain there were several points of skin-to-skin contact visible. Then she dropped and rolled under the bed just as we heard the doorknob turn.

Closing her fists to mute the light from her remaining motes, she pulled her aura in tight. Quietly, she turned her head toward the intruder. The black boots were military issue, as were the pants tucked into them. An American male's voice quietly sneered, "awww… the little Sandman whore is traipsing through her target's dreams. Isn't it tragic that she'll be trapped in his head for as long as he lives?"

It sounded like he unsheathed a weapon. Sopora cupped her hands like a woman in prayer and tensed.

The man sprang forward with a sudden, killing stroke. Sopora released a mote right up through the bed.

Tenseness hung in the air, then the attacker pulled back. A rivulet of blood dripped down the side of the bed and started pooling on the floor. The attacker whispered, "Sweet dreams" with a malicious tone in his voice and wasted no further time in letting himself out.

Sopora stayed still on that dirty, smelly floor beneath the bed much longer than I had held out in the clean, comparatively spacious stairwell of the hotel. When she finally rolled out through the pool of blood it wasn't even remotely disturbed by her passing. Standing, I saw what the attacker had done. He had stabbed a huge combat knife between her phantasmal shoulder blades. The mote she had released at the same time must have been to create a believable reaction… the blood.

She again transferred her few remaining motes to her left hand. With her right she grabbed the handle of the knife and smoothly pulled it out of the illusion. As she did, her simulacrum degraded and quickly dissipated into nothing. The guard remained in his induced sleep completely unaware. She tucked the knife into a belt under her jilbāb and left as quietly as she'd come.

As she made her stealthy way off the property, I wanted to ask her how she could just leave these murderers alive. She has seen the truths in their own minds, and done nothing to bring them to justice. I didn't want to advocate she kill them, but I had hoped she'd call the authorities or something. I tried speaking to her, but she didn't react. I tried thinking at her as loud as I could. I mentally imagined screaming at her. Even though she'd done things earlier to make me believe she knew I was there, she gave no indication that she was aware of my attempts to communicate. It seemed I was only an observer, invited but silent.

I gave up when I saw the guard at the front gate. He'd been killed by a knife to the neck. Sopora shook her head sadly and made her way back into the anonymity of the town.

Chapter Six
2012 – Leaving Milwaukee

There was one more thing I needed to do before I could really go off on this crazy trip. I had to take some time off of work. If the Sandmen knew anything about me, then they'd most likely know my car and have my workplace staked out. I spent my time in the shower at Nate's place mentally rehearsing the call I'd have to make to Cal.

"James," he answered instantly, "I hope you're not stuck in traffic." Was it too much to ask that I'd get to leave a message?

"Uh… no…" I hate that feeling where your brain screeches to a halt and goes completely blank.

"Ok, good. Your 8:00 am appointment is already here waiting with the receptionist."

I didn't have any appointments on my calendar. I instantly assumed it was Sandmen, which only made me mildly surprised they were trying a direct approach. "I can't come in Cal, there's been a death in my family and I have to head back… west."

"James, don't pull my leg. Not to be indelicate, but we know you didn't have parents."

"I still had a foster family, Cal." See? I resisted the urge to call him Jackass. And people say I can't censor myself. "I also don't know who shared information from my personnel file, but I'm pretty sure what you just said is a huge breach in my privacy rights that I'll deal with when I get back. I'm asking you, please, let me take personal time." Either someone in Human Resources has a big mouth or Little-Miss-Social-Media has done some serious cyber-snooping. It was almost like Fate wanted me to get out of there so badly she was smacking me upside the head.

"Oh, hey now, there's no need to talk like that." I could hear the fear of employment law in his voice. "Of course you can have bereavement leave. Standard is three days for an immediate family member." The more he spoke, the more I hated my company. "What about your 8:00?"

"Let Jeni handle it. She's vying for my job anyway. Here's her big chance."

"Now James, that was unfair. She's just an eager beaver out to climb the corporate ladder."

I bit my tongue before the words Beavers Don't Climb Ladders Asshat rolled out. Instead, I took a breath and replied, "If you say so. Either way, she's in my division and if she doesn't cover for me it looks like you'll have to."

"Perhaps I should coach her to cover in your absence."

I had to squash another sarcastic comeback in order to say, "That's a great idea. I think she'll be just super. And thank you."

The rest of my morning preparations were spent hoping the Sandmen were unkind to Jeni-with-a-heart. Before I left, I used Nate's computer to disable my social media accounts. I was also smart enough to know that most phone apps tracked location these days, so I dedicated the time required to figuring out how to shut down ALL location services for

ALL apps except navigation. I didn't see any reason for a giant flashing arrow to flicker on and off over my head.

THE HIGHWAY

Nate's '92 Jeep Wrangler felt old, loved, experienced, and adventurous. The fact it was still running was a testament to its pedigree. Nate took good care of his things these days, but he hadn't always. I happen to know that this Jeep had been in two accidents, and had multiple system replacements. He'd tried to sell it twice, and both times he came to the conclusion it was cheaper to keep it. I suspected he loved his old Jeep and couldn't bring himself to get rid of it, even though he always drove his newer, more fuel-efficient car these days.

He had given me the key from his key ring at dinner, and had me park my car in its place in his garage. He had also packed a backpack with road food for me and loaned me two tubs of the camping gear we used to use. It'd be warm for another couple months, and any night I could pitch a tent so I didn't need to pay for a room would be a good night.

I wasn't even completely out of town before I wondered again if this was unthinkingly stupid of me. If following these dreams answered a lifetime of questions then this was absolutely the right thing to be doing. But I had to entertain the idea that I was perhaps not thinking as clearly as I should have been. What if I was crazy? I didn't feel crazy... but when does crazy ever feel crazy? I know it's not a very nice way to phrase it, but I had to face the possibility. If I had to choose between telling someone I had dream powers or was losing my mind, I don't think I could actually say, "dream powers" out loud.

But what about agent Bruadair? He was in the first dream I'd had of Sopora's life, and then I saw him in the library and followed him to the hotel where he almost caught me on the stairs. His appearance in my life had to mean something.

The miles flew by while I argued with myself.

By the end of the day I was two tanks of gas poorer. I wouldn't have to empty my bank account entirely for this trip, but it'd make a serious dent into funds I couldn't afford to spend frivolously. I was also getting tired. Stops for gas, food, and bathroom breaks weren't providing the refreshing wake-up I had hoped. After a full day doubting my sanity and reasons for going, I was also feeling mighty alone. It was completely stupid and irrational. Realizing I wouldn't actually be able to bring myself to tell anyone what was going on only enhanced my feeling of isolation.

I tried calling Nate, but he was still working and asked if I could call back later. I tried calling Michelle, a friend from the gym who went by 'Chelle and was always up for a good talk, but only got her voicemail. On a whim, I tried Justin. He answered on the second ring, but it sounded like he was in traffic and I asked if it was a bad time.

"Oh no, I'm good. I'm on the bus headed for home." He hesitated. "I wasn't sure if you'd actually call."

I could tell from his voice he was feeling a bit vulnerable for admitting that. So I tried for funny, "I thought the two day wait was still stylish? Did I screw that up?"

Thankfully he laughed, "Nobody waits anymore. Texting is instant. Hey, did you get out of the library before some idiot pulled the alarm?"

"Text instantly, duly noted. No, I caught the tail end of the commotion. What was it about?"

"They said some maniac picked up a chair and rammed one of the downstairs emergency doors."

I forced myself to ignore the mirror. I didn't need visual confirmation of the sheepish look that crept over my face.

Unaware, he continued on, "Did you ever find that closed-up restaurant you were looking for? Why'd you need to find it?"

"No, I didn't. I think it was in my family at one time. Like I said, I saw several pictures of it in a scrapbook I recently inherited, and I just wanted to know more."

"I can keep looking if you want? Hey, what are you doing tomorrow?"

"I'm actually on the highway heading out of town on business, but have hours ahead of me on the road if you wanted to talk. If not, that's cool... but, um... I shouldn't be texting."

"Oh, that's cool. I can talk for a bit. Where's business? What do you do?"

On a whim, I decided to try my cover story on for size, "I've made a recent transition to dream research. Most of the better facilities are on the east coast, so I'm headed to Rhode Island for a while. What about you? Is the central branch of the Milwaukee Public Library your end goal?"

"OH hell no! I mean, it's part of the path for sure. But I'm actually trying to get in with one of the large national libraries, preferably the research department. If not research, archives would be cool too. I love some of the stuff you can find if you know where to look!"

"You should try looking in people's heads some time."

"Huh?"

"Oh, sorry. Dream research, people write down the strangest things when they're still half-remembering their dreams.

Sorry, didn't mean to interrupt. You were telling me about you. Is there a Mr. Justin?"

He laughed a good, solid laugh. "You're good looking and all, but I probably wouldn't have exchanged numbers if I already had someone. I tried the open relationship thing once, and it just ended up messy and painful."

"I've never tried. I'd like to think I'm open-minded enough, but I really don't think I am." Hell, I knew I wasn't. I had never even made it past knowing my exes had been dreaming about other guys.

"It's okay. I'm not ready to go back that way again. So, no, there's no Mr. Justin. Would you be interested in applying for the job?"

Ouch. I didn't even know if I should be impressed with his candor, or worried by the suddenness. "I think an interview over dinner, and maybe a follow-up interview would be in order before I can answer that question definitively."

"I like the sound of that. What about you? Is there a Mr. James?"

"Nope. Caught the last one entangled with someone else and it hurt way too much. I almost pushed you away at the library, which had nothing to do with you and everything to do with that particular event in my past."

"I wondered why you changed your mind." He thought for a second, "You're not still holding on to that lost love, are you?"

"No. Right there in the library, I realized I was initially trying to avoid getting hurt again. But in hindsight, my ex's name didn't even pop into my head. I think I've been using the experience, but not the man, to protect myself from the good parts of living. Once I'd convinced myself it was unhealthy, I figured I should let you ask me out to dinner."

I could hear the laughter in his voice. "So we're telling people that I'm the one who came on to you?"

"Well it's true!"

"Okay, maybe it is."

We talked for over an hour. For the most part we shared first date banter. His favorite foods are Italian, mine are anything spicy like Cajun or Thai. He has a cat, I currently have no pets. He went to a state college, I had been a liberal arts guy. Stuff like that to fill the time. We eventually had to stop, but I was grateful to him.

He gave me a lot of new distractions to consider, which was good for keeping me awake. Because once the sun goes down and you cannot see the countryside, road trips are mind-numbingly boring. I didn't want to risk slipping into a dream while driving. Having someone new to think about, someone who is full of possibility and excitement, did wonders for my energy levels.

I finally admitted it was time to pull over and stop. The night's weather didn't require a hotel, and a rest stop with camping facilities presented itself. I peed, set up camp, locked the Jeep's doors, and prepared for Sopora's next installment. I had just laid back to rest when my phone rang.

"Hi 'Chelle."

"I'm going to quit my job!" The drama in her voice came through loud and clear.

"Uh oh. What happened?"

"My new boss is a self-obsessed megalomaniac. He set up a project schedule and screwed up everyone's job. He had me running errands! Me! The art director! And we're stuck with it until we can get HIS boss to realize what's going on."

"How long will that take?"

"Well he'd have to get his ugly butt back from Ohio first."

I smiled at her graphic honesty. "Well… it may not be artistically fulfilling, but you could always just enjoy getting out of the office and running some errands on company time."

She laughed deeply, "Oh I thought that through already. I may have even set up a personal appointment or two with doctor hair stylist and doctor Botox."

"Ha ha ha!"

"But that's not why you called me. You know I don't talk on the phone, I'm like a twelve year old girl with texting. What's up? Did you hear what happened at the gym today?"

The plush, downy, soft, cuddly sleeping bag suddenly got very uncomfortable. "I was there when Gregory died. I can't go back for a while."

"Oh James, I'm sorry. I heard about it, it sounded terrible. I can't imagine seeing it." And then the twelve year old girl kicked in, "Was it bloody? Did anything come out his ears? Or nose?"

"Okay, stop! It was really bad. I needed to take some time away."

"Well come by tomorrow for dinner."

"I can't, I'll be in Rhode Island."

"That doesn't… huh? Rhode Island, Massachusetts?"

"Rhode Island's its own state. I decided to follow up on a job offer and go ahead with the interview."

"I just thought you meant time away from the gym. Damn. You meant away away. Tell me about this job, you certainly hear enough about mine."

While I was telling her what I'd told Nate, I watched headlights fly by on the interstate. Nate and 'Chelle knew each other through me, but didn't generally chat with each other. Still, I had figured Nate would be the analytical and critical one, so when he seemed okay with the story, I thought it'd be okay for 'Chelle too. She's generally pretty open to anything from New Age wisdom to pseudo-science. Man was I wrong.

"Dream research? What the fuck is that? Is that like Freud and shit?"

"Kind of. People sleep in a controlled environment, and their eye movements are monitored. When they reach the end of a dream stage, they're awakened and asked to write down everything they remember."

"Mmmhmmm. Sounds fishy. And what in your life, exactly, makes you qualified to do this research?"

"I'm re-inventing myself." It hit me she had no idea how true that really was. "Besides, when the dream research is over, the company will move on to a new project. Mostly they just catalogue, analyze, and then archive the data. They're not the researchers, just the information gatherers."

"Doesn't sound like you at all. It sounds stuffy and boring."

"Well in case you hadn't noticed, the sexy, exciting job offers haven't been setting my inbox on fire."

"Wait. How're you getting to Rhode Island? I don't hear a plane."

"I borrowed Nate's old Jeep."

"The Death Buggy???"

Okay, so maybe it was Death Star gray. And maybe Nate had once smashed into the back of a city alderman's Cadillac. And maybe, just maybe, I was the guy who gave it that nickname. But Nate's willingness to loan it to me last night had been a kindness and I was willing to defend him a little.

"Yeah, the Jeep. It's not that bad."

"Not that bad? Aren't you the one who said it strikes fear into aldermaans all over the city?"

"That's not confirmed. And, anyway, it was awesome of Nate to loan it to me."

"You know I'll give you my frequent flyer miles!"

There it was, The Competition. "I know you would, but then I'd have nothing to drive when I get there. Rental cars are stupidly expensive. And if I fly and use public transportation, I'd have to get a room. This way I can sleep in the Jeep."

"YOU'RE SLEEPING IN THE DEATH BUGGY?"

Shit. "In a tent, mostly. Unless the weather turns bad."

"Look, I'll be happy to miss my glamorous week of running fucking stupid errands. I'll make up some disease that the Megalomaniac doesn't want to catch and I'll burn some of the sick time I've been building up. At least pick me up in the morning and I'll go with you."

"I can't."

"You're already there, aren't you?"

"Not exactly. But, umm. I am on the far side of Ohio. Hey! Do you want me to find your boss's boss and clue him in to what's going on in your office?" I offered as a lame, tension-diffusing joke.

"Oh shut up. Look, if you need anything, anything, you call or text me. Ok? This isn't the Stone Age. Our little phones allow instant communication at any distance. I can put money in your online account if you are stuck somewhere."

"Okay."

"Uh uh. You gave that up too easily. And I can't check to see if you're crossing your fingers, so I can't make you promise. So instead, I'm going to issue you a threat."

"Are you serious?"

"James, if you're in need and you don't fucking call me, I will make sure you hear about it from me daily for the rest of your life. And when you die, I will dig up your decomposing ass every day and make sure you hear it some more. And when the Goddess finally calls me home I will find your afterlife and I will make sure you fucking continue to hear all about it for the rest of fucking eternity."

I'd never heard her issue so dire a threat. A car with a bad muffler drove past. "You mean that, don't you?"

"With all my eternal awesomeness, jackass. Eternity and beyond."

I solemnly agreed to her terms and she calmed down enough that we could say our goodbyes without any lingering weirdness. It actually felt good to know I had friends that cared so much. If this trip bore fruit, leaving them would be heartbreaking.

I looked over at the Death Buggy. Nate and I had put a lot of the miles on that Jeep together. Memories of simple runs around town, day trips to local wineries, and adventure weekends away were all ingrained into the faded fabric and dashboard scratches. Aldermaanians all over the city might fear the Death Buggy, but to me it was a comforting sanctuary.

THE NEXT MORNING

Morning dawned. The sun was hitting me square in the face. I looked around expecting Sopora to tell me to remember, but I was still in my tent next to the Death Buggy. I was not in a woman's body. Also, I had to pee again. Since I had never once felt any of my own bodily needs while in one of Sopora's dreams, I deduced I was wide awake in the real world. I felt a strange emotional emptiness that I think I had expected Sopora's dream to fill, almost like a next chapter in her story. As much as the dreams were messing with my sanity, and my life, I hoped I wasn't done having them.

I looked at myself critically in the cloudy metal mirror of the rest stop bathroom. The second day of beard scruff was coming in nicely. I wished I looked exotic and Mediterranean with my facial hair. But though my stubble was dark brown, it was only good for about four days before it started looking sparse. Sometime around day six it'd cross the line into patchy and I'd get frustrated and shave it all off. But not today. I washed myself with a packet of body wipes from my camping kit and tried to see myself as some kind of Dreamworld Avenger. It sounded infinitely better than Captain Suck-O-Vision.

Exiting the restroom, I noticed something I hadn't seen in the dark – RVs and semis parked behind the brick visitor's center. If Sopora's dream from the previous day was meant to show me something, and if I was in fact like her, then I should be able to gather a dream mote from a sleeper. It was still really early, surely someone was still asleep. I put my toiletry bag in the Death Buggy and walked over towards the large vehicles, trying to form my hands into gathering claws just like she had. Walking up and down the aisle between them, I tried to feel a connection, any connection, between me and any potential dreamers. I was quickly starting to feel like a creep, when I felt a vibration. It was just a slight tremor in my hand, almost like a muscle spasm. I looked down, and saw a dim mote phase through a semi and come to rest in my palm. I stopped walking and pulled it up close. I could make out details on the mote. It was like I could telescope my vision in and see the dream. The man was on an island of nude women who wanted nothing more in the world than to… eww. I put my hand down. I didn't really need to see his dream in that much detail. But that was exactly what Sopora had been trying to show me when she had pulled her own hand close. She'd wanted me to focus in and see the dream within the mote.

Turning, I started back towards the Death Buggy. On a whim, I tried to transfer the mote to my other hand. It slid over easily.

I knew I had to try one more thing before I lost the mote. I tried painting with it. It smeared across reality, looking like a floating ribbon of muddy color. I had tried to paint a tree branch. It didn't look anything like a tree branch. It looked like a toddler with finger paints had tried to paint a colored smear and mostly succeeded. I say mostly because the quality of the color wasn't up to finger paint standards.

People were going to be up soon. I put my hand on the smear, and felt the faint tremor again. Interesting. I then focused on absorbing the dream energy into my body like I had with my aura. After a second, the smear started coming apart. Soon enough, it was gone completely. I was stunned. It was harder and harder to pretend I wasn't becoming the Dreamworld Avenger!

Pleased with myself, I jogged back to the Death Buggy and fired it up, hitting the road again. Another full day on the highway stretched out before me. I tried to mentally replay Sopora's first dream where she was driving to the Agency's compound. I would have to recreate her drive, and I was desperate to keep the information fresh so I wouldn't miss any clues. Plus, it helped pass the miles.

PROVIDENCE, RHODE ISLAND

I reached Providence by dinner time. I had done my internet research while waiting for Nate. Rhode Island's largest city is also its capitol. It's easily twice the size of any other city, and the only one I would actually consider a "city." The next most populous was technically a large town.

Her dream had started with her heading out to the country. I had decided to try driving out of the city on the main highways first, working my way down to state highways and then county roads if I needed to.

The first two highways didn't jog my memory in any way. The third, Highway 6 heading west out of town, felt right. Cities can change a lot over a couple decades, but large buildings are slower to do so. As the sun was setting I noticed a familiar skyline. Feeling good about it, I kept going. Sopora's dreams had all been vague about how much time was passing. I had yet to figure out how I could accurately time the duration of anything she did. So I had no idea how far I needed to drive.

There were a lot more suburbs now than there had been in Sopora's time. I feared that the most prominent landmark, the gold and red barn where Sopora had turned to enter to the Agency's complex, stood a very good chance at being gone completely. Thankfully, even if I drove beyond the barn's original location I'd reach the One-Eyed Roe. I strained to see any landmarks as the sky turned golden, and then eased into black.

Rather than risk zooming past something important in the dark, I started looking for a place to camp for the night. I didn't see any convenient campgrounds, but I had passed a Wal-Mart Super Center south of here along I-295. It wasn't ideal, but tolerable because it'd likely have traffic most of the night, so I stood a chance at being unnoticed.

I parked the Death Buggy farther away from the entrance, where I hoped the night employees parked. I locked the doors, laid the seat back again and stared at the ceiling for a few minutes. Is this what my life had been reduced to? Sleeping in parking lots? I hoped I'd get beyond this soon. I was convinced there had to be a reason the Sopora dreams had started. If the Death Buggy had answers, it held on to them tightly. I drifted off to sleep thinking about my favorite superpowers.

CHAPTER SEVEN
1972 – NAIROBI, KENYA

"Remember!"

I don't know why I was relieved to be staring at Sopora's reflection where my own should have been, but I was. Missing one night of her memory dreams had been more jarring than I'd thought it would be. I don't know if I considered her my mentor or just someone whose story needed to be remembered. Probably both.

She looked around. The daytime sun was bright and hot. She stood on a wide pedestrian avenue in front of a glass and steel building that had offered the reflection she'd needed. The name over the door proclaimed in English "Co-operative Bank of Kenya." The other pedestrians were dressed fairly contemporary, for Sopora's time, in Western-style pants and button up shirts. She walked along the pedestrian mall to a busy street and blended into the foot traffic.

She covered several city blocks, surrounded by what looked like government buildings. At first, I thought Sopora seemed to have a destination in mind. Then I noticed she was scoping out restaurants, cafés, and other places where people gather. I couldn't tell if she was looking at the venues themselves or the people.

One restaurant held her attention, and she found a nearby vendor who sold her a newspaper. She grabbed a place across the street where she could sit and read while keeping an eye on the restaurant's outdoor seating. Once again, time passed and I had no way to track it effectively. The majority of the patrons coming and going wore military uniforms. They were the ones she was most interested in.

One officer in particular gave her a reason to fold up the paper. She squinted, and I saw an aura through her eyes for the first time. The people around the officer had dull, thin variations of energy and color, but his extended powerfully a foot in all directions. Where the normal auras were fairly static, his swirled violently with shades of grey and black. It was active and coruscating, and made him appear larger and more powerful than everyone around him. If this was how we looked to each other, I understood why Sopora had become a prized field agent. Her ability to hide her aura meant the people of this secret world would generally ignore her.

Sopora pulled hers in tight and waited. Having closed up her paper, she started looking up and down the street, though always keeping the officer within the edges of her field of vision. Was she looking for someone else? Soon enough, a woman with her own powerful aura approached the officer. Unlike his dark, powerful aura, hers was red and enticing. Hers spoke of lust and desire, and dreams fulfilled.

She smiled coyly at him, and even I could spot the start of a flirt. What Sopora was helping me see was the way her aura operated. His had defined borders, but hers faded into a misty obscurity. I could see the red mist wrap around behind him, but aside from being overtly supernatural it wasn't creepy. It almost looked like her aura was caressing his, hugging it.

The couple was still talking, and I saw his hardened military demeanor soften. And then he smiled. He offered her a seat, which she took, and he motioned to a waiter. They ordered drinks and kept talking. Sopora kept watch.

Throughout the course of the first drink, her aura continued to wrap around his. It was never forceful. Instead, it waited for a grey swirl or a dark eddy in his aura, and then her passion-red mist would just flow into the momentary space. By the time they had finished their first drinks, her aura had made inroads to several key places through his aura–most notably his mind, his heart, and his groin. Her seduction seemed to be working, and he made several gestures to indicate leaving together. She played a little hard to get, which only inflamed his interest.

Eventually, she assented, and allowed him to pull her up and lead her away. He looked pleased with himself as he hailed a taxi.

Sopora didn't seem remotely anxious that they were getting away. She watched calmly as the officer helped the woman into the car, got in behind her, and gave the driver an address. She waited for an awful lot of traffic to pass before she stood from the bench, walked purposefully to the street, and hailed her own cab. In the accent she'd been using for her cover identity, she gave the driver an address and he laughed deep and loud.

"It is good for you that I speak the English!"

Sopora laughed lightly and airily, "Oh thank you! It really is my lucky day! I love it when a driver can tell me about his city. Is there anything I should know?"

"Ahhh! Yes! We call Nairobi 'The Green City in the Sun!' Have you ever seen such a large city with so many beautiful parks?"

She dutifully shook her head, "No! They're fantastic! Like that park? What can you tell me about that one?" she asked him excitedly.

His tone wavered, "That park is named for another famous English who built hotel. But in front of that park, many people died to give Kenya freedom."

Sopora's gaze lingered on the small park, though whether it was part of the act, or she was honestly looking for something, I couldn't tell. "I'm so sorry... I mean... not sorry you have freedom, but I am sorry people had to die."

"It was bloody times. Now, look there. Jevanjee Gardens!" he pointed grandly.

Indeed, it was a much nicer park, and the driver had some obvious pride about it. They turned just beyond the gardens, and the driver kept pointing out landmarks until they were out of central Nairobi. The address was a nice boutique on the edge of a residential neighborhood.

"It looks like they are to close for the day very soon. Do you want me to wait for the ride? You pay now, but I wait?"

"Oh no, I'll be okay." Sopora paid the man, and it must have been on the generous side because his eyebrows bounced a little when he saw the cash. She went inside and started looking through the racks of clothes that appeared to be a random mix of African and European styles. She kept glancing out the window, but the cab hadn't moved.

It must have been near, or past, closing time. The shopkeeper kept coming up to her and offering her better and better bargains in an attempt to speed her out the door. After the third time, Sopora gave him a handful of cash and begged for just a few more minutes. The shopkeeper immediately answered in much clearer English than he'd been using, "As long as you need, gentle lady." He returned to his creaky stool behind the counter and prepared to offer assistance to the woman who tipped so well.

During her second full circuit of all the racks, the woman with the red aura walked in. After a cautionary glance around the boutique she stormed over to Sopora. Gone was any pretense of flirtation, she was all business. "I have done as you ask, Walker-in-Dreams. He drank the whole thing. My debt to you is paid in full. Hound my steps no more."

"I am very grateful for your help. And yes, I confirm that your debt is paid in full."

"I now give you warning. You know I could feel his emotion in my blood. He is full of rage, and hate, and vengeance. Leave while you can. He is a very dangerous man. You know he is of Death, but you do not understand how much he relishes killing and death. It is more than the heritage in his blood. He has been hurt, and causing death is the only thing that truly slakes his lust. We in Kenya who are born Outside-the-Normal stay far away from him. You should too." She didn't wait for a reply. She turned on her heel and stormed out.

Ironically, she got into the cab that was still waiting and argued with the driver for a minute before he agreed to take her fare. Sopora smirked as the cab drove off, "That's one favor I'll never admit she did for me."

While she paid the shopkeeper another tip for his time, I mused on what I had seen of Sopora's world. She was very obviously tied to an Agency where they could enter people's dreams. Sopora seemed able to quite a bit with it, but it didn't sound like Bruadair could. None of his modern associates had shown me anything when they'd nearly caught me in Milwaukee.

I had powers like Sopora. At least, mostly like her. I just needed a lot of practice. I had also seen something supernatural when Gregory died, and Sopora hadn't shown any such tendency. Then there was the man who was present at both of the assassinations–the man in the black coat. If his black scythe was any indication, he could foresee deaths just like I had in the gym. But Sopora couldn't. And now there was this African woman who made the officer lust after her, but she clearly considered herself different from Sopora. In fact, it appeared that Sopora called in a favor because this woman could do something she couldn't–she could entice men supernaturally. Was I being shown a third power that I might have? Oh god, what if I could only make women lust after me? That'd be a cruel joke. Useful if I went into spy work, but cruel all the same.

Sopora stopped walking, cutting my musing short. The house was only a few streets over. She walked right up to the front and let herself in as though she belonged. She locked the door behind her, and once inside slipped into a stealthier form of movement. I could hear snoring from upstairs, but she took her time casing each room, making sure the rest of the house was empty. When she had verified they were alone, she entering the bedroom.

The officer was lying across the bed at a bizarre angle. His shirt was mostly unbuttoned, but he'd never gotten his pants off. A tumbler lay on the floor where it had rolled out of his hand. Going to work, she rolled up her sleeves. She placed one arm over his, but the other she placed on his bare chest. She avoided touching him anywhere else.

Seeping into this man's inner world was vastly different than the last two. For starters it was much more difficult, as though his dark aura knew what Sopora was and it resisted her instinctually. After being blocked several times, Sopora started testing his aura's responses. Wherever she tried to pass through, it strengthened. Marshalling her power, she sent a strong surge of energy down her arm on his chest. Predictably, his aura at that point of contact tightened against her attempt. While she kept up this blatantly inelegant assault on the aura over his heart, she was very slowly insinuating her aura into his through her point of contact on his arm. Every time his arm's defenses would shift, she'd batter another spike of power into his chest, forcing his aura to return its focus to defend his core. She'd then gain a bit of ground on his arm. Her hammer-and-silk technique eventually got her into his dream world, but she had to earn it.

I'd thought the hatred in her last target was off-putting. I was in no way prepared for this man's psyche. His mind's ocean was a sea of copper-smelling, hot blood. He protected each of his dream islands with some form of barrier. Some were trapped behind iron and rust bars, others were encircled by bone fences with strips of flesh still hanging from them. Behind each barrier was a single scene, each depicting someone dying over and over. Floating above them all, watching like some sort of hungry death god, was the officer. Only in his dreams he was a giant, and much more heavily muscled than in the real world. He wore armor of an African tribal design and a crown made of pieces of skulls. When I realized he'd been watching us the whole time, I nearly panicked myself right out of the dream.

"Show me Tom Mboya," Sopora commanded him.

The officer just laughed a deep, booming, African man's laugh. It was a laugh that started in the dark caverns of the earth below his toes and projected out to compete for volume. It was easily the most evil and mocking laughter I had ever heard, and I've seen a lot of movies.

"I'm serious, Reaper. Show me what I wish to see."

"You are puny, Walker-in-Dreams. You will die here. I will place you on an island, and that island will have a fence made of my hatred for your kind. I will never allow you to leave my mind."

"You're wrong."

"SILENCE! I am the god here, and you are less than a bug who has come chittering into my domain."

"This is your last chance. Show me what I wish to see or I shall tear your mind apart looking for it," Sopora threatened.

"You can try. In fact, I hope that you do try. It has been far too long since I've tasted blood."

Sopora wasted no more time talking to him. Instead, she dove like a hawk towards the nearest island.

The officer shouted, "No!" and I felt the entire sky move as he dove after her.

Sopora was faster. She hit the island with her hands in that familiar claw shape. Instead of collecting motes, though, she ripped into the dream fabric that comprised the island. Pulling up two chunks of it, she spun just in time to deflect the officer's giant fist with a piece of his own memory. It held against his punch, though the force of it drove Sopora back. He punched again, and again, only to have Sopora block his attack each time. I wanted to hold my breath, afraid to distract her even the slightest.

He then lunged to choke her with both hands. She blocked with both pieces of dream island, but his feint had fooled her. At the last second he twisted his hands to grab the top of her two shields and forced them down. Once he had created the space, he snapped his neck forward intending to head butt her. She let go of the pieces of island and narrowly jumped back in time. He pressed his advantage.

She ducked his next swing, and hooked her clawed fingers into the sand of the dream island again. Instead of pulling out two chunks, she stretched the landscape and pulled up a wall of distorted dream material as tall as he was. When his fist hit it, he snarled in rage and pounded it again. The wall held firm.

"You're making me work for your death. I shall relish killing you all the more," he snarled viciously.

Sopora had backed off as far as she could. She reached down into the dream island's turf, and threw up another giant wall. She sidestepped, and pulled up another at a different angle, and another at yet a different angle. He was not able to batter through them, but he did move around them more nimbly than his bulk and size would have led me to believe. Sopora backed up and created two more at odd angles.

I thought she might be dodging and weaving between them. But she wasn't. As she kept creating walls, I realized her plan. She was slowly building a cage.

When she had all the walls she needed, Sopora stepped into the blood sea. She reached down with both hands and grabbed the edge of the island. With a roar, the giant officer saw the trap and tried to float up into the sky.

He was too late. Sopora expended a mighty effort, both physically and mentally. With a titanic heave, she snapped the sides of the island up as though it were a giant fly trap. The series of walls she had made fit together like the teeth of a bear trap, with the thinnest of cracks between them. His primal roar poisoned the atmosphere with hatred and venom. He furiously battered at the very fabric of the cage.

"Yes, destroy the cage. Destroy the dream it's made of, and chase me to the next one," Sopora cajoled. "How about that one? Does that one mean anything to you?" She pointed to the nearest island and floated toward it.

He attacked his prison with rage-driven fury.

Sopora flew down and landed on the new island. She looked at him, making sure he was watching, and plunged her hand down into the turf of the dream island. At first I didn't understand what was happening, though he must have because he started insulting her in his native language. He then switched to English and demanding she stop her dream-witchery. She merely took a centering breath and continued.

Then I saw it. The island was shrinking. She was absorbing its energy. She was pulling its very essence into her aura. Much like the dream motes on previous nights, she was absorbing the very fabric of this dream construct to store it as energy.

"Stop."

She glared at him.

"I'll show you that which you wish to see."

She pulled her arm out of the ground, but I noticed, or rather felt, that she retained the energy she'd gained. "Where?"

He pointed behind her, "that way."

She started flying the direction he indicated, and I heard him shout, "Now release me!"

Stopping, she spun back around, "Not until I've seen the dream memory. I'm looking for a detail that is not about you.

I have no interest in condemning you. When I've seen the dream, I'll free you so you can return to your life and we'll never cross paths again."

Flying over the islands, she summoned a glow around her hand to guide the way. She must have had a vague idea of what she was looking for because she didn't slow down for many of the scenes. The only ones that held her interest were those that had cars and streets.

Every island had a violent scene–each and every one of them depicted a gruesome display of blood and death. She was flying low to examine one when the officer burst forth from the island below her. Had Sopora's reflexes been any slower, he would have hit her dead on. Instead, he glanced off of her hip and she did a mid-air roll to one side. Coming up, they faced each other. He had shrunk down to her size.

"I see you figured out the trap."

"Yes, Dream Witch. I just had to think puny like you," he sneered.

"Or deflate your ego. It depends on how you look at it."

"It matters not. Now you die." He sprang at her again. Fortunately he wasn't any faster in the air than she was, and Sopora proved she was the more practiced flier. He made several grabs, but she was always ready for him, and stayed out of his reach. A couple times she tried coaxing him down to an island, but he was wise to it, and instead tried to grab her from above, forcing her to roll and gain altitude lest she remain pinned between the officer of death and the bloody scenes on his islands of memory.

His anger swirled around him in roiling black clouds. When he failed to grab her yet again, he switched tactics and lashed out with his black aura. It came at her like a stinger made of black venom, and it was whip-fast. Sopora only just interposed a small explosion of bright dream energy from her hand before being hit by the stinger. It lodged in the nebula of energy barely inches from her palm, and then he retracted it.

Laughing evilly, he created a second one and whipped them both out towards her. She smeared some of the dream energy in an arc in front of her, and the stingers stuck in the makeshift shield. This time, because it wasn't anchored, he was able to pull it down when he retracted his weapons.

"I can keep at this, Witch, until your hands are empty." He lashed out again. Sopora leaned away from him, using her body to hide the way she was angling her hand toward the ground behind her. She then released a burst of energy like a propulsion jet. She rocketed between the lashes and shot past him. He cursed and grabbed for her, dropping the stingers to do so. Had his hands initially been free, he might have succeeded, but she slid through his grasp and left him trying to hold a shimmering con-trail.

The short burst of flight burned through her stored energy quickly, but it provided her a three island lead. Dropping down onto an island showing a particularly gruesome knife-fight in which the officer was ecstatically remembering himself disemboweling another man, Sopora turned to face her pursuer. He was two islands away and closing. She reached down through the island's turf once again. She strained everything she had to tear apart the fabric of the island. Within moments it was shaking apart as though an earthquake was sundering it in half.

He was only one island away.

Screaming from the effort, Sopora gave one last mighty

pull, and angled the front half of the island up to intercept the officer, holding him at bay with a giant half-island shield. The turf of the back half started to flow up her hand, calcifying around her as it went. She was forming earthen armor out of the fabric of his dream.

The officer pounded on the barrier once, and then started climbing to get over it. He appeared above her, standing on the lip. "Your tricks will not save you." He held out his hand and his aura flowed forward into a long, black, curved headsman's sword with wicked barbs that dripped inky black death. One of the drops hit Sopora's armored shoulder. It sizzled itself out of existence, forcing her to regrow armor over the hole.

He dropped right toward her, meaning to use the momentum of the fall to cut her in half with the blade. She wasn't done though. While I'd been watching the armor, she'd been extracting a spiked shield from the piece of island he'd climbed over. She snapped that arm up to block his attack, and he saw the peril too late. As the front chunk of island splashed back into the blood sea, his eyes focused on the manhole-sized disk with foot-long spikes that suddenly appeared right below him. It was too late to pull out of the dive. She locked all of her joints, strengthened by her stony armor, allowing him to impale himself on his own dream material.

As soon as the spikes entered his flesh, she slammed him down on to the piece of island bobbing in the sea before her. She twisted the disk, digging the spikes into the ground beneath him. He made a feeble slash with his blade, but it bounced off the rocky armor on her shin. Reaching down with her other hand, she sunk it into the ground for a moment.

"My interest has never been in you personally, butcher. I only came to learn about something you might have seen. I've bound these spikes to the island beneath you. If you try to break free, you'll tear yourself into several pieces. I doubt your psyche will survive. If you allow me to see what I came to see, I will release you as I leave your dreams."

"NEVER! I will hunt you to the end of your days! I will extract your soul, imprison it here, and have my way with it over and over! Then I will hunt down other dream witches and torture them before your eyes, killing them and feasting on their souls while you watch. You will never know peace!" He made another furious swing with his blade, this time glancing up her leg toward her torso.

"Wrong answer."

Angrily she grabbed his wrist, taking control of the blade's momentum. His chest was protected by the shield that now capped the spikes, so she continued its arc around until it bit into his thigh. One of the envenomed thorns sank in deep. "I assume," she said bitterly, "that you poisoned the thorns so I'd die a slow death?"

The look in his eyes was all the confirmation she needed. "Good. That should give me plenty of time to find what I need."

"I promise I will find a way to kill you, witch." Malevolent hatred rolled out of him, filling her with his seething anger. She nearly broke his wrist swinging the blade around to slam it into his other thigh, "And that is for calling me a witch."

Levitating up, she ignored his thrashing and threats of violence. She flew several islands away maintaining her dignity before she allowed a sob to escape. I didn't realize she'd started crying. The blood sputtered where her tears touched it. She cried quietly, waiting until the sea was quiet again before gathering her composure and moving on.

Searching from island to island, she pulled up short and gasped when she saw Agent Bruadair behind a bone-and-flesh fence. Floating closer, she spied on what the dream had to show her. Though the entire scenario was on an island, Bruadair was creeping through the very house in Nairobi where her body was touching the officer. Bruadair went into the small bedroom next to the Officer's. When Sopora had checked it was empty. In this dream fragment, Bruadair approached a crib. Reaching in, he lifted the baby out. "I hear your daddy's a powerful Reaper. Morpheus thinks you'll make a fine subject..."

Bruadair was interrupted by the officer coming into the room. Upon seeing a strange white man holding his baby, he drew his handgun in one hand and instantly created his curved black blade with his other, "Put my son down now, dream walker, and I kill you honorably."

"No can do, Butcher. My boss wants this boy."

The officer snarled, and lunged at agent Bruadair. Bruadair took the tackle head-on, slapping his bare hand to the officer's cheek. By the time the men and baby hit the ground, the officer was sound asleep. Bruadair stood, gathered up the screaming baby, and left.

Sopora was mortified. Sniffling the last of her tears, she shot up away from that island.

Calling tiny pebbles from her armor, she formed them into a squad of dream motes that she whispered to and sent in all directions. She made wide swooping circles as she flew, giving the motes the largest search radius possible. Once again, not being able to track the passage of time made this part of the dream simultaneously fly by and drag on.

The search took longer than Sopora had anticipated. She spent energy more freely once she noticed some of the islands cracking at the edges and crumbling into the blood sea. It was like watching time-lapse photography of sand sculptures on the beach. Sopora increasingly became more worried as more and more of the islands lost structure. She coaxed out a second squad of motes to speed up the search, but more and more islands were starting to come apart. Some of the smaller ones already had cracks running into their interiors.

The motes were whizzing around faster than I'd seen her push them before. She gave up more armor and sent out a third squad. Islands were now losing chunks to the sea. Most of the fences and barriers had fallen in by this point. The blood looked like it was getting darker. When Sopora glanced to the horizon, I saw a curtain of black. None of these inner dream seas had ever possessed a border before. I had a horrifying moment when I realized his death was closing in on her as his mind was shutting down.

One of the motes shot up into the air and popped brightly. Sopora moved immediately. Though the island was in bad shape, the people in the dream carried out their play oblivious to their crumbling world. A handsome black man came out of a pharmacy near the small downtown park she'd seen earlier. A car drove by slowly cracking apart like the ground of the island. I saw the officer roll down his window, raise his gun and fire at the handsome man. Though Sopora noted this, she knew it was not what she'd come to see. She looked around wildly, finally seeing him in the park. Seated in plain view, was the man in the black trench coat. He was completely unaware that the bench beneath him was falling into the blood sea. Playing his part for the last time, he shook his head sadly at the violent assassination playing out behind her. The car accelerated, shedding pieces of itself into the pools of black blood that were claiming the dream. As the car crested his position, the man in the coat stood. Because the dream's owner had gotten a clear look at him, Sopora did too. He was movie-star handsome. His hair and eyes were both a warm dark brown, his skin a medium tan. He seemed sad. There was a silver pin of a swan on the lapel of his coat. He cracked apart as he made his way toward the dying man. The blood sea claimed him before he reached his target.

The island was falling in on itself, consumed by the now black sea.

Sopora flew up and put her hands behind her again, palms away. She started burning through her remaining armor, converting it to propulsion. She rocketed along the path that had the largest island remains still visible. There weren't many. Sopora looked back, which I thought was unlike her until I saw what she was confirming. The black curtain was mere islands behind her and moving fast.

The officer's hateful voice boomed across the sky, "If I am to die in my own mind, Witch, yours will be the last soul I claim..."

"Like hell," was all she said, and she converted more of the rock armor into thrust. I could feel it pushing against the soles of her feet as well as her hands. She was quite literally giving it everything she had. Zooming past jagged rocks and outcroppings that had once been islands, she was losing the race.

The blackness caught up to her.

The nothingness caressed the bottom of one foot like a

feather of oblivion. Sopora gasped. She was almost out of armor. Looking around, the blackness was closing in on all sides. There, ahead of her was the last shred of island I could see. There was a man pinned to it, laughing feebly.

Sopora adjusted her path and shot right at him. Her foot disappeared to the ankle, and the blackness caressed the bottom of the other one. His death trap was snapping shut. She was out of armor to burn.

As the numbing blackness of oblivion visibly closed in on her, she lost altitude and speed. He was so close. He was so far. Everything was going black.

She couldn't see.

It was cold. She could barely feel her own skin.

Sopora hit something and screamed.

My head exploded.

CHAPTER EIGHT
2012 – CRANSTON, RHODE ISLAND

I gasped. My head felt like it'd been ripped inside out.

"Sopora?" I called out before I realized I was lying on the asphalt of a Wal-Mart parking lot.

A woman in a cheap windbreaker several stalls away squawked and pulled her flappy, gigantic purse close. She sped up, in a sudden hurry to reach the shopping extravaganza that awaited her.

My clothes were wet.

I looked down and was momentarily stunned to see I was covered in a thin layer of frost that was melting quickly in the warm air. I didn't realize my feet were numb until I tried to stand and almost toppled over. Four yards may not seem like much, but it's a nigh impassible distance when your feet are betraying you. It was an agonizing hobble to reach the Jeep. When sensation returned, it felt like Hell's Hordes were jabbing cocktail stickers into my feet with all the vengeance the infernal pits could muster. It only intensified the throbbing pain in my head.

I wanted to climb into the Death Buggy, but the doors were locked. That caught me off guard. I looked the Jeep over, but didn't see a single broken window or means of exit. And yet, there I was on the outside. Which also meant the key was still hidden under the passenger seat cover where I'd put it before going to sleep. Yes, I was becoming that paranoid. A quick check of my pockets confirmed I didn't have the key on me. Nate had thoughtfully put the Death Buggy's hard shell roof on, so I couldn't just peel back a corner. I'd have to remove it, and that required a screwdriver unless I could get inside to pull the release handles.

Wondering at the extent of my powers, I concentrated on the lock, willing it to unlock. I scrunched up my forehead. I even made a few Jedi-like passes with my hands. Nothing.

Sighing, I hobbled my way up to the Wal-Mart.

The frost on my pants was mostly melted. I say mostly, because the ancient man they had greeting shoppers helpfully pointed out, "You've got some ice on you, buddy."

"Air conditioner's busted. I need a screwdriver."

"That'll be back in hardware. Need a cart?" He pushed one toward me.

"For a screwdriver?"

"Ya never know what you'll find."

"Thanks, I'm good."

He shrugged and went back to sucking on his teeth and staring at the girl trying to open the coffee and concessions stand.

Stores like this are completely surreal to me. Right up front are inflatable yard statues next to gallon jugs of predator pee designed to ward off critters. The very critters who, apparently, posed for the inflatable yard statues. I guess the Wal-Barons can't make a profit if people actually enjoyed looking at nature as it went about its business.

My wet shoes started squeaking on the dirty tile and the

sound went right into my pounding head. I angled off toward the clothing. The racks were on that weird industrial carpeting. It also meant I'd have to walk past the women's undergarments. I suspect every man in America–whether gay, straight, bi, or transgender–probably feels like a pervert walking past women's underwear in Wal-Mart. Specialty underwear stores at least try to emulate some sort of boudoir atmosphere where a woman might feel empowered and beautiful. Not the Wal-Mart. Nasty panties on plastic hangers hung forlornly right next to the wall of unsexy industrial bras. I didn't understand why they didn't just sell the women's undergarments in Valu-Paks of three like they did the men's, but trying to make sense of it made my head pound even more.

My shoes had stopped squeaking by the time I reached Hardware. I found what I needed for breaking into the Death Buggy. Nate used to lock his keys in it all the time, so we eventually broke, I mean rigged, the tailgate lock so that it could be coaxed open with a screwdriver. Or "jimmied open" as Nate used to say just to annoy me. He knew I hated it. He said it anyway. Every damned time.

I decided to detour through Wal-Mart's grocery section. My go-to food when I had a headache was beef jerky. I can't explain why it made me feel better. The protein was probably the magic. I grabbed two bags. As I was leaving the aisle, I saw a black suited agent run toward the back of the store.

I froze.

What the hell?

My aura! I pulled it in tight like I'd been practicing. The very sensible part of me told me to wander like a spaced-out Wal-Martian to the checkout and get out. The adventurous, and might I add cocky, side of me wanted to follow the agent. I followed.

He met up with another agent back in Hardware. I walked past their aisle and wandered down the next one, straining to hear their conversation.

"... entire parking lot is covered in dream bubbles and frost. Morpheus is positive it's him."

"Your bubble analogy is weird. Has anyone but Bruadair even laid eyes on the guy?"

"Negative."

I imagine the momentary silence carried a meaningful look regarding Bruadair, but I couldn't see it.

"The trail stops here. Or it heads back the same way."

"Let's go."

I heard them moving in the direction of the food, so I walked the opposite way and stayed hidden behind the endcap. They followed my trail to the jerky without another word. I knew right then they could follow me if I didn't keep my aura pulled in tight. And something about my explosive exit from Sopora's dream had sent out a strong signal. I'd have to be more careful. Somehow.

I wandered around the back of the store looking at all the sad cast-off items that weren't good enough for the main aisle shelves. In a place like Wal-Mart, that meant I was looking at all the junk. I couldn't help but feel a bizarre, poetic kinship with this stuff. All the other merchandise that had shipped with these items had gone on to a home and was being used for its purpose. Yet these random things were here alone, un-used, and maybe even a little undesirable. None of them were currently in season. On the bright side, none of them were predator piss either. Wal-Mart keeps that stuff near the door.

Reaching the back corner, I turned and started toward the front of the store checking that my aura was pulled in tight. I didn't run into any more agents, just the windbreaker woman from the parking lot with a six-pack of dish towels in her hand. She froze when I came around the corner. She was up to something. Hating myself for doing it, I looked at her gargantuan purse. It was bulging and not so flappy anymore. I must have still been reeling from the dream because a high-pitched whine started ringing in my ears.

I turned and walked the other way. I didn't need any part of that. I had snitched once back in second grade. I had been beaten until I was bleeding every night after school for two weeks as a lesson of what happens to tattle-tales. No thank you. I didn't need one of the people of Wal-Mart pounding me into the ground. Sopora's missions were doing an adequate job of that already.

Having no desire to walk all the way back past the aisles of misfit merchandise, I turned a few aisles over. It was thankfully, blissfully empty. As I neared the front, I couldn't help but notice one of the agents sitting in the concessions area. I didn't see his partner anywhere. I knew that suddenly turning around would look really strange, so I checked that my aura was pulled in tight, tried to walk casual, and I went to pay for my screwdriver and jerky.

Only one register was open, and the old cashier with her magenta-colored hair and vibrantly pink lipstick was being inordinately chatty with the dude in front of me. He looked miserable.

"Oh, Greek Yogurt! I read that's really good for you. Better than 'Merican yogurt, but don't tell anyone I told you."

The guy mumbled something like, "I just like the taste."

"Bananas, there you go. Those are always a really good deal here. Are you sure you wouldn't want a bunch that's a bit greener? They'll last longer?"

"No..."

"And look, Band-Aids. I hate it when I run out. That's always when I get a paper cut that bleeds and bleeds."

He didn't even try to interrupt. I'm pretty sure he had just decided it would go faster if he didn't give her any conversation to latch on to. I tried to nonchalantly make sure most of him was between me and the agent, but not entirely. I didn't want to look like I was hiding. I noticed the back of his neck was getting redder by the second.

"Beard dye? Oh, you couldn't possibly be old enough to need this. Is it for your father?" She looked at him with her watery eyes.

He just shook his head, "nope, mine." He started fidgeting with his wallet, pulling his bank card. I could tell he was hoping and praying she'd shut up and finish the transaction in peace.

"Ah." She reached for his last item, the one the poor guy had been dreading.

He swiped his card much harder than necessary.

"Oh." She continued undeterred. "Preparation H?" She held it up as if seeking his confirmation. "Oh don't worry hon, hemorrhoids are the worst. This'll help, though. You know what else I do?"

Please don't make me hear it. Please don't make me hear it. PLEASE oh PLEASE no...

"I alternate sitting on a baggie of ice cubes and a hot water bottle. Switching temperatures like that helps the healing process."

Oh god, not only did she go there, she kept going.

"Of course, water bottles are kind of old fashioned. If you don't have one, a warm bath is nice too. Oh, and make sure you buy some moist towelettes. Dry toilet paper will only aggravate it. We have some nice medicated ones in the pharmacy."

The poor guy and I were both stricken mute by the idea of this old woman's aggravated fanny. There was nothing we could do to un-hear what we'd just heard.

Nobody escapes the Wal-Mart unscathed. Nobody.

She handed over the receipt, gearing up to say something, but he grabbed it and his bag and bolted. I didn't blame him. Run for your life, brother.

She turned to me and smiled, "What've you got for me today?"

I set my items on her tray.

"Beef jerky? Oh, I can't eat that. It gives me gas." What was with this woman and her bowels?

"It's not for me, it's for my car."

I watched the gears in her head grind to a halt while she tried to process my answer. She obviously needed more information for that to make sense. She held up the screwdriver, "So what's this for?"

After she'd inflicted her rear on that poor guy, I was feeling like a smartass, "Oh that's for me." She looked at me, really confused. So I offered, "It helps me unwind."

Click. Click. Click... Delayed blast joke-bomb. "OH! Ha ha ha ha!" She had the dry raspy laugh of an old woman, but she must have truly thought I was funny. It was a bad move on my part, because the agent looked over and scrutinized the situation. So I shook my shoulders like I was chuckling with her and tried to project the idea that she and I were old friends, therefore I was local.

Her laugh finally wound down and she was able to give me my total. I paid cash, gathered up my bag, and walked for the exit. The greeter called after me, "Thank you for shopping at Wal-Mart! Come back real soon!"

I resisted the urge to turn and see if the agent was following me. Instead, I surveyed the lot. The other agent was sitting in a dark grey Ford Taurus idling in the parking aisle right in front of the Jeep. He was blocking it in. His head snapped my way, but I surmised by his glazed look he was using his Aura Vision. He didn't have much reaction to me, so I walked to the side of the parking lot with a bus terminal and sat down in the Plexiglas shelter to wait, apparently, for a bus.

The bus stand faced the street, so I couldn't turn and look back at the agent without being obvious. So instead I put my back in the corner and angled myself to see if they drove out either of the exits, which were thankfully both on this street.

Unlike in Sopora's dreams, I could quite acutely feel the passage of time. I had no desire to actually get on a bus, and the stand gave no indication as to whether multiple lines stopped here so I could skip one or two. I pulled out my phone to check the time and immediately felt like a dumbass. I chalked my stupidity up to my pounding head and I searched for the local bus schedule.

Two lines served this stop, and they alternated each half-hour. Which meant, if they were on time, I could wait forty-five minutes before I had to logically get on a bus. If you've never waited alone at a bus stop with a splitting headache while two agents are nearby looking for you, then you have no idea how long forty-five minutes can be.

I tore into the beef jerky. That only killed about three minutes. Forty-two to go.

The first bus, the one I was pretending wasn't mine, showed up on time. It dropped off five hopeful shoppers. One of them lit up a cigarette the instant his foot hit the sidewalk. He inhaled deeply, almost medicinally.

Inhaled.

I used the five shoppers as an excuse to turn around. The Ford hadn't moved. I turned on my Aura Vision. The entire parking lot was awash in a nebulous cloud of shifting hues. That's what the agents had seen. I'm guessing, that's what the agent in the car was keeping an eye on. Though I have no doubt they'd taken stock of the vehicles in the lot, there was thankfully no incriminating variation in the energy near the Jeep. Just the Wisconsin plates.

Taking my cue from the smoker, I began to slowly pull the energy into me. Careful to not make it look like I'd suddenly turned on a vacuum, I instead tried to imagine the cloud seeping into the ground, and I pulled it up from the ground through the soles of my feet. Interestingly, my still slightly numb feet stopped prickling as I did so.

It was a good exercise in moving the energies around. In addition to not being obvious about where the energy was going, I had to make damned sure my own aura never flared.

I kept reminding myself I had a half hour, and there was no reason to rush.

The agent in the car must have alerted his partner somehow. The concessions agent came running out of the Wal-Mart right into the smoker. They had an awkward moment while the agent in the car got out. They ignored the shoppers and scoped out the parking lot. They walked the perimeter, and I was damned careful to slow down when they were near. It might not have mattered, they were more interested in why the ground was devouring the dream energy they'd been sent to investigate.

I couldn't help but feel like the Agency's training program had gone downhill in the intervening years. I mean, I'd just witnessed Sopora take on a butchering, assassinating death god in the playground of his own mind. Yet these agents were being fooled by an untrained novice.

Except, maybe I wasn't exactly untrained. What if Sopora's dreams were a sort of advanced training I'd accidentally tapped into?

No, she traveled under the last name Gardner.

My last name.

I couldn't ignore that coincidence. Sopora had also learned at least one trick from Margaret that the Agency didn't know how to do. It was possible Margaret had trained her in quite a few techniques, and I had been receiving the benefit of that while I slept. I just didn't know, and my ignorance was going to get me hurt.

Though maybe not today.

By the time I'd drained all of the energy out of the parking lot, my headache was completely gone. I wondered if I had just exploded my own energy all over with the violent end to last night's dream. Or maybe I could heal myself with dream energy? More things I didn't know.

The agents were both on their phones. Though their conversations were obviously different, their body language was clear. There was nothing else to see here. The target must have moved on right away because the phenomenon had faded. I dared to hope that some god was taking pity on me for having heard all about the checkout lady's hemorrhoids.

The agents must have been ordered to perform one more sweep. They half-heartedly complied, cutting corners and moving along so they could get on the trail they probably believed would be growing cold. As they were opening the doors of the Taurus, the woman with the completely stuffed-full purse came out. In addition to her gargantuan handbag, she had a plastic Wal-Mart bag that had something small in it, like a tube of toothpaste. Or hemorrhoid cream.

The agents took an immediate interest in her. She noted them at the same time, and she screamed and took off at a run. She had a split-second lead on them, but they were in far better shape and one grabbed her arm, pulling her to a halt. She screamed again, fumbled out a whistle from somewhere in her windbreaker. Before the other agent could stop her, she put it to her lips and blew.

And the whole world turned sideways.

A shrill wave of sonic energy burst from the whistle, shattering car windows in concussive waves that coruscated across the parking lot. When the first one hit the bus stop, I fell backwards into the Plexiglas trying to cover my ears against the pain. Battered by wave after wave of sonic energy, I could do nothing but hold my head and try to shut it out. And I was on the far side of the parking lot.

One of the agents was on the ground. I could not tell if he was dead or passed out. Blood was streaming from his nose and ears. The other agent was down on one knee, pulling his gun. Her eyes widened when she realized he was resistant enough to at least draw on her. She bolted again.

Running took enough of her concentration, and I'm assuming most of her breath, that the intensity of her whistle abated slightly. The agent stood and took a shot at her, clipping the strap of her purse. It fell, bouncing off her rising thigh and sailing out of her grasp. Her five-finger discounted items spilled out across the parking lot. She cursed, which ended the whistle assault completely. Choosing to live, she ducked between two cars and didn't go back for the stuff.

The utter lack of any sound made me realize I'd been deafened. I pulled my hands away from my ears and noted a small amount of blood on them. I rubbed my nose, but thankfully it wasn't bleeding.

The agent pursued the windbreaker woman a short distance, but she was keeping low and weaving. I could tell he'd lost track of her among the cars, and he couldn't hear her footsteps. Frustrated, he went back to his partner, did a quick check for pulse, then lifted him by his underarms and dragged him to the car. He got his partner into the back seat, jumped into the driver's side, and sped off. I watched them zip down the road and turn a corner.

Not wanting to end up a witness, I bolted for the Jeep. The side windows were gone, but the front windshield only had a few cracks. I reached in and unlocked it, throwing the now useless screwdriver into the back seat. I grabbed the key, fired up the Death Buggy, and shot out of the parking lot the opposite direction the Taurus had taken. I'd figure out a destination later, I just had to get away.

Nobody escapes Wal-Mart unscathed. Nobody.

Several miles later, I pulled into the lot of a Next Level Fitness & Athlete Training Center. I had used some wipes to clean away the blood. I kind of wanted a workout and desperately wanted a real shower. They didn't have a day rate, but the basic membership was twenty dollars per month with no commitment. I paid for a month and disappeared into the unfamiliar room to try clearing my head with weights and iron and sweat.

I had a lot to think about, and I just let it all ping around the back of my head while I focused mainly on losing some fat and pushing my muscles. If today had taught me anything, it was that my new world was physically dangerous and I needed to be at the top of my game. It may not have been an Olympic-level workout, but I felt better when I was done.

The shower was infinitely more cathartic. The soap and water held no more answers than the iron weights had, but it was something I needed in order to feel human again. I also noticed my hearing was returning to normal. I only had an annoying flat tone in my ears, and the pressure felt much reduced.

I bought myself a protein shake on the way out, sat in the Jeep and surfed my phone's internet for a nearby shop that might be able to repair the Jeep's windows. Finding one that looked promising, I pulled up, explained to the mechanic that some crazy psycho had shattered all the windows at the Super Wal-Mart, and that I needed them repaired so I could continue my trip. When he asked for my insurance information, I said I'd just submit his bill to the insurance company so they could reimburse me. He shrugged noncommittally. As long as he got paid, it didn't seem to matter.

He then quoted a number. I was sure my hearing was still funky, but my look of disbelief prickled his predatory tactics.

"Hey, you're just going to pass that on to insurance, right?"

Unbelievable. "Well, I still have to be able to afford it today, here, and now, or you don't get my business. If you can do it for something I can afford, I'll stay."

He sighed and gave me a lower number. I didn't like it, but I'm fairly certain I wouldn't have liked any number. He filled out the work order, I signed it saying I agreed to the price he quoted, and he took the Death Buggy into the work area. I went up front and sat my battered body down in a plastic chair.

CHAPTER NINE
1972 – ATHENS, GREECE

"Remember."

Sopora had gotten out of the death god's head! She was bruised, and looked like she'd gone ten rounds with a prize fighter, but she was alive. She was putting the finishing touches on some cover-up makeup. I had seen better cover-up jobs, which made me think she wanted some bruises to show through. Seemingly satisfied, she left the bathroom, grabbed a sketchpad from her luggage, and went to the phone beside the bed. It was old, and huge, and gaudily plastic, and reminded me that she was operating not only far from America, but far into the past as well.

She dialed the operator and gave the number to which she'd like to be connected. While I heard the noises of an international connection being made, she was looking at the drawing on the pad. Someone, Sopora herself I assumed, had done an amazing shoulders-and-head sketch of the man in the trench coat. She'd captured not only his rugged features, but also his sad expression. In one corner was a smaller inset of his full body, but because the trench coat lacked any uniquely discernible features she hadn't spent a lot of time on it. The other corner had a fairly detailed sketch of the swan pin.

The call went through. Sopora merely said, "Connect me to the boss, please."

A man's voice said, "One moment." Cheesy on-hold music came across the Atlantic scratchy and incomplete.

"This is the Section Chief. The line is secure on this end."

"Not on this one, boss. I'm calling from my hotel."

"Understood. I assume you forgot a detail about our pending merger? Why else would you be calling from your vacation?"

"A minor detail, I sent the notes via the usual courier last night."

"Will you hold while I go check the mail room to see what the holdup is?"

"Of course."

More on-hold music.

"The notes were received. Are you sure about this?"

"Completely. There's no doubt that our associates at Blackwell and Blade were not responsible for the corporate losses in Africa."

"No, but they seem to know something about it. I'd like you to make an appointment with our local office over there. I'll ask my secretary to set it up. Until you hear from me, enjoy your time off."

"Thanks boss."

She hung up the phone and looked at the drawing once more. Picking up the phone, she gave the operator a much shorter number. A woman answered in a foreign language.

"Dor, it's Janet. Will you meet me at the old family homestead?"

"Janet? Of course. Give me an hour."

Standing, she went to her luggage and started pulling clothing out, laying outfits on the bed. Selecting one, she dressed, did her hair, and put the sketch pad in a large purse that looked expensive. She went out to hail a cab, and I figured out pretty quickly that we weren't in Nairobi any longer. The signs looked like they were in Greek, with a smattering of English. She confirmed it when she told the driver to take her to one of the sites on my personal bucket list–the Parthenon.

Hollywood does a much better job with the monument than reality. That, or it has been significantly cleaned up in the intervening years. It was crumbling, dirty, and not at all what I would have expected of a monument to the gods. I saw a small group of tourists, but they appeared to be finishing their visit. Sopora waited for them to leave, and then wandered deeper into the monument. Behind one of the columns, a young woman, barely more than a girl, motioned us over. Sopora gave her a big hug. The girl smiled widely and returned the hug.

"Janet, you know it isn't safe for you here." She was enunciating slowly, her Greek accent getting in her way a bit.

"I know, and I won't stay long. But I need your help. I need to know if you can identify someone for me. I think he's a Reaper."

Dor froze, looking wide-eyed. "You know I can't do that! Especially not after what happened in Nairobi!"

"I'm not asking you to divulge anything relating to what your people are doing, or even his identity. I just need to speak with him. He saw something related to that case. It's something that affects all Outré, not just Sandmen or Reapers. I just want to ask him for his witness's account to a couple events. That's it. Look, if you are more comfortable, I'll show you his picture, and then I'll tell you the hotel where

I'm staying. Tell him that he can choose to contact me if he's willing to help."

Dor bit her lip. "I could get in trouble."

"Not for delivering my request to meet. He can remain completely anonymous. And we can do it in a very public place."

"Ok. But only because it's you… and because I believe you."

Sopora pulled out the sketch pad, "Thank you, Dor."

The girl looked at the man's face. "I know him. But you have to promise to leave Athens. For your own safety. Where's your next stop? I'll give him your next hotel."

"That's just it, I'm stuck. Whatever he can tell me will determine my next stop."

"Janet, you know the Reapers here will kill you outright if they find you. What you did last week sent a lot of people out hunting for you."

"I know. But I tell you, it was self-defense."

"That much came out in their investigations, but you know as well as I do that they cannot just let it go. They're demanding restitution."

Sopora took a slow breath, "If I complete this investigation, the reputation of the Reapers will be improved by removing their association to several global conspiracies. Certainly that has to be some sort of restitution?"

Dor looked thoughtful for a moment, then nodded. "Go to Cairo. Get a room at the Mena House. I will tell him to contact you there if he is willing."

Sopora nodded. "Cairo? But the death cults there..."

"... hate all other Reapers for our ethics and beliefs. I choose it because it's unlikely the hounds chasing you will venture into that territory. Plus, the death cults will probably throw you a hero's feast if you let them."

Sopora smirked, "That would not be the low-profile I need to maintain. I'll go. And Dor... thank you again." The women hugged tightly for a moment, then Dor took off first, disappearing among the columns.

Sopora wandered the monument for a few minutes, her thoughts as unknown to me as they always were. When enough time had passed, she left the way she'd entered, hailed a new taxi, and returned to her room to pack.

Giza, Egypt

I fully expected to wake up, but the dream shifted and we were suddenly in courtyard that would have taken my breath away had I been breathing. The giant U-shaped building behind us dwarfed many sizeable a palaces. Its arms pointed toward a hill upon which towered the great pyramids of Giza. The courtyard itself was a lush oasis, made all the more opulent when contrasted to the hot desert I could see beyond the arms of the hotel. We were shaded by cool palms. There was a pool being enjoyed by visitors. Camel handlers with their animals just up the hill waited for eager tourists to leave the safety of the hotel. Sopora was in a deck chair and had just put away a compact makeup case. I assumed she'd had it out to start the memory in the small mirror, but I didn't know for sure.

A man was approaching.

He'd shed his trench coat in exchange for a loose cotton shirt and pants. He had a drink in his hand, and looked more curious than cautious. "Do we have a mutual friend who goes by Dor?"

Sopora smiled, "We do. I had been hoping she'd make the introduction."

"We haven't been introduced yet. And, frankly, I'd like to save introductions until I know your story."

The smile she'd been wearing as he approached slipped away. "I understand. You probably think I'm a killer."

"Actually, I think the man you killed was a killer." He took a sip to punctuate what he was saying, "Which I think makes you even more dangerous than he was."

"You're not like the others."

"I've been out in the world, and I've seen things they refuse to imagine. Their self-imposed seclusion is not exceptionally conducive to street-level awareness. That doesn't change the fact that you are a dangerous woman."

"I suppose it doesn't. For what it's worth, I never intended him to get hurt, let alone," she stumbled on the words, "kill him."

Pondering her hesitation for a second, he chose to sit in the deck chair next to her. His curiosity was still tinged with a bit of wariness. "Go on."

"I only needed to know about Mboya's death. He was tied closely to a dream that worried the Oracles. I was sent to ascertain any truth to the rumors that the Reapers were starting a bloodline war."

He raised an eyebrow. "Are we at war?"

"I could not tell. The officer's dreams were so bloody and violent. Every image I saw showed him killing someone new. I don't know how many were memories of actual kills, versus how many were just kills he was contemplating, or wishing he'd made. But nothing about his dream confirmed or denied Reaper aggression against the Sandmen."

"Which means you saw me at the incident through his eyes. What did you hope to gain from me today?"

Sopora nodded, "Yes, you were there. You were calm, observant, and I assume you did your job by helping Mboya's soul move on before it was devoured? Because I could only witness what the officer remembered, I didn't see much after the killing shots were fired. I expect you had to fight just to carry out your duties?"

"Only a panicked crowd. The shooter sped off." There was no element of bragging in the man's voice. If what she'd seen of his previous fight where he displayed mastery of his dark scythe was any indication, he was no stranger to combat. His matter-of-fact tone spoke of a great deal of modesty, but it was oddly wrapped in some sadness.

"I was hoping your apparent impartial neutrality would allow you to clear up the confusion in my investigation."

He didn't answer, but took a drink. Seeing that she didn't have one, he offered her a sip of his. "You really should stay hydrated out here in the desert." She took it and leaned back to wait. He didn't say anything else, though.

Sopora didn't push it. The moments of silence stretched out between them. Oddly they seemed comfortable with it. A waiter came by and Sopora ordered something fruity with an umbrella. The drink came, and the waiter left them alone. Still the silence dragged on.

"That was not the only death I'd witnessed that year," he said barely audible. "You have to understand, even though we can sense pending death, most of us can't do anything to prevent it. We might get lucky if the situation has an obvious threat and we stick around intending to act at the right moment, but otherwise we don't get much chance to save anyone. So we are often frustratingly helpless when see the spiritual energy of a death occurring. Those of us who can shepherd a soul on are uncommon. When a shepherd's discovered, the elders send us to specific targets. We're not allowed to refuse."

"Three years ago was a dark year. So many nations in Africa were fighting bloody wars for their independence, or staging military coups. The elders sent me into every one of them. I thought we were investigating the possible involvement of one of you other bloodlines. But death after death did not support that accusation. For each death with circumstantial evidence that could be pointed at one of the Sirens, another could be attributed to a Reaper, or a Temptress, or a Myrmidon, or a Sandman." He motioned to Sopora. "There was no apparent tie, except that nationalism and independence were sweeping across the continent. But where there is war, men will see conspiracies."

I couldn't fault his logic, though I did not recognize the groups he spoke of. What surprised me was that I wasn't shocked to learn there were more like us. I was interested that he called us bloodlines. That made a lot of sense, and supported my growing suspicion that I was related to Sopora. Deborah. Janet. He had also exactly described my experience with Gregory's death in the gym. Something Sopora had yet to show me. She was looking at the man, and asked the exact question that went through my mind. "What shall I call you?"

"I should give you my handle, but I'd prefer it if you called me James."

I froze. To. My. Core. Froze. Was I seeing my parents' first meeting? I scrutinized his features in more detail. My eyes and hair were dark like his, but my skin was much lighter. I certainly did not have his strong nose. I had always thought mine was kind of small.

"Well," Sopora interrupted my comparison, "if we're giving first names, then you should call me Deborah."

As a child, I'd had wild mood swings centered on who my parents had been and why they'd abandoned me. On my more forgiving days I imagined my parents' first meeting had been one of honesty and love, celebrated with champagne and roses. Usually, wondering about who they were hurt too much and I eventually put those thoughts in a box on an emotional shelf so I wouldn't have to deal with the pain. Though a desert oasis in the shadow of the great pyramids isn't a bad start, I was irrationally mad at her for giving her alias. Maybe I wasn't quite ready to take my parents out of the box I'd put them into.

"Well, Deborah, have I assisted your investigation? Or have I sparked a new bloodline war?"

"I think your answer helps us avoid war. I'll bring it back to my Agency."

James laughed derisively. "Agency. Who would have thought the dream runners would be the ones to modernize and formalize what they do into a structured organization?"

"Well, it beats a mysterious enclave of shadowy elders who pass down incomprehensible commands." I felt her smile at one corner of her mouth.

He smiled back, and she must have felt encouraged. "Did you see any other Outré at any of the assassinations?"

Considering her question for a moment, he finally shook his head. "No, it's as I said. Evidence might hint at one blood-line or another, but there was never anything conclusive."

They shared a look, and then glanced back up at the pyramids.

He cleared his throat, "Is it true you can invite other people into your dreams? To show them things?"

Sopora nodded, "Only some of us can do it, but yes, that is a skill I learned."

"I think you should meet my Elder. Invite him into your dream. Show him what you saw. He has worked very hard to distance the concepts of assassin and murder from the reputation of the Reapers."

"I don't mean any disrespect, but perhaps your bloodline should start using a different name?"

It was James' turn to nod. "We've tried. Psychopomp was the favorite in the sixties. Before that Shepherd and Guide were popular attempts. None of them stuck. So instead, we're trying to change what the Outré associate with the name they won't let us shake. Your dream testimony could be very helpful. And I hate to speak ill of the dead, but now that you've ended the reign of the Butcher of Nairobi, we stand a chance at cleaning up our reputation."

"You realize that showing an Elder what I'm capable of, giving up my bloodline's secrets, will ostracize me for sure."

"The Reapers would stop hunting you. It might even be a really good first step towards our bloodlines working together. Nobody denies the investigative acumen of the Sandmen... and women. But you also cannot deny our uncanny ability to be where death is going to happen. I would think that would provide a lot of opportunity to work together. Who knows, in time it might even be the thing that clears your name with both bloodlines?"

"My section chief may not go for it unless I can prove the

Reapers are not trying to start a war."

"To do that, you're going to have to talk to one of the Elders, who adamantly believe the other bloodlines hate us and would never work with us."

"In our defense, Mboya's killer was not exactly a good ambassador for your cause. What'd you call him? The Butcher of Nairobi?"

James sounded angry, "No, he wasn't. But what you did is still considered a direct attack on a Reaper until you can prove the reason was not because the Sandmen are starting a war."

"So you want me to prove that we weren't doing the very thing we think you were doing."

"In a nutshell."

Sopora downed her drink. "Fine. Let me clear it with my section chief. But you might as well start talking to people on your end so they can plan the meeting."

They looked up at the great pyramid allowing some silence signal the end of that topic. Eventually Sopora asked, "I've always wondered something. What's your relation to the death cults of Egypt?"

James didn't look away from the pyramid. "None if we can help it. The story goes back to before biblical times, when tribes of man were still coming up with the notion of territories. They say two brothers from my bloodline parted ways. The brother who believed in peace and guiding the dead to the realms beyond made his way into the mountains of what we now know as Greece. His philosophy became the ideal of the Reapers. The brother who believed the bloodlines were gods to be worshipped and served made his way to the Nile where he started the death cults." James hesitated.

"There's more, isn't there?"

He nodded. "Many believe in a third brother, one who championed reincarnation and traveled to India. But the Elders would have us believe that's just a sub-sect of the Reaper belief of helping the soul transition."

"You're not convinced."

"I'm convinced that this world is larger and more mysterious than we're allowed to know."

"In that belief, you and I are a lot alike."

A few moments of silence stretched between them. Then James said, "For what it's worth, I'm sorry for what he did to you."

"For what it's worth, I'm sorry I killed him defending myself. I should go call my chief."

"I'll call the Elders." He glanced at the hotel, "The Mena House serves a famous dinner. Will you meet me tonight? We can go over what we learn from our calls."

Sopora smiled a genuine smile, "I'd like that."

SOPORA'S ROOM

This time she got through on a secure line. There was, apparently, a bit more to the Mena House than opulence.

"Chief, I think he's right. I think an ambassador to the Reapers could clear up a lot of animosity. I'm the one they want right now, so I'm the logical choice. I'm ready for this."

"I know you took down one of their strongest warriors, Sopora, but we haven't even had your full briefing on that situation. You killed a man from within his own dream! That should not have been possible. His mind's failsafes should have woken him up. Everyone's calling it cold-blooded murder, and the word is out. Now the other bloodlines are rumblings that we have a small cadre of dream assassins. I forbid you to meet with them, or anyone, until we've had time to review your incident and analyze the situation."

"The longer we wait, the harder it'll be to patch things up."

"Now you have some wisdom? As the agent of his death, you will find friendly overtures completely impossible. They're too riled up about you. Do you copy? I'm not against making nice with the Reapers. I just think it has to be handled properly. You're trained for field operations, and you're damned good at improvising when you're out there. I wager you're one of the finest alive. But you're not a diplomat."

"Nobody trusts diplomats. When a diplomat walks through the door, everyone immediately expects half-truths, false smiles, and cover-ups. My gut tells me that the honesty and integrity of a field agent admitting the mistakes she made, and then apologizing, will allow for real negotiations."

"The answer is no, Sopora. Pack your bags. I am ordering you home. Your flight itinerary will be at the Mena House front desk within the hour. Do you read me?"

"Yes, chief."

She hung up the phone and bit her lip. I wasn't used to indecision from Sopora, but she was at a crossroads. Hell, I wouldn't have known what to do. The chief's assessment was solid, but so was her instinct. I'm not convinced she'd made her decision yet. She changed her clothes into something akin to a safari outfit for women. Pausing to look into the mirror, I expected her to tell me to remember, but instead she said, "I could go for coffee and scones anyway," and laced it with an emotional push. I was sure that was for me.

Grabbing an overly-large tourist camera from her bag, she strode out into the courtyard and up the hill.

"Pretty lady, nice scarf. Pretty lady!" The vendor tried to get the scarf around her neck, but she brushed him aside. He tried again, "Is very pretty, for very pretty lady."

"No," she said insistently. "I am looking for a camel and driver. Do you have a brother who..."

The vendor did not let her finish, "Yes! My brothers give rides! Come, pretty lady. Come!" He motioned her up the hill to the plaza.

There, in the shadow of the great pyramid, Sopora negotiated a ride out into the desert. Climbing on the back of the smelly beast, the camel's driver launched into his running diatribe.

"The camel used to have name Kennedy! But then Kennedy is shot, so I think is bad name for camel."

Sopora all but grunted, "Naming an ornery smelly beast after a much-loved American president? I don't imagine people liked it very much?"

"No! So I think to myself, the camel needs a new name. So I think, name him Mickey Mouse!"

The camel chose that moment to make a deep ululating bellow that sounded like a roar coming through the throats of a hundred old smokers. It was clear what the camel thought of his name.

Unabated, the driver continued on, "but every time I say his name, the camel makes unhappy noise. Listen. Mickey Mouse."

Again the camel angry bellowed, this time accompanied with a fist-sized gobbet of spit.

"I assume," interjected Sopora, "that he now has a new name?"

"Yes!" The driver was thrilled to have an involved listener. "So I think, he needs a new name. He needs the name of a warrior god. So I name him Horus."

"Horse?" mocked Sopora.

"No, Horus. Egyptian god of the sun."

"Oh," continued Sopora, again playing dumb. "I thought that was Ra?"

"Ra too! But then gods united and became Horus-Re."

"Oh."

Sopora's answer didn't give him anything to springboard off of. He thought a moment, then said, "You have camera. You want best picture of pyramids in all Egypt?"

"Oh, yes please! I would love that!"

He continued bantering on, showing a keen insight into current American politics. Sopora even remarked that he seemed well-read.

He gushed at the praise until finally bringing Horus to a grunting stop. The camel began levering himself down onto the sand using a sickening see-saw motions, finally allowing the driver and Sopora to step off. I'll say this for the driver, he was right. From atop the dune, when we looked back at Giza plaza, there was no sign of Cairo spread out below. One could only see pyramids and desert far behind them. This was surely where every photographer stood. Sopora began dutifully snapping pictures. The driver even allowed her to include Horus with his carpet saddle and rope harness in several of them.

What the driver had no way of sensing was her feet in the soil. She was drawing dream energy up through the earth. I thought I understood. This was a place of power. Anyone who had ever looked at pictures and dreamed of Egypt dreamed of this spot. They dreamed of standing in the desert and seeing the pyramids beyond the dunes. If this spot was a source of dream energy, I wondered if that meant the pyramids were a source of death energy? Was James there now, filling his aura?

Once she felt full, she wound down the picture taking. "Oh, I think I've used up all my film! Can you take me back to the Mena House?"

The vendor gave a slimy smile. "The ride back to Mena House is extra charge."

"What?"

"Is extra charge."

"Fine, I'll walk."

"You will get lost, you should ride. The ride is extra charge."

"I'm not paying extra."

"You only paid for the ride to the desert. I have to feed Horus, he eats very much food."

"I'm healthy. And look! I can navigate using the pyramids, so I won't get lost. Good bye!"

She stomped off.

"NO WAIT!" The vendor sounded scared.

"Please, one dollar? If police see you walk back, I get into trouble."

"One quarter."

"Two quarters."

"Fine."

The angry, shamed driver had no more stories. It made for an eerily quiet ride back.

CHAPTER TEN
2012 – OUTSIDE PROVIDENCE

I woke with a start. The mechanic was shaking me by the shoulder. "Hey buddy, the windows are done." He motioned to the cash register. I got up, wiped the drool from my chin, and paid him cash. His eyebrows bounced a bit at that. I wasn't about to start using my card yet. I had pulled a great deal of cash for this trip so I could stay under the radar. This expense of new windows for the Death Buggy prophesied having to use the plastic sooner than I'd like, but not quite yet.

Back on Highway 6 I wanted to find a place to lie down and sleep. I'd never gotten hooked into soap operas on television, but dammit. I think my parents' story was unfolding in my dreams, and I wanted to know everything. The nagging voice of reason reminded me I also needed to verify it against what I could learn in the here and now. So I kept driving.

Right until I saw half of a decayed gold and red wall. Slamming on the brakes, I skidded to a stop and pulled onto the side-road that should lead to the Agency's complex if that first dream was accurate. Which meant the One-Eyed Roe was up the highway a few miles.

Looking around, I realized enough of the barn remained that I could hide the Jeep behind it pretty well. I found some brush and debris and did a passable job considering my lack of survival training. It certainly wouldn't be visible from the highway. Someone turning onto this country road would have to be watching the barn, not the intersection, in order to pick it out. That would have to be good enough.

Trying to jog down the unnamed road, I ended up covering the miles to the complex at a quick walk. So many thoughts were pinging around my head that I wasn't paying as close attention to my surroundings as I should have. Reaching the gate, I was surprised to see that not only was it no longer manned, but had fallen into disrepair and was hanging open. Looking beyond, I saw that the rest of the buildings were also in states of neglect and decay. Damn. They'd moved offices. Probably.

I'm no tracker, but I'd played my share of role-playing games. I've also seen quite a few shows and movies. The asphalt road wasn't going to tell me anything, but the debris might. It was too early for leaves to have fallen in any numbers, but recent storms had shaken loose dead twigs. I scanned over the tree debris on the road a few times, and think I saw a pattern of broken and snapped wood that might indicate tires.

I remembered to pull my aura in tight. Moving a bit more carefully, I approached the gate. I noticed something down low. Though the gate was hanging open, there was a live eye-beam across the entrance. Lacking a utility belt with a handy-dandy fogger I couldn't actually see the beam itself, but I saw the dim light inside the apparatus. It was high enough that most critters would go right under it, but cars and people would trigger its warning if they weren't aware of it. I looked up and down, but only saw the one projector-receiver pair.

Taking extra care, I swung one leg and then the other high over it. I quickly scooted to the side of the yard behind an out building. There were very few trees on the grounds, making it tougher to hide and creep forward.

In Sopora's dream, she had parked beneath the barn. She'd then walked far enough away that I'm guessing the offices were below either the house, or the add-on office building. I was closer to the house. I don't know if it was true in this case, but it seemed fitting with traditional command structures that the leaders would be beneath the authentic house and minions would be relegated to the sore-thumb of an office building. Keeping the out building between me and the drive, I made my way around the back towards the house.

Once I was at the corner facing it, I had no desire to cross the open expanse. It looked abandoned, but from here I could just make out a pinpoint of red light under the porch. Because of the angles, I never would have seen it from the drive. The active sensor equipment on the gate and house were deterrent enough. I wasn't trained for this. I didn't want to get any closer. Maybe I didn't have to.

I'd been fairly keyed up at the Wal-Mart, but in hindsight I had extended my Aura Vision across a large parking lot. Trying again was a better alternative to being exposed on the porch. Leaning back against the out building, I tried to focus on seeing auras. Once I was certain I was in the right state of mind, I started trying to coax my vision down into the ground beneath the buildings.

The first couple times my concentration hit the solid earth it was snuffed out. I wasn't giving up that easily. Based on what I knew of physics, energy either bounces off objects, or finds crevasses and bounces inward, or changes state and vibrates through. I tried to vibrate my focus through. My belief that since vision has to travel in straight lines thanks to those pesky photons, the whole vibrating through on a different wavelength should serve me well. I concentrated on that while staring down toward where the house's basement should be. It was really slow going, like pushing sponge cake through molasses, but I felt like I was making progress.

Suddenly I saw a faint form. I'd made it deep enough that I felt like I was watching one of those shows where people use thermal imaging. It was barely noticeable, like the color of a soap bubble, but I saw it. Pushing harder, I soon saw a second. And then another. Success is a great rush, and pretty soon I saw four auras beneath the house. Three were stationary, but one was on the move.

I stopped immediately, returning to my normal vision. I didn't think I'd triggered any alarms or all of them would be on the move. I also didn't want to risk any of them sensing the extra energy I was pushing out to do something like this. I started my slow creep out of the complex. If at some point in her dreams Sopora reconciles with the Agency, I'd certainly be able to return here and introduce myself to them. If the dreams play out another way, then I wouldn't want them to find me ever.

My mind may have been buzzing with thoughts and contingencies, but I was more aware of my return to the Jeep than I had been coming in. Nothing impeded my motion, and I made it back to the Death Buggy without incident. Checking the highway, which seemed more used now than in Sopora's time, I uncovered the Jeep and got back on the road. I was sure Sopora's comment, "I could go for coffee and scones anyway," had been for my benefit. It was time to find that diner.

THE ONE-EYED ROE

As predicted, it came into view a couple miles up the road. The parking lot was still gravel, the building had a bit more wear and tear, but the paint wasn't chipping and the neon sign was still mostly lit. Parking the Jeep in the empty lot, I calmed my breathing and relaxed. I was grateful that mid-afternoon turned out to be an odd time for a diner so far from anywhere to have customers.

Stepping inside I could not help but focus on the woman behind the counter. Her once brown-and-steel colored hair was now entirely white, but she still piled it in large curls on top of her head. Her matronly form had shriveled and shrunk with age. Her green eyes had faded to a dull gray and now peered out from behind a pair of librarian glasses on a thin chain. She wasn't smoking, but the smell and lingering cigarette cloud betrayed her continued habit. She hadn't bothered with her nametag today. She didn't need to.

"You don't have to stare," she greeted me defensively, "I know I shouldn't smoke the damned things, but they're not what's going to be the death of me." Her voice was more brittle around the edges, but Margaret still very much sounded like she had in the dream.

I attributed my sudden inability to speak to cruel, vicious, irony. She was the first person from these dreams with whom I wanted to speak, and I didn't know where to start. Blurt it out? Play casual?

"You're a long way from home, you must be hungry? What can I get you?"

"Y... you know me?"

She pointed to the window, "Wisconsin license plate." She set a menu down in front of a seat at the counter for me.

"Oh... I'm a dumbass." I really felt stupid. I had wanted so badly for her to recognize me on sight and tell me my whole history. I didn't look at the menu. "I'd like coffee and a scone please."

Behind her glasses her eyes sharpened to a predatory focus and some of the green came back. "A scone? We stopped making those over ten years ago." She held up her hands, knuckles swollen, fingers locked into a cigarette-holding grip. "I can't knead the dough any more, and most of the bakers around here wouldn't know a scone from a pile of dog shit."

Her use of profanity shocked me, and it must have showed because she laughed an odd barking laugh at my expression. "We get all kinds in here, but the truckers use the most colorful language." She shuffled down the counter and turned to go into the kitchen. "I've got something better than scones for you. Why don't you come around and pour yourself a cup of coffee, then take the table in the back corner. If you keep your ears open, you might just learn a thing or two from today's truckers."

Okay, that was pointed. Still, I was willing to play along if it meant answers were forthcoming. I poured myself the coffee and sat in the booth she indicated. Several minutes later, she brought me a steaming bowl of chili. It smelled amazing. "For the best listening experience," she confided, "you'll want to put your back to the door and look like you're reading something." She pulled a cheesy, dog-eared copy of an old The Phantom novel out of her apron pocket and offered it to me. I took the book, and the advice, and switched seats.

The chili was awesome, and I told her so when I got up for another cup of coffee.

"It's my own recipe, perfected over the years. The bacon

in it was intentional, the coffee instead of broth was a happy accident." She beamed. "Now go sit back down, they should be here soon."

A brand new, black Taurus was pulling up as I reached the booth. It looked like a hybrid. I looked at Margaret before sitting down, "Truckers?"

"Hush! Sit and listen... and keep it to yourself."

Shit, my aura. I pulled it in tight, and she nodded. That answered everything. No time to ask her my million questions now. The door jingled open as I was situating myself back in the naugahyde seat.

"Rasui will live," the woman was saying, "but he will likely have permanent hearing loss. The doctors won't know for a while."

The man clucked his tongue, "That really sucks. Were you in the circle that got to read Arman's report?" Bruadair. He sounded conversational and light, like he had when I first saw him interact with Sopora.

"Yes." The tone of her voice changed when she addressed Margaret, "A diet coke, please. And today's soup if it's gluten-and-dairy free. If it's not, then a salad, no croutons, no dairy."

"Today's special soup is chili. Plus we always have French onion or chicken noodle. But for you, no noodles."

"The chili, no crackers. I'm gluten-free."

Margaret had obviously dealt with this regularly. She didn't miss a beat, "The delivery truck brought those rice crackers you like. Want me to substitute those?"

"That's fine."

Recognizing his turn had finally come, Bruadair placed his order, "and I like all that stuff she doesn't. So I'll have your shaved roast beef and gravy with those garlic-cheese mashed potatoes you make. Two slices of Texas toast, and a big glass of milk."

"Do you want the dinner plate? It'd include the toast and milk, plus a side salad."

"Yeah, fine. But give Lourdes here the salad. And make sure no croutons go anywhere near it, or we'll all hear about it."

Margaret and Bruadair shared a chuckle at Lourdes' expense. Lourdes clearly wasn't going to laugh. I'm guessing she was one of those people who are utterly incapable of poking fun at herself. I heard Margaret get their drinks, hand them over, and shuffle back into the kitchen, and the two agents sat down a booth away from me. My armpits were starting to sweat.

"She's gone, continue," he said. Interesting, I seriously doubt trained agents would have missed the guy in the far booth. I sat very still wondering if Margaret had 'clouded their minds' to protect me like The Phantom often did in the novel? If she had, I didn't want to move and give the game up.

Lourdes took a drink. "Arman's report simply does not support the latest bug Morpheus has up his ass. The report clearly states the Siren had been at the Wal-Mart when they arrived, as had the two males. She filled her purse with as much shoplifting as it could carry, one man bought groceries and personal items, the other a screwdriver and some jerky. Neither man had an aura. Mr. Personal Items drove off in a sedan with local plates before the Siren attacked. Mr. Jerky witnessed the attack from the bus shelter, but was far enough away to not sustain visible damage."

I was relieved to be considered inconsequential Mr. Jerky and not targeted with a huge red flag as Prime Suspect Number One.

Lourdes continued, "There was no evidence of the Siren having fought with a Sandman prior to the agents' arrival, or they would have noticed sonic damage already at the scene. And Arman clearly described her aura in his report, and nothing about it mentioned any latent or ancestral dreaming ability. She scanned as pure Siren."

After a beat, Bruadair asked, "I heard some of Morpheus' rant. Why does he still think the event's related to the guy from the Milwaukee?"

"First, proximity. It occurred halfway between Providence and The Farm, just south of the highway we all use almost daily. Since Mr. Personal Items checked out as having been local all his life, Morpheus is convinced it is Mr. Jerky. Second, Arman reported a Jeep with Wisconsin plates."

How in the fucknuggets did they not see the Jeep when they walked in? Between that and being moved up to Prime Jerky Number One, I was sweating pretty badly.

"Do you really think he can hide his aura?"

I wished I could see Lourdes' body language. She spoke like some sort of high-level analyst, and if she was intent on the question, then I'd know how seriously they were looking for me.

"I doubt it. Nobody's been able to do that since Agent Sopora. She had been an only child, and the reports clearly indicate the Reapers killed her before she was old enough to have met a man and produce an heir. The researchers have begrudgingly admitted that after decades of failure trying to replicate that particular ability it may have died out with her bloodline."

I stayed very still, praying my sweat wouldn't start to give me away. The ability hadn't died out. I had it. Not only did

Margaret have it, she was somehow obfuscating an entire vehicle. It suddenly dawned on me what a dangerous game Margaret was playing working so close to The Farm. She flew below the radar of every agent who came in here. Except Sopora. She had known. Margaret had taught her to use the ability right in Morpheus' back yard.

Bruadair finally asked what was truly on his mind, "Have the researchers mentioned whether the ability to kill a dreamer from within died with her as well?"

"You need to stop fixating on that Bruadair." I was inordinately pleased Lourdes was on to him. "You nearly got thrown into Tartarus for trying that on a mission. They've been watching you closely ever since."

"Yeah, but you're not going to turn me in, are you?" That bastard was trying to charm her! He was still a weasel.

Lourdes sighed, "No, I'm not. I just want you to be careful. And the answer is yes, after twenty years of lab and field testing, not to mention some really expensive cover-ups, the researchers formally declared that the ability to kill a mind from within its own dreams does not exist. Since Agent Sopora only allegedly did it once, and it was never duplicated or satisfactorily verified, they are not considering the incident a documented fact. It's merely unproven hearsay. The Reaper's own autopsy showed that she had drugged the man..."

"So it was a drug that weakened his mental protections?" Bruadair's interruption betrayed his desire.

"Okay, we're dropping this. I told you the researchers tried for twenty years to re-create the event. Do you think they neglected to try drugging their subjects?"

"Well, no... but..."

"Drop it or I'm done sharing."

He was silent for a moment, but he took her threat seriously. "Ok, fine." She tried to engage him in non-Agency talk, but I could hear in his reply that he was brooding. As with Sopora, it sounded like Lourdes may have been a lover of his for a short time, though she didn't seem to be currently.

Margaret brought their food out. Asked after their needs, and then shuffled back into the kitchen, "I've got to get ready for the dinner rush. Holler if you need me, dears."

Moments after she was gone, Bruadair asked, "What are we going to do about Morpheus?"

"Nothing if you want to stay out of his cross-hairs."

"Oh, that's so easy for you to say. You're the Golden Girl right now. You-Who-Can-Do-No-Wrong. He watches my every move like a hawk out of his one good eye." Some people never change.

I could tell she was answering carefully. "You have been plotting to take his place for years."

"So? He has to retire eventually. Besides, there's no proof of that."

"We're an Agency of near-psychic investigators. I'm pretty sure your desires in the matter aren't a secret. And I wouldn't put it past him to hold off his retirement just to spite you."

"Exactly!"

"If you're so unhappy, why haven't you transferred to the Australian offices?"

"And work for the Aboriginals? No thank you. And before you suggest it, there's no way in hell I could work for that Italian poofta either." I instantly hated Bruadair even more than before.

"I'm just saying that what's going on between you and Morpheus isn't helpful to anyone, and a separation might be in order."

"Separation? You mean you want me gone."

"I didn't say that."

"You didn't have to. I'm a near-psychic investigator. I deduced your meaning."

"I quit." She sounded frustrated. After a second, I heard a zipper and a snap. "Here's my share of the check. I'll walk back." She stormed out, and he just sat there. I couldn't see what he was doing, but his fork kept scraping his plate.

When Margaret came out later to clear away the dishes, he merely volunteered, "She got a call." They went through the motions of ringing him out and he left. I didn't budge until the car was well down the highway.

"James?" Called Margaret from the kitchen. "Why don't you come back here and help me with dinner?"

It was time for answers, I hoped.

She didn't wait for me to say anything, "I saw by your body language that you recognized him. And I know you knew who I was when you walked in. Mind if I smoke?"

"Uh... in the kitchen? Isn't that illegal?"

"The inspector owes me more favors than he can pay off in one lifetime. I get a few allowances." She lit up a fresh one.

I couldn't wait any longer, "You knew my mother. Are we related?"

"I was her aunt," she handed me an apron and pointed me first at a sink, and then to a big silver bowl. "Please mix that up. Use your hands. Meatloaf is best mixed with your hands." She went about setting out six meatloaf pans while she talked.

"I bought this diner a year before she signed up for her training at The Farm. I wanted to be nearby in case she needed me. But when she needed me the most, she was far, far away."

"What happened to her? Who was my father?"

"I never knew your father. And I am sorry, but by the time she met your father, she was in it so deeply that she and I didn't have a chance to sit down and talk again. I would have loved to have heard all about him. But after an incident in Africa, we had to communicate in dream fragments. I assume she left a series of them for you, or you would not have walked through my door asking for a scone."

"So the dreams I've been having are real, and on purpose?"

"They sure are kiddo. And I'm glad she found a way to leave them for you. I wasn't sure she'd be able to anchor them in such a way they'd stand the test of time."

So many questions fought to be first..."What on... I mean. I have to know, why did she get rid of me?"

"To keep you from Morpheus. Has she shown you, or have you overheard from the agents, the full story of what happened in Nairobi?"

"Where she killed the Reaper from inside his own dream?"

"Yes. You know all the details then?"

"I was there. I mean, in these dream fragments, I see things from her eyes. I saw what she saw in his head. I'll never be able to un-see it."

"Then, to my knowledge, you are the only person still alive who may have seen it. I doubt Morpheus was able to extract it from her. She may have shared it with your father, but he vanished into thin air after Morpheus grabbed your mom. More realistically, the Reapers have hidden him from Morpheus."

"These Sandmen are spies, though. How can you believe what they told you is true?"

"Well, for starters, nobody tells me anything. I'm just the

cussed old broad who runs the diner. But as you may have noticed, I overhear a lot."

"They were talking really blatantly about things that should have been hush-hush. Unless they didn't clue in to the fact I was sitting a booth away."

She raised a hand in supplication, "Guilty as charged. Over the years I may have woven a subconscious compulsion or three into the walls of this place. And maybe it is just subtle enough that they don't notice they're letting down their guard and spilling secrets. Bruadair knows, or suspects enough to have figured out there's something about this diner. He once looked around for some sort of Temptress ward. Though he didn't find anything that I didn't want him to see. So now he brings Agency women here all the time so they can get around to spilling their secrets. He's actually heard enough damning evidence to bring Morpheus down for good, but I don't think he's smart enough to piece it all together. That, or he's doing it for Morpheus. Bruadair's only real danger is his ambition. Lucky for us, if you're not in his way you might as well be invisible."

I was squeezing the meatloaf ingredients to a fine mash between my fingers. It was kind of therapeutic. "So, will you tell me all about my mom?"

"Yes, but not now. Once you get those pans filled and in the oven, you're going out back and waiting in my trailer until the Agency folk have eaten their fill and gone home for the evening. You should move your Jeep to my carport. It's a bitch to make people believe they're not really seeing it. If you don't mind waiting until I wrap this up and come home, I'll tell you everything."

CHAPTER ELEVEN
1972 – GIZA, EGYPT

This time I had no doubt–I was staring into my birth mother's eyes. "Remember," she'd just said. Now that all of my suspicions had been confirmed it wasn't likely I'd ever forget anything she had to show me. She was in the Mena House lobby. She'd just checked her lipstick in her reflection, and I noted that though she was wearing a stylish black evening gown, she'd paid some attention to the fact she was in Egypt by covering her bare shoulders and arms with a lacy shawl. Her hair was pulled up into an intricate braid, and her make-up should have been on a magazine cover.

James walked in from the oasis courtyard moments later. His tuxedo was simple, but timelessly stylish. The silver swan was pinned discreetly to the lapel. He looked her up and down, and his eyes complimented her more than words ever could have. She laughed and offered her arm. If he was taken aback by her forwardness, he didn't show it. Together they went up a couple of steps into the restaurant. The host welcomed them to the "restaurant where generals, kings, and presidents have dined for the last two centuries." James had put the reservation under the name Paulo Stephenos, and they were taken to a semi-private table for two in a corner.

"Business first?" he began, "or pleasure?"

"Business please, I want to end the evening on a good note."

He raised his eyebrow like he had earlier in the day. I noticed he used it in place of actually asking a question out loud.

"I was told 'no' in no uncertain terms. I'm to pack up and be on the midnight plane to the United States."

He looked confused, "There's no midnight plane out of Cairo International."

"Not domestic, no."

"You're in trouble at home too." He didn't make it a question.

She nodded slightly, "They're doing an awfully good job of making it sound like a simple debriefing, which set off all my warning signals."

"If I may be so bold, your gown is setting off all of my warning signals."

She smiled.

"How will you handle it," he went on.

"I guess that depends on your side."

"My news is significantly better, though potentially no less of a trap. The Elder would love very much to meet with you. He was willing to let you choose the meeting location, though he'll propose a change if he feels it isn't secure enough."

The waiter arrived with a bucket and champagne that James had obviously requested ahead of time. I was taken aback by the label. He was spending some serious dough. They made light conversation with the waiter about the vintage, and then returned to their serious conversation when he left.

"So," she said, "That means I have the hard choice to make. Honestly, if your Elder had declined outright, or laid out a blindingly obvious trap, I would face going home and dealing with my people. But you've just delivered the nicest invitation I've ever heard of an Elder making. It's hard to pass that up. So, even if you are leading me into a trap, I'll at least have this fancy meal."

He raised his champagne flute, "Then here's to fancy meals, questionable motives, and this dangerous life we lead."

She toasted him, brought the glass to her lips, but actually stopped the flow with her tongue. She bobbed her Adams apple for effect.

He watched her for a moment, and then asked, "It didn't tickle your nose?"

"It may have," she said with a comically stoic face, "but I wasn't going to be one of those girls who tittered about it."

"No, I suppose you're a bit beyond tittering."

"WELL beyond tittering."

They shared a laugh.

Sopora stared at the flute in her hands, watching the play of lights in the liquid.

"You're thinking something."

"How badly would he receive a request to a meet at the place in the United States where my people are going to pick me up?"

"Very badly."

"My chief said he didn't want me making contact because I'm not a trained diplomat."

"Which is probably the biggest reason the Elder agreed to meet with you. He thinks diplomats are a waste of time."

"Precisely. But this way he would have your people in his retinue, and I would have mine. And maybe, just maybe, they'd start trading words instead of blows."

"Are you really that naïve?"

"No. Just... hopeful. Since I have something both sides desperately want."

He raised his eyebrow.

"Me," she answered.

He shook his head. "The only way I'd even attempt to manipulate that meeting into happening was if I planned to sneak away during the crossfire."

"The thought had occurred to me."

"Don't. If you pulled off your initial disappearance, you'd have both sides actively hunting you. Right now, you're just a casual person of interest."

She sighed.

"I love the movies where the hero does something like that and then gives a heroic speech and both sides get those dopey thoughtful looks and everything ends well."

I sympathized with her. Me too, mom. Me too.

His thoughtful sadness returned, "This isn't the movies."

"I'm well aware."

They were interrupted again by the waiter, this time to see if they wanted to order. James must have seen the menu earlier because he'd never picked his up, but he ordered anyway. Sopora took only a minute, found a pheasant that had an interesting blend of spices, and ordered that.

I felt Sopora give her crooked smile. "Is this the part of a first date where normal people tell stories about themselves?"

James nodded. "I think so. I'm pretty sure I read a briefing where it's an attempt to both appear enticing and find common ground."

"Common ground? I wouldn't even know where to start."

"Oh come on, it's easy. Ask me when I first discovered my superpowers."

She smiled, "Well, Paulo, when did you first realize you were Outré?"

"In my teens. I saw black flitting shapes hovering around a girl in class. At first I thought she had flies. But as the day progressed, they started attaching themselves to her skin until she was covered in them. I teased her, but nobody else could see them. I'm sure I'm the one who ended up looking like he was having a bad drug trip. She died that night in a car accident. They held a moment of silence for her the next morning, but I couldn't stop thinking about the implications of me seeing those flies. Your turn."

"I don't think I can name a time I wasn't able to see the dreams of those near me. Even as a little girl, though at that young age I had to have skin-to-skin contact. And for the record, dogs do hunt in their sleep."

He smiled at that.

The conversation lagged for a minute, and he brought it back to work. "You know there are many Reapers practiced in bringing death? What you did in and of itself isn't shocking to us, except that you're the first Sandman to do it."

She nodded, "I guessed something along those lines. I've been thinking I'd be safer with your people than my own for that very reason. It's part of why I wanted to talk to you."

"Transfuge?? I don't know of anyone who's ever switched allegiances in our lifetime. The bloodline nature of our abilities doesn't lend itself to thinking that's even a possibility... but... I guess you're no stranger to being the first."

"I'm trying to avoid making it a habit."

He smiled at her. Everything about it looked and felt genuine. I wanted very badly to believe he'd protect her. He hadn't offered yet, but I suppose in their line of work it might seem false no matter his actual intentions.

I felt the change in Sopora's physical anxiety a split second before she spoke. "Very well. Let's go. After dinner. To your Elder."

James considered it, then nodded.

"You're not going to try to talk me out of it?"

"No. You're a very capable agent. I trust you know what you're doing."

She laughed, "I wish I had your faith."

At that moment, someone in a full desert robe strode into the dining room, looked around, and made his way to their table. James looked annoyed.

"Güçlü büyücü, I have watched as you commanded. The pyramid dancers come this way."

"Teşekkür ederim, Muavin."

Sopora didn't know what they'd said any more than I did, but she at least recognized both the language and the urgency. When the robed man left, she opened her mouth to ask James something, but he cut her off. "Not now, we have to go. The death cult is headed this way." He threw a wad of cash onto the table, found the waiter on the way out, and apologized profusely as they walked by him.

"We need to get someplace visible, public and with a lot of people who aren't practicing religion. Is there anything in your room you'd like to grab in case we don't make it back?"

"Yes, a few things, but I can get them into one bag."

They hurried and, as promised, she threw everything into a single bag. She pulled a small handgun from a concealed compartment in her luggage, but left the bulky bags behind. They stopped in James' room next. He grabbed only a few items, all of which he secreted into pockets of his tux.

"Thought of anyplace yet?"

"What about the Khedivial Opera House? I can get us in to whatever show is..."

James cut her off as they stepped outside, "It burned down last year." He waved to a cab.

"I suppose the museum is out?"

"All their ancestors are housed there. You don't want to risk them waking up angry great-great-great-grand-uncle Khufu to help hunt us down, do you?"

She laughed as she ducked into the back of the cab. "No, I don't."

"Do you mind a bit of British Imperialism?"

"No. Maybe?"

He told the driver to take them to Windsor Bar, downtown Cairo.

Sopora looked around, but didn't see any death cultists creeping up on them. James noticed her furtive glances. "We should be ok. Muavin is very good, and he moves quickly when he needs to..." His praise for his companion petered out when he saw dark shapes advancing on the cab. "Step on it," he commanded the driver. When the driver didn't show any initiative, James dropped a bill over the seat. The cab sped up, and then slammed to a stop.

The cab was hemmed in by cars on both sides, preventing the driver from swerving to avoid the shadow in black robes who had just jumped out of the bushes wielding a huge curved blade. My role-playing days kicked in and I realized I was seeing a real, functioning khopesh.

The driver shouted "MEDJAY!" and bolted from his cab. He hadn't taken the car out of drive, so it immediately started rolling forward unguided. The warrior stepped to the side where James sat and waited for the car to roll closer.

James and Sopora each kicked their doors open and jumped out. The car kept rolling, completely empty. People were scattering out of the way of the whole scene, but staying close enough to witness what might just be the best entertainment any of them had ever seen. Sopora had pulled her handgun from her bag. She checked the rounds, finding only two remaining. She looked over at James. His baton was out and already had the black scythe tentacles rippling off of it. He and the death cultist were facing off, but no blows had been exchanged yet. Sopora looked around. A cult means more than one by definition. Sure enough, the shadows were watching James.

"That's a switch" she muttered under her breath. Not needing to shoot anyone immediately, she chased down the rolling car. Jumping in through the open driver's door wasn't easy, but she managed it. Gaining control of the car, she threw the gears into reverse. The bumper tagged the cultist, pinwheeling him off a fancy car and into the shadows. The cab shifted momentum and she brought it to a stop right behind James. He flipped around the side and dropped back into his seat. Sopora accelerated so quickly the doors nearly shut. James pulled one and then the other tight so they wouldn't blow open.

Several blocks away she looked at James in the rear-view mirror, "They weren't after me."

He looked up at her, "Didn't appear like they were."

"Keep your secrets if you want, but we're quickly getting tangled up in each other's dramas."

He shrugged, "It's entirely possible I'm not supposed to be here in Egypt. And since we're speaking hypothetically, about the only time the death cults unite and come for blood like that is when someone reclaims an object the cults most likely stole from someone else centuries ago. Or a hated enemy has ventured into their territory. Or they hate men in tuxedos. We may never know for sure. They weren't horribly forthcoming with conversation."

"For the record, I have no idea where the Windsor is, if that's still our destination."

"It is. I'll give you directions. For now, head for downtown Cairo. We'll be able to stay the night and get to the airport under the nice bright light of day."

James and Sopora were both fairly alert for the majority of the drive. He guided her through the downtown maze. When they'd arrived at their destination, they gathered their belongings and he gave the keys to a teenager nearby. The cab was gone in seconds.

Sopora looked at James like he'd just committed a felony.

"What? I checked his aura. He's not going to die from this. And if the cult marked the cab in any way, they won't be storming in here looking for us."

She sighed, but didn't say anything.

Stepping into the Windsor was exactly like stepping into a British pub from the last century. Imported European wood, booths and tables delivered the traditions of that faraway land. Absolutely nothing Egyptian dared to be seen. James explained, "This used to be an officer's club. They kept it this way to remind travelers of home."

"It's jarring, but I like it. Come on, let's not sit near the windows."

Grabbing a table near the back, James went to order, and returned with two glasses of wine that were nowhere near as fancy as the champagne. "We also now have a room upstairs if you want to sleep before we leave."

"Probably not a bad idea. But dinner first. I'm getting really hungry."

In almost no time, the bartender brought over fish and chips. The last thing I clearly saw was them in their formal attire enjoying simple pub food immensely. The dream started fading while they ate. I saw brief flashes of them in a room laughing. The bed was simple, and the room European in design. In one flash, James was helping Sopora out of her gown. In another, she'd removed his tux jacket and had a hand up his shirt.

I suddenly understood she was selectively editing out the romance, allowing me to only see enough that I'd get the idea. I both appreciated that and hated it. She was my birth mother, of that I had no doubt. I strongly suspected he was my birth father. Like most children who've grown up not knowing their parents, I wanted to know everything. I was old enough to handle the idea that my parents had had sex. More painful was my need to know everything about them. But she had set this fragment aside for me long ago, and all my wishing wasn't showing me more than she wanted me to see.

TURKEY

In the morning, she was attired for travel in a plain dress and sensible shoes. There was a travel bag on the bed, so I surmised someone ran out to buy some new clothes. He was just finishing getting dressed. They kissed once before leaving the room. It was a lingering kiss of new love.

They held hands in the cab to the airport. Whatever identities they were using held up as they boarded a plane for Istanbul. In the air they made a game out of sharing their cover identities and making up details for each other. James decided Sopora's cover's father was Michael Gardner, a loving widower and philanthropist with a penchant for philately. Again I was struck by the use of part of my name–my middle name as well as last name this time. I guess it wasn't just the use of my name, it was potentially the origin for my name. Holding her own, Sopora came up with James' mother, Katherine, a serial crafter and cook on a knitting kick. She had a huge dog, he had a cranky cat. Back and forth the story creation continued for the duration of the short flight.

A limousine awaited them in Istanbul, but it merely took them to a train station. James bought their two tickets to Göreme. Sopora waited until the train was in motion before asking if they were going into the famed Cappadocian caves.

James laughed, "No. If that were actually an Enclave for the Elders, you wouldn't be anywhere near it. Those caves have nothing but tourists these days. However, the Elders like them to be weighing on peoples' minds during meetings... wondering what's down in the dank and dark. So they use the caves as a backdrop regularly."

Sopora looked shocked, "Did you just spill trade secrets?"

"Well, if I did, then I must be comfortable that you're at least considering us as an option."

"I've officially disobeyed a very strict direct order. My options are limited."

"Probably not as limited as you're imagining, but I understand. I've been on the naughty list before."

"Oh really?"

"Yep. And that naughty list too." James winked at her, making her laugh for a moment. Then the serious feeling returned. James didn't interrupt her this time, but let her watch the scenery roll by.

Göreme was beautiful. One and two story white stone buildings nestled among stone chimneys, spreading out over rolling green and stone hills. If I hadn't seen it through Sopora's eyes, I would never have believed such a place still existed. I kind of hoped we'd get to see the famous cave cities they'd mentioned.

A black sedan waited for us at the train depot. Sopora acted a bit like a tourist, head swiveling back and forth to take everything in. We were not taken to a cave, but to a two-story building that looked an awful lot like a church. The interior was lit only by candles, wooden shades pulled across the windows. Incense was burning somewhere, but it wasn't cloying.

Coming down a short hall, we entered into what could only be called an audience chamber. There was a chair on a dais, but it looked like they were carved from the same stone as the building. On the chair was a figure in heavy velvet robes. I couldn't tell if it was male or female. A woman in similar robes was standing to the right, a man to the left. The woman spoke, "Sandman, have you come to confess your sins?"

Sopora tilted her head. "I have come to tell the truth by sharing the dream-vision of what really happened. I will confess the truth of my actions, though I do not believe them to be sins."

The woman looked at the man beyond the seated figure. They waited for a sign from the seated leader, a barely perceptible nod.

The woman continued, "Very well. Share the vision with me."

"We will need to sleep near each other."

The woman turned and motioned Sopora to follow. James nodded encouragingly. Heading deeper into the building, the robed woman led Sopora to a room with two beds. She moved directly to one and laid down in a funereal pose. Sopora recognized the woman's ability to enter her meditative state and moved to the other bed and tried to relax herself as well.

She showed the woman the same dream I'd seen of her time in Nairobi. As she had with her romance the previous night, she again edited past the dream for my benefit. I was glad I didn't have to go through that ordeal again. It was still plenty vivid in my memory.

The robed woman screamed. Sopora woke in time to see the woman's death aura flare out in all directions, reflexively trying to protect her from harm. Sopora rolled off her bed away from the woman. Seconds later, the Reaper's aura had calmed and she lay on the bed breathing heavily, blood trickling from her nose. She sat up and stared at Sopora.

"Stay here," she commanded. Leaving the room, I clearly heard a key locking the door. Sopora was amused by that. I didn't doubt she possessed enough training to get out of this room. She stayed.

More untrackable time passed.

When the door did open, the man who had been standing opposite the woman merely set a tray of food on the bed and left, re-locking the door. Dinner looked delicious, and Sopora really enjoyed everything she sampled. It made me want to visit all the more. When she was done eating, Sopora played with the dream energy she had stocked up on in the desert. To her it looked like vapor, but it still made more sense to me to think of it as a sort of cohesive energy cloud. She was moving it from one hand to the other. She was sending it around her body in various ways, forming it in to various shapes, and then reabsorbing it. I understood she was showing me techniques I needed to practice. These were obviously the stepping stones to forming armor and phantasmal walls. She kept at it until she heard a key in the lock.

By the time the woman opened the door, Sopora was sitting silently on the bed.

"Come," she commanded.

Back into the audience chamber, the man and woman flanked the figure on the chair again. Wooden chairs had been brought in for James and Sopora. They sat.

The seated figure looked up, and enough light made it under the folds of the hood to reveal a skull. If it had been my body, I probably would have jumped. Sopora didn't.

The skull spoke, "You who are known as Agent Sopora, we have considered your confession. The only crime we find you guilty of is entering where you were not wanted." The leader's skull was remarkably flexible and emotive for solid bone. I wondered if maybe it was a trick of the death powers. "You offered many reasonable opportunities for cooperation, and only defended yourself."

"Further, it is also our wish for the bloodlines to cooperate, and we believe you were trying to prove there was no Reaper conspiracy. In that vein, we are prepared to make you an offer. If you will renounce your blood ties to the Sandmen, we will indoctrinate you into the Reapers. Once complete, you will be afforded all of our protections. In exchange, you will continue your career as an investigator on our behalf. You will defend Reapers and our interests with your life as if we'd always been your family. Do you need time to consider these terms?"

"One night, please. I shall have an answer in the morning."

"Very well. In the morning." He didn't stand, he floated up. His lieutenants moved just like normal people as they stepped in beside him. But the skull floated with no sign that he needed or even had legs. They left the building, but did not lock the door this time.

Sopora turned to James, "Was that good or bad?"

"Really good. I think it's probably the best possible outcome. Who knows? I might even be the one who gets to show you the ropes."

"Ropes? Now that's an idea. There are beds in the back, but no rope that I saw."

He raised his eyebrow encouragingly.

She smiled conspiratorially, "If you'll put up with my questions about what being a Reaper is like, I might be so grateful that I'll repeat a few things from last night."

"Oh... my..."

Chapter Twelve
2012 – The One-Eyed Roe

I woke in a strange living room that had definitely seen a lot of living. The chair was overly poofy, but had a dent where a smaller, slightly bowed body had been sitting comfortably for years. I remembered coming into Margaret's home, exploring the combination of awesome trinkets from around the world and old-lady comforts. I'd made the mistake of sitting down in her big easy chair, and had made the bigger mistake of being happy when I discovered that it had working heat and vibration controls. As if my narcolepsy had needed the help.

If I had any complaints, it was the decades of cigarette smoke that had suffused everything. Apparently, my shirt was not immune, and I could smell the burnt-and-stale smoke already deep in the fibers. It was dark outside, but the front door was being unlocked. I struggled to get up out of the chair, but Margaret caught me anyway.

"If you're done napping, I could use your help cleaning up." She didn't wait for an answer, but turned and shuffled her way back across the yard.

She was at the dish sink, loading a tray. "Go out and clear a table. Think about the one question you most want me to answer. When you return to drop off the dishes, I'll answer. Then you'll go clear the next one and repeat. This is hard for me too."

I hadn't realized this could be hard for her. She didn't have great big gaping holes in the knowledge of her life. I grabbed a grey bus tub and tried to let go of my self-focused thinking. It was hard. I'd spent my entire life wondering why someone had given me up. Aside from some guided therapy, I'd never spent much time wondering about the other side of the story. The sudden realization made me feel a little guilty.

I came to a complete stop when I saw the dining room. Every table was dirtied, as was every seat at the counter. Sighing, I hurried for the first table. I already knew what my first question would be. I'd been asking it most of my life.

"Why'd my parents get rid of me?" I asked as I walked back in.

To her credit her shoulders didn't droop, but she took me seriously. "They didn't. Section Chief Morpheus had your mother in a holding cell so he could take you to a lab as soon as you were born. Back then he was the ranking leader at the local facility. He's had major setbacks, and come back stronger each and every damned time. He's the effing Director now—which means nobody's above him in the Sandman hierarchy." I was about to ask a follow-up question, but she cut me off. "As far as I can tell, your father never knew your mother was pregnant. As I said, I wasn't able to find him after everything went to shit. Your mother died within minutes of giving birth to you. Jan would never have given you up willingly. And by now, I'm sure you've seen how well she could fight?"

I nodded.

"Good. Next table."

I took care to not break anything, but I practically swept everything off the table in one movement. "Was James my father?"

She barked a quick laugh, "I would have thought she'd have shown you that much by now. Yes, she told me about him, but like I said, I was never able to find him. In a perfect world, I'd have been able to point him to where you were fostered. In that, I've failed you."

Mulling over my thoughts while I cleared the next table, I had to decide the order of things I wanted to ask in case she cut me off. Even after I had carefully decided on an order of questions, I blurted out the one I thought I should have saved for the end, "Why didn't YOU come for me?"

"I fucking deserved that." She took a deep pull on a cigarette she'd been trying to hide behind the stock kettle. "You'd been placed with a normal foster family. Morpheus had his damned agents hunting high and low for you. He wanted very badly to experiment on you. When they finally found you, you hadn't developed powers. When your teen years came and went, and it looked like you were completely mundane, he reduced surveillance on you. By the time you turned thirty he'd given up on you manifesting abilities from either bloodline and turned his full attention to other matters." Margaret looked old and tired. "I hope the foster family was good to you. I've been hiding in the effing Sandman effing backyard for over a lifetime. Janet was not the only person I've taken under my care. So for me to suddenly acquire the child Morpheus desired so badly would have put a lot of people in jeopardy. You appeared safe, and it looked like you'd live out your life unmolested by his effing schemes.

You saw all the souvenirs in my house? I bought every one of those damned things while looking for your father. Having him claim you as his son would have been the best thing for a great many reasons. I never gave up watching over you, but there was no way for me to safely bring you here. I'm not a fighter like your mother was." She shooed me out, but not before I saw her eyes tear up.

I stayed out in the dining room a bit longer this time. I also decided that since she was putting dishes into racks based on function, it made more sense to get all the dishware in categories. So instead of everything off a single table, I cleared all the glasses from across the dining room.

When I returned, she smiled. "Now you're getting the hang of it."

I tried out my father's eyebrow raise as a question. Her expression didn't show that she recognized it as anything other than my curiosity, "You have the power to change a few rules in this world. I told you to clear one table at a time, but you noticed that's not how I was doing the dishes on my end. So you changed the rules. Remember this lesson. Changing the rules was your mother's greatest strength. Did you have a question for me?"

"Many."

"One per trip, them's the hard-and-fast rules."

I nodded. "Very well. I've found you, and my father could still be alive. Do you know of any other relatives I might have?"

"You have two cousins on your mother's side. They're not very nice, and one of them is in prison. Some Reapers I know owed me a few favors, but I'm still an outsider to them. I never was able to find out anything about your father's side of the family. So I don't really know about that one. They might tell you more if you prove yourself to them."

Back in the dining room, I opted for all the silverware. It made for a heavier tub.

"Should I find the Reapers? Should I find some of my mom's old friends? What should I do now?"

"I suppose that's up to you. I sense that Jan's not done showing you things yet. She may have something to show you that might lead you to your father, or to something she needs you to do. That I don't rightly know, but even if she doesn't, what you do next is ultimately a decision you have to make for yourself every day, whether Outré, or mundane."

"Outré? That word's come up several times in the dreams."

She put a bony hand on her hip, "That seems to me a whole new line of questioning, which means some clearing is in order."

I hurriedly grabbed all the saucers and cups.

"Some damned hoity-toity Frenchie," she continued when I returned, "came up with that name for us back in the seventeen or eighteen hundreds. It means something like 'strange' or 'unusual.' We mostly define it as 'supernatural outsiders' today. But it's the term that refers to all of the bloodlines, the ones we've documented as well as any new ones that pop up."

I raised my eyebrow hoping she'd elucidate.

"Nice effing try. Get the bowls."

I did.

"You're obviously familiar with the Sandmen and Reapers..."

"And have painful, first-hand knowledge of Sirens," I interrupted.

She scrunched up her wrinkled face, "Oh, ouch."

"Yeah."

She barked a couple laughs. "Well, bloodlines come and go. But some of the more common include Temptresses who have the ability to cloud the mind with lust. Then there are the Myrmidons, gifted with battle powers. Each one of them is very different. One might have effing hard skin like armor where another will have supernatural skill with blades or guns. Let's see, oh. The Maenads. They pretty much bring all your worst emotions to a damned boil and turn you loose to cause some mayhem. The last major bloodline is the Oracles. Their lot is the gift of prophecy. They're rare, though I think it's partly because they have the easiest time rationalizing their powers as a series of coincidences and lucky guesses. However, they're high in demand if they have a record of accuracy. Minor bloodlines are usually narrower in scope, and haven't withstood the test of time like the major ones."

Plates were next, creating another heavy tub.

"So, what exactly can I do?"

"HA! Boy, what can you imagine yourself doing?"

I must have looked perplexed because she laughed those short raspy laughs at my expression.

"I've lived a long time, and tried a lot of shit. And if there's one thing I've learned, it's that we are each individuals. If you can imagine a dream-themed ability, you can start to practice it. If you're doing it right, it'll manifest. And the cliché "Practice makes perfect" is annoyingly accurate in this case.

She took a drag off her cigarette and powered on, "But we're kind of lucky. Dreams are malleable. We humans expect dreams to change and do fantastic things. Think about it. Death is kind of static. You're either alive or you're dead. Not a lot of room for growth, is there?"

I shook my head.

"Same with the Myrmidons. What do they do? They fight. Could they do more? Probably, but they don't imagine themselves doing more. Well, when we enter a dream we imagine we can do anything. And that's our edge. Jan understood that intuitively. She practiced transforming thought into action, and she was brilliant at it. Too brilliant, Morpheus may not have understood that this was what made her powerful, but he very badly wanted what she had."

She motioned me back into the dining room, but aside from collecting the creamers and assorted little ceramic serving dishware, there wasn't anything left to do but throw out napkins and wipe down tables. I saved those for the next time she sent me out.

"Butter dishes and creamers already? Your help has really sped this along."

I grinned, perfect tie in, "Can I stay with you and learn from you?"

"Nope." She dismissed me so quickly it hurt. I'd just found a link to my birth family, and was told I couldn't stay. "I didn't say we wouldn't keep in contact, but you can't stay here."

I must have looked like I was building up to argue with her, because she cut me off again. "I'm not as strong as I used to be, and I can't keep masking your aura every time you forget."

Damn it. I pulled it in tight.

"Better, but if I hadn't been ready for you to slip, they'd have been pounding down the damned door by now. We're too close to them." She pulled an envelope and a key with a huge white plastic fob out of her apron.

"The address of the hotel is in the envelope. I want you to stay there. It's built over an energy nexus that is friendly to the Myrmidons. It should be enough to hide your burgeoning abilities in case you slip. I assume Jan is subtly training you through your dreams?"

I nodded.

"I thought she might be. Teaching by example?"

"Yep."

"That's my girl." When she said that, I felt a tightening in my chest that had nothing to do with Outré powers and everything to do with finding my family.

"I've also called a friend who owes me big to protect you. If she feels it's safe, she's to introduce you to the local Reapers. She's younger, and spry, and has no tie to the dreaming. She's affiliated with one of the Reapers' northern branches. Not the main center in the Mediterranean area. You can see auras by now, I assume?"

"Yeah." I didn't think it appropriate to tell her I called it my Suck-O-Vision. I had a feeling that ability was about to become far more useful.

"Good. Almost all of us Outré can see them. And almost none of us can hide them, if you take my meaning. It's how we recognize each other, and how we keep from showing off in front of the mundanes."

She noticed my discomfort, "Oh I hate calling them that too, but calling them non-Outré is even more effing awkward."

"Good point," I laughed.

"And if you don't think they'd start a whole modern witch hunt for us, guess again. Humanity is dangerous when it's scared."

I nodded. I saw it every time I turned on the news.

"Where was I?"

"Auras."

"Right, well, everyone's aura is a combination of their bloodline abilities and the way they see themselves. Remember that, because if you're perceptive it gives you some pretty important insight into people. The young Reaper I asked to help you was in the process of selecting a shadow name when I called. I don't know what she'll introduce herself as. But her aura wraps protectively around her like black raven wings."

"Selecting a shadow name?"

"It's kind of an Outré rite of passage. You name yourself, and in so doing kind of declare both your allegiances and roles in our hidden world."

"You chose Margaret?"

"No, I chose She-What-Must-Not-Be-Named-Lest-She-Spit-In-Your-Soup. Of course I effing chose Margaret. I needed to hide in plain sight." She laughed her raspy bark for a few minutes, and it devolved into a wet-ish sounding cough. She took a hit on the cigarette trying to calm the spasm.

"Sorry, my lungs ain't what they used to be."

"Apologies not necessary. Ok I can go wait for her. Then what?"

"Then stay the hell out of trouble and learn to use your damned abilities. At least bone up on hiding if nothing else. I'm guessing if you ask her nicely, she might show you some Reaper abilities too. I'll come and go as I can, but you'll learn more about the dream abilities from Jan than you would from me."

I nodded, putting the envelope and key in my pockets. I wasn't ready to leave, and she wasn't forcing me out. Instead, she pointed at a sink with a few giant pots and pans left to scrub. I went over to do the heavy scrubbing and let the silence get comfortable while we both worked. I finally had to ask one more question, "Can I call you Aunt Margaret?"

She smiled warmly, "I'd like that very much."

That was all I needed right now. I wanted to make sure she wouldn't leave me now that I'd found her, but that was an irrational side of me. I tried to sit on that and make it go away. When the pots were clean, I swept up and took out the trash while she tidied up the front counter. Eventually we were out of chores.

"Don't take this the wrong way, cuz I'm grateful for your help today. But I ain't as strong as I used to be and I have to get up damned early. So, you need to get going."

I nodded. "Thank you, Aunt Margaret. Thank you." I gave her a huge hug that made her squawk a little.

As she walked me to the diner's door, she was saying, "Remember, keep your aura hidden at all times. If you do nothing else, you keep practicing on hiding it. The ability to appear mundane is better camouflage than anything else you've got. I'll check in on you regularly. If you need me, come here in the off hours. But not until you're strong enough to keep your aura hidden. Got it?"

I nodded, "Got it. I'm ready for this."

"Oh? We're never effing ready for this, kiddo. It's thrust upon us unasked for. However, I do think you're up to the challenge. Good night, Nephew James."

I laughed as she closed the door. She watched me get in the Jeep and drive off. She didn't twist the lock until I was turning onto the highway.

OLD FURNACE STATE PARK, CONNECTICUT

The hotel she'd set me up in was across the state border into Connecticut. It was easy access to I-395, not far from Old Furnace State Park. I spent the whole drive making sure my aura was pulled in tight. In the parking lot I focused on my Aura Sight, dun-dun-dun-daaaaa! I struck a heroic pose, made all the more comical by my flab being unheroic. I couldn't help it. Things had gotten so serious I needed to blow off some steam.

My room was nice in a mass-produced, cookie-cutter corporate way, and therefore utterly boring. Admitting to myself I had a long way to go before my heroic pose meant anything, I changed into some running clothes and headed for the park.

As I jogged up to the entrance, a sign proclaimed "Closed at Sunset." Well, damn. That gave me less than an hour. Who was I kidding? I'm not sure I'd ever run for a full hour. I picked up the pace determined to set a personal record. I practiced keeping my aura dampened while I exerted myself through the cycles of walking and jogging. The park was gorgeous. I ran along a waterway with a bubbling brook. I clambered over stone formations and looked out over the park from high up. Being slightly curious, I gazed around with my aura sight. What I saw explained why Aunt Margaret had chosen this particular hotel. Ghosts of battles past were locked in their eternal struggles. There were Native American warring tribes. There were colonists fighting tribes, and then colonists fighting colonists over an iron furnace. The place had a history of battles... and a heavy miasma of death. I suddenly didn't want to be there after dark.

CONNECTICUT COUNTRYSIDE

Showered and tired, I lay on the bed with a frantic clashing of thoughts whirling through my head. I had an aunt. I had superpowers that let me see other people's dreams AND ghosts. I had a crappy job. But I also had some of the best friends in the world. What the hell? I grabbed my phone.

"Hey J, do you have the job?"

Of course Nate would ask me that right off the bat. Shit. "I don't know. I mean, I think it went well, but I need you to talk me off a ledge."

"Ledge?"

"I think I found my birth mom's aunt. And, I think I want to stay and find out if I have more family."

His initial silence carried more condemnation than the words that followed. "Damn... James... you didn't have a job interview did you? You went out there chasing family. Why didn't you just tell me?"

I hated myself for a minute, but realized this was a better way to avoid the whole crazy bloodline conversation that would probably get me committed to a nice medically green institution.

"I take it by your silence that I'm right."

"Maybe."

"Look, you know I would support you in that endeavor more than finding a job. That's been the largest mystery in your life. You just... ahg." He took a moment to compose his thoughts. "Tell me about her."

"Well, she's old."

"Great Aunt? She'd have to be."

"She's quirky, thoughtful, well-traveled, and has a mouth like a trucker. She lives alone, but I have the feeling there are a lot of people in her life. She even mentioned distant cousins."

"How'd you even find her?"

"I spent a lot of time on an ancestry website trolling around. I chased down every family line with my name."

"Gardner? That had to be an exercise in dead ends."

"You have no idea."

"You had a lot of free time, didn't you?"

"Yeah, I really did. It's amazing how much time the standard j-o-b sucks out of our waking lives, and what you do at night to forget your long, monotonous day. Anyway, I found a woman who had to have been my mother based on her time of death. Turns out they put her family name on my birth certificate. My whole life I've been searching for paternal Gardners, not maternal."

"How sure are you about this great aunt?"

"Relatively. She was able to describe the first foster family where I was placed. Not in huge detail, because her knowledge was limited to what she knew before I was placed, but enough that it had to be her."

"Is she willing to take a genetic match test?"

"Gee Nate, I didn't think to ask an old lady if she'd donate some genetic material to soothe my lifelong hurt feelings."

"Don't get snotty, it's a valid question. In the absence of actual legal documents proving any sort of relation, it would be a really good way to verify it. I'll help pay for it if you need me to."

I needed to steer this conversation a different direction, I couldn't tell him I'd checked her aura and it was like mine. "I'll talk to her about it, but I think it's too early for that. There's something else."

"She's loaded, so your disparaging comments about jobs are well justified?"

"No. Actually, I think she's burning through her retirement fund just to afford this world that got way more expensive than her generation ever thought possible. No, it's about the Death Buggy."

"What'd you do to my Jeep?"

"I didn't do anything. Some creep broke the windows in the parking lot."

"Fax me the police report and I'll report it to my insurance."

Shit. "I didn't stick around. I was afraid he'd break my head because there was nothing in the Jeep to steal."

"Did you at least take pictures?"

"Er... no. But I have the receipt from the garage where I already paid for the repairs. I can send that to you and the insurance company can call him to verify the damages. It's something."

"Find, send it. I'll see if I can get some of your money back. Probably not all, and possibly none without the police report."

"Sorry. My safety felt more important."

"Yeah. It is. Just. Be careful."

"I was. I got out of there."

"I mean about the family stuff too. That kind of hurt doesn't heal like a broken bone."

"I know. I'm sorry I didn't tell you right away. I just wasn't ready for... it."

"Yeah. I'll give you a pass on that one. One pass. You've used it. Now I know, so no more stories about crack addled research jobs. Ok?"

"Ok. I haven't even asked how you are. I'm a shitty friend."

"Oh stop, I'm fine. Work as usual, then home for more work, so I can sleep and dream about work."

"Gosh you make it sound appealing."

"Heh. Look, keep me updated on what you find about your birth family. I won't say anything to anyone until you tell me you've told them."

"You mean 'Chelle?"

"I sure do. By the way, the longer you wait to confess to her, the more she'll box your ears and kick your shins for not telling her something so important."

"I know, but I want to tell her in person if it works out. If this is just a dead end, I want to wallow on your couch in complete lonely misery."

"Lonely?"

"Yeah, you'll be at work."

"Ass. Take better care of my Jeep."

"I will, sleep well. Dream of handsome hunks."

"Thanks, you too."

Hanging up, I couldn't help but wonder if I'd have been able to implant that dream for him if we were closer. Or maybe even at a distance if I'd given it enough oomph. Oh! I was in a hotel with sleeping people!

I made claws of my hands and tried to draw dream energy to me. Nothing, but it was early. I set the alarm on my phone for 2:00 a.m. so I could try again and then practice moving the energy around like my mother had tried to show me.

I laid back on the bed and smiled myself to sleep. I had a birth mother who was trying to talk to me.

CHAPTER THIRTEEN
1972 – GÖREME, TURKEY

Sopora's eyes were staring at me from under a black velvet hood. "Remember," she said with the familiar emotional push. She was in a stone room above ground. Orange sunlight was streaming in a window behind her, but whether sunrise or sunset I couldn't immediately tell. She had no makeup on at all. Most disconcertingly, I could feel that she had nothing on under the robe.

Leaving the mirror, she sat cross-legged on an ottoman in front of the window. She calmed her breathing down to virtually nothing. "Practice," she whispered, "letting air move through your lungs without pumping them. Do not breathe. Do not give the signs of life." After several minutes whispering that over and over to herself, she pulled a single fluffy feather from the cushion near her. It was one of the light curly feathers, technically a down feather unless we've bastardized the meaning of that name. She thrust her lips out like she was going to kiss someone, and rested the feather on her upper lip in front of her nose. She then practiced letting air move through her lungs under its own power.

The first several tries she blew the feather off her nose. With a lot more patience than I would have had, she merely picked it up, sat back down calming herself, and tried again. Eventually, she had it to where she only ruffled the light fronds of the feather, but didn't blow it completely off. She held remarkably still considering it was tickling her nose.

She was able to maintain that level of calm through the setting of the sun. When the last sliver of the sun's disc dropped below the horizon, I noticed air movement ruffle the feather counter to the direction of her breathing. She did too, she dropped backwards off the ottoman and rolled into a crouch, ready for action. A black scythe whirled soundlessly through the air over her head. The feather was completely gone.

"Crude weapons," was the last phrase she uttered out loud for a while. Jumping back, she summoned forth a small trickle of the dream energy she'd pulled from the desert. I was amazed that she'd held onto it for this long. She conjured up the mental construct of that nightmare where you cannot hold on to something, and coaxed that dream into a thin barrier. I just realized she'd had her aura out and sort of large, she pulled it in tight now and ducked back into the shadows away from the window.

Across the room, a dark figure was soundlessly retrieving the scythe from where it'd clattered to the floor. I felt Sopora shake her head. Moving as silently as her attacker, she began to make her way around the perimeter of the room.

Something I couldn't detect gave away her position, and the attacker threw the scythe again. It arced through the air with its wicked-sharp blade spinning around. Sopora mostly dodged, but it would have nicked her if not for the shield she'd erected. Instead of embedding in her shoulder, the final centimeters of the blade skidded off the slippery-nightmare shield.

She tried to keep sneaking, but even in the darkest parts of the room, the attacker tracked her motion easily. As it moved for the scythe once again, I felt her trickle out more precious dream energy. This new construct also felt like a thin field at first. Then she stepped sideways out of it, and I saw the simplicity in her plan. She had created a phantasmal duplicate of herself. It continued sneaking around the perimeter of the room, much like she had.

Her duplicate somehow held the attacker's full attention. We were a short way from where the attacker had picked up the scythe. This time, it seemed we were unnoticed. Up close, I could see the attacker was the woman from the audience chamber, the one Sopora had invited into the dream. Sopora noticed it too and started releasing a trickle of dream vapor beneath her robes. The woman swung the scythe, and the duplicate raised its arm to block. I was stunned when the blade stopped against the illusion's arm. The attacker paused for only a second, then like lightning pulled the scythe back and readied for another swing. The duplicate took a fighting stance. The woman came in high, forcing the duplicate to block high. At the instant before contact, she shifted her angle and slashed across the duplicate's chest. Dream vapors leaked out. Sopora grimaced, but concentrated on keeping the duplicate in play, gaping chest wound and all.

The woman realized something was very wrong, and stepped away from the duplicate, looking around for the real Sopora. That's when she noticed the floor was slowly becoming a pool of blood beneath her feet. Until the woman reacted I hadn't even noticed that Sopora was slowly shaping the low vapors into a copy of the blood sea. Instinctually her attacker took several steps back, slipping on slick, sloshing blood. Coming to her senses, she glanced around the room, clenched her jaw, and sent forth a wave of pure, unreasoning, primal fear of dying.

It hit Sopora so hard the duplicate faded in a vapor cloud. She scrabbled backward a few steps, thudding into the wall behind her. The thud was all the attacker needed to pinpoint Sopora and rushed her with the scythe.

The sudden threat snapped her out of the deathly fear, and she focused not on the scythe's blade, but on the woman's chest. Sopora conjured up that twitch we often get just at the moment of transition from drowsy to sleep, the one that shakes the bed. She delivered that twitch to her attacker along a bolt of dream energy. The woman's body convulsed and she dropped the scythe.

Sopora rushed forward, feinted with a kick, and grabbed the woman's skull in her hands. She burned a lot of the stored energy to slip into the woman's waking mind.

She landed at the water line. The dream sea with its islands stretched out behind her. In front of her was a continent, solid and unforgiving. I could see across it for miles. In the center was a huge stone citadel. Commanding from a platform at the top was the woman. She stood naked, but blackened bones were part of her skin, almost like an inverse skeleton costume.

Sopora adjusted her position back a step into the water. I realized that the woman could not see into her own dreams while she was awake, but Sopora could see her. Looking over her shoulder, she scanned the closest islands. Each of them seemed to hold a fairly mundane event playing out. Floating up over the water, Sopora chose one with other robed figures.

"... make her face her own death" the leader with the skull

head was saying. "I don't care how you do it, but she must
come to terms with dying if she is to be a Reaper."

Sopora nodded. I had read once that our dreams are our
minds trying to categorize parts of our day. New memories
must form here in the shallows until our mind sleeps and can
deal with it. I'd have to ask Aunt Margaret. Sopora levitated
up and floated to the next island. Not seeing anything useful,
she moved past and looked at several more. There. Caged, but
near the surface was a beast. It was larger than an elephant,
but quadrepedal for the most part. It had the eyes and mouth
of a great shark, but an armored hide unlike any creature I'd
ever seen. Its paws had giant rending claws, and it looked to
be far more nimble than an elephant. It was eviscerating the
robed woman. Sopora let the dream start over. The creature
hunted the woman through a dark city. It pounced on her
from an impossible angle, and ripped her to shreds while she
screamed helpless to stop her own nightmare. Then the woman, still alive in the dream scenario, had to watch the creature
feast on her own entrails. If I'd have been in my body, I would
have thrown up.

Sopora flew back to the point between that island and the
shore, and stretched her hands out, releasing some dream
vapor. She slowly formed a misty bridge. She didn't bother
giving it any weight or solidity that I could tell. She merely
made sure it was perceptible. She then flung a mote at the
nightmare beast, getting its attention. It let out a trumpeting
snarl and sprang toward us. Sopora released another mote
that morphed into the woman in her robe, coming to a stop
on the bridge beneath us. The creature's full attention shifted
to its eternal prey. Sopora turned her hand, palm up, and the
new duplicate screamed and ran for the mainland, making a

bee-line for the citadel that housed the woman's real waking consciousness. The creature shrieked an ear-splitting howl and gave chase. Its wicked talons sunk into the vaporous bridge, but not all the way to the dream sea.

Upon reaching the mainland, it chased the duplicate toward the citadel. Sopora lowered herself to the dream sea as she watched them go. When her feet hit the water at the edge of the now empty dream island, she dipped one hand in as I'd seen her do and replenished her depleted dream battery. She left enough island to re-cage the beast, and then exited the woman's inner world.

In the real world, Sopora let go of the woman's head. The scythe forgotten, the woman crumpled into a fetal position and whimpered, fighting off her own nightmare in a battle we could no longer see.

Picking up the scythe, Sopora went to the window and lobbed the scythe out into the night. Turning, she exited the room through the door. The hall outside her room was pitch black. She strained to hear, at the same time, she brought to mind her own lesson in quiet breathing. Her senses detected nothing. She crept down the corridor, keeping one hand lightly on the wall.

An opening to her right brought her to a halt. Senses straining, she inched her fingers into the space. The door was ajar. She considered for a brief moment, and then slipped through the open door. I don't know how she knew, but she ducked milliseconds before a scythe would have taken off her head. From her crouch, she kicked out and connected with a knee. Neither Sopora nor the new attacker made any noise. The scythe arched down, but Sopora rolled deeper into the room. Hitting a small chair, she turned her standing momen-

tum into an over-the-shoulder throw. The chair hit a wall, but
the shuffle of feet indicated her aim had been good.

There was a momentary standoff in the dark. I felt Sopora
check that her misdirection shield was still intact. Calling
energy to her hands, she strained to hear anything. I thought
I heard the lightest rub of velvet robe against a piece of furniture. Before I was entirely sure I had even heard it, Sopora
let loose a burst of white light, closing her own eyes at the
last instant. The attacker grunted in pain. Sopora spun like a
dancer, and I heard the scythe whiz blindly through the air
where she'd been standing.

The man's deep and accented voice resonated through the
room, "your dreams will not affect me again."

I felt Sopora reach down and grab the woven rug. It shifted ever so slightly, and she pulled for all she was worth. The
man had been ready for a phantasmal assault, but not that.
He went down on his ass. A brief glow from Sopora's hand
showed her where the scythe had fallen. I thought for sure
she'd dive for it, but she grabbed an end table instead. She
smashed the table down onto his head as he rolled for the
scythe. His skull bounced from the table and cracked the
carved stone floor. He stopped moving. She picked up his
scythe and took it with her.

Continuing her sneak down the hallway, she entered a
large, cavernous space. In the center was the skull-headed
robe man. Next to him a single lit candle. He motioned to
the floor in front of him. Sopora approached him as he was
pulling the hood back, revealing his unnatural skull head.
She offered him the scythe, but he didn't take it.

She set it down on the floor next to where she lay down,
head pointed at the candle. The Elder nodded once, and then

walked off into the dark. "Sleep now, it's time for you to visit your own dreaming sea," was all he said.

She closed her eyes and slowed her breathing. It took her almost no time to reach her own inner world. Her sea was actually a sea, covered in sunlight that sparkled on jewel-toned aquamarine colors. It reminded me strongly of the Caribbean. Flying up over the water, she passed island after island. I had no idea how she knew where she was supposed to be going.

In the quiet moments like this, I wished I had a way to communicate with her. This was my mother. My birth mother. In her past she had known enough to plant these memories for me, allowing me to get to know her. But I had questions, thousands of questions. And there's no reason I shouldn't have been able to ask them of her. Except I kept trying, and I couldn't because it was a replaying of a memory in dream form.

There was something dark on the horizon. Of course we were headed right for it.

Getting closer, I made out a whirling dark cloud large enough to be protecting an entire island. Coming to a stop before the black hurricane, Sopora hesitated.

Plunging in, we were buffeted by the winds. She smoothed the journey a bit, but it was still pretty rough. In the eye was a single island. On that island was a large house. It was too small to be rightly called a manor, but it had several gables and was larger than most. I thought it looked a little like the Addams Family home. Sopora floated closer, hesitated, and looked around. "Figures."

She never set foot on the ground, but floated to the front door. It opened for her and she floated in. Screams echoed up the stairwell to the right. She looked that way, floated up over the bannister and began her descent. Several levels below, she followed the screams down a sterile hallway tiled with something orange that did not feel natural. Sopora avoided touching it.

She stopped in front of an orange door. This one did not open for her. There was a small inset window. Sopora floated over to it and looked in. She was looking at herself strapped to an orange table, screaming. Turning, she exited the way she came in.

Once outside the black hurricane, she turned and glared at it.

The black hurricane trembled, and then tightened. Slowly, inexorably, she was crushing the house and the island. It was one of those things that was hard to believe when you were there watching it. She was controlling the forces of nature, using them to destroy the constructs in her own dream realm. The house was being shredded, and coming apart the way I always envisioned a house might fare against a tornado. The island, however, was simply being erased as the circumference of the storm shrank.

Within minutes, there was nothing left but warm, blue-green water gently dappled by a sun that wasn't in the sky.

Sopora turned and flew out.

Waking up on the stone cold floor, the candle had burned itself out. That didn't matter, a lone door had been left open. Warm gold candlelight invited from the other side. Picking up the scythe, Sopora went the way she was expected to.

It was the audience chamber. The Elder was back on the raised seat, the woman with her recovered scythe stood in her usual position. The man, empty-handed, stood in his.

Unlike previous audiences in this room, there were maybe twenty other individuals present. Each of them was similarly robed, though only about half of the hoods were pulled up. Sopora saw James, and he nodded, seeming pleased.

"Come forth," the Elder commanded.

She did without hesitation. There were whispered muffles when she reached the dais, and I wondered if she was supposed to kneel in supplication. She did no such thing, but instead handed the scythe back to its owner, handle first. I swear a slight grin pulled up the corner of the skull's mouth.

The Elder stood, and all whispering ceased.

"You have faced my daughter," he motioned to the woman. "Instead of fighting her physically, you turned her own nightmare against her."

The daughter held her head high, making an obvious show that she had re-chained her inner beast. Sopora nodded.

The Elder then motioned to the man, "You then faced my son. Instead of fighting him in the realm of the mind, you knocked him prone, and then knocked him unconscious."

The man did not hold his head as high as his sister, but instead glared at Sopora. To her credit, she merely nodded to the Elder.

"I then sent you to face your own death. Your actions were unique there as well. Tell the assembled what we saw."

Sopora's raised her voice so that all could hear, but she kept her eyes locked on the Elder's. "You constructed a possible death in my mind. Something you thought would frighten me. Instead, you merely showed how very little you know of me. You see, Elder, when Death comes for me, I'm going out fighting–not screaming helplessly."

Silence filled the audience chamber as though the night

waited in anticipation.

Then the Elder smiled. His damned skull actually smiled. "You are a welcome addition to the Reapers. Do you, before the assembled Outré witnesses, hereby renounce your ties and allegiances to the Sandmen?"

"Yes."

"And do you swear loyalty to the Reapers, vowing to undertake our sacred duty of assisting those who've died in finding their way to their afterlives?"

"Yes."

"Your Sandman name will die with those ties. What shall you be called among the Reapers?"

"Somnoleni," she answered without hesitation. Several people nodded approval, and I committed that to memory phonetically. I needed to know what it meant.

"Welcome, Sister Somnoleni."

The assembled Reapers then came forward, starting with the Elder's children, and greeted her. Some gave a formal hand on the shoulder, others barely uttered an unemotional "welcome." A few, the Elder's son first among them, merely gave a cold glare and nod. I had the sense nobody dared go against the Elder's pronouncement, but junior seemed to know how much dissention would be tolerated.

James was last, and his greeting included one of the rarest things of all–a smile. It appeared the ritual was over, and Reapers were filtering out into the night. Most had street clothes on under their ceremonial garb, and shed the robes on the stairs leading to the street.

James leaned in close, "I've got a real hotel where we can go tonight. I'm done with this stark building if you are."

"I'd really like that. And a shower."

"It might have to be a bath, but I'm sure that can be arranged."

Looking around, my mother noted the Elder was gone though he had not been among those to leave by the front. His daughter came toward my parents. "If you'll be staying around, I would really love the opportunity to spar with you and trade some fighting techniques. I think there is much we could learn from each other."

Somnoleni looked at James, inviting him to chime in. When he didn't, she replied, "I think I'd like that. Though I may need a day or two to recover from the ordeals."

"Then tomorrow I will arrange a tour of the cave cities and surrounding countryside, and we'll plan for sparring sometime after that. Again, welcome."

GÖREME, TURKEY

Alone in their room, Somnoleni asked James a question I'd had as well. "I didn't know there was a formal transfuging ceremony."

"Well, I don't think you can change the abilities in your blood. Though I believe they'll develop along a more Reaper-like theme from here on out."

"You know the Sandmen aren't going to let me go that easily."

He nodded. "I know. The Elder does too. He's already called a convocation of Elders to decide how to handle your old employers when they come knocking."

"If they knock. Asking nicely won't be their style. They'll sneak in at night when your guard is down."

James chuckled, "Well that is pretty standard for all Outré.

I have some faith that the Elders and the dream agents know enough about each other to make this interesting. I also believe between you and I we know enough about disappearing to get out of the limelight for a while?"

"That is exactly what I'm trained to do."

LATER

She edited out her bath and romance with James again, but picked up after James had gone to sleep. She was lying next to him, slowing her breathing. Reaching inward, she took me again to her inner world. This time, however, she flew far higher than ever before. She never looked down, but the brilliant azure sky soon gave way to grey, and then blackness lit only by stars. Moving through the blackness, she crossed through an odd silver cloud. It felt like the powdery vapor given off by dry ice or smoke machines. How she navigated through it, I'll never know. Soon, we were descending through the emptiness of space into a darker blue sky. The ocean below us was a gray-green. Not unhealthily so, but mysterious. It was the type of sea that regularly cloaked itself in fog. She touched down on the continent, though this one was blanketed only in forest. I saw no citadel, or buildings of any kind. Stepping farther inland from the beach, she went to a nearby tree. In the crook of a branch was a piece of typing paper and an old Bic pen.

She opened the paper and started to write:

Auntie,
I'm sure by now you've heard the rumblings from the
farm. Most likely you're hearing bits of truth, but they're

going to be distorted. A murderous Reaper tried to kill me in his dream islands, and during the fight, I had to kill him to save myself. It was not easy, and I did not escape unscathed, but I did escape. I sensed the lies behind Morpheus' orders for me to return home, and have instead taken up with Reapers in an attempt to smooth over the fallout from that disastrous murder. Things have gone well, and the Reapers have offered me protection while we sort this out. I am safe in southern Europe.

Beware Bruadair. He's at the center of a project Morpheus is keeping secret. They had previously secretly stolen the baby of the man I killed. I don't know exactly what they're doing with the children, but the man learned enough from Bruadair that I can assume they're experimenting on offspring of powerful Outré. Bruadair seems to be Morpheus' primary collection agent. Something they've both managed to keep secret from me.

I've met a wonderful man. He is Outré, but he's a Reaper not a Sandman. He's not turned off by what I can do, and he's offered me unfettered access to his inner world whenever I want. So far, I haven't wanted to go there. He understands I may accidentally slip in while we sleep, and that comfort alone keeps me from feeling like I have to go looking. I've never known what a normal girl in love is supposed to feel like. But I think that's where I am.

I will update you as things progress. Just know that I'm safe, and I love you!

-Jan

She folded the note, and tucked it and the pen up back in the crook. She then hugged the tree, and it felt as though the tree hugged right back, solid and strong and comforting. Bolstered by that feeling, Somnoleni took to the sky and returned the way we'd come.

Chapter Fourteen
2012 - Connecticut Countryside

My alarm dutifully woke me at 2:00 a.m. I stared at the dark ceiling trying to hold on to the feeling of my mother hugging that tree as though it were Aunt Margaret. As with all dreams, it faded as the noises of the real world intruded. A car sped by on the highway outside. Someone closed their room door. A female's voice in the hall said, "I know you're awake, I heard your alarm."

I shot bolt upright.

I had no stored dream energy, but suddenly wished I did. I clawed my hand and tried to attract some. I felt a light tingle, and an instant later a lone mote flew through the wall into my hand. It was something. Maybe it'd be enough to make a bright flash in an emergency. "Who are you?" I called through the door as I pulled pants on.

"Your Auntie M sent me. If you don't believe me, she wanted me to tell you that you could sleep in her chair any time."

"What side of the family are you from?"

She paused. Then sounding amused she replied, "The farming side of the family. We mostly guide sheep and cattle to their pastures."

I liked her sense of humor. What the hell... I was expecting a woman, it stands to reason Aunt Margaret would have told her which room she'd rented for me. I left the door latched, but opened it a crack.

I don't know what I expected, but she wasn't it. I think I wanted a mysterious robed woman, or a badass biker. The blonde woman who looked back at me was in jeans and a t-shirt. She was on the athletic side of curvy, and she was so tall she could look over my head without standing on her toes. Her hands were in her pockets. I didn't see a bag.

She looked down at me.

Right. Her aura! It took me an uncomfortable second to shift into my aura sight. Once I'd managed it, I saw the black wings folded protectively around her. Damn it, I forgot. I pulled in my aura.

She nodded slightly, "You should have been cloaked already." She shifted her weight to her other foot, obviously waiting for me to spontaneously generate some manners.

"I guess you can come in." I closed the door to unlatch it, and then opened it for her.

"You guess?" she asked as she came in, looking around. "That your Jeep out in the lot?"

"Borrowed, but yes. Why?"

"The Wisconsin plates are a give-away."

"Apparently. You're the second person to comment." I wasn't sure where this was going.

She shrugged. "I know a few guys who could strip it down, add some wicked grills and rims, put on some flames and get you some fake tags."

I gaped like a fish, which only made her crack up. "Relax, I'm teasing. Big scary death girl is trying to put you at ease.

We'll figure something out."

"Okay, but I'm already a little weirded out by everything. This is already so far outside anything I understand. I feel like I'm in a comic book where the writers have decided to mess with me."

A look of sympathy came across her features, "I get that. And Margaret said you've had no guide, which probably makes it all doubly weird."

I nodded. "More than double. So... now what?"

"Sleep. We'll figure out something in the morning."

"Sorry, I won't be able to sleep. I haven't had anyone to talk to about this. Well, Aunt Margaret for barely an hour. And if you're here to help me, I want to ask you everything."

"Everything? There's probably not enough vodka in the state for that."

"Then start with the basics. Anything."

"Look, Margaret said you had the rare ability to hide your aura, and she said the Sandmen were looking for you. Which probably makes your life hell. I can't hide mine, but I pretty much live with my aura sight active. I actually have a tough time not seeing auras. I owe Margaret and Gestur big time, and I promised I'd keep you safe. So primary rule number one, if I see your aura show I'll interrupt whatever's going on and tell you to hide it. Beyond that, I'll answer your questions if I'm able and show you some of the basic techniques we show young Reapers. Hopefully they'll translate into whatever your bloodline is. You can call me Halldora."

"Is that a codename? I wasn't given one. I guess, for now, James will have to do."

"You'll hear it referred to as a shadow name. You mostly get to choose your own unless you sign up with a bastard mentor who goes really old school and slaps you with one that carries on his legacy. It's pretty typical to avoid using your real name where you can. I've taken the name Halldora Odinsdottir because it has a lot of meaning to me."

"Daughter of Odin? Cool. Does the secret identity help you protect your family?"

She looked at me oddly for a moment. I was used to explaining my geekdom, so I continued on, "You know, every superhero uses the identity to..."

"Yes, I know. I read a couple comics growing up. Most of my family is aware of this side of reality, though, and they're more than capable of handling themselves in case it comes to a fight. It's more like you choose a shadow name so Big Brother can never use your real identity to track you down."

"So, that part is really a thing? The whole secret shadowy agency?"

"Yes and no. It's certainly not as much of a global-conspiracy as you might be imagining. We do keep hidden for obvious reasons, and each bloodline has some level of organization to a large degree. Even the oldest among us cannot deny the utility of modern communication."

"So, I have to be always ready, always alert?"

She didn't try to soften it, "At least for a while, yes."

I nodded, thinking that over. If that's so, I probably needed to always have energy available to me. "Okay, then I need something. This is going to sound really odd, but I need to head down to the lobby for a second. Will you be okay here?"

She shook her head. "I don't like it. If you don't mind, I should stick with you for a while. Unless you're pooping or something. You get to do that alone."

"Uh... ok."

She motioned to the hall. "Come on. Let's make your lobby run."

I pulled on a shirt and grabbed the key and we walked down the hall. Keeping the hand opposite her low at my side, I tentatively moved my one lone mote to it. I then concentrated on drawing dream energy to me. Several doors later, I had another. And then another. It was tricky to do that and keep my aura hidden, but I tried to split my consciousness into supporting both tasks.

By the time we reached the lobby, I had five motes. I walked across the lobby to the ice machine and filled one of the buckets next to it to bring some ice back to the room. Halldora looked at me with quizzical eyes.

I wasn't able to gather any more dream motes on the way back to the room. Halldora obviously knew something was up. When I'd closed the room door behind us, she asked, "What were you really doing? That wasn't about a bucket of ice at two in the morning."

"I was... I don't know if it has an official name... I was gathering dream energy from sleepers."

"So, you've chosen then?"

I didn't know what she meant. "Huh?" Damn I'm eloquent sometimes.

"Chosen, a bloodline."

"I didn't choose anything." She was about to say something, but I barreled on, "What are you talking about? I was born to both bloodlines wasn't I?"

She got a theatrically surprised look on her face. "Oh my goodness, yes! That's right!" she twittered. "Of course, that's it! That's why they want you!"

I knew she was mocking me, but I still didn't understand, "Is it?"

"No, dumbass" she dropped the mocking look. "You think you're the only person to ever be born to two bloodlines?"

"Well, I don't know. I mean, Sandmen are hunting me, people are acting like I'm some great find. I thought maybe the dual bloodline gift was special."

She laughed, "And I suppose you think some shirtless she-wolf and sparkly vampire babe are going to drop out of the sky and fight over you? Or maybe that you're some long-prophesied wizard prince?"

Holy crap, she thought I was straight. "Well, no but..."

She laughed in genuine humor, "You need to quit reading teen girl novels."

"Hey, I don't read those!"

"Mmm hmmm... whatever you say, Boy Wizard." She grinned. "Okay, seriously, being born to two bloodlines happens more often than you'd think. Bloodlines aren't supposed to mingle, but forbidden passion burns hottest and all that poetic shit."

"So, there are other Reaper-Sandmen out there?"

"No, there aren't. That's what I was telling you. Look, you were born with the potential for both in your blood. But once you develop the advanced abilities of one, you essentially align your blood, your soul, your fate, your whatever, with the energies tied to the abilities you've developed and that becomes your bloodline. We call it 'Making The Choice.' It's possible your immediate children might have some residual choice, but usually once you make the decision to work on advanced abilities, you permanently imprint to that side, and the other one fades away."

"So, if I keep using my dream abilities, I will lose access to my Reaper abilities?"

"Dream abilities? Like collecting dream energy? I'd say you've already gone beyond the basic ability."

"Wait, which one is the basic?"

"Oh my god, you are a newbie. The basic dreamer ability is the ability to enter another's dream as a witness. We're all careful to not sleep anywhere near a Sandman for that reason. The basic death ability lets you see death moments before it takes someone. What else have you done?"

"Well, hiding my aura as you already knew. And I can gather dream energy."

"So you have chosen. You've denied the Reaper abilities from yourself then." It was a statement, not a question.

"Well wait, what's the next Reaper ability? What did you learn next?"

"It's too late for this."

"Please?"

She gathered her thoughts for a moment, "To some degree, you'll determine the direction your abilities develop based on what you try to do with them. Many of us learn the abilities our culture associates with our bloodlines, but I'm sure that's just tradition guiding what our imagination comes up with it. In my case, I learned to see in the dark."

I thought of Sopora's battles in the dark before being indoctrinated into the Reapers. It suddenly made sense, the Elder's children could see in the dark. My mom couldn't. I nodded, "okay, I get that. But, how?"

She took a deep breath, "Okay, you're jumping right ahead to training. We need to talk about getting you to a safe place first."

"I thought I was staying here so I could go see Aunt Margaret if I needed to?"

"Ha! Like hell." She motioned that I sit on the bed. She then took the chair and faced me. "You're playing with ancient deadly powers that are being wielded by near-fanatic conspiracy experts in an attempt to capture your ass. You need to stop thinking of this as some sort of summer camp for fledgling superheroes. We need to stay mobile. If you stay in one place too long, you'll get comfortable, which means you'll get sloppy. And that's when they find you."

"No, that's not fair!"

"You're how old?"

"Sorry, she's my only family, and I've only just found her. I'm not ready to just drive away from the only link to my past. Can we at least make periodic trips back?"

"Okay, fine. We can figure something out. For now, get some sleep, we'll leave in the morning."

"Can't sleep. It's too much."

She took a deep breath. "My god you're a kid. All right, a few more questions then it's nighty-night time for Boy Wizard. Go ahead."

"You. Start with your story. What part of the Reapers are you from? Aunt Margaret indicated you were from a neutral Reaper group."

"We're descended from a Norse lineage that has a tradition of female shieldmaidens who served Odin. We guide the spirits of the nobly dead warriors to their eternal reward in Valhalla. I consider myself a Valkyrie."

"Cool! And I ask this in the best kind of jealous way–do you get the busty armor and a sword?"

"No, though I could probably have some commissioned.

Growing up, I always wanted the winged wolf mount legend says I get to ride into battle, but I've never seen one of those."

"That sucks. That's got to be the best part of taking on a prestige class."

She looked lightly amused, "Prestige class? You're a gamer geek, aren't you?"

"I used to be, though I've not been in a group for many years. But the terminology is helping me understand some of this."

"It's okay. One of my boyfriends used to let me play with his group. I know just enough to attend a geek con."

"So, the Choosers of the Slain are neutral?"

She grinned, "Where these inter-bloodline feuds are concerned, yes. We make it really clear that we want nothing to do with bloodline bickering and we pointedly carry out our duty to help the dying get to their final resting place."

"So you helping me…"

"…is officially repayment of a debt owed."

"Got it." I was about to ask about Sandmen factions, but she interrupted.

"I have a question. If you're already gathering dream energy, then I don't believe you will have Reaper abilities. What other dream abilities do you have?"

"Aura sight."

"You may have surmised, but that's actually a quite common ability for all Outré. Hence you being able to hide your aura being a big deal."

"I also was able to absorb a small cloud of dream energy, roughly the size of a parking lot."

She considered it, "Which is similar to what you did in the hall. Arguably, it's the same ability to collect energy just on a larger scale. Anything else?"

I held out my hand so she could see the motes. She looked at my hand, but shook her head confused. She couldn't see them... that's useful to know.

I forced one mote to my fingertip. I pushed it against the air between us and mentally charged it, envisioning a gold ribbon arcing through the air. As before, all I was able to create was a multi-colored smear across the space between us. It barely had the luminescence of a candle, but she saw it.

"I think," I explained, "that I in time I'll be able to create short-lived phantasms that actually look like things. But this is all I've managed so far."

She studied it in a bit of wonder. "It's so different from the energy a Reaper draws. Where I draw upon the very energies of death and darkness, you draw on the energies of light and hope."

My shoulders slumped before I could catch them. She looked at me quizzically, so I explained, "my mother found a way to turn dreams into nightmares. It's not all light and hope."

"I wasn't going to mention her so soon, but yes. There is a dark side to dreaming, just as there is a peaceful side of dying. Still, the energies spring from vastly different sides of the human experience. The dead don't dream, and the living aren't dead. Don't be hard on yourself. Just recognize that there are differences for now."

"I hadn't really thought about where the energy comes from. I guess. I've only touched it a couple times."

"The sooner you study it, the faster you'll master it. That much I believe. Anything else?"

"Please humor me for academic purposes. Let's say I want

to know about seeing in the dark. How do you manifest it? What does it feel like?"

First she looked like she was going to dismiss my request. But then she gave in. "I've never tutored anyone, so, forgive me if I'm not practiced at explaining this. It's a lot like aura sight. Only... only it's like trying to read the aura of the darkness itself. My mentor described it as seeing the death of light, but that never worked for me. The aura sight analogy was something I could conceive and put into practice."

I mulled that over. "Mind if I try?"

She shrugged, "Nope. Knock yourself out."

I got up and turned off the light. I then reached deep inside, trying to remember if I'd felt anything when Gregory died. I couldn't remember. I brought about my aura sight and turned it against the dark. At first it was merely dark, but then I saw a pillow speeding towards my head. I got a hand up to kind of block it. It still bounced around my wrist and slapped me in the forehead. "Ach!" I flicked on the light.

Halldora looked kind of amazed. "You saw it coming."

"I think so, I'm pretty sure, anyway."

"How is that possible?"

"I'm a quick study?"

"No. Seeing in the dark has never been a recorded Sandman ability. Ever. You created the phantasmal smear of dream energy, so you should be unable to pierce the dark. Yet you saw the pillow coming seconds after the lights went out. There's no way your eyes would have adjusted to the complete dark, let alone shifted to seeing through the dark." She wasn't quite sputtering with disbelief, but she was certainly agitated.

"I don't know what to say. I never really considered having limits." I was genuinely confused.

"Say nothing. We will definitely explore that some more, because I don't think your bloodline has been locked in. You don't realize how huge that is."

"Honestly, I don't think it needs to be locked in."

"Since when is anything ever up to the boy wizard?" She laughed. A moment went by while she stifled a yawn. "It's really late, and we both need sleep. Don't argue. I've traveled really far very quickly to help you, and I'm beat. I'll take the chair." She got up and pushed it in front of the door. Nobody was coming in without hitting her.

"Thank you," I motioned to her precautions.

"Tomorrow, we get a room with two beds and we push yours up against the door."

"Ok... that's fair."

I closed my eyes and tried to sleep, but couldn't. First, because there was a strange woman in the room who for all I knew was staring at me with creepy death vision. Second, I realized she didn't have a suitcase or anything, and that sparked a whole new line of questions she wasn't going to let me ask.

CHAPTER FIFTEEN
1972 – DERINKUYU, TURKEY

Janet and James were running in the dark. It felt weird not using my mother's agent handle, almost like she'd ceased to be the superhero I'd just started getting to know and suddenly become someone else. I guess in a way she had. I might grow into liking 'Somnoleni.' I kind of hoped I did because it was an identity she chose for herself. She had paused to look at her reflection in the serrated combat knife she now held, "Remember."

And then she was running again.

"What was that?" James asked from behind.

"Nothing," came her breathless reply.

They were running through a huge cavern with three other people. I recognized the Elder's son and daughter flanking her, but not the backside of the third. Somnoleni held the only light, an old silver flashlight, in her off hand. The others weren't avoiding the light. Instead, they held to a tight formation near her.

"To the right," the Elder's son commanded in his bass voice. As a unit, they cornered and I saw them angle down a narrow hallway.

"Iskandar," came the clear voice of the Elder's daughter

as she addressed her brother, "We will run out of city soon. Where do you take us?"

"The poison well," he said simply as if that answered everything. The man in the lead grunted unhappily.

Now that they were running through a narrower space, I could see more in the light. This place was amazing. They weren't in caves like I initially thought. They were sprinting through an underground city. I once heard about the fabled underground cities in Turkey, and had done a fairly thorough internet search on them. At the time, available information had been sparse. For starters, they are more extensive than I'd have thought. When lit only by flashlight, and running at breakneck speed, the passages took on nightmarish qualities. Smooth stairs, crazy curves, and a few inner terraces that were little more than drops of death suddenly appeared out of the dark. I saw spaces flit by that may have been where families once hid from invaders. Or maybe they were dark yawning caverns of death. It was hard to tell.

"Umara," Somnoleni asked through heavy breaths, "why is it called the poison well?"

In fantastic fighting shape, the Elder's daughter wasn't having as difficult a time talking while she jogged along, "It is the only water source for this city. In ancient times invaders would try to poison it when people were hiding in here. Though it was almost never used for water during times of conflict for that very reason."

The man up front was shaking his head, "We will be trapped in that well. We should try to reach the passage to Kaymakli."

"And be caught in a three-mile tunnel they might be fully aware of?" came Iskandar's reply. "No, we should go to the well and jump in."

"Trust him, Husni, he knows this city better than anyone," Umara supported her brother.

The man in the lead grunted, but didn't object further. He led them down a tight group of stairs with no side railing. Somnoleni's flashlight beam didn't reach anything in the yawning dark to that side.

They came into another vast, open, dark space. Somnoleni was straining herself listening, and very faintly I thought I heard a gas motor. But as I tried to filter out details, the sound faded and came back, almost like a bee on the other side of the yard. It was a persistent threat, but not an immediate danger.

"They are starting the generator," Iskandar explained.

Husni sounded upset, "That is not good. We have to cross through the sector open to tourists."

"Be alert, everyone. Somnoleni, let us know if there is dream power about. You'll sense it before we will," James said. "We will have to slow to a walk if there are visitors ahead."

An electric humming echoed around us, and lights buzzed to dim life. Somnoleni shut off her flashlight. They were in a mostly carved cavern. Spaced around the edge were large, deep alcoves that might have been family living areas looking out on a communal center. The floor was littered with the detritus of a half-finished excavation, but the path through the center was relatively clean. They were stopped by an iron gate with a padlock that looked recently added. All eyes turned to Iskandar.

"I did not have time to request the keys. I shall have to amend this later." He reached out and put his hand on the padlock. Somnoleni shifted to her aura sight, and she saw his power as black smoke. He was corroding the padlock, aging it... killing it. Within seconds, it crumbled away in bits of rust and steel. He pulled the rest off of the door, "Come. We must walk like we belong."

The lights were brightening as the generator's power reached normal levels. I noted that the Reapers were all wearing black military fatigues with no insignias. Most of the many utility pockets seemed to be bulging. They were prepared for something.

This sector of the underground city had been fully excavated for tourists. The walkways were all clear, and little plaques here and there indicated various bits of trivia that they didn't stop to read. Husni walked purposefully towards the voices. As they neared, he indicated they stop for a second while he crept forward. Precious moments ticked by. A baby cried. Husni reappeared and motioned the group forward, "It is a group of tourists. We will camouflage ourselves with them for a bit."

"Not dressed like this we won't," James pointed out.

"James is right," Umara agreed. "Can we get ahead of them and pose as guards?"

Iskandar nodded, "Derinkuyu has many levels. Come." He led them off to the side and into some tunnels that were a lot rougher and uneven, though the lighting made them easy to traverse at a quick walk. Rounding a tight corner, there was suddenly a narrow, steep set of stairs down. They descended into passages that were partly natural, partly hewn, and in some cases partly supported by modern masonry. He led them through a twisting set of tunnels, to a stairwell leading back up.

He and Husni seemed satisfied they were on the other side

of the tourists. They struck off at an angle that positioned the voices mostly behind them. I don't know how to accurately describe the extensive nooks and crannies, halls and stairs. This place could be home to twenty-thousand people plus their livestock. It quite rightly qualified as a city, but entirely carved from stone. Underground. My little role-playing heart was beside itself with glee. The only thing tempering my excitement was the grim look on each face in this group. This was not sight-seeing. They were being hunted.

Rounding a corner, they came face-to-face with a man who had a rifle aimed their direction. Husni dove forward into a roll, Iskandar dodged one way, Umara grabbed Somnoleni and rolled the other. James dropped to one knee pulling out his baton, flaring the scythe blade. The rifleman fired, but James was faster and caught the bullets in the black-tendril blade. When Somnoleni looked away from James, I saw that Husni and Umara had already closed on the assailant. Before he could fire again, Husni had slit his throat and Umara had cut off his trigger hand. They looked at each other over the body.

"Now we can't question him about their plans or numbers," Umara said matter-of-factly.

Husni merely shrugged.

Somnoleni shook her head, "He didn't have an Outré aura at all. He was a hired mercenary. The Sandmen don't tell hires the plans, just assign them tasks. He probably didn't have to die, but he wouldn't have known anything."

Iskandar came over. "No time to remove it proper." He put his hand on the mercenary's back. Somnoleni's aura sight was still going strong, and I watched the black cloud decompose the man's body in a matter of horrifying minutes. Husni scooped up the clothes and rifle.

Checking around corners, the group moved on quickly. "More auras ahead, both mundane," Somnoleni warned everyone. Umara gave them a hand signal, and they stopped. Pulling two grenades from her hip pockets she pulled the keys, stepped forward and threw one down each hallway. Dodging back as the guns fired, the grenades detonated in flashes of bright light and smoke, but no concussion. Using hand signals, she motioned they hold for a second. The mercenaries fired at precisely the instant you would have expected someone to move in after the grenade flashes. They heard bodies hit the floor as the shots stopped. Umara motioned forward quickly. Dropping to a crouch, they flitted past the hallways.

"We need the advantage, can we kill the lights?" James asked as they moved on.

"Junction box is not far," Iskandar replied. He guided us to it. Using his ability to bring about the death of objects, he quite literally killed the junction box.

"Don't turn on the light," James said to Somnoleni quietly. "Take my hand, I'll guide you."

She held hers out, and I felt his warm hand take hers. He guided her to his side so she could use his motion as well as his hand. I heard the others take the lead, and then felt him guide her forward.

Interestingly, she could see auras when they were near, but not walls or stairs. She kept the group far enough away from remaining mercenaries that the darkness was enough to allow them to slip by.

"We are near the well," Iskandar warned everyone.

Somnoleni pulled back on James' arm. "There's an Outré aura ahead. That'll be the agent in charge."

"Anything we should know?"

"Strengthen your mind. It's rare that an agent can affect the physical world, so most likely if you see something a little unbelievable, you should not believe it. Just like I told you."

"Spread out. And remember, don't let the Sandman touch you," Umara finished.

She saw their auras flare, each one differently. Umara surrounded herself in black armor that had properties like black metal. Her brother's aura was shifting and swirling like a cloud that distracted attention. Husni's was more like black tendrils from all directions. Though it faded a few feet from his body, I couldn't help but wonder if he imagined it as connections to the world around him. James' aura was how I imagine my own, like a nebulous energy field.

They spread out, but not as far as the warnings would have indicated. I guessed they were still in a tunnel. My suspicion was confirmed when, moments later, Iskandar disappeared to the left and Umara to the right. Husni moved forward toward the coalescing aura I saw deeper in the room. James kept Somnoleni back in the entrance to the tunnel.

"I can hear you," a man's voice called from the center. "Agent Sopora, you have been ordered to stand down and come along peacefully. If you resist, you will be knocked unconscious and extracted against your will."

I felt her energize her vocal chords before she spoke. Even though her mouth was moving, I heard the words emanate from across the chamber, "You hired mercenaries who shot first. I know procedure well enough to know what that means. I will not accompany you to my death. I renounce my ties to the Sandmen. If you stand down and walk now, there will be no fight."

"Nobody leaves the Agency, Sopora. You know how it is. You were Morpheus' protégé, you know the rules better than anyone."

"Sadly, yes I do."

"Then you know I dare not return without you, alive or in a body bag."

"You're a long way from the Farm, agent. I plan to disappear. You can always claim you didn't see me."

"You know I can't do that. They'll find out."

"Don't kill him if you don't have to," she said for the benefit of the Reapers. I saw a confused ripple in the Sandman's aura. He hadn't heard the Reapers, he'd only heard Somnoleni. More interestingly, he hadn't seen their auras. Had my mom been hiding them? Had she taught them to hide theirs?

The Reapers reacted instantly. James stepped in front of Somnoleni, but she watched over his shoulder. Husni and Umara moved in on him with scythes made of black energy. The Sandman's aura stepped down off something and the room flared with light. The Reapers cringed, and it was the opening the agent needed. He threw a handful of sand into Umara's face and she slumped to the floor. He ducked and pulled his gun, bringing it to bear on Husni. As his finger squeezed the trigger, Iskandar's scythe blade hooked the agent's wrist and yanked just enough to make the shot miss.

Dodging towards the fallen Umara to buy a moment of time, the agent reached into a pocket and I saw him grab a handful of sand. So did James. My father whipped his weapon forward, releasing the scythe blade. It flew through the air cutting the Sandman's forearm. He lost control of his fingers and the sand spilled onto the floor.

"Don't kill him," whispered Somnoleni.

"He's not dead," James whispered back.

Their position was once again foremost in the agent's mind. He swung his good hand, the one with the gun, and aimed right at James. I saw his aura channel into the gun as he pulled the trigger. So did Somnoleni. James snapped a new scythe blade up, but the dream-enhanced bullet tore right through it. Somnoleni thrust out some of her own dream energy into a raw, unmolded cloud of vapor. It didn't stop the bullet completely, but reduced its velocity so that it only hit James' shoulder with the speed of a professional boxer's punch. It threw him back into Somnoleni knocking them both over, but he wasn't bleeding.

Husni reached the Sandman and kept him busy while my parents stood back up. Every time he brought the gun up to fire, Husni would knock it aside with the world-tethers of his aura. I couldn't see Iskandar.

Footsteps behind us were the only warning. Somnoleni pushed James down and forward into the room a split second before the mercenaries behind us opened fire. James cursed, and Husni muttered something about leaving enemies alive behind you. My parents each crawled to flank the entrance to the hall and remain out of the mercenaries' line of sight.

Where was Iskandar?

Knowing it would take the mercenaries a second or two to reach the room, Somnoleni scooted sideways to grab Umara's arm and drag her back. Looking to James, he nodded to her and then readied to cover the hall. My mother reached down and touched Umara's neck. We entered into the first layer of her inner dream world. I sensed a calmness similar to what I had experienced when we left the message for Aunt Margaret. Umara was completely comfortable with who she was.

Her calmness, though, was the contemplative calmness of a well-tended graveyard. Umara's father had referred to her as the more physical warrior, but her mind was like a tranquil place you came to set out flowers for those you loved and remembered.

Somnoleni called to her, softly and encouragingly. Looking around, we found her on one of the first islands, asleep on a bed adorned with brass and exotic wood. "Wake up, Umara," she called. "This sleep isn't for you." My mom created a gentle mist of dream colors and sent it over to moisten Umara's face.

Umara blinked awake. "What happened?"

"He used a highly volatile, chemical-based sleeping dust laced with dream energy. Are you ready to return to the fight?"

Umara nodded, and we pulled out of her inner world quickly.

Back in the cavern, Umara's eyes fluttered open.

"Mercs in the hall," Somnoleni warned her.

Umara nodded, quickly re-summoning her death armor, "Where is Iskandar?"

Husni replied tersely in Turkish. Umara and James nodded. Dammit, why hadn't my mother learned more Turkish? Then I understood. The agent didn't know what had been said either.

"Get ready to run," Umara warned my mother. She unhooked another flash grenade and lobbed it around the corner into the hall. The instant it went off, Husni backflipped away from the Sandman. The agent turned, expecting to see his mercenaries ripped apart in a spray of shrapnel. He was not prepared for them to fire blindly when their world exploded in a burst of light and sound. He took at least one bullet. It dropped him but didn't kill him instantly.

When the hail of bullets stopped, the remaining Reapers and Somnoleni bolted for the other side of the room, down a tunnel and around a corner. Husni in the lead, there were no words spoken. When they ran out of light, my mother snapped the flashlight back on so they could keep up the pace without lighting up hallway access lights and leaving a glowing trail.

Coming to a stop in a small room that had a rope and pulley contraption over a small hole, Husni motioned a stop. He listened down the well. "Iskandar is almost done, step back out into the alcove to the left and do not move lest you attract their attention."

Their?

Everyone complied, though I sensed Somnoleni's unspoken question. James just shook his head at her, "Not now."

Moments later, quick, staccato noises of stone clicking and scraping on stone echoed up the hole. They got louder. Something was climbing out of the well. James tried once to avert my mother's gaze, but she would not look away. After a final attempt, he accepted her decision.

Momentary terror seized Somnoleni's spine when the first bony hand reached up over the lip of the well. The odor of putrid flesh assaulted her nostrils. She almost emptied her stomach. James put a steadying hand on her forearm as the creature hauled its bloated carcass out of the well. It was a god damned zombie. Holy crap. Not just one. Four more followed. Each one of them reeked of watery decay.

Iskandar had called up a squad of god-damned zombies.

I felt a panic overwhelm me, but whether it was mine or my mother's I couldn't separate. The Reapers were completely motionless. The zombies looked around hungrily, inching closer. They were attracted to the light! Shit! One of them was making wet, snuffling noises like it was trying to smell our warm flesh through a nose swollen with a bucket's worth of scummy water.

A shout echoed from somewhere behind us. Five bloated heads made squelching noises as their attention all snapped that direction. They reacted like a school of undead, bipedal piranha more than anything. Skin hanging in glistening strips, eyes white and dead, teeth bared, they moved in unison with a feral speed to hunt down and devour their prey.

I didn't realize my mother had stopped breathing until she started up again. The smell that hit me almost made me vomit through her. Bile rose in her throat and she took several deep breaths to quell it down.

"Come," James motioned. "They won't be long, and they'll return to where they were animated once the food runs out. And we don't climb as quickly as they do."

"Ah," Husni said, "but we know how to use a rope and pulley." They put Somnoleni in the bucket and lowered her first.

Iskandar was leaning up against a wall, thigh-deep in the putrid waters. His black aura had vitriolic green striations in it, and I realized he was barely able to stand. Somnoleni moved to help him, but he pushed her away. "No. You don't touch me. Ever."

She nodded, accepting his rejection as though they'd already covered this. Umara was next down. She immediately went to her brother, supporting him. "Iskandar, you really should not have done it."

"It was best way to slow the Sandmen. We need time to get away. With her 'no kill' mandate, this was best way."

Somnoleni made a questioning face, so he continued. "If the living retreat up into the sunlight, the dead will not follow. They will be alive as you requested. If they stay and fight, the bullets will most likely win, but it will take time. Even then, they will be alive as you requested." He needed to stop and catch his breath. "Either action on their part will give us time we should make best use of. Prepare to swim."

By the time his labored speech was done, James was down. Husni dropped the upper end of the rope down the hole. Using a pair of gloves, Husni used his hands and feet to control a slide down the rope. "Is everyone ready?"

Everyone nodded. Husni cut the rope and pulled it through the pulley. Both ends fell down into the hole. The only means up or down was a treacherously slick, rocky climb.

Iskandar pointed to a dark corner of the well room. When my mom shone her light there, I could see nothing but inky black water.

"Is a tunnel with no choices." Iskandar explained. "Keep one hand on the wall to guide you and swim forward. It will lead to a lake where you'll see the sunlight above you. I hope you hold your breath a long time."

My mother looked at the old silver flashlight. She had already strapped her knife, but I could tell she was trying to determine the light's waterproof rating. Looking around, she asked, "Me first?"

"No," came James' reply. "I will be able to see the tunnel in the dark, you won't. If you need to, you will hold my belt and swim with me."

She nodded. Together they cleared their lungs a few times, took deep breaths, and plunged under the water.

The flashlight barely got her to the tunnel opening before it gave out. I felt her drop it and use both hands in the dark to assist the swim through the tunnel. She was a powerful swimmer, I could tell from the kicks. This tunnel hadn't been carved by rushing water. The water had merely seeped in and filled it. Somnoleni's hands were getting bruised and cut as she blindly bashed into outcroppings and jagged rocks. I realized she was watching the dodge and weave of my father's aura, trying to use it to orient. She was doing better than I would have, considering she couldn't see the walls. But it was still hard going.

When her lungs started aching, I felt James take her hand and put it on his belt. She swam as near to him as she could without fouling his own kicking. It sped up her progress a little bit.

I do not recommend gallantly throwing yourself into a body of water and staying under just to experience what they mean when someone says their lungs are burning. It hurts, and I was only getting it second hand. Every survival instinct wants you to breathe to make the fire stop. When your lungs ache with the need to breathe, your vision starts to tunnel and go black. I felt her kicks faltering. She wasn't avoiding the walls as well as she had been. I thought maybe she saw a dull light ahead, and that renewed her with a bit of new energy. Mostly, though, it was her grip on James' belt that saved her. I don't remember the ascent to the surface of the lake, though whether she was blacking out or editing the dream I couldn't tell.

The next thing I knew with any clarity, James was kissing her. And she was coughing. My mother hacked wetly, spitting out lake water. She looked up into James' rugged face and chose that moment to edit the dream. I know they kissed, dammit, but she faded that out anyway.

When she allowed me to see again, we were still wet, but there was no lake in sight.

"You must leave Turkey. It is no longer safe for you here," Husni was saying.

James nodded, "I agree. We need to get north to my people."

"We can send you along our network to Prague," Umara offered. "You will drive the back roads and stay with loyal friends. After that, you will have to find your own way."

"That is very generous," Somnoleni said, "Thank you."

My parents hugged everyone but Iskandar who merely stood to the side and scowled. It only took him a moment to decide to speak what was on his mind. "The war you have started has begun. Today was the first battle, and you fought it here, in my home. The Elder may have accepted you into our clan, so I will fight beside you. But I lay every death in this war at your feet." With that, he stomped off.

Umara looked after him sadly, and then hugged my mother again. It was a simple gesture, but it meant the world to her.

CHAPTER SIXTEEN
2012 – CONNECTICUT COUNTRYSIDE

I sat bolt upright. Halldora was staring at me. "You just mumbled something about zombies. Bad dreams?"

Shaking my head to clear the fuzz I answered, "No, I had a very good dream. It just happened to have zombies."

"That's a switch. I've never heard of a zombie cameo ending up good for anyone."

"Well, I don't think it ended well for the folks the zombies wanted to take to dinner. Umm... So... what'll we do today?"

"Travel."

"Right, I mean, work on a new power? History lesson? Twenty questions? OH! Did you know my father?"

"Good gods, I need coffee before I can deal with you." Halldora went into the bathroom, closed the door loudly, and then pointedly locked it. Well... hell.

I got up and did some stretching. Out of habit, I checked email on my phone. Aside from the usual junk, something stood out. It was a message from "The Dreamer." Yeah, that's not fishy. I thumbed it open.

Dear Mr. Gardner,
If you are the party I'm seeking, then this will make

sense. I think I knew your mother before you were born.
I recently had a dream about her, a dream in which
her son was seeking her. It's taken me some weeks, but I
think I've found you. If any of that made sense to you,
I think I can answer some questions about what your
mother was like. I am sorry if what I'm about to say is
unknown to you, but your mother died in childbirth.
All I can offer is my memory of her, but I am willing to
share what I can for her son. She meant a great deal to
me and I would be happy to do this for you. I've enclosed
my email and my telephone number in my signature.
Please accept my offer.
    –M, The Dreamer

"Hey... Halldora? Are you pooping?"

"Why would you even ask me that?" she called from behind the door.

"You talked about me pooping in private yesterday. I figured it was a big deal for you."

"Argh. Hang on." There was some shuffling, then a flush. The door opened. "What is it?"

I handed her the phone and indicated she read the email. "Is that who I think it is?" she asked in a toneless voice.

"If I'm right, it's Morpheus."

"James, where are you getting your information?"

"Dreams. Packets of dream information I think my mom left for me."

"Shit, shit, shit. Morpheus personally wants you?"

"Umm. Maybe? He was my mom's boss."

"Shit."

"What's...?"

"Shit. We need to go. Now."

"Ok, explain. Then I really do have to poop."

She looked a little disgusted, "Morpheus… The tyrannical leader of the Sandmen in the United States. He's terrifying. Rumor is he hates and mistrusts all non-Sandmen Outré with a vitriolic passion. He polices all of the Outré under 'his jurisdiction.' Thing is, nobody gave him police power. He just does it. He commits executions of Outré who he feels are not adhering to his laws. They say his agents catch you sleeping and keep you sleeping. Then they just take you away in the middle of the night."

That didn't sound like the Morpheus my mother had shown me. "Are you sure? I mean, that kind of thing doesn't happen in America."

"Wake up. This doesn't happen in broad daylight. We Outré keep ourselves fairly isolated, so I guess our disappearances wouldn't be as noticed as a mundane's would be."

I processed that. Things had changed. Drastically.

"You said, 'his laws?' What are his laws?"

"Let's see. If a duly-appointed representative of the Agency makes a request, Outré will comply. Failure to comply will result in imprisonment in the Tartarus facility. Committing violence against another Outré will result in imprisonment. Murdering another Outré will result in imprisonment and likely death. Every Outré will train at and serve the Agency for two years upon reaching adulthood. Blah, blah, blah. His rules are byzantine. And, like I said, nobody elected him or appointed him."

"So, wait. I thought my mother worked for him?"

Halldora got really quiet. "Look, I'll tell you what I know, but I'll tell you on the road, okay? Can we just go?"

"Sure. Can I poop first?"

"Yes, hurry. I'll pack up and grab breakfast from the lobby. Oh, and this phone?" She held up my mobile menacingly.

I lifted my eyebrow in question like my father did. I kind of liked how that felt.

She smashed the phone down on the table. Hard. It shattered, though not as dramatically as I think she'd have hoped.

"HEY!" I shouted.

"The phone is compromised." Snarling she pushed me aside and carried it into the bathroom. I tried to grab it, but she dropped it into the toilet and flushed it. "If you ever see an email that could potentially be from him again, delete it. Do not open it."

"I... my... you said the conspiracy wasn't as big or global as I imagined."

"Well I didn't know how good your imagination was. And if I'd given you all of the details, you would not have slept."

I was speechless. I pushed her out and closed the door. I was still staring at the mirror when I heard her leave.

ON THE ROAD

We didn't speak again until we were in the Jeep. She started the conversation, "Head north."

"That's it? You tell me we're under the jurisdiction of a madman while we remain hidden in a world that doesn't know about us, oh... and my mother worked for the grand dictator... and all you have for me is head north?"

She considered it all and nodded, "Yep."

We drove for a couple minutes while I thought it all over. "Let's set aside the important topic like this Agency and come back to it later. Do you, or did you, know my father?"

"Only by reputation. He's actually considered a paragon of the Reaper's duties. A unique manifestation of his gift always seemed to make sure he was at the right place and time to witness the right death. They say what he learned could lay entire governments low."

"Wait, you're talking about him like he's still alive?"

She shrugged, "I wish I could confirm or deny that. His legend may be larger than the man ever was, or it could all be true. You have to understand, he would have more good reasons than most of us to hide from the Agency."

I stared at traffic, trying to not to make eye contact.

She continued on a bit softer, "He was involved when everything went down with your mom. Morpheus used to declare that any Outré who helped your father would be put to death immediately. About a decade later, he announced that your father had been captured and executed. However, rumors of your father's activity have continued to surface. Unconfirmed sightings, friends of friends who saw him, odd pronouncements by the Elders, all hint that he's still doing the Reapers proud."

"If there's any truth to that, then my father may be the coolest man alive."

She nodded. "He's kind of an underground hero, snubbing Morpheus' self-appointed godhood by continuing to do what he's meant to do. If any of it is true, he's the expert on staying several steps ahead of Morpheus."

"It almost sounds like being in the right place at the right time includes not being in the wrong place at the wrong time."

She looked a bit impressed, "That's a really good interpretation."

"Thanks. Okay, so the Agency?"

She motioned an exit that would take us northeast and I took it. "The Sandmen have become like the bogeymen. Morpheus makes sure nobody knows their faces. They're trained to stay far enough away so their auras aren't detected. When you're finally asleep, they move in. They say the Sandmen loyal to the Agency are all trained to keep a sleeper in deep sleep. They trap you in your own mind and then barge in, taking what they need to know. If they consider you guilty of breaking Morpheus' laws, they keep you asleep and take you to Tartarus."

"I've heard mention of Tartarus before. You've indicated it's a prison. How can something like that exist unknown to the government?"

She stared out at the countryside. "Tartarus serves as a prison, research facility, and training facility. They say it's the new headquarters as well."

"So, the Farm isn't used anymore?"

"I don't know. It's probably still used for something."

"Where is Tartarus?"

"Nobody knows. Nobody who's ever been a 'guest' at Tartarus has ever returned. Only agents come and go, and like I said, they keep their distance and move like ghosts."

"That doesn't make sense. The agents who were looking for me at the Wal-Mart looked like traditional Men in Black. They stuck out like movie villains."

She chewed that over. "Tell me about it."

I started with me pulling up and walking into the store. I don't know why, but I wasn't ready to share waking up in a frosty puddle on the ground. But beyond that, I shared everything.

"That doesn't sound right at all. It lacks all subtlety. I wonder what their game was?"

"No clue. Hey, where are we going?"

"Maine."

"Okaaayyy... I assume you have a plan?"

"I do. For now, we keep moving. If we need to discreetly cross a border, I know a place in Maine."

"If he has no jurisdiction in Canada, why haven't more of us moved north?"

"He claims global jurisdiction, but he has to play by the rules of the existing governments to remain unnoticed. Besides, it's never that easy to leave your home behind."

Yeah. I suppose it if was I'd have let my townhouse go. And Nate, and 'Chelle. Crap. My phone. "So, can I get a burner phone or something?"

"Burner phone? Do I look like the local CrimeMart?"

"I just assumed you were more adept at living life in the shadows than I am."

She nodded, "Whatever. I probably am. We can get you one. Next time you see a super-cheap mobile phone store, pull over. Don't go to one that is controlled by a specific carrier. I'll show you what I know."

She was feeling chatty, so I kept going. "Last night you mentioned someone along with Aunt Margaret. Gashtar?"

"Gestur. It's Icelandic."

"Who is it?"

"Just the guy who trained me. He knows Margaret from way back, though that's a story you should definitely ask one of them."

"Is it good?"

She shrugged, "more like ancient history and I wouldn't

want to get it wrong."

"Ok."

We drove on in silence for a bit.

Finally I broke the silence. "So... when do we talk about the fact that I could collect dream energy and see in the dark?"

"Now if you like. Let's start with needing to know if you've manifested any other ability?"

"I saw a man's death less than an hour before he died. Everything else you know about."

"Pull over at the next rest stop. If it's empty, we'll try a couple small things and see if any spark."

"Tell me about yourself in the meantime."

"I'd rather not."

I didn't expect that. "Oh. I get it. In case Morpheus gets ahold of me. The less I know about you the safer it is? I understand that."

She sighed. "No, that's not it. This isn't a first date. I'm fulfilling a favor for Margaret. We don't need to be friends."

"Okay."

We drove on in more uncomfortable silence. Miles later, I saw a place to pull over. It wasn't a state-run rest stop, but it had picnic tables and no people.

Halldora acted like no weirdness had happened. "Why don't you sit at that table?"

I did as she asked. She collected a few items and brought them over.

She pushed a clump of dirt my way across the table. It had some grass growing out of it. "Hold your hands over this."

"What about these motes I collected last night?"

"Motes?"

"The dream energy."

"You're still containing it?"

"Yeah, why?"

"Why? You slept. You're telling me you retained energy through unconsciousness," she was completely incredulous.

"I take it that's another no-no?"

"It's not possible. Ever. Our abilities don't just run on autopilot. We have to consciously manifest them. There is no record of them ever being maintained through unconscious states. That's what makes Sandmen so terrifying. They have the ability to keep Outré unconscious."

"Noted. You know... I'm not sure I feel like binding myself to rules about what I'm supposed to and not supposed to do. Maybe all Sandmen can retain dream energy and they're just hush about it? I mean, dreams and sleep are sort of the Sandman playground." I needed to change the subject, "So, what's with the grass?" I shifted the motes to my left hand and put my right over it like she'd indicated.

"The motes?"

I nodded to my left, "Over there."

She looked, but blankly. "Don't use them. We need to see if you can use an ability more difficult than merely sensing someone's pending death." When I nodded, she continued. "Causing death is a very common ability. Fortunately for everyone involved, the more complex the target is organically, the more difficult it is to snuff out its life. Grass is fairly simple, invertebrates are more difficult, vertebrates even more difficult, and something with a thought process that can will itself to live is the most difficult. Aside from severe, rage-fueled accidents, it's impossible to use our abilities to kill another person without years of practice. So, I want you to envision this grass dying. I don't care if you see yourself sucking out its life force, or projecting the energy of death into it. Find the imagination construct that works for your mind and make it happen."

The thought of killing anything was abhorrent. I mean, sure, I'd swatted mosquitoes, but I always considered that self-defense. This was an entirely different thing. Then I remembered seeing mercenaries aim and fire at my parents through my mother's eyes. I was now part of a secret world where the stakes were for the ultimate prize: staying alive one more day.

I shifted focus back to the grass calmly growing out of the nourishing soil. In a moment of inspiration, I tried to see its aura. The aura sight was coming easier now, and I saw Halldora's across the table from me. Nothing for the grass. I turned the clod of soil. There. One blade was broken. At the point of the break there was a faint disturbance. It was slightly less noticeable than heat rising off a warm rock in the sun... but at least it was something. I hoped it was a break in the plant's aura, its very life field. I focused in on it a bit more, and saw that there was something surrounding each blade, but only noticeable by its absence where there was a break or tear. I touched the broken point of the blade with my right index finger. I could push the aura a few millimeters from the blade, but it returned immediately. Much like the distortion over the hot rock in the sun. You could wave your hand over it causing a ripple, but that didn't stop the rock from being hot.

I could shade the rock, though. And it'd cool where the shadow of my hand prevented the rays of the sun from hitting it. I messed with the blade's aura again, this time trying to insert my fingertip between the grass and its small energy field. It was extremely difficult, and if I moved one millimeter too far, the nearly-invisible aura returned to its place sheathing the grass.

Armor. The Reapers my mom had fought alongside all formed some sort of armor from their own auras. I was merely getting under the grass's armor, but not doing anything about it. Starting at the break, I used my fingertip to push it ever so slightly aside. Once I'd succeeded in moving it a scant distance, I tried to summon up the black vibrations of energy I had seen around Gregory at the gym. I shivered when I felt a cold chill travel up my spine, and that was enough to interrupt my progress.

I started over again, nudging aside the aura from the blade of grass. I then focused on the black vibrations coming from that same finger. I was ready for the chill this time, and steadied myself. My finger started to lose sensation, but through my aura sight I saw faint black waves of energy start to work into the grass. I pushed a bit harder, and suddenly my senses filled with black, nauseating pain as the skin on my fingertip split spraying blood and black energy onto the grass. As I jumped involuntarily to get away from the pain, I saw the blade I'd targeted as well as a few near it wither and blacken. Halldora gasped and jumped back from the sudden blood spurt as well.

"Jeesus!" she swore. "I said kill the grass, not yourself. Let me see your hand."

I held it out while I tried to clear my vision and return my heart rate and roiling stomach to normal. She inspected my finger. "You'll be fine," she pronounced.

I looked, it wasn't any deeper than a bad papercut. The spray had been momentary, because now there were just a few small beads of blood seeping through the split.

"Quick," she said, "Paint me a picture with those motes."

Still trying to mentally qualify what I'd just done, I smeared my left hand across the space between us. An ugly ribbon of color filled the air between us.

"Unbelievable." She was staring at both of my hands under the ribbon. I was too. After a moment, she picked up the clod of dirt and showed me the withered blades of grass near one edge.

"You just demonstrated advanced abilities of two separate bloodlines within seconds of each other."

"Okay, you said yourself that I was nothing special. What if this does happen, and people keep it a secret because it's not supposed to happen? I mean, you said we're all secretive and shit. What if us dual-bloodliners know enough to just keep our mouths shut?"

"Oh come on. You know human nature. Do you honestly think through all of history this could have been kept quiet?"

My finger was starting to throb, making me feel a bit argumentative. I didn't care. "Look, you can't confirm the life or death of my father after all these years. Is it really that hard to believe that something rare could have been kept secret successfully?"

"I'm not ruling it out, but it's extremely unlikely."

I looked at my hand again, the edges of the split were slightly black. I thrust my finger in Halldora's face, "is that dead skin natural?"

She nodded, trying to keep up with my chaotic topic changes, "Yes. Until you train your body to accept the energy of death, that will happen. It'll take about the same amount of time and effort as training your body to accept heavy weights in a gym."

I nodded, "I think I can relate to that."

"You work out?"

Ouch.

She turned and started walking.

"Are you leaving me?"

"No, freaky Boy Wizard. The coffee kicked in. I'm going to find a place to pee."

Somewhere in Massachusetts

In the next town, I found the kind of mobile store she'd mentioned.

"Still up for helping me get a phone?"

She nodded, "Yeah. What's your spending limit in case I have to do some bargaining?"

"Negative dollars," she shot me a wry look. "I dunno, is under a hundred reasonable?"

She shrugged, "We'll see. C'mon."

The guy inside looked like he was in his early twenties and had all the ambition of a garden slug. He was draped across the counter watching something on an oversized phone. Halldora walked right up to him and stood there making him uncomfortable until he finally hit pause on his screen. "Yeah?"

"Do you work on commission?" she asked smartly.

"Maybe," the kid's suspicion was apparent.

"Fast sale, quick commission. We need a pre-paid phone loaded with minutes." She was doing something with a front jeans pocket, and it took me a minute to realize she was flashing cash.

"Yeah, okay." He went to the back corner behind the counter and grabbed a box. He plugged it into the store's computer. "You know I'm supposed to register it, right?"

She nodded. "I sure do. Here's the I.D. with the name on it." She slapped down two twenties.

"The phone for him?" he pointed at me.

She nodded.

"See, he looks like a Benjamin to me."

I almost interrupted, but Halldora turned and looked at me, winked, and then turned back. "How very perceptive of you. His name's Benjamin G. Jefferson, Jr."

The guy looked thoughtful. "Of course, I'll need to see the I.D. with that name. She fished out more twenties. There were a total of six on the counter for a brief second, then they all disappeared. He started typing.

Several minutes went by while he talked his way through the setup screens. He wrote something down on a scrap of receipt paper. "Here's your new number."

He finished the setup. I heard the computer chime and he unplugged it. He handed it over with the box. "You want a case or anything with that?"

Halldora shook her head, "Not my Benji, he lives dangerously." She grabbed the phone and box and herded me out of the store.

Back in the Death Buggy, I paused before starting the ignition. "You didn't use a single supernatural whammy on him, did you?"

She shook her head, "No need. Money is still one of the greatest powers of all. Speaking of that, you owe me a hundred bucks. Consider the last twenty my gift."

I pulled out my wallet and counted out the last of my cash.

Well, not entirely, I had now had six dollars on me. Halldora saw that.

"You weren't very prepared, were you?"

"Ouch. Meanie. Remember the Siren I mentioned at WalMart? She broke all the windows in the parking lot? I used cash to get these repaired."

"Where do you bank?"

"A credit union."

"Ugh. Consider keeping some funds in an international bank from now on. If you're really going to keep pursuing information on your parents, consider an offshore bank with really good privacy. We all assume Morpheus has some top-level people watching financial transactions for him. For now, call someone back home with signatory powers and ask them to withdraw some cash and find a bank specializing in international transactions. Have them set up an account for you at the Danske Bank in Oslo."

"What? Nobody in my life has 'signatory power' for something like that. And do you realize how weird that request would be?"

"Not nearly as weird as Sandman agents grabbing you in your sleep because you used a hometown credit union debit card to pay for a hotel room."

"Ha!" I pointed to the back seat. "Camping gear. We can avoid hotels for a while!"

"Oh? Am I going to snuggle up with you in your sleeping bag? Brush with your toothbrush? Maybe we're going to eat bark and moss, Wizardly Adams, because I don't see any food back there. Or were you planning to point that finger at a deer and bring home some venison?"

"Point taken."

"Look, your instincts are good. And you're a fast study. But this is for keeps. You can't bribe the GM with a Coke if the dice don't roll your way."

"You ARE a gamer girl!"

She looked mortified. "No... I was trying to speak your dorky language."

"Totally busted. I'll bet you played elven wizards."

"Oh shut up."

"Tell me I'm wrong. And remember, I can see your aura."

"I said shut up."

We bickered about games for a while to pass the miles. Turns out we'd played several of the same ones. We then discussed where to sleep. She'd get a cheap motel room for the night if I agreed to call someone back home for banking help. She then had me walk around the motel and gather any dream energy I could. We rounded out the night's training with more attempts at seeing in the dark. By the end of the night I could see a pillow coming at my head two whole split-seconds before it hit me, instead of just one.

And I was right, she totally had a thing for elven wizards.

CHAPTER SEVENTEEN
1972 – PRAGUE

Somnoleni was looking at her reflection in a small lady's mirror at a window desk. "Remember." She was looking out over a huge city. Most of the buildings stood silent as sentinels clad in the gothic stonework of old Europe. A large river flowed through the city. From up here, the view was enchanting and full of rich histories and centuries of stoic grandeur. I hoped I'd get to know the city in greater detail.

My mother looked around the room, she was alone, but there were two travel bags near the bureau. One was the bag she grabbed in her flight from Egypt. She stood and went over to the bed. Lying down atop the covers, she began her deep breathing, and I felt her push herself into her own dream realm. Once again, she ignored the islands and took to the sky, flying higher and higher.

Crossing through the silvery dream barrier, she came down on the shore where she'd left the message for Aunt Margaret. The tree was still there, though the message was long gone. She sat and waited.

"Jan!" called a familiar voice. As before, the voice was stronger than I'd last heard it.

"Aunt Margaret!" She jumped up and spun around. Aunt

Margaret was standing there with open arms. She looked like an idealized version of herself. Her hair was up in a perfect beehive hairdo, her dress and makeup were the height of Kennedy fashion.

They hugged deep and tenderly. Then Aunt Margaret held my mother at arm's length and looked her up and down. "You look well. I've been worried. The Farm is a hub of frantic activity. The code is that the farmers are all looking for a lost sheep that apparently killed a wolf!"

"Auntie…"

"Don't auntie me. Did you really kill the Butcher of Nairobi in his own head?"

I felt a powerful sadness creep over my mother. She was quiet long enough that her silence became her answer. Tears formed in the corners of her eyes.

"Oh Jan…" Margaret hugged her again, this time consoling her. "I hate that they sent you into the mind of a killer. You never should have been put in that position."

My mother sobbed into her aunt's shoulder for several minutes.

"Let it out. Get rid of all of those negative emotions. You know we're more susceptible to them than most. You're safe here. There, there."

She continued to cry. I saw a few dark snake-like tendrils leak out of my mother and into the grass under the tree. Wherever they touched the ground, the very aspects of nature attacked them, ripping them apart. Leaves became nets, grass became miniature blades, twigs became spears, and they worked in concert to trap and kill the negativity. Aunt Margaret looked uncomfortable until the tendrils were all destroyed. She pulled my mother a short distance away, and sat down with her, holding her hand. When Somnoleni was all cried out, she said something softly.

I was experiencing the dream through my mother's senses and I couldn't hear her. Aunt Margaret didn't stand a chance. "What's that, dear?"

"There's more," she sobbed quietly.

"Better tell me then."

"He hated Sandmen."

"So many Outré do!"

"But few have as valid a reason as he did."

"Is this what your note was about?"

"He'd had a son once. A beautiful boy."

Aunt Margaret just squeezed her hand and let her talk.

"Bruadair snuck in and kidnapped the baby, taunting the officer."

Aunt Margaret, who I considered pretty worldly, looked shocked. She even put her free hand over her mouth to cover her gasp.

"I'm kind of surprised that whiner had it in him."

"I think all his whining has been a cover for what he's really doing. After all, as long as people think his missions are the most boring ones Morpheus could possibly assign, then they aren't going to scrutinize him very deeply. It's a perfect smokescreen."

Aunt Margaret looked like she was both impressed and sucking on a lemon.

My mother kept going, her emotion pouring out of her, "When the officer caught him over the crib, Bruadair said his boss wanted the baby."

"We knew he was slimy, but kidnapping children?!?" Something dawned on Margaret, "Is there any chance he was saying that to frame Morpheus? It's not like a highly-trained agent to let someone live after a statement like that."

"Bruadair told the baby he'd make a fine test subject."

The color drained from Aunt Margaret's face. "Tartarus? He's experimenting on babies in Tartarus?"

"It seems so."

Thunder cracked in the distance.

"Auntie… we need to be extremely careful."

"Oh I know, sweetie. I've built my life around being careful. That doesn't mean I don't get pissed off from time to time. Like when I found out what he had you doing out 'in the field.' Oh, you should have seen the storms raging here that night!"

My mother laughed through her tears.

"I don't think it's all that funny!"

"Oh, I'm only laughing at what I imagine you would do to Morpheus if he was here!"

Aunt Margaret looked like she wanted to list off all the things she would do to Morpheus and his anatomy, but sensed that perhaps it was best to let her niece have the momentary laugh instead. After a moment, her eyes softened.

She asked, "Something doesn't add up. The Butcher of Nairobi had the connections and influence, why didn't he go after his son? It wouldn't have been that difficult for him to start working through Sandman offices, torturing and killing until he had the name of the man who matched the description of the kidnapper."

"I don't know. His memory hadn't been hidden or changed in any way I could detect. It was fresh and visible as though it was a dream, well, nightmare he re-lived often."

"We need to know what's going on there. If that same force

is brought against you, I need to know how to undo it."

"I'll let you know everything I learn. Like I always do."

They looked out at Aunt Margaret's powerful ocean with its lifetime of abundant dreams.

"How shall we save the babies?"

My mother looked up at the sky for a moment, absorbing the atmosphere. "We need to find out where Tartarus is before I can figure out what its defenses are."

"That's not going to be easy. You know the agents with clearance to know that information aren't allowed to talk about it."

"Right, but now there's a new agent to consider. Bruadair. He always complained that even with his years of service he's never been on the 'in the know' list, but he obviously takes the children somewhere. And he never brings them to the Farm. I've never even smelled anything remotely baby-like on him, not powder, not poop, nothing. So he's delivering them and cleaning up."

"Yes, and he's more dangerous than we suspected," Aunt Margaret commented. "That damned jerk has had me fooled all this time."

"I saw him face the Butcher. He put the man to sleep with a touch."

"Are you certain?"

"It was a dream, so it could have been distorted, but I don't think it was. It lacked any of the telltale haziness. The Butcher's dreams were clearer than most, and he seemed in full control of his unconscious mindscape."

"Do you have any reason to believe Bruadair can put someone to sleep at a distance?"

"Not based on what I saw or he'd never have allowed a

pissed off Reaper wielding a headsman's scimitar conjured from death energy to get that close to him and his mission objective."

Aunt Margaret looked like she was contemplating several steps at once. "Very well. Now that I know what to listen for, I'll be more persuasive about directing conversations at the diner. I'll ramp up the chatty meals. If Bruadair comes in, I'll make sure his drink of choice is especially potent. I'll find out what I can."

"Auntie, be very, very careful. They've already sent one agent to bring me in, or to eliminate me if I failed to comply. I'm now unquestionably an enemy, and you don't want to be tied to me."

"I know, I know. I've been careful for longer than you've been alive." Aunt Margaret narrowed her eyes, "Does Morpheus know you saw the abduction in the Butcher's dreams?"

Somnoleni nodded, "I'm operating under the assumption he does. Which explains why he needs to bring me in and control the situation."

"He had better never come into my diner."

"Auntie, don't expose yourself. You walk such a dangerous line as it is."

She hugged my mother, "I know, sweetie. I'm no good to any of us if I'm discovered."

"I just worry about you, so close to them all the time."

"It's what I'm good at."

They sat side by side for a minute, looking at the sky.

"I had better get back."

"I'd better get to the baking and organizing for breakfast."

"I'll be sneaking home soon."

"Then you need to be far more careful than me. I don't have to get past any customs agents any time soon."

"I know. But they trained me for this, so... naturally... I'm going to have to find a way to do it that isn't in their playbook."

"That's my girl. Leave me notes periodically and let me know you're okay. I'll leave one if I learn anything useful."

"Thank you, Aunt Margaret."

"You're welcome sweetie." They hugged one last time, fiercely.

Without making it awkward, Somnoleni lifted up into the sky and returned to her body in Europe. There was a moment of blackness, then she was waking up in the hotel room. James was there, sitting on the edge of the bed, watching over her.

She stood, smiled at him, and then averted her eyes. "I have to return to America."

"I expected that eventually. What'd you learn?"

She bit her lip.

"It's bad, isn't it?"

She nodded.

He seemed content to let her get around to explaining on her own time. Instead of prying he asked, "Where in America? I may have options."

"Anywhere on the northeast coast. Boston would be ideal, but I don't need to be that picky."

"Let me make a call."

He got up and moved for the phone, but she stopped him. "Wait." He stopped and turned, raising his eyebrow.

"It's my people... my ex-people. The Sandmen."

"Obviously."

'They had kidnapped the Butcher of Nairobi's child. I have reason to believe they've been doing this for a while."

I saw him putting the pieces together. "That explains a lot about him. So you were gathering intel so they could find a way to set me up for it. I don't want to know what they're doing with children, do I?"

She shook her head. "I don't know every detail about what they're doing, but I needed you to know. In case they get a lucky shot and I die, you need to know so you can carry on the fight."

He looked like he was about to reassure her, but she cut him off. "They're experimenting on Outré. I don't know the nature of the experiments, but it can't be good if children are being stolen for it."

"All the more reason to keep you alive. If anyone stands a chance of fighting the Sandmen in their own heads, it's you. Let me see what I can do about getting us across the pond."

She nodded and sat back while he made a call in a language that, I'm ashamed to say, made me think he was talking to the Swedish Chef. He spent a long time on the phone. When he was done, he smiled. "Fancy an Atlantic cruise?"

"Yes! But do we have time?"

"We need to make time. I still have a lot to show you about fighting like a Reaper, and it seems that most of the airports are being watched. Your old boss wasted no time having you declared armed and dangerous," he pretended to read a briefing, "a rogue agent with her own agenda, extreme caution advised."

"Wow," she sounded impressed. "I have quite the legend to live up to."

The Atlantic Ocean

The dream fuzzed out and back in. They were boarding a large, commercial ocean cruise ship. It was white and pristine, and the crew had unveiled the pomp and circumstance for the horde of people who were coming aboard. Names were checked off of lists, fake passports were checked, and champagne was handed to my parents while they leaned on the railing to wave good-bye to crowds of people who were there to send other people off.

She let me see snippets of them enjoying little discoveries about the ship, but she came back into focus that night in their small room. He was in a t-shirt and jeans and had his baton out.

"The thing about our abilities," he was saying, "Is that they flow from the final parts of life, but that means they're still tied to life. By extrapolation, it means we affect things in the physical, living world. Everything I've seen of the Sandmen indicate they only affect the psychic world."

Somnoleni drew on some of her stored dream energy and sculpted a dream baton. "You might need to update what you know, I can affect the physical world too."

James squinted for a moment. "Are you sure?"

She waved her baton at him.

He went to his bag and pulled out a Polaroid camera. "Hold your baton up." She did, and he snapped a picture. He snapped it back and forth rapidly like you were supposed to. After several minutes, he looked at it and handed the picture to her triumphantly. In the photo, her hand was shaped like it was holding a baton, but the baton didn't appear in the Polaroid image.

"I see the baton when we face each other, but I'm assuming

that's because you're making my mind see it."

"So, I shouldn't try to deflect bullets with this like you do?"

"Absolutely not. I think it'd be best if you looked like you had a Reaper's scythe, but instead were making yourself appear to be a short distance to the left or right. Not so far that the sound of your movement gives you away, but far enough that it looks like you're deflecting the bullet when in truth it's just missing you. Are you ready to try?"

She nodded, and I felt dream energy envelope her like a nebulous cloud. She tried a couple movements, but she was burning through dream energy quickly. She stopped and looked frustrated.

"What's wrong?"

"Well, I can do it, but it requires a lot of energy because I'm so large…" she trailed off.

"What'd you just conclude?"

"I'm only facing you, right? Not a crowd?"

James nodded, not sure where this was going."

"So, I don't need to burn a lot of energy making it look like my body is elsewhere. I only need to burn a tiny amount making your brain think I'm elsewhere."

"Can you do that?"

"At this range, I should be able to. Distance would make it difficult. Mind if I try?"

He indicated that she should, and I felt her draw a much smaller bead of energy up to her forehead and then mentally push it towards James. I don't know how else to describe it. She didn't move physically at all, she just… thought it towards him and it dutifully went.

"Now," she said tentatively, "Throw something at me."

He grabbed a pillow from the bed and lobbed it at her. It

landed two feet to her left.

"Perfect," they said in unison.

Oh… Halldora would never again hit me with a pillow!

They practiced it for a while. He showed her how to move like a Reaper. She even made her baton black and gave it a scythe blade like his. In turn, she was showing him how to see through, or slip out of the mindgames Sandmen would be trained to use against him. After an hour, she called a stop.

"I need to gather more energy."

He raised his eyebrow, "You guys run out?"

She shrugged, "If I was in your dreams, I'd use your own energy against you infinitely. But here, in the physical world, we have to store it unless we have a supply nearby."

He considered it. "I suppose that makes sense. There must be enough atmospheric… death? Entropy? Something for us to maintain a steady pace with our abilities. We're certainly stronger if there's a death nearby, but there's always at least a little to draw on."

"Lucky. I'll be back shortly."

He must have tidied up a bit while she was out. When she returned, he was flipping through the ship's large binder of activities. Casually he said, "We missed the Captain's dinner."

"We have to go to those?"

"I have no clue. Sounds like we were supposed to."

"If it's all the same, I'd rather not be out for long periods like that."

"Fine with me."

"James, you said your abilities are tied to life. How was it Iskandar was able to crumble the padlock?" I'd wondered that myself.

"A few rare Reapers can bring about the 'death of objects.' It stands to reason an Elder's son would be able to, but it's certainly not common. Personally, I think he redirects the wet decay of organic material into the object hastening its own rusting decomposition. It's only a theory, though, I've never been able to reproduce it."

She hesitated, then asked, "And the …"

"Zombie servitors?"

She nodded.

"That, unfortunately, is far more common that any of us are comfortable admitting. For a while, Elders tried to ban it completely, but that only made it more appealing to Reapers who wouldn't have sought it out otherwise." He held out a hand to her, "The very act floods the body and soul of the necromancer with necrotic energy, decaying it a bit more each time. It's not pleasant, and certainly not without repercussion."

"I hope I never have to see it again."

I agree.

CHAPTER EIGHTEEN
2012 – SOMEWHERE IN NEW HAMPSHIRE

I woke before Halldora. I don't know why I expected her to be a rise-n-shine militant, but I was kind of surprised to find she wasn't. Since I had a moment of peace to myself, I decided to get up see if I could find a place to work out and maybe grab some breakfast. No matter what powers I was discovering, simply wishing I was lean and muscular wasn't getting me anywhere.

The motel wasn't much for a gym. I ended up just pulling my aura in tight and focusing on keeping it under control while jogging down the highway and back to get my heart rate up. Breakfast looked disgusting, and that was being charitable. A dirty placard at the front desk billed it as an amazing continental experience. After the first pass I was fairly certain they didn't ever eat this crap on any continent. I stared at the soggy tray of donuts and allowed a pack of questions to run freely around my head.

In the lead was my uncertainty regarding where I was supposed to go from here. The Valkyrie didn't sound like they hosted a formal training program. Though a Camp Big Scary Death Girl t-shirt would be kind of hilarious. Not to diminish Halldora's skills, but I would rather be learning from

Aunt-Margret. Not only was she my only link to a family I'd long ago given up hope of finding, but she also had experience training people who needed to stay hidden. It sucked that it was too dangerous for me to stay with her. Actually, the hardest part to swallow was that my own inexperience could get her killed.

If what I just dreamed was true, I was terrified about the new shadow world I was entering. I mean kidnapping children to experiment of them? That doesn't happen outside of movies. It's just... I thought we had come farther than we have as a society. And yet, the Sandmen were still as black hat and mirrorshade as ever.

Standing there in the dingy foyer that counted as the motel's lobby, I tried to put my thoughts in order. First and foremost, I have to know if my mother and James were successful. If they stopped the flow of children to Tartarus and stopped the experimentation, then maybe because of them the world of today is a better place than it was in their time. But if they hadn't succeeded, I think that means it's my job to pick up where they left off. Why else would I be receiving these particular dreams instead of light fluffy dreams showing what loving and caring parents I could have had?

If that's what they want me to do, then that's a whole new level of terrifying because I don't know anything about being a secret agent, or shadow warrior, or big scary death guy. I don't know how to pick a lock. I don't know how to break into a super-secret facility. I don't really even know how to shoot a gun. I certainly don't know how to use these new abilities effectively. And... dammit... I don't know anything.

Looking down in disgust one more time, in case some new and appetizing food had magically appeared while I had warred with myself, I came to one decision–we were not going to have motel breakfast. Instead we'd find something a little healthier on the road. Looking across the lot, I could see the lights were on, which meant Halldora was up. I went back to the room and let myself inside. She was sitting there looking angry.

"Were you pooping in the woods?" she asked.

"No. I went for a run and tried to find some breakfast."

"What did I tell you about being alone?" she admonished. "You can't be doing that right now. Not right now. I know this is new and you're probably not taking it as seriously as you should, but you're going to have to listen to me."

"Okay fine. But I sometimes need to have a moment alone when I'm not pooping."

"For obnoxious male reasons, or because you're confused and are trying to sort your head out?"

"How do you know it wasn't both?"

She shrugged, "We're going to lump the first one under 'pooping.' If it's the second one, try to make sure I'm nearby visually. I don't mind you having some space, but you're really vulnerable right now."

"Vulnerable?"

"Yeah. If you forget to shield your aura, you're a beacon. You don't know how to fight, don't have a firm grasp on your abilities, and you don't have one bloodline or the other vouching for you. Vulnerable."

"Oh… I… Vouching for me?"

"When you hear someone talk about it, it's going to sound a bit like you're claimed property, but yeah. You need someone with some respectable power to say you're a member of their bloodline so the others stop looking at you like fresh meat. Morpheus already made a few overtures. Do you want to throw in with the Sandmen?"

I shook my head vehemently.

"Ok, based on what you know so far, do you want to throw in with the Reapers?"

She was watching too keenly for my reply. "I can sense a trap when one's laid out. What is it that I don't know about the Reapers?"

"Everything."

"How so?"

She took a deep breath, "Well, the Sandmen have organized, right? Chain of command, facilities, paychecks and government Fords, etc."

"Yeah, though they're kind of like the evil empire."

"True, but the evil part is irrelevant at the moment. They have one globally unified command structure. Reapers have never come anywhere close to that. We're still just pods of independent Reaper groups. Some work well with others, others most definitely do not. Some, like the Valkyrie, have very noble goals and a code of honor. Others, like the ghûl of the desert, do not have humanity's best interest on their minds."

"Great."

"I know it sounds like a pain, but that fractious nature has allowed us to remain nimble and difficult to infiltrate or take down. It's how we avoided the church and the inquisition. It's how we keep the Sandmen and everyone else at bay. Do you realize how many powerful people would enslave us to see if we can fight off death on their behalf?"

I raised my eyebrow. "You can do that? Challenge the Grim Reaper to a chess game where the stakes are no less than a person's life?"

"You are such a geek. Nothing so cool. You said death looked like a black energy tendrils? Well, we can try to hold that off. It doesn't always work, and it's certainly not a civilized chess match. It doesn't change a dangerous environment or situation, and someone who gets shot still bleeds. But we might be able to slow the advance of those tendrils and keep the heart beating a few moments longer."

"Wow."

"Yeah, well, it's amazing how many desperate men and women think a few extra heartbeats equal immortality. Even at our best that kind of fight is no substitute for emergency medical care."

"Yeah. I'm not looking forward to someone grabbing me just to make me fight off their death. So, there's no Central Reaper Agency. But what if I joined up with one of the factions? Like the Valkyrie?"

She laughed.

"What, you don't like the C.R.A.?"

"No, well yes. But no, I was laughing at you as a Valkyrie. You aren't nearly enough of a warrior."

"Har har har, meanie."

"Seriously, you're not. Yet in spite of that, I am taking you north to meet them if you're up for it. If nothing else, we'd have other Valkyrie nearby while I worked on training you."

I nodded, "I think that's as good a starting point as anything." While I was throwing my stuff into my bag, I asked, "What else do you know about Tartarus?"

"I know enough to not go looking for Tartarus."

"Let's say you had to."

"Nobody has to."

"I kind of think I have to."

"I wish you didn't."

"Yeah, I wish I didn't either."

"Then you're going to have to work really hard on the exercises and training I put you through."

"I'm up for it."

"You realize that probably won't even be enough?"

I took a deep breath, "Look. I'm serious about this. I think I'm more serious about this than anything I've ever been serious about. Because this isn't just about my wants, it's actually about something important."

The look that crossed her face said she'd heard what she was waiting to hear. "All right." She grabbed her phone, "I'm going to make a call. You shower, and poop," she grinned, "and we'll get on the road. We can be there by tonight."

A New Hampshire Highway

Once we were in the Death Buggy heading out on the road I had to ask, "What were you doing for me yesterday if not preparing me for this?"

"Margaret asked me to teach you a few basics and help you work on keeping your aura hidden full time. Until this morning, I figured you were going to eventually go back to whatever life you'd had. I'm still not convinced you understand what you're getting yourself into with this search for Tartarus. Even a boy wizard has to realize that's not something you just casually toss around in conversation. So I'm at least convinced that you think you're serious about this. And that's enough for now."

"You think I'll change my mind."

"Not at first. But to be fair, I think everything's going to get stupidly hard. I think you're going to get frustrated and hurt. I think I'm eventually going to be ordered to stand down and not accompany you any farther. And then I think you'll finally see the scope of what you're up against. Just remember, dead is dead. If you need to retreat, rethink, and strategize–there is no shame in living to carry on the fight. And if you didn't get goosebumps just now, allow me to reiterate. A Reaper is telling you that dead is dead."

Okay, I'm man enough to admit I may have sprouted a goosebump or two.

"Anything I should know about your... people? I don't even know what to call you? Cell? Branch of the family?"

"We tend to think of ourselves as families. The abilities are ultimately bloodline based. Mine is a bit heavy on the Norse symbolism, but it gives some of them focus. Women are Valkyries, men are Einherjar..."

"Odin's reincarnated warriors?"

"Where the hell did you learn that?"

"Roleplaying games mostly. You should get back to playing them."

"We don't have time for games. But yes... Einherjar. In essence, we're guiding souls to their final rest and prepping for the end of the world."

"So... happy fun deathy stuff?" I said as light-hearted as I could.

She laughed, "You've seen too many cartoons."

"You can never see too many cartoons. Go on."

"Well, we can't have big old mead halls like they did in the past, but I don't think variations on a pub will ever go out of style. So we have a series of bars and pubs at which we gather. When we have to refer to ourselves as a group within the greater appellation 'Reaper,' we call ourselves fjárhirðir–it means shepherd, or far-herder."

"That's incredible."

She looked confused, "What is?"

"You sounded just like the Swedish She-Chef!"

She punched me hard in the bicep.

"Ow!"

Several moments of silence rolled by with the scenery.

Yeah. That was my fault.

"I'm sorry."

She didn't budge.

"Really. I am sorry. I'm so far out of my element all I have left is humor."

"You are going to meet a lot of people who are very old and very powerful. Elders who control supernatural abilities with precision and deadly force."

I started to say something lame like, "I know..." but she steamrolled right over me.

"AND those people are going to be from all corners of the world. Since I don't want to waste my time training a dead man, and I'm reasonably certain Margaret won't let us use the Roe as a meeting place anymore if I let you get dead spouting off to an Elder, you need to check your mouth."

It was my turn to sit in silence. I had that coming. I let several miles go by.

"I cannot evaluate my life any longer. I have no way of knowing where I'm going."

"We are Outré. Do you know what that means?"

"We're outsiders?"

"Yes. But it's more than that. The French word has elements

of 'fantastic' in it, and we're that too. You are predisposed to being outside. So quit trying to evaluate your life. You will never be able to. You are going to meet people who can join you in your dreams, people who can entice you into believing they're the only other person in the world, and people who can see death coming and maybe fight it off. You can't evaluate that. Because the instant you land on an explanation you think is right, you'll meet someone who can punch you with the force of a cannonball in flight. You just find your purpose in this fantastic world and do your best to uphold your belief in your purpose. And you're not going to figure it out in a couple days, so cut yourself some slack."

I had a lot of food for thought.

"What else should I know?"

She looked at me disbelieving. "I can't just... where does one start?"

"Where did we Outré come from?"

She dropped her head back against her seat rest, "I have no idea."

"Sorry."

She took a deep breath, calming herself. "No, don't be. You're just curious. What I do know is that we Outré have gone through cycles of being visible and being hidden. It's really hard to know where we come from. That said, we have our stories as well."

"Like the brothers who became the Elders?"

She smiled, "That's one, though it's a very biblio-centric point of view and not very popular right now. There were people with death-related abilities in other parts of the world who are in no way descended from those brothers."

"So, we aren't all descended from one Reaper?"

"Odds are against it, but I can't defend a theory any more than you can say all humanity came from Adam & Eve."

"Fair enough. Umm... where are we going?"

"North, Miss Tessmacher."

I smiled like an idiot, "Now you're speaking my language! The Reapers have a Fortress of Solitude?"

"Several. Loads of fortresses. We each get a fortress upon graduating from Deathwarts! You'll get one when you join the team, along with a uniform and a plaque. However, until you sign up, I'm only taking you to Maine to meet the others."

"Fine, but you owe me a trip to the Fortress of Solitude now."

"Whatever. Dork."

A MAINE HIGHWAY

Hours later, I took my turn as the passenger. I wasn't anxious or nervous... I was bored. Halldora wanted some time to drive without me pestering her. My complete inability to meditate led me to the realization I had had so much on my mind that I hadn't called Nate to let him know about my new number. Having nothing else to do, I made up my mind to call him.

Yeah. Stupid new phone. None of my normal contacts were in it. Why? Because the numbers hadn't been ported over. Why? Cuz Halldora had flushed my old phone down a motel toilet. I had several long, painful minutes where I tried to log into my primary email service on the teeny phone window so I could get the few numbers I might have in there.

Fortunately, Nate put his number in the signature of every

email he sent. Once I'd copied it to the new phone's contacts, I called his office number. I could tell by his hesitant answer he was being cautious about answering from a number he didn't recognize.

"Nate, it's me."

"Oh, hey. Are you all right?"

"Yeah, my phone got flushed down a toilet," I shot Halldora a meaningful glance. She rolled her eyes. "This is the temporary number until I can get everything cleared up."

"No, I mean, good to know. But no, some guys in suits showed up and asked if I had seen you."

"Guys in suits?"

"Yeah, it smelled fishy. I said I hadn't seen you in a while, that you were away visiting family. Then they said something weird, they said, 'he doesn't have family, do you want to amend your statement?' I mean, my statement? I wasn't aware I was on trial."

I was getting really worried.

"Shit, then what?"

"I said you'd actually found someone who might be a birth relative, and you'd gone to verify it."

"Did they ask you anything else?"

"No, they thanked me for my time."

I looked at Halldora. She looked concerned, and she'd only heard my side. She mouthed, 'his dreams' really pointedly.

"Nate, this is going to sound really weird, but have you had any dreams about me since then?"

"You know, now that you mention it, I did have a dream about you meeting an old lady and telling her she was related. I'm pretty sure she gave you cookies and milk, and I think you were wearing a propeller beanie and kids' clothes. Weird, right? I guess they had me pretty shaken."

"Not as weird as you might think. Dammit. Please, let me know if they come back. I have to make a call."

"Wait... what..."

I hung up.

"How much of that did you understand?" I asked Halldora.

"Enough. What did he see in his dream?"

"Me with an old lady."

She grew forebodingly still. "How much did he know about Margaret?"

"I specifically had not told him anything useful. Nothing like her name or what she did for a living. I only told him that I may have found my mom's aunt."

"Shit. Shit. Shit."

"Well, I had to tell him something–I needed his Jeep because they would have had my car watched. But it's not like he knew enough to implicate Margaret. I mean, she's spent her life not being of interest to the Sandmen."

"How far from the Roe did they see you?"

"They don't know it was me... but my guess is they sensed my dream energy at a Wal-Mart halfway between Providence and the Roe."

"Shit." She found the nearest turn-around and we started heading back south. While on the way, she pulled out her phone and had more Swedish chef conversations. Three of them. I heard Margaret's name a couple times.

When she was done, I asked, "What language was that? And what's the new plan?"

"Icelandic. And we're headed back to Providence to meet a few other Reapers who are friends of Margaret's. The new plan is to distract the Sandmen, dangling you as the prize, and draw any possible scrutiny away from her."

I was bait for saving Aunt Margaret. "I'm in."

She floored it.

Funny thing about narcolepsy. When high emotion wears off you don't realize how suddenly exhausted you've become. I don't remember falling asleep in the passenger seat.

Chapter Nineteen
1972 – Reykjavik, Iceland

"Remember."

My mother was in a lovely room, looking into a wood-framed mirror. It looked a lot like a bed and breakfast decorated with an odd blend of rustic material and smooth modern shapes. The lights were on, contrasted to the black night outside the windows. A warm fire crackled in a circular fireplace. I could hear two men speaking in another room, one sounded like my father. I didn't speak their language, but I was starting to recognize it as Icelandic.

She moved down the hall and into the room with what turned out to be three men. The other speaker looked like some sort of professional. He was older, his hair was greased back, his suit was perhaps a bit too tight around the middle, and he was very animatedly discussing something. When my mother stepped into the room, he looked up, frowned, and pointedly shoved some papers into his briefcase.

The man sitting silently at the table was extremely old. He epitomized the saying, "he was a bag of skin and bones." He had been weathered by a hard life working outdoors, which made him look like an ornery old cuss. I could not tell if he was angry at the proceedings or if this was what he always looked like. My mother's entrance didn't improve his mood, but didn't seem to worsen it either.

James had a smile, but he was the only one happy to see Somnoleni. The business man pursed his lips and looked to James to say something. "Well," my father said ignoring him, "We're not being run out of Reykjavik at gunpoint. But I'm not permitted to teach you anything. Or even help you. Or, if Halfdan here has his way, even so much as buy you coffee."

My mother nodded, "I understand. I'll go fight for their children alone. It's okay." Well that cleared up the mystery of where I got my bitter, snide commentary.

The old man further furrowed his already furrowed brow, but Halfdan exploded into angry conversation first. James raised an eyebrow at him, but listened politely to every word. When the tirade wound down, James smiled, "It seems they're also not happy about a woman playing hero."

The businessman exploded into another stream of angry comments. At one point, he took a breath and the old man raised his hand to silence him. Everyone looked to him expectantly.

I figured he'd sound like he looked, like someone old and raspy, but his voice was deep and strong. He spoke English, but it was heavily accented, "In the days of our father's sagas, our women, the Valkyrie, were every bit the warrior as their men. I hear from the honored dead that this woman Jörmundur has brought to us is very much a warrior like women of old."

Jörmundur? I suppose if my mother traveled and worked under an assumed identity, there's no reason my father should be much different. He was, after all, known for being present at the right death at the right time. I wouldn't be giving out my real name either.

"Gestur," said the businessman "She is not one of our women."

This couldn't be the same Gestur Halldora had mentioned. I wondered if it was a title that was passed on. Gestur, narrowed his eyes. "Well, Halfdan, she is not theirs any longer, and she wants to be ours. I think maybe we work with her."

"Bah. She is a spy," Halfdan proclaimed, as if it would be enough to cement the argument.

"Umara has been in her head. Umara says she is real."

It was Halfdan's turn to narrow his eyes. "What if Umara lies to make us look stupid?"

The old man shook his head, "You know Umara can be trusted."

Momentarily silenced, Halfdan turned away. He wasn't ready to cede the final word, "That does not mean she," he referred to my mother, "can be trusted."

Gestur dismissed him with a flick of his hands.

James looked to the old man, who nodded. Beckoning my mother over, Gestur took her hand, "Our children go missing, and you have brought the first real clue. The Sandmen take our children, this is our fight too." He looked at her knowingly for a second. They shared something in that look, something I didn't understand, or feel.

Nodding as if satisfied, he said, "Tell us what we need to know."

Once again, she told the story of what she'd seen in the dreams of the Butcher of Nairobi. This time, she focused on what she had heard and seen of Bruadair's mission. Gestur listened intently, but James watched Halfdan's reactions. What I saw of them showed him to be resistant and unwilling to give Somnoleni any credit or authority.

"So," she concluded, "we first have to find Tartarus."

Halfdan snorted. "Tartarus used to be the place all Elders could imprison the most dangerous Outré from their bloodlines. So we used to be able to trust our Elders to come and go from Tartarus, couldn't we? But then your Elder Morpheus was put in charge of mollifying the prisoners to keep them subdued. Then one day the Elders could not visit because of a dangerous 'situation.' We wondered why it was taking such a long time to contain. Then, once Morpheus announced that was cleared up, the Elders came to survey what the situation had been. But the old Tartarus was empty. Wasn't it? Your Morpheus had moved it. Hadn't he?"

"He's not my Morpheus. I don't want him. You can have him," was my mother's reply. "But in essence, yes. That is what I heard as well. I wasn't involved, though I remember hearing that Tartarus was on lockdown at one point and we weren't to bring anyone in for imprisonment until that was lifted. I'm not surprised it was a ruse to cover the relocation. Dreams are almost always symbolic of something deeper, it stands to reason everything Morpheus does has a deeper meaning." She paused, "I may still have people I can talk to for information, but it will be tricky."

"We are not," Gestur said, "without our own methods of gathering information. Perhaps we should try our way before you accidentally alert someone to your intentions?"

She nodded, relieved. "Please, let's do it your way!"

He creaked his old bones up out of the chair and retrieved a shoulder bag I hadn't seen near the door. Pulling a bundle out, he laid down a rich fabric as a work space. He then set down a small silver bowl, a small curved knife, a human skull, and what looked like a skeletal hand with thin metal wires where cartilage should have been. He positioned them methodically, everything in its place. Halfdan and Jörmundur lost interest in the preparation, but Somnoleni watched intently. When he was ready, Gestur nodded to my mother, "Welcome to the Reapers."

He picked up the knife and gashed his finger. He spilled the blood into the silver bowl and set that in front of the skull. Finger still bleeding, he painted blood on the teeth of the skull, and then on the index finger of the hand. He then held his bleeding hand out in front of his face, and blew on the cut. It was like watching a time-lapse-animation of a flower bud closing at night. The wound 'peeled' shut. Satisfied, he turned his attention to his workspace. He blew on the bowl of blood. A fine reddish-black mist formed and enveloped the skull, exploring and writhing into the openings where it could.

The skeletal hand flexed its bony fingers ever-so-slightly.

Taking a deeper breath, Gestur blew again. He didn't blow harder this time, but pushed it out for a lot longer. Little twitches were manifesting in the bones, a finger here, the jaw there. When his breath ran out, he inhaled again and spoke, "Draugur, ég veit þú heyrir til mín. Ég hef þörf fyrir þig." I'd have to ask Halldora to teach me the language.

A ghostly imprint of a man appeared over the skull. I picked out fur and leathers, but beyond that couldn't tell much about him. He hissed, as though air was difficult to come by. Gestur gave him commands in Icelandic. Though I didn't speak the language, the meaning was clear. He was ordering the spirit to seek out the new location for Tartarus. When the spirit had enough to work from, it hissed. Gestur inhaled and blew so hard on the blood that it evaporated out of bowl. It swirled through the apparition taking it around the room and up the chimney.

"He will be gone a long time," Gestur explained simply. "Get some rest." He then ambled over to a comfortable-looking chair by the window and dropped into an instant nap.

Halfdan gathered his things, sparing a few dark looks for Somnoleni. Without a word to anyone, he stomped out. James, or Jörmundur I guess, took my mother's hand and led her back to the bedroom.

She spoke first, "I'm destined to have detractors wherever I go, aren't I?"

"Yes, probably. I wish I could sugarcoat it, but you know that what you did stigmatizes you."

She nodded, "I know. But Gestur makes the second Elder who's been supportive. So that's something."

"That's actually something very big. If the Elders were against you, the Halfdan's and Iskandar's of the world would be free to give in to fear, hatred, and prejudice. They'd attack you as the whim grabbed them."

"I don't ever want to go up against either of them."

"No... but you're no slouch."

She smiled, "Thank you. But I am inexplicably tired. We should take Gestur's advice and sleep."

My father pulled her close for a second. Then she let the dream fade in and out. I saw them ready for bed, then they were in bed, then they were falling asleep...

Then suddenly she was puking. Same suite of rooms, though there was faint light out a window. She used a moment while cleaning up to reinforce her "remember" command.

"Are you okay?" my father called from the other room.

"Yes, just queasy all of a sudden."

She finished up and got dressed. "I'm going to go make some coffee."

Alone in the kitchen, it seemed to me she was trying to order her thoughts more than make coffee. Gestur calling from the living room snapped her out of her thoughts. "He is returned."

She hurried in, as did Jörmundur moments later. The ghost was floating above his skull. Gestur gave him a quick command. As the ghost spoke, Jörmundur translated for Somnoleni:

> "*Travel, you must, north of the Lake of Egypt,*
> *West of Eldorado, yet east of Old Man River,*
> *Layers beneath the famous shark will you find the*
> *dream cages.*"

The spirit finished with a flourish. It then raised its hand, though whether in salute or an obscene tell-off I couldn't distinguish. It vanished in a tempestuous swirl of red mist that faded a second later.

"Did that mean anything to you?" my father asked my mother.

She shook her head, "Just 'research time.'" She found a notepad and quickly scribbled it down.

"Good," said Gestur, "Library is not far. You go research. I have calls to make, and people to make ready. I will come back here when I am done."

He took his time gathering up his implements, making pointed glances towards the kitchen. Jörmundur chuckled and made the Elder some toast and coffee to take with him while my mother showered and got dressed.

THE UNIVERSITY OF ICELAND, REYKJAVIK

In the early morning light, my parents were nearing the University of Iceland. Luckily for me, the signs were easy enough to translate. The main building was fairly unique looking, stately and white-gold in the light of the rising sun. Crossing a circular field, my parents heard a whistle, and spun to look.

"Morpheus," my mother hissed. They sprinted for the building.

Several footsteps sounded behind them, as did a wet, slapping sound. They didn't initially turn to look, but I felt my mother's panic rise. Jörmundur was faster, though he slowed to stay by her side. Together they raced to the front of the building. I felt my mother conjure a dark armor-like aura out of stored dream energy, and through the corner of my eye saw blackness flicker around my father.

As they raced up the front steps, I heard the slapping noise getting closer than the footsteps. Jörmundur reached the door first, and moved to fling it open. Locked. Cursing, he pulled out his baton while he spun to face the incoming danger. His eyes widened in horror.

Spinning herself around to look, my mother also cursed. A sleek monster was coming up the steps behind them. The slapping noises were its webbed claws coming down to propel it forward. It had shiny black fur plastered to its body like a seal, but its face was pure carnivorous rage. Crowning its back were long spiked tendrils that were reaching forward toward my parents. The thing's eyes flashed red and it hissed, baring its fangs. I felt a tremor of fear vibrate down my mother's spine.

"Those are only legend!"

"Kind of like Sandmen who can overcome the mind's defenses and kill from within a dream? Come on, we've got this." My father sprang forward.

"JAMES! NO!" My mother flung her arms to the sides, putting up a multicolored wall around my father and the creature. The outline of four Sandman agents suddenly appeared in the wall's glow. They'd been sneaking up invisibly.

Jörmundur backpedaled, switching from offensive to defensive. An agent fired first. My father snapped up his black scythe blade and absorbed the bullet. It only took two more shots before they realized he was going to continue blocking them. The agents switched tactics, and one of them shouted, "Attack!' He pointed at my parents.

The beast pounced.

My mother dropped and rolled toward it, allowing its leap to take it clear over her. She sprang up behind the creature. My father had dropped to one knee, planted his baton, and spun the scythe blade so the point angled towards the monster. If it continued its leap, it'd impale itself just to get to him.

The threat of pain didn't faze the creature in the slightest. It took the blade to one shoulder and tried to bite my father's arm. He flung himself back in time, but was suddenly without his weapon. As soon as his hand left the baton, the scythe-blade dissipated. As the baton fell, my father deftly caught it in his off hand, and brought it up like a club under the creature's chin.

"It's a nightmare," my mother explained, "It's tireless and can't be physically harmed."

"Dammit."

She had her own problems. She was holding one of the thing's back-tendrils at bay while also dealing with an advancing Sandman. "But it won't survive daylight."

I saw my father glance to the horizon, the sun would rise above it any second now. "Ok." He jumped to the side, taking a swipe from a tendril spike to his armor. It knocked him around a bit, but he recovered and landed in front of a Sandman agent. The agent brought a glowing hand forward, but my father was wise to it. He blocked with his baton, blocking the dream energy with death energy. He then launched a powerful kick at the guy's knee, dropping the agent for the moment. Keeping in motion to keep forcing the beast to turn, he moved sideways to the next agent.

My mother had the spiked tendril in her hand, and was exercising a small amount of control over the dream material from which it was made. She was using the tendril as an improvised weapon to slash at the agent that had moved in on her. The final agent had taken a firing stance, and pulled the trigger. My mother ducked, and the bullet sailed harmlessly through the nightmare creature. Angrily, she rammed the tendril's spike into the agent in front of her. He didn't defend himself in time, having expected his partner to shoot her. He shuddered violently when the tendril hit him. Somnoleni ducked behind him, using him as a living shield, as the other agent fired again, narrowly averting his shot at the last instant.

The agent leapt to tackle my father, but hadn't been aware of the death armor. As soon as he made contact, there was a sickening sound, and it looked like years of his life peeled off of him and a cascade of dust and dried flesh. Jörmundur just said, "Dumbass." He flicked his scythe blade out of the baton and brought it down into the man's forehead, killing him instantly and decaying him within the next few heartbeats. The agent whose knee he'd hurt, gasped in revulsion getting my father's attention. Which was the only reason he was able to dodge a silent lunge from the beast. He squared off against the monster.

"Where'd Morpheus go?" my mother called out. Nobody had an answer for her. The agent directly in front of her was pulling the spike out and told her where she could go. Pissed, she grabbed his hand with her free one and said, "sleep" punctuating it with a wave of drowsy energy. The man dropped to the ground out cold. The agent with the gun sensed his chance and started firing wildly as she ducked and tried to roll away from my father. Coming out of her roll, she raised a hand and pointed a blinding flash of light at him. He cursed, and twitched sideways to avert his eyes. She used the distraction to get close to him and wrestle him for the gun. The instant she felt his skin, she put him to sleep too.

Jörmundur, still fighting the beast, called over, "How the hell?"

"I figure if Bruadair could do it, a toddler could probably do it."

"Argh!" my father called as the agent with the wounded knee hit him with a poorly aimed glowing blast from his hand. My father looked like he was going to pass out for a second, but the creature renewed its attack bringing his attention back into focus yet again. Having disabled her two agents, my mother joined the fight. She was too far away to affect the remaining agent without shooting him, so she plunged her hand into the nightmare beast. Just like she had with the dream islands, she started siphoning energy off the monster.

Where bullets had failed, that got its attention. It forgot all about my father and spun to destroy this threat that was hurting it. My mother stayed put, but her hand ripped at its body's cohesion when it spun. It roared in obvious pain. The sound was an ear-shredding blast somewhere between a thousand nails on a blackboard and an elephant-eagle hybrid. I felt the concussive shock from the roar hit and damage my mother's eardrums. Somewhere beyond the creature, my father yelled in pain again, but the sound was muffled.

The creature was attacking more frantically now. Instead of leaping away from the hand that penetrated it, the enraged nightmare was trying to kill this woman that was hurting it on the inside. My mother held her ground, draining its very essence away. Its edges were losing some of their so-lidity. The monster brought all of the tendrils along its back forward. The creature lunged with all tendrils driving the sides of the spikes into my mother like clubs, pushing her back far enough that her hand was no longer in the creature. She braced herself, and managed to stop moving before she topped backward down the steps. Looking over her shoulder, she didn't see Morpheus anywhere.

"He's invisible," she shouted. She could barely hear her own voice and wasn't sure if Jörmundur heard her, so she kept the beast's attention with little sparkles of color. It coiled its hind legs and sprang. She didn't quite dive to the side in time, and took some of the beast's weight to her shoulder, knocking her down.

My father had been slicing at the beast with his scythe. He chased its pounce and positioned himself next to my mother, reaching down to help her up while the beast turned to attack again.

Standing side-by-side, my parents readied for the next assault. Instead of using its tendrils the creature opened its maw wide, as if to roar again. My parents covered their ears.

A staccato stream of bullets shot out of the nightmare's mouth and carved into my father, cutting his chest open six, seven, eight times before he fell out of the way. My mother's instinctual dodge got her to the side, but she crab-crawled right back to him. A wave of fury and grief washing over her, she snapped up to the beast.

It was coming apart in the rays of the sun. Everywhere a lance of golden light hit the nightmare it turned to vapor and dissipated. A lone man was standing inside the beast.

Ignoring him, my mother put her hands to my father's wounds. So much blood was gushing out of his chest and mouth, he could no longer speak. She tried to stop the bleeding, she tried to hold him together. "No," she was crying. "No, no, no…" She tried using some of her stored dream energy to stanch the bleeding, but he bled anyway. I could feel her fury subsiding as she tried frantically to find a way to save him.

As the beast melted away, Morpheus made 'tsk tsk' sounds. "Pity," he said dryly, "he would have made good breeding stock."

"I'LL KILL YOU," my mother shouted at her former boss.

He nodded condescendingly at her, "I believe you want to. However, even you aren't strong enough to fugue my senses before I can fire this." He motioned with the automatic rifle he had pointed at her.

"You've got Outré around the world riled up. I had to see you fight for myself, up close so I could evaluate it. I believe you really are as good as the rumors and whispers claim. I never taught you some of those maneuvers, and I know you didn't learn them from the Reapers. Tell me, Sopora, who else have you been learning from?"

"Don't call me that, ever again. Go to hell." She hadn't looked up. She was trying to keep my father alive with her own willpower.

"Oh, we'll go to hell together soon enough. I have a very special hell set aside just for you."

My mother was crying now. She saw my father's spirit rise from his body, and I felt the same death energy I had experienced in the gym. Jörmundur's spirit looked her up and down lovingly, he raised an eyebrow when his spirit-sight reached her abdomen. "I have one attack left to me." His faint spirit voice said to her. "Make use of it. Run. Get away and keep him safe. I love you."

"No!" my mother cried.

Unable to see my father's ghost, Morpheus thought she was still talking to him, "Oh yes, I had to prepare an extra-powerful cell to hold you, but it's ready and waiting."

My father's spirit rose up and dove over my mother's head, ramming into Morpheus' chest. The Sandman leader clutched his heart and pitched forward face-first.

My mother lingered over my father's body. "Run!" came his disembodied voice.

Somewhere deep inside her, years of pragmatic agent training took over and she sprinted across the façade of the building, heading for the corner. Her vision was obscured by tears, and her ears were still ringing. I thought I heard

Morpheus call out, "Shoot her, dammit," but wasn't entirely sure until I felt something stick into her back. Another sting hit the back of her thigh. She looked down to see a small red arrow attached to a needle that had just gone into her leg.

"Dammit," she cursed. She tried to run, tried to keep going on adrenaline alone. Two more darts hit her, one bouncing off her shoulder at a weird angle, but the final projectile penetrated her neck on a bull's eye shot.

The dream went dark as she crashed to the ground mere feet from the corner of the building.

Chapter Twenty
2012 – Back Through Massachusetts

"AAAGGHHH!"

Halldora nearly jumped out of her skin, "WHATTHE-
FUCK?!?!" She pulled the steering wheel and Jeep back under
control.

After a moment, she asked crossly, "What are you screaming for?"

I was breathing heavily. "I'm sorry, my mother just showed
me how my father died."

She was silent a moment, and I felt myself start to cry.
When she looked over and saw my tears, she asked if I was
okay.

"I just," I sniffled, "I hadn't realized until just now how badly I was holding on to some hope that he might still be alive."

Her voice softened a bit, "Is there any chance it was a symbolic dream?"

I shook my head, "I doubt it. This one was just like the
dreams that led me to the Farm and Aunt Margaret, and
those were both exceptionally accurate."

She nodded.

Some countryside went by in silence. Tentatively she
offered, "If you saw enough to identify the place, I could

make some calls and ask for verification? Some Reapers can actually see events of past deaths if they can find the place where the death occurred."

"What good would that do?"

"None for your father, though it would allow others who knew him in life to be rid of their doubt and mourn him. This probably sounds stupid right now, but more immediately it would establish both your reputation as someone helpful and go a long way toward confirming your lineage in their eyes."

"Fine, I guess. University of Iceland, front steps of the main building. It was a big white stone building on a circular field. They never made it to the library."

She pulled out her phone and speed-dialed someone. They held a conversation in Icelandic while I stared out the window in a daze. I picked out the word for University, but nothing else. Look at me go, a budding linguist even in my depression.

She seemed comfortable letting me take my time coming to terms with the vision. So I did. I didn't really think too deeply about anything, I just let the miles roll by while I allowed images and implanted dream memories roll through my consciousness. The only time she interrupted was to remind me to pull my aura in. I did without a word.

Roughly an hour later, we crossed back into Rhode Island. Her phone rang while we were sitting in rush-hour traffic in the suburbs of Providence. Yet again her conversation was in Icelandic. But this time she did a lot of listening. When she hung up, she took a minute to put her thoughts into order.

"You up for hearing this?"

"Sure," I said pretty dully.

"They found the site. Gestur himself performed the…"

"Gestur the Elder? You mentioned him once before as knowing Aunt Margaret. He's still alive??"

The wheels in Halldora's head came to a crashing halt, "How do you know about him?"

"He had been helping my parents on the day my father died, though he hadn't gone with them to the university. He was ancient then."

She snorted, "He's always been ancient. Most of us are pretty sure he was born ancient. That explains why he took personal interest in this today. Back when your parents disappeared, he had searched near the National Library several blocks away and never found anything. I wonder if he felt responsible for your father's death?" She put her thoughts back on track, "Anyway, he just returned from the University. He said I was to test you with a couple questions. Are you okay with that?"

"I guess."

"How many agents were there?"

"Four plus Morpheus on the ground. I don't know how many snipers." My heart started pounding. It was too soon.

"Can you describe the equipment they brought with them?"

"Not unless you mean the nightmare monster."

She nodded, "I do. Sorry. It wasn't my idea to try to trip you up."

"A black ugly carnivore with webbed feet and spiked tentacles on its back."

"Final question, who committed the first kill?"

"My…" damn. "My father."

She seemed satisfied with my answer. "Gestur fears Morpheus will hide behind that fact as justification for his actions if we go to any other bloodlines with this."

"But Morpheus was going rogue long before that. He moved Tartarus out from under the noses of the Elders before my parents ever even met."

She looked at me a bit incredulously, "I didn't know Tartarus had had multiple locations, or that the Elders had ever had access to it. My whole life it's been just a Sandman thing. I wish you could take me with you on your dreams, they seem very educational."

"Yeah, they are. My mother once shared a dream with Umara in Turkey. I bet with the right training I could bring you into one." I didn't say that Gestur's confirmation erased any doubt regarding why my mother needed me to see this story. She needed to make sure I knew the truth because neither she nor my father could find me and tell me. And because someone had to take up the fight.

"I need to let Gestur know you confirmed what he saw. Do you mind?"

"No, I figured that's why you were asking me the questions."

She called back and had another, shorter conversation.

After hanging up, she informed me, "We're meeting some of the others in Providence shortly. Is there anything you need or want to do first?"

"No. Maybe stop crying like a damned child, pee and blow my nose."

She pulled off to a wayside. We freshened up, then she offered to keep driving because she knew where she was going. I didn't mind.

PROVIDENCE, RHODE ISLAND

The house was right on the cusp of where city became outlying areas. It was a well-loved older neighborhood. Kids played in the streets and people were out in their yards chatting with their neighbors. People here still cared about their community. It occurred to me that if this place had a neighborhood watch with a social media group, it would provide its Reapers with valuable warnings about strange activity. I was shocked to realize I was starting to see the world from an Outré viewpoint.

Halldora pulled the Jeep into the drive of a big, old house. Someone inside opened the garage, and we parked next to a trendy black hybrid sedan.

There was a man about ten years younger than me at the garage door button. Once we were all the way in, he pushed to close it. He was thin, but wore stylish glasses and a nice shirt with no pattern or logo. His jeans and sneakers were timeless American.

"That him?" he asked Halldora the instant her door was open.

"Yes. Tyler, has…"

"Gestur's riled up." He turned to offer me some brotherly advice, "Dude, it's usually not a good idea to get Gestur riled up."

"I didn't mean to. I didn't realize the old guy'd still be alive."

"Of course he's still alive. Someone like Gestur doesn't just die."

I raised an eyebrow, but when he didn't answer I turned to Halldora for help. "Later," was all the information she gave me.

Tyler continued on, not in an annoying way, but as if con-

firming a longtime theory, "So it's all true. The Slumberscythe
left us what we needed to end the war?"

That was new, "Slumberscythe? War? Don't 'later' me on
this one, Halldora. What's this about?"

"Thanks Tyler. Jackass."

"You didn't tell him?!?! Some mentor you turned out to be."

"I said SHUT IT, Tyler."

"Actually," he needled her, "you didn't tell me to shut up.
Well, until just now, but you hadn't previously."

She stormed in past him.

He looked to me, "I love my sister. She's just too damned
serious all the freakin' time!"

I laughed. "I'm James. Ummm… Slumberscythe?"

"Oh, yeah," he motioned me inside. "Some of us started
calling your mom that in honor of what she did."

"But she wanted to be called Somnoleni." The house was
nice on the inside. The wood trim had been lovingly oiled at
regular intervals, and shone with a warm light. The floor and
walls were clean, and the furniture all looked hand-carved in
a Norwegian style. This was a comfortable home.

Halldora was in the kitchen talking angrily to a tall lanky
guy. His hair was meticulously messy, and he had that intentionally smoldering look to him. I'm sure he was a lovely guy,
but everything about his style screamed rocker-poser fake.

"That's Atli," Tyler supplied. "Halldora's ex-boyfriend."
He tapped me on the arm and moved me past the confrontation in the kitchen. In the living room was a guy who
was so hugely muscular I couldn't help but stare. My inner
monologue wondered if he used steroids before I could stop
it. Once I had my inner thoughts under control, I realized
he could probably give me great workout advice on losing

weight.

"This is Alan," Tyler pointed. Alan caught me staring a bit too long at his chest muscles. Before he could say anything, Tyler introduced me like he had been the one to find me, "And this is Slumberscythe's boy, all grown up!"

To Tyler, Alan said, "Dude, chill." He stood and came to shake my hand, "Welcome." He looked to the kitchen, then back to me. "I'm assuming that since Halldora brought you here she doesn't know you're gay?"

I was about to thank him for the welcome, but choked after that last bit. "What? No… it never came up… Why?"

Alan and Tyler shared a knowing look. "It's not our place to say. Just be kind when you tell her. She's…"

"She's going to go ballistic!" Tyler supplied unhelpfully.

Alan glared at him a second, then turned back to me to offer a sympathetic look. "It won't go well, but it's not your fault. Hey, they're right – you do hide your aura!"

Tyler looked heartbroken that he hadn't thought of it first and scrunched up his face, "O-Em-Gee! He does hide it! That's wicked!"

"How do you do it?" Alan asked.

Gah. I didn't know if I was supposed to keep that a secret. It obviously had been an ace-in-the-hole for both Aunt Margaret and my mother, but it's significantly less helpful if people know about it. I opted for new-guy stupid until I had a grasp on the situation, "I'm not sure how to describe it. I just do. Kind of like when you focus all of your hearing just to listen for a tiny pin-drop of a sound. I promise I'll share it when I can explain it better."

Alan nodded, "You're on bro." He scowled at the kitchen. "I'll go get them. We need to get started."

He stalked off toward the kitchen. Tyler leaned in close, "He's cranky whenever he has to referee another Halldora and Atli moment."

"Oh? Umm... bad breakup?"

"For Halldora, yeah. And recent. She jumped at the chance to go get you so she could get some space to think."

"Ah, that explains a bit." I looked around pretending to ignore the raised voices in the kitchen, "Hey Tyler, do you have a computer or laptop I can use?"

Tyler nodded and brought me his tablet from a nearby room. I started searching for references to the lines in the riddle of Tartarus' location as brought back by the ghost Gestur had summoned. After I crossed off any attempt at poetic references, I started taking the lines of the stanza literally.

"Travel, you must, north of the Lake of Egypt,
West of Eldorado, yet east of Old Man River,
Layers beneath the famous shark will you find the
dream cages."

Old Man River was easy, I'd been hearing the Mississippi called that most of my life. Yay for Wisconsin folklore. Turns out Lake of Egypt and Eldorado are places with those exact names. The shark reference kept throwing me at first. Once I narrowed down to the town that fit the first two lines, I scanned its official page. The geographic area had a real prison, still in operation.

By the time Alan, Halldora, and Atli came in with drinks, treats and frosty silence, I had it figured out. I scribbled down the stanza and the clues as I had solved them. I gave the paper to Halldora.

She read it over, "Are you sure?"

"As sure as I ever am where dreams and the internet are concerned."

"What's it say?" Tyler asked, trying to sneak a peek.

Even Alan and Atli looked interested.

She read it over again. "It says that Tartarus is beneath the Federal Prison in Marion, Illinois."

The three men looked stunned.

"How reliable is that?" Atli asked. His Icelandic accent was very heavy.

"In 1972 Gestur conjured a ghost who took off and came back to deliver that riddle. That also means it's been forty years since this information was asked for. That's a lot of time." I realized what I was saying only as the final sentence left my damned mouth, "And Gestur has had that riddle all this time and never done anything with it."

Tyler and Halldora looked at each other.

"Was the ghost male, wearing furs?" she asked.

"Looked like it, yes. It was hard to tell."

Tyler nodded knowingly, "That was his brother. His brother's never wrong. But…"

Halldora interrupted, "…but his messages can only be heard by the person who needs to hear it."

"That means," Tyler was on a roll, "That James here was the one meant to receive the message!"

I shook my head, "No… my father translated it for my mother. Gestur was standing there listening to my father translate it."

"Oh." Halldora and Tyler said together.

Atli shook his head, "It does not matter. The mystery

of that incident made all the Elders pull back and go into hiding."

Halldora shot an angry look specifically at Atli, "He saw his mother's memory of how Morpheus killed Jörmundur."

"It was really murder then? So, this is why Gestur's involved?"

She nodded.

Alan interrupted, "Do we have direct orders?"

Halldora nodded, "We're to go check on Margaret."

"Margaret?" Tyler asked.

Halldora looked at me, allowing me to spill it the way I chose.

I didn't see anything but the truth being even remotely helpful. "Margaret was my mother's aunt, and we think Morpheus might be gunning for her."

"Shit, let's go," Alan said, already in motion.

We hustled out to the garage, and they all started getting into the hybrid. "Some of us could take the Death Buggy?" I motioned to the Jeep. The four of them just stared at me. Oh shit. Yeah, I just said 'Death Buggy' to a room full of Reapers. That's me. I'm a dumbass.

Alan laughed first, "Normally I'd prefer the Jeep, bro. But not with those plates. Get in." He took shotgun.

It was apparently Tyler's car, so I climbed in the back allowing Halldora to have me between herself and Atli.

We were well out into traffic before Atli said, "I have many questions for you when we get home tonight."

"Okay. I also want you all to hear the story my mother's been sharing with me. I think she wants this story known."

Tyler made great time through traffic. We pulled up to the One-Eyed Roe, and there were quite a few cars in the lot. I checked my aura, but realized theirs were big black beacons. "Guys, wait." I tried experimentally to dampen Halldora's like I had the dream mist residue around my apartment, but nothing changed. I had a brilliant idea of painting a null aura around her using some of my small supply of dream energy, but with my lack of skill she might end up glowing like a Christmas tree.

"Guess not. Your auras stand right out and I can't dampen them. Want me to go in quiet-like and see if she's ok?"

Everyone turned to Halldora. "I don't like sending you in alone, but you're right. They'll pick us out in a heartbeat. Go."

I jogged across the lot and went in.

Some other lady was behind the counter. I tried to scrutinize her aura, but I didn't see a thing. If she'd been trained by Aunt Margaret she might be hiding hers like I hide mine.

"Excuse me, is Margaret in tonight?"

The lady looked startled. "No. She called me this morning. Said I needed to cover for her. I do that sometimes."

"Please, I'm worried about her. Did she say where she was going? A hospital?"

The lady looked worried for Margaret's health, "A hospital? Is she sick?"

"I hope not. I just really need to find her. She might be in danger."

"Look, I don't know anything. And you didn't hear anything from me." Not only was that an odd answer, it didn't take a professional to see she was hiding something and extremely nervous.

"Margaret's a dear friend, always has been. I help her whenever she needs it. If you hear anything… anything at all… you be sure you call me first. Right away."

Dammit, dammit, dammit. My inner monologue had
watched as much television as I had, and it was screaming,
"She's an informant!"

I tried to keep cool. "Thank you, you've been very helpful.
I'll try to get to her if I can. Will you be available to open the
restaurant for a couple days?"

"Oh sure, sweetie. I'm retired. You just remember to let me
know if you learn anything."

"I will." What name did my father use in Egypt? "I'm Paulo."

"I'm Ida Lynn."

"Thank you, Ida Lynn."

"Sure thing, sweetie."

I bolted back out to the car. "They have her. Someone
named Ida Lynn came in to open for her, but every instinct I
have says she's an informant… or plant…"

"Gods dammit!" Cursed Halldora.

Tyler drove us out of the parking lot and back onto the
highway. "Well," he said, "I guess this means we all pack for
Illinois."

"What if they took her to the Farm temporarily? Just while
they're preparing to move her? It's close by," I asked.

"I'd heard it was decommissioned," Tyler said. Alan nodded.

"I don't know about that. I snuck onto the grounds when I
first got here, and though it looks empty, there were auras in
the sub-basements."

"Fuckin' hell, of course they have sub-basements," commented Alan.

Tyler was nearing the turn by the run-down barn, "Yes or
no people?"

"Yes," said Halldora definitively.

Tyler was just putting on the blinker when a black SUV shot out at us from my old hiding spot behind the barn. "FUCK!" he cursed, swerving but managing to stay on the main road. He hit the gas, but there was no way the combined hybrid/electric engine was going to accelerate with all five of us in the car. The SUV adjusted course to ram us. At the last second, Tyler swerved and pulled the hybrid off the road.

"Fight time," Alan said, tumbling out his door. I saw him clench his fists and start to sheathe himself in his version of black armor.

Atli pulled a black blade from his boot, and Halldora pulled a small gun from his other boot. Those two had obviously trained together. I hoped they could patch things up. Tyler was frantically shutting off the car, but when he exited, he kept it between himself and the Sandmen.

I jumped out on his side as well, not sure what the hell I was going to do.

The SUV did one of those three-point turns you see in car chases and crunched into the other side of the hybrid. As we leapt away I heard Tyler squawk, "That's my car, bitches!"

I ducked back down behind some crap as three Sandmen agents piled out of the SUV. Alan immediately got up in the first one's face and they started trading blows. Halldora fired a shot, but it didn't hit any of the agents. They moved into melee with us. Things were a bit of a blur while I tried to figure out who was facing whom.

An agent with his own knife was on Atli instantly. The tall Reaper hadn't seen the blade in time and got a serious gash for his inattentiveness. Tyler moved in to help him. The third agent stayed back, talking into his wireless headset, "...the waitress didn't realize the target had multiple conspirators. Request backup. Repeat, request backup. Target plus four Reapers."

Well I'll be damned, I was right. Ida Lynn was a lying bitch. "Hurry guys, he just radioed for help."

I heard Halldora groan at the news. She fired at the one using the headset, but her shot went wide. I heard her whisper, "four."

Meanwhile, Atli and Tyler were giving their agent a workout. Between Atli's expert knife use and Tyler's anger at the damage to his car, the agent was being harried on both sides.

Alan was doing a remarkable job with the one agent, but he was alone. I jogged over and took a kick at the agent's leg. It broke his concentration enough that Alan landed a solid punch. I saw him smile approvingly, but he didn't say anything.

Bringing some dream energy to my hand, I reached up and tried to smear it into the agent's eyes. He was moving around so much avoiding Alan's blows, though, that I only succeeded in making a colored smear in front of him. Still, it caught him off guard when he expected it to do something impressive, allowing Alan to land another thunderous combination of blows to his opponent's abdomen and head.

I heard Halldora fire again, but there was no accompanying cry of pain.

Then Alan did something I'd have to try, he backed up and touched his leg to a withered old stump. I saw the flickers of black energy, then the stump decayed a bit. He reached down and pulled out two stakes. He threw them overhand at the Sandman, reached down and grabbed two more, throwing them while the agent was still deflecting the first ones. He then barreled into the Sandman who was trying to deflect the second barrage, tackling him to the ground. He got his strong hands on the agent's face, but instead of squeezing, he sent black energy down his arms into the agent's head. The Sandman screamed. Assuming Alan was okay for the moment, I looked up.

The headset agent Halldora had been firing at had his back to me. I rushed over to help. I launched another kick, this time at the new Sandman, and connected solidly with the backs of his legs. He grunted as his legs buckled, but did not deposit him on the ground.

I tried to grab his head and emulate Alan, but only managed to get my fingers in front of his eyes. Not hesitating, I released some dream energy in a bright, blinding flash. He cursed and pulled his hands up. I nodded to Halldora and stepped away.

She maneuvered around the car and shot his leg. My stomach clenched. I saw flashes of my father getting shot, and felt a little light headed. I backpedaled away from the bright red spray of blood gushing out of the man's leg.

Coming around the back of the SUV, I was taking deep gulps of air. The back door flew open, and a female agent sprang out with a weird gun in her hand. This fourth agent was well-trained. In less than the amount of time it took for my brain to register that there was danger, she had the gun aimed at me and she fired. I felt a needle prick, and saw a little red feather sticking out of my pectoral muscle.

"Shit... HALLDORA?" I called like an idiot.

I saw her head snap up. She couldn't see the agent, but I know she couldn't miss the tranquilizer dart.

"Agent," I pointed at her and shouted. She fired again, and another dart penetrated my chest. I saw Halldora crouch into a ready stance and sneak around the other way, out of my sight.

I tried to back up so she'd wouldn't be facing the direction Halldora would come from. The world spun a bit, and my head drooped. My legs were getting weak, I was losing feeling in them.

The fourth agent grabbed me and man-handled me toward the back of the SUV. I still had some fight in me, and I didn't make it easy for her.

"Bruadair warned me your mommie was a fighter, but you're a pathetic sissy." That voice. Lourdes! She must have misunderstood my shocked expression. "That's right, I read the intel on you," she explained.

"Bruadair's got 'n agenda," was I slurring? "He's usin' you."

"Save it, homo."

My vision was tunneling really fast. The dumb voice in my head pointed out that two darts had probably been over-kill. Overkill. Killing was bad. As Lourdes was pushing me headfirst into the back of their vehicle, I heard Halldora say something brutal and nasty. It was followed by her gun firing, and then Lourdes' body hitting the dirt behind me.

My feet were still on the ground, but I was bent at the waist pitched face forward into their truck. I didn't have the strength to do a damned thing about it. From where I was, I could only hear the fight and smell the weird car-fabric smell in the back of the SUV. Alan was still going strong. I could hear the metallic noises of Atli's knife being deflected by something. The most silent was Tyler. I couldn't tell what he was doing. He better not be hurt because of me.

I was fading quickly.

The fight raged on, and I saw Aunt Margaret's face, beehive and all, coming at me out of the tunneling mist, "Don't you try busting me out of The Farm, kid. It ain't effing worth it. Tell Halldora I said to keep you hidden."

I tried to speak to her, but I couldn't.

"If you get the chance, kid, come to the tree beside my dream sea. You know the one. Left some stuff there for you."

I wanted so badly to let her know we were coming to save her. That we'd free her and she could go back to traveling the world and collecting tourist mementos. But my mouth was no longer working. I heard Alan snarl, and call someone a dick. I don't know why it was funny. What was I doing? Oh, Aunt Margaret! I called to her, but she had faded away. Maybe I was the one fading away? Maybe the SUV was fading away?

I don't effing remember.

Chapter Twenty-One
1972 – The Farm

Her voice was really faint, "Remember." She was looking at her reflection in the side of a surgical bowl on a table near her head.

"What'd you say?" someone in scrubs with a full facemask asked angrily.

She wasn't faint, she was pretending to be out of it.

"Don't speak to the subjects," said a disembodied voice through a speaker. The proceedings were under observation. That was also good to know.

The medic at the bed grabbed and secured her elbow painfully, holding her still. Her wrist was bound, and she didn't have a lot of room to move. He stabbed a needle into her arm, not caring about comfort. He drew out the blood he needed, then yanked the needle out. He pushed the side-table with the silver bowl away. There was a buzzing, and we heard the medic open a door and the cart was wheeled out. The door slammed shut.

My mother was strapped to a flat hospital bed, there were tight leather restraints on her wrists and ankles. The room was a bizarre orange pink, and very brightly lit. I could feel extra weight on her bladder, and realized she was several months into the pregnancy. My pregnancy.

For a brief second I felt like someone walked over my …
cradle? I don't think there's any language for dealing with the
messed-up nature of this particular situation.

Some time passed, and the buzzing sounded again. Another person in scrubs and a mask wheeled a new side-table
in. I smelled nasty, organic hot mush. The attendant brushed
up against my mother's hand at the edge of the bed, and I
felt a brief contact of skin-to-skin. In a situation where they
weren't supposed to talk to the subjects, that should have
been disallowed as well. A warm and melodious voice filled
my mother's thoughts, "Do not react. If I am caught, I will
have big trouble on my hands." A sense of calm filled my
mother.

It was Anoushka.

"Morpheus plans to take your baby to Tartarus when it's
born, but not you. He is afraid you have a way to tell people
where it might be. So he will keep you here. Even I am not
supposed to know where the new Tartarus is. What a bunch
of bureaucratic nonsense. I saw most of the purchase orders
for the non-medical equipment," Anoushka's voice continued
in my mother's head. "Did they think I wouldn't wonder why
so much medical equipment was shipping to Illinois?"

"I have much to tell you, and only the amount of time it
takes me to feed you." She put a spoonful of the hot mash
into my mother's mouth. It tasted like it smelled. Some
nutritionist had pureed all of the vegetables they deemed
necessary for health, and mixed them into this paste with
no spices. Then they heated it for good measure. It was like
eating warm compost. No wonder babies spit this crap out.

Anoushka was trying to be gentle. "First is this gruel.

Bruadair now makes jokes that Morpheus is using a soporific to sedate Agent Sopora. As usual, he is as witty as a dog's ass. When nobody was looking, I concocted a buffer medication for you and put it into tonight's meal. You should no longer be stupefied day and night, though it is in your best interest to act like you are." She offered another half-spoonful. "My blend will make you highly resistant to the standard sedatives they have on hand. So this probably tastes worse than usual, but it is worth it." She lifted another spoonful. My mother ate slowly. "If they bring in completely new drugs, I will need some time to come up with another antidote."

She offered another bite, but wasn't forcing it down. My mother saw the wisdom in eating it, though, so her senses were once again assaulted by the horrid flavor.

"Second, your old friend reached out to me one day while I was having coffee and a scone." Anoushka knew about Aunt Margaret. I had to add her to my list of people to find. "I understand to some degree what's at stake now." Her thoughts continued to radiate calm. I wondered if she was doing it on purpose so my mother's heart rate wouldn't jump in case they were monitoring her vitals. "I am on your side, and started making calls from a secure location. Your new man's friends have been alerted. Hopefully his friends will put his family in contact with me. When that happens, I should be able to direct them here."

"Third, I will try to help you when and how I can. But I am no good to you if I too am locked up. I may send help in the strangest of ways, so be alert and be vigilant."

My mother nodded imperceptibly, and accepted another bite.

"Which brings me to my final point. Growing up, our

people in my homeland had a fable. It would seem that at the heart of the fable is something you might be able to use. However, I offer a word of caution – none who tried have ever survived. I only mention this because you seem to excel at the impossible."

"This tale says there was once a dreamer. She was prisoner to a demon of chaos and destruction who shackled her every day and sent her out to do its errands. The dreamer longed for a day when her body could leave the physical world. A day when nothing would prevent her from living wholly in the world of dreams where the demon could no longer hurt her. Whenever she was out to do its errands, she would seek out other Wise Dreamers. She could never talk to them for very long, for the demon did not understand time the same way we do. It would eventually wonder where she'd gone. When time permitted, she would say to the others, "Oh Wise Dreamer, I wish to enter the Dreamworld with my body as well as my spirit."

"The Wise Dreamers would laugh, or cry, or raise their fists at her. One by one, they all told her basically the same thing, 'Child, nobody can take their body into the dream. It is not done.' But the demon kept hurting her, so still she searched and still she asked."

"For you see she believed in her heart that it could be done, and for us to believe in something is a very, very powerful thing."

"So she continued seeking. Eventually there were no more Wise Dreamers to ask, but she did not give up. She asked the sky, and the sun and the moon. She asked the trees and the rivers. No matter who or what she asked, none had an answer for her."

Anoushka offered another spoonful.

Her voice took on an almost whispering quality. "Do you know what she did?"

I sensed a brief negative reply, and realized I had not been hearing my mother's side of this mind-to-mind conversation.

"She started exploring her inner dream sea for answers," Anoushka answered. "When the islands had no answers, she flew through the barrier of the sky. Up in the dream heavens she met a many-armed god, and he took pity on her. 'I know what you seek, Dreamer' he said to her. 'I am pledged to destroy demons. I will tell you what you seek, but in return you must help me slay your captor.' She agreed happily. He began teaching her how to turn herself into the gateway to dreams."

I sensed some hope in my mother's heart.

"Easy, my friend," Anoushka cautioned. "This tale does not have a happy ending. It only serves to warn you. When the dreamer thought she was ready, the god came to collect his promise. 'You agreed to aid me, now is the time.' But the Dreamer wasn't willing to be risk being hurt by her tormentor any longer. The many-armed god called for her to honor her promise, but she slunk away.

Alone without her help, the god fought the demon as best he was able, but he could not kill it without her. Angrily, he ceded the fight to the demon."

"The god found the dreamer's trail, and stalked after her. He found her in meditation with a sliver of the dream gateway open through her chakras. When she saw the angry god coming for her, she tried to step through herself into the realm of dreams. He narrowly caught her by her silvery cord and ripped it away, making her scream spiritually as well as physically. To this day, none have ever stepped bodily into the dream realms. They say that still the angry god waits on the threshold for us when we try."

Anoushka was uneasy. She covered her nervousness by delivering another bite of food. "The dreamer did everything she thought was right. Only when she stepped through her own portal did she realize her error. You see, she was stepping through herself without a tether. The god had ripped away the cord that binds her mind to her soul to her body. She died in her own maelstrom to the shouts of a betrayed god."

Anoushka delivered the final bite of compost mash.

"Still, I think there is something in the fable that can help you. And maybe there is one last thing I can do for you."

I felt dream energy pour out of Anoushka and into my mother where their skin touched. I had no idea how much anyone could hold, but she felt really full. "Use it wisely, I don't know when I'll be able to sneak back here with more."

I could not hear any replies my mother thought back to her.

The dream faded a bit. The pink and orange lights were dim. I sensed my mother's relaxation techniques. I hadn't realized how badly she'd been drugged until I experienced the absence of the drugs. Clarity is remarkable when you're not used to it.

Quickly entering her own inner sea, she flew up through the sky and crossed over into Aunt Margaret's inner realm. I paid a lot of extra attention to how she found it. I worried I'd have to find it on my own very soon.

When my mother landed on the familiar beach, the younger Aunt Margaret was waiting under the tree.

She pulled my mother into a big hug. "You just say the

word, Jan," Margaret began angrily, "and I'll come in there and turn their heads inside out."

My mother laughed in spite of herself. "I believe you would, but things have changed, Aunt Margaret. He threw out all the old rules of engagement. Morpheus is using snipers at a distance. He knows we're strong up close, and he's using that against us. Plus I don't know exactly where Tartarus is yet, just that it's in Illinois. Anoushka does, and she'd tell you. Thank you for sending her."

"Can you tell me what happened?" This was the first time I heard Aunt Margaret sound genuinely scared.

My mother told her everything since the last visit I had seen between them. Aunt Margaret sat and listened to it all silently, not interrupting at all. She smiled when she heard Gestur's name.

When my mother stopped, Aunt Margaret shook her head. "I don't want you to try to create a dream door. I've heard such nonsense as well. Anoushka is right, you'll die."

"I'm still thinking through what her tether comment could mean, but I promise I'll share any insight with you before I try anything. But even death would be preferable to being Morpheus' personal breeding experiment."

"No, Jan. Do not die! Be strong, and we can get you out. You have to be strong for you and for that little baby."

"That's the other thing, Aunt Margaret. I don't want you to tell anyone you ever knew me. Not even to other Outré who have always been friendly. If Morpheus finds out I have a blood relative out there, you'll be on a table next to me."

"We'd be together…"

"No! That is a fate worse than death. Besides, IF I am going to escape, I'm going to be weak and I'll need you on the outside and at full strength. At the very least I need you to set up a way for me to disappear… and to do that, you're going to have to remain completely anonymous. Please?"

Aunt Margaret didn't like it, but she also didn't say no. Though she looked far from convinced.

"Promise me, Jan, that you'll come here every night you are able to slip away. Even if only for a minute."

"I will, I'll be here every night I have the strength to enter my dreams."

"That's my girl."

They shared another strong hug.

The dream faded again.

LATER ON THE FARM

She was back in her body on the table. Her stomach felt larger. Morpheus was in the room, and he looked like hell. His face was crumpled and blotchy, and the iris of one eye was a dead white. He leaned heavily on a cane. The worst was his neck, it looked as though the skin leading down to his chest was dying.

With him were two doctors. They were all shouting.

"What do you mean, you can't figure out how she hides her damned aura?" Morpheus was livid. "What am I paying you to do?"

"Sir," one of the doctors tried justifying, "You know we still know very little about any Outré abilities themselves. We've only just begun to understand what makes us different at a cellular level." He sounded like a weaseling dipshit.

"Then work HARDER. I expect results!"

"The most difficult part, sir, is that her aura seems permanently hidden. We've never had a chance to witness the transition."

I realized my mother was sitting there with a drugged look on her face. I thought for sure she was going to fake-drool any second, but she kept that in check and just listened.

Morpheus, full of anger and menace, limped over. He put his hand on her cheek. I marveled at her ability to not flinch and pull away. He tried to work his way into her mind, but she was ready for him. Rather than throw up a wall, which he would have just battered away at, she shifted and undulated her aura so he was always carried along a current and then deposited a little ways away. When he tried punching his mind in hard, she allowed her defenses to give like a rubber sheet, and then redirect his energy off to one metaphysical side or the other.

Again and again he tried to batter away at her psyche, but she had the stamina to redirect him and ride it out. Finally his weakened body betrayed him, and he pulled away in a coughing fit. He was so angry his aura visibly seethed. "You," he pointed to Tweedledipshit, "and you," he motioned to the other, "come over here and help me slip past her defenses."

They came over dutifully and laid their hands on her bare arms. In her mind I felt them coming. They were clumsier than Morpheus. It was evident he wanted them to be the brute force distractions so he could slip in on the sly. The doctors came at her head on from different directions. She bounced them around and redirected their efforts with ease. She spent most of her energy watching Morpheus and just toyed with the doctors absently.

I watched as she lay a funnel or crevasse for Morpheus to find. He'd dive in thinking he had successfully found a way in, and she'd use his momentum to direct him around so he would collide astrally with one of his doctors. This went on frustratingly for a while before the doctors admitted defeat and pulled out, followed by Morpheus.

"There, do you see? Her mind's autonomic defenses are incredible."

"Yes, they are," the other doctor said keenly. "You know, we could learn a lot from her just trying to get in like this." He snapped his finger right in front of her nose. She didn't flinch, but gave a few delayed blinks. "She's still so drugged she barely knows we're here, yet her mind defends against intrusion. She's really remarkable."

Morpheus was so drained he looked like he was on the verge of falling over. He sighed angrily and leaned heavily on his cane to reach the door. "I want you to figure it out. Figure out how she does it and submit a full report, and I want it sooner rather than later." He was buzzed out of the room.

The doctors conferred with each other for a moment, and then decided to try again. They approached from opposite sides of the bed, as though that would confuse her. After what I had witnessed her do with Morpheus they didn't stand a chance.

As I expected, she treated them to the same channels and shuffling around she'd given Morpheus. She would show them something they might expect to see, like a weakness or a hole, and when they came in for it, she'd redirect them. She only ran them into each other when it was obvious they'd blundered into the same trap together. Too much, or too regularly, and it'd look like she was perfectly coherent.

At one point during the assault, I felt something a little different. It was so minor and weak, I almost didn't believe it was there. Very imperceptibly, she was siphoning energy off of them. She was just taking tiny amounts, like the thick fabric of a sweater capturing tiny droplets of moisture on a humid day. She was only taking the excess energy from the little eddies caused when their auras moved quickly or slid along her psyche's barrier. It was damned brilliant. Had she been even remotely obvious, they'd have been on to her. Instead, she merely harvested fractions of the imperceptible wasted energy.

Doctors Tweedledipshit and Tweedledumbass tried for a good long time. I admired her extreme patience and undetectable touches. I couldn't help but wonder again what her purpose was for showing me. Did she just want me to know what my parents had gone through? Did she want to scare me into staying as far away from the Sandmen as possible? Was I to pick up the mission where she had failed? Did she think I'd ever be as good as her? If so, I had a long way to go.

The doctors obviously wanted to impress Morpheus with something to show for the day's work. Yet, they could not match my mother's staying power. By the time they admitted defeat, they were really low on energy and my mother's store was unsurprisingly topped off again.

"The subject's protections are utterly remarkable, and still completely intact," Dr. Tweedledumbass was saying into a blocky recorder's microphone. From the corner of my mother's eye I could see the purple bruising that had formed under his eyes. He'd been trying really hard, and it had taken a toll on his body. "Her aura senses any incoming contact and redirects the energy in a way reminiscent of Eastern martial arts. Note: verify subject's combat training with Section Chief Morpheus. Note: subject's ability to hide her aura may in fact be the ability to redirect visual cues."

Meanwhile, Dr. Tweedledipshit had grabbed my mother's arm. I couldn't see him, but a moment later I felt the inflation of a blood pressure cuff. "Vitals are on the high end of acceptable for sedation level," he shouted across the cell to the recorder. "Subconscious defense obviously causes changes in biophysical and biochemical states of rest."

The doctors cleaned up the tools and continued chattering into the recorder. "Tomorrow will begin coordinated attacks into the subject's defenses. Note: invite a third and fourth specialist. The confusion theory should work if we have a large enough number trying to get through." I was already getting tired of Tweedledumbass's notes and wished he'd go away.

They only mumbled to one another for a few minutes longer, and finally had everything on the wheeling side-table. They were buzzed out, and I thought we'd have a few moments of quiet time. Instead, I heard a voice that made my mother's skin crawl.

"So, the golden child has been put in a cage?" It was Agent Bruadair. My instinct was to jump up and beat the guy's head in with his own smugness, but my mother barely moved.

He walked around so he could sit in her field of vision. "Let me guess what you learned from the Butcher of Nairobi. You dug too deep and learned about my true missions for Morpheus. Ah... Janet. Dear, sweet, wrong-place-wrong-time Janet. If only you'd told me who you were chasing down like I'd asked. I could have saved you so much of this heartache. You'd still be in the field on your high profile assignments, attracting all the attention from the Outré folk while I go about my business quietly in the background. Morpheus was careless when he assigned you. He had to know you'd find out. He..."

Bruadair paused. A look of paranoid understanding crept over his face. "Dammit. Morpheus sent you on purpose, didn't he?" The whiny hysteria in his voice was rising. "Didn't he?? Tell me!" He grabbed my mother's shoulder and shook her hard. To her credit, she stayed limp, "You have to tell me. JANET! DID MORPHEUS SEND YOU TO SPY ON ME?"

My mother didn't even groan in a drugged stupor. I assumed she was trying to let him undo himself through his own deep paranoia. It was working. He looked like he was feverishly trying to mentally analyze all recent interaction he'd had with Morpheus. Disgusted, he quit shaking her and just stared.

"You're worthless now," he said icily. "I'd kill you myself for the trouble you've caused me, but I had to log my visit and I'm not going to be the one who took away Morpheus' new project. Mark my words. As soon as he's done with you, I'm coming back to kill you."

He didn't leave right away. He just sat there, staring at her. Until this point, I was glad she'd decided to play up the glazed-eyes-empty-stare. Only now I didn't want to see what she was seeing. Some internal war was playing across Bruadair's face. It was ugly and obviously touched on something very deep. Twice he moved, as though he was about to do something, and then stopped himself. Both times he looked up behind my mother toward something on the wall. Both times were menacing as hell.

With one last snort, he stood and strode away. He practically ripped the door off the hinges when it was buzzed, and as his footsteps receded down the hallway I heard the word, "asshole" barely escape my mother's unmoving lips.

Chapter Twenty-Two
2012 – The Farm

My chest really hurt. It felt like I'd smashed it into a rocky outcropping during a fall off a really tall cliff. I still felt a bit of vertigo like I was falling. I was on my back in a big SUV's cargo area. Halldora and Atli were above me, examining something. Atli had an empty syringe in his hand.

"I told you that was the antidote," he told Halldora quietly.

Her mouth was a grim line, "The specter of death around him has faded." Her eyes were smoldering hatred.

"What hit me?" I tried to sit up and couldn't marshal the strength.

"Some kind of tranquilizer. Atli assumed..."

"Correctly," he interjected.

Halldora raised her voice to shut him up, "... correctly assumed that the other syringe in the shooter's gun case was the antidote. Nothing was labeled."

"Thank you. Both. How is everyone?"

Halldora glared at me. Atli filled me in, "Tyler took a nasty blow to the head, but he'll live. Alan put a field bandage on the gash for him, so it's not causing any current trouble. I have already bandaged my knife wound. The rest of us are okay. Alan appropriated an earpiece, but there's been nothing transmitted yet. We've probably only got a few minutes before they demand a status update. We're going to steal their SUV and get the hell out of here. We just wanted to make sure you were alive first."

"I'm alive, but we can't leave. They're holding Aunt Margaret up the road at The Farm. She appeared to me while I was out. They're probably preparing to move her to Tartarus. We have to press our advantage now while security is light and they're not expecting us."

The air around Halldora chilled as she laid into me, "Press our advantage? Do you think this is a movie? And what do you know about anything? You've been tranqued and can't even stand. My little brother's been cracked upside the head AND has a car accident to call in..."

Alan approached while she was talking and tried to diffuse the rant, "I say we go after Margaret. Slumberscythe junior here may be useless in a fight," he winked at me, "but if we need to contact Margaret it sounds like we can knock him out and send him into dreamland with a message. Think of him as a really big, narcoleptic cell phone."

In a lighter situation, that would have made me laugh out loud. Instead, I latched onto his enthusiasm trying to appeal to Halldora's reason, "And we have their SUV. And I've seen how my mother got into the place. And I've seen where agents parked."

"Your fucking stone age information nearly got us killed! For all I know you're working with them to bring us in."

Atli let his composure slip for the first time today, "Your fight is with me, not him. His intel's the best we've ever had. Plus, Gestur would want us to free Margaret."

"You would take his side." Halldora stomped off a few steps

and stared down the road. I moved to sit up, but Alan motioned me to stay put.

Halldora must have reached her decision. "Margaret saved Tyler and me from the Sandmen years ago. We owe her." She turned and glared at me, "I don't give a fuck anymore if they grab you. We'll get Margaret out. Since she cares for you, we'll try to get you out. If you get shot, don't disappoint her by bleeding to death. I have no bandages for you. Alan, hide Tyler's car and keep that earpiece in your ear. Let me know if there's any chatter at all. Atli, get the fuck out of my sight and check on Tyler. If he's not ready, hide him in his car. I'll get James ready. Hurry."

Everyone jumped to action. I noted that everyone deferred to Halldora once she started giving orders. I tried to get up, but Halldora pushed me back down. "Seriously, don't piss me off. Don't move until I'm convinced you're helping us." That's when I noticed the handgun in her hand. She wasn't pointing it at me… yet.

"You heard what Lourdes said about me, didn't you."

Halldora glared at me, daring me to continue.

"Look, I don't know what's changed. Everything is so damned confusing right now. Help me get Margaret out of there, and I'll go away with her so you never have to see me again."

"That will be Margaret's call," she said coldly.

Not having much else to do, I turned on my aura sight. I saw something flare around her eyes as she looked at me. Holy crap, I was seeing her use some sort of sensory power.

"You're using Death Sight on me!"

She frowned, "Being a drama queen will get you shot right now."

"But you are, aren't you?"

She clipped each word angrily as she answered, "Yes. But it's not like some on/off superpower. It's not like that."

"Fine. You can give me the full lesson later. But if I see something similar in there, I need to know what I'm seeing."

"Fine. Now get away from me until we're ready to move."

"Thanks." I sat up to a sudden wave of light nausea. It passed quickly enough, so I tested my legs. By the time I was leaning up against the tailgate of the SUV, Atli was bringing Tyler to us. There was a livid red bruise poking out from under a bandage on the side of Tyler's face, and I've no doubt it extended under his hairline and down his shirt. He was limping too, but mostly able to walk without Atli's help. "Let's give'em hell," was all Tyler said. He then walked past us and went to the driver's door. I heard him rummage around, then call back, "We need to check pockets for keys."

"You do it," Halldora ordered Atli.

Atli just nodded back, and started going through the pockets of the dead Sandmen. I pushed away from the SUV and moved to help him. Lourdes had been shot twice. No amount of television could have prepared me for the amount of blood on her clothes and the ground around her. I had a stupid moment where my brain conjured up some factoid about there being ten liters of blood in a body. Ten liters spreads far when it's out of the body. Then, on the side of the road, right next to where people were recently dead, I started to get tunnel vision.

Initially I thought I was going to pass out, and I probably would have if I'd not seen the black tendrils. Inky black energy seeping away from the corpses as the individual bodily cells died one at a time. Neural energy may have ceased, but the actual living tissue took a bit longer to die... and my Reaper side could see it. I was fascinated and repulsed. I knew I should help the others, that time was of the essence, but I couldn't force myself to move. Atli was stepping over and around the black tendrils, confirming my suspicion that he was aware of them.

Then I noticed Atli trailing his hands in the energy, collecting it as my mother had collected dream energy. Death energy didn't move like dream energy. Where dream motes behaved like weightless particles of colored light, death energy was reminiscent of black smoke seeking the lowest point. It was inky and dense compared to the bright lens flares of dream energy. I'd spent all of my dream energy trying to blind these Sandmen, so I wasn't currently charged. Knowing that there would likely be more fighting, I tentatively reached into a black tendril like Atli had.

I immediately snapped my hand back. It was cold, far colder than I would have guessed in even my most poetic moments. Steeling myself, I reached out again. Atli noticed what I was doing, and he showed me how he played with it, almost as if teasing it into accepting him. I focused on trying the same.

He found the keys and motioned me over. "They call us Reapers, but this is the only reaping we usually do. Collect this energy. You will be able to use it to add crude strength to your armor and attacks. In time, you may develop finesse and special tricks. But even today, the crude abilities could save your life."

His voice was calming and contemplative. I hoped he would consider being my mentor since it appeared Halldora was done with me.

I trailed my hand in and out of the black tendril as Atli watched. I tried to imagine the dark energy coming into me. Within a few seconds my bones started feeling cold.

Atli must have sensed my success. "It feels like cold death filling in the empty spaces in your living body, yes?"

I nodded. "I feel like it's freezing my bones."

"That's good!" He looked encouraging. "Collect as much as you can. I'm going to help Alan hide that car so we can move. We've spent too much time here already." With that, he moved away and left me to my tendril. I toyed with the deathly energy, pushing it around and pulling it in. I finally concluded it was like the negative of fire. If you hold your hands very close to crackling flames, you can sometimes feel the licks of the flames. Well, either that or your imagination supplies the tactile illusion to go with what your eyes see. In this case, the energy felt the same, but it was a chilly life-taking instead of a warm life-giving. Right. If dream energy was very much like thought photons, death energy would be like negative fire. I could work with that.

Suddenly it made sense that I could store and use them both. After all my heritage was tied to both, and apparently my blood didn't exclude the use of either.

I was just getting the hang of reaping when Tyler started the engine and Halldora called, "Everyone in, let's go."

I stood, got used to moving with the cold in my bones, and took my seat in the SUV.

Halldora turned to face me, "I don't care what-the-fuck happens in there. I don't care what-the-fuck you think you know. You will follow my orders. Understood?"

I nodded.

"Good. My goal is to get everyone out alive. If you think

you know something, past or present, you fucking tell me and I'll make a decision. Stay the fuck behind Alan at all times. His armor's the best, and he's the most used to protecting people. Tyler, you're wounded..."

"Not that badly."

"Tough, still wounded. I also want you to hang back. No arguments."

"Okay," he said meekly.

Having cleared that up, she turned back to me, "What do we know?"

I ordered my thoughts. "Ok. When I was here earlier, I noticed an eyebeam across what looks like the abandoned front gate. The vehicle may have something used to disarm it or allow us to pass without tripping an alarm. There's a similar eyebeam shooting out from under the front porch on the main house. However, I don't think we'll need to go that way. When my mother arrived back in her day, she drove into the barn. The floor would lower her car down to an underground garage."

Tyler immediately started searching, and found the row of buttons along the bottom of the rearview mirror's plastic housing. "I wish these were labelled," he muttered. "Halldora, can you peek into their near past and see if the agents used them for anything?"

"Not easily, no."

Tyler shrugged, which appeared to needle her. She reached her hand up to the mirror, closed her eyes and slowed her breathing. A couple minutes of scenery went by as we approached the gate. "Starting on the left, they open and close the barn's main door, lower and raise the floor, defrost the mirror, and the last one isn't used enough for me to get a good read on it."

"So we bust on through the front gate?"

"The gate'll be open," I supplied. "Just has an eyebeam."

"Righto, we'll bust through the eyebeam then!"

Halldora didn't look like she liked the option, but she didn't voice an objection.

The Farm looked as I remembered it, old and abandoned. We drove through the gate at a reasonable speed. Everyone but Tyler looked at Alan who was listening to his appropriated earpiece intently. After a few seconds he shrugged, "Nothing."

Tyler guided us to the barn. The main door was wide open. Given the generally clean nature of the interior, I guessed the door was normally closed, but had been left it open by Sandmen in hurry to catch me at the Roe. Tyler pushed the button to close the doors. Once they were shut, he pushed the next button to lower the floor. The car lift was smooth and swift, and the sublevel clean and shiny. I pointed to the left, "The agents used to park their personal vehicles over there. So company vehicles..." sure enough. To the right was another black SUV. "That hallway on the right used to lead to the section chief's office."

"Armor up," Halldora commanded, "And keep your faces hidden."

Everyone else in the car tapped into the world's residual death energy to create their personal armor. Atli's looked like something a Viking ranger would wear, black metal pads over black leather areas, lined with black furs. A black, horned helmet covered his face. By contrast, Alan's was new and sleek, almost space age. Halldora and Tyler both had supple armor, almost as if they were wearing monk-style tied leggings and shirts. I knew I didn't have time for finesse, so I just pulled my aura in tight and then released enough death energy to coalesce around me in a cloudy vapor.

"Dude," Tyler commented quietly, "You look like a vampire becoming mist. So cool."

Halldora made a hissing noise, "No more speaking unless necessary. Everyone ready?"

Everyone nodded. At a signal from Halldora, we exited the SUV.

Atli took point, followed by Halldora, then Alan, then Tyler and I brought up the rear. Atli moved to the hallway I'd indicated, the rest of us in tow.

We met with no resistance. Halldora motioned to Alan's earpiece, but he shook his head. I couldn't see her face, but her body language was tense. She turned back to the hall and hustled after Atli.

Passing under the yard, we made it to the main house. There was a sealed door with a strange multicolored palm plate blocking our passage.

Halldora motioned me forward, "Expect a lot of these, it most likely senses for dream energy. Put your palm on the plate."

"But I'm all out."

"It won't matter."

Trusting her, I mentally pulled back the death energy and put my palm on the plate. I felt a tingle, and the door shooshed open. I followed as they moved through quickly. The hallways remained empty as we made our way deeper in. I tried to remember the path my mother used when I saw her here. I haltingly guided the others through the complex quietly pointing the direction I believed we should go.

Remembering I had only seen a handful of auras down here, and doing a quick count of how many agents had come after us, I realized we might be quite alone down here. I tried to engage my aura sight and look around for Sandmen. After several attempts, I gave up. It was significantly more difficult to do while moving and leading people through someone else's memory of corridors.

Alan huffed. "They're asking for a status update."

Which meant there was someone here. We looked to Halldora. "I don't know," she admitted. "Try to give an agent-like response."

Alan reached to his ear and tabbed the earpiece, "Negative. Subject not in custody."

He listed for a moment, then, "Affirmative." Tabbing off the earpiece he listened a second to make sure he wasn't transmitting. Then he tilted his head, "They've ordered us to return to The Farm." I heard a smile in his voice.

"That gives us a few moments more until we're seen," Halldora said.

Tyler shook his head confused, "The eyebeam? The garage? Shouldn't they know we are back?"

"There were only a few auras here when I scanned it before meeting Halldora. They're probably operating on a skeleton crew," I offered quietly.

"Don't get complacent," was the only warning Halldora offered.

We moved past the abandoned office desks, remnants of an era before the office cubicle. The sector chief's door was closed, but it looked like the lights were off. I motioned to the next long hall, the one that lead to the break room where my mother and Bruadair had their meeting, and the area where

Anoushka had had her equipment warehouse. If my mental map of the grounds was accurate, beyond that would be the point farthest from the sector chief's office, a logical place to detain prisoners. An escapee would have the farthest to travel to reach both the leadership and vehicles.

We had to cover that distance as well.

The break room was empty. As we moved past it my mother's memory of the room came back to me. The door to the equipment and clothing warehouse had a window in it, so I peeked in. The dim security light was enough for me to see that most of the room was completely empty. If the abandoned corridors hadn't been indicative, the bare hangers let me know that primary operations had moved on.

After another palm plate, we entered the final long corridor. Voices echoed from the far end. As a group we paused, checked our various armor and readiness. In my case, I made sure my aura was pulled in tight. Halldora and Atli motioned us to stay back while they crept forward.

They were incredibly silent, like two black shadows.

I don't know who noticed whom first. I just know that the voices at the end of the hall stopped at the same time I saw Halldora duck back. Instantly, Alan drew a handgun and moved forward and I had a moment of despair. I did not want people to die. I wanted this to be like the movies where the heroes could get in and out without bloodshed-getting nothing more than a few bruises for story tension. But this wasn't the movies. It was a crazy shadow life that I'd had no clue even existed a month ago.

Halldora dropped to the ground. There had been no shot, but Atli and Alan responded immediately by jumping into the room. Tyler and I rushed to Halldora, checking her for injuries. We didn't find any. She was sound asleep.

"Bruadair," I said out loud.

Tyler continued his check on Halldora but asked, "huh?"

"Agent Bruadair worked with my mother. He could put people to sleep."

"That would have been handy to know," he pulled his sister to the side of the corridor.

"He's also Morpheus' primary agent, though his missions are usually not recorded."

Atli and Alan had gone into the room, and we heard the fighting begin. "Stay with her," I said. "I'm going to try to help."

"You shouldn't. We're supposed to stay back and let them handle it."

"I know, but since our fearless leader went down, I at least want to see well enough to know if we have to grab her and run."

He nodded uncertainly, so I moved forward. They were fighting in a small area with a guard station and waiting chairs. An imposing door on the far side looked an awful lot like the kind of door used keep prisoners contained.

Atli wielded a knife in each hand, keeping two agents engaged at the guard's desk. They didn't look like they'd been ready for a fight. One still wore an operator's headset and microphone. Atli must have knocked the guard's gun away, because it lay on the floor off to his side. Alan and Bruadair were squaring off in the center of the room. If Bruadair had tried to put Alan to sleep, it hadn't worked so far.

I momentarily entertained the idea of crawling to the gun on the floor, but gave that up quickly. Even if I made it, I still didn't know if I could bring myself to kill with it. I started thinking through the things I thought I'd be able to do with death energy. Annoyingly, this hallway lacked handy, rotten tree stumps.

Screw it, time to be mundane. I darted around the corner, grabbed one of the waiting chairs, and underhand-lobbed it at Bruadair's back. It wasn't a stellar throw, but it knocked him way off balance. Alan's jab caught him under the jaw and knocked him backward over the chair.

I didn't have the chance to savor Bruadair's predicament. One of the agents on Atli peeled off and lunged at me. Someday I'll be athletic, but I wasn't ready for his attack and he grabbed my forearm. Instantly, my head flooded with images and noise, and I was taken aback by the wave of vertigo that came with it. I think my butt hit the floor. Then I'm pretty sure something landed on top of me and threw up.

I tried to shake away the visions.

When the phantasms cleared, I was lying on the floor. The guard was on top of me. One of Atli's knives was protruding from between his shoulder blades. He hadn't vomited on me, he had sprayed blood as he died. My vision tunneled again, and I felt the nausea return. Dammit, I'm not a fighter.

Through my haze I could see Atli and the other guard. Though Atli was down to a single knife, the lone guard didn't stand much of a chance. I could see the telltale flares of dream energy being directed at Atli, but they appeared to bounce harmlessly off his armor. After a few lunges, the second guard had a couple new knife holes in his chest and he fell to join his counterpart.

The guard's desk blocked my view of Alan's fight with Bruadair. Atli looked over to see that I was moving. When I nodded at him he leapt over the desk to help his friend. I couldn't just lie there, and tried to stand. My legs were shaky, but they were under my control. As my vision cleared, I stood up to see over the desk. The fight with Bruadair was largely at a stalemate. He had backed up to the prison door and was fending them off with powerful flashes of dream energy. I'm not sure what he was trying to do, but neither Alan nor Atli seemed willing to be hit by one. He had to be at least sixty years old, but the guy could fight.

As I stood, Bruadair locked eyes on me. "It's you," he said a bit incredulously.

I didn't feel like bowing or acknowledging him, but suddenly realized I might have a chance to make it look like the Reapers weren't doing this willingly. "Finish him off boys," I said sinisterly, "and your debt will be paid."

In hindsight, the effect of my statement was hilarious. Bruadair looked completely baffled, and Alan hesitated. Atli rolled with it, lunging under Bruadair's guard in the confusion. Seeing Atli's movement, Bruadair backpedaled. He grabbed the prison door and spun, dangerously turning his back for a split second. Atli's knife sheared through Bruadair sideways, but there was no resistance. No blood. No contact. The image of Bruadair melted, and the real Bruadair laughed. He'd been roughly a foot from the illusion he'd been projecting. He'd been close enough for a chair to hit him, but too far for a smaller knife blade. He slammed the prison door shut and we heard the lock click angrily. Bruadair's shadow retreated from the small, wire-reinforced window.

"Shit," Alan cursed. "Shit, shit, shit."

"He wasn't the target," Halldora said from behind me. "They were going to know what we did here whether or not any Sandmen got away from us. Focus. We need to find Margaret and get out before they can mobilize a response. Move people!"

I stepped back as they snapped into action. Tyler looted a guard's keys and moved to try the door. Atli cleaned his knives, then sheathed one and kept the other out and ready. Alan lifted his shirt to check a nasty bruise that was forming on his side. I started wiping blood off my face and arms. When I looked up, Halldora was glaring at me.

"What?"

"You were supposed to stay back, that's what."

"You were down and they needed help."

"My orders remain in effect, even if I fall. Do you have any idea..."

Atli cut her off, "His distractions were exceptionally helpful. Cut him some slack."

"We are not running this mission by committee," she snapped. She needed a second to calm down. "We'll discuss it later. Get that door open."

When the key alone didn't unlock the door, Tyler poked around the guard's desk. He found the predictable button on the underside, and buzzed us through. Bruadair was nowhere to be seen.

"Stay alert. If this is a prison, he didn't get out through a back way. Be ready for an ambush."

I cleared my throat. "Now is a good time to mention that some of the Sandmen involved in killing my father could do some sort of invisibility."

Each of them swore. Then Tyler said, "I got this."

Through my death sight I saw thin tendrils creep out from his armor in all directions. The farthest only went about twenty feet. When we started moving, I understood. Anything that moved through one of his tendrils vibrated it and he was instantly aware of the direction. I smiled at him.

We resumed our formation and crept forward. I let my senses fade from the real world, tapping into the newly familiar aura vision. "He's ahead on the right."

Alan whispered back, "How do you know that?"

"I can see his aura."

"You can see through this interference? Any other surprises? What about Margaret?"

I tried to understand what I was seeing that they weren't. The whole place resonated with dream energy, it was emanating from an area right behind Bruadair. "His is the only aura I can make out. He's right next to the source of the disturbance. If Margaret is here, she's hidden, maybe behind it or within it? I think I can filter it better than you because I'm a little more tuned to dream energy. Maybe?"

Everyone absorbed the information, checked their weapons, and glided silently ahead, taking the next right. Bruadair wasn't standing out in the hall, but the door next to the disturbance was cracked open. His aura, however, was on the other side of the corridor. Classic.

I tapped Halldora. When she looked, I pointed to the open door and shook my head. I then pointed to the closed door with his aura and mimed a fist clenching. She got it, and moved forward to warn Atli and Alan with similar gestures. They both nodded. Atli sidled over, and took a position next to the door out of sight of the viewing window. Alan waited for his nod, and then made a show of checking the open door. Instantly, the door behind him sprang open. I saw the shimmering bolt of dream energy hit Alan in the back. His armor deflected some of it, but the brutal force of it punched through to hit him directly. Alan slumped to the floor much like Halldora had. Atli spun knife-first into the room. Halldora jumped in right behind him.

Tyler shuffled forward to pull Alan out of the way. Looking up, I saw a shadow moving behind the viewing window of the room emanating the disturbance. I heard Halldora grunt, and Tyler twitched like he was going to step in to help. He was hurt worse than I was, and I stopped him. "Let me, she's already geared up to ream me out for disobeying." He just grimaced, but stayed with Alan.

I slid over just enough to peek into the room. A strange glowing energy membrane had encased Atli. He was trying to slice his way out of it, but the ephemeral material was just curving lightly against the blade. Halldora was squaring off alone against Bruadair. He must have clobbered her once because the side of her face was bright red.

"All out of chairs to throw?" he taunted me. "You're not half as quick on your feet as your mother."

Rage flared, and I charged into the room. Halldora yelled for me to get back, but I didn't listen. Bruadair smiled and launched a bolt of dream energy at me. I dodged instinctively, and only got out of the way because I could see it as clearly as he could. I completed my charge by ramming my fists into his stomach.

He bent a little, giving Halldora an opening. She took it, punching his jaw solidly. He spun towards her, treating her as the greater threat. I backed up.

Watching the fight between Bruadair and Halldora, I placed my palm on the sheath around Atli. It was solidified dream energy. The Reapers couldn't do a damned thing with it, but I could. I tried absorbing it into my hand. Much like the knife, it resisted me at first. I don't think I would have succeeded if Halldora hadn't been occupying the majority of Bruadair's attention. I applied more mental will, and the energy started flowing into my palm.

In less than a span of two punches, Atli was free and I had a supply of dream energy as well as death energy.

Knives out, Atli returned to the fray to help his ex-girl-friend. Once again it was obvious they had trained to fight together. They took up positions on either side of him and started harrying him. Atli thrust in with a knife, Bruadair deflected with a burst of dream energy. Halldora flung a dark bolt at him, and he knocked it aside with a sudden flare. Each motion brought them a step closer to me. Guessing Brua-dair's intent, I dodged out the door. He grabbed at me, but pulled back before he lost his fingers to a razor sharp blade. I didn't want the occupant of the other cell, I assumed it was Margaret, to become a hostage. So I stepped away from that door. Tyler was alternately trying to wake Alan and keep his eye on his sister's fight.

A duplicate of Bruadair peeled away from the original and squared off against Halldora and Atli. As I was shouting a warning, the real agent spun out into the hallway, slamming the door and trapping the Reapers in a cell together. Shit.

He turned to face me. Double-shit. The wily old agent squared off against the chunky new guy.

Tyler twitched, looking vaguely toward the Sandman. He obviously didn't see Bruadair who must have still been under his phantasmal invisibility. I pretended to look slightly past him down the hall, as though I was trying to focus on something. I must have been convincing because Bruadair smirked. "Blind as your mother," he sneered under his breath.

Giving no further warning he lunged forward with his hand charged to put me to sleep.

Something inside me snapped.

A lifetime of frustration at the world for abandoning me to utter loneliness supercharged my current fear at losing the family I'd just found. Anger pounded in my eardrums. This villain was stealing children. This killer had helped put my parents in the ground. Now this asshole was taking Margaret from me. I blasted all of that pent-up emotion forward into Bruadair. Dream energy laced with death energy arced forward carried by my cry of rage. There was nothing calculated about my attack, it was an emotional barrage of conflicting energies.

Hitting him a hair's breadth before he touched me, the dream energy I'd stolen from his membrane negated his own dream armor, leaving him wide open to death energy. My blast hit him the way my father's dying curse had hit Morpheus. The skin of Bruadair's face and neck decayed before my eyes. I felt his heartbeat stop. Bruadair's body betrayed him, aging rapidly under the onslaught. He collapsed at my feet. Black tendrils of death rose up and snaked down the hallway toward him.

I wanted him dead.

I didn't want to be a killer.

Not understanding how I was doing it, I tried to stave off the tendrils.

Tyler, wide-eyed with fear and confusion, saw me take on death's advances. "Keep him alive?"

"Yes," was all the breath I had for answering.

Instead of messing with the tendrils coming to claim Bruadair, Tyler pounded his fist down on the agent's chest.

I strained my willpower to keep the tendrils from making contact. Again Tyler pounded Bruadair's chest. A third time. I was losing inches to death's inevitable advance. The old man coughed.

The tendrils stopped pushing forward, but did not retreat.

I do not blame Tyler for not wanting to give Bruadair mouth-to-mouth. Instead he kept giving chest compressions until Bruadair's shallow breathing and faint heartbeat happened on their own. Slowly, the inky black tendrils sank back into the floor.

I stood over the man I had nearly killed. My heart was pounding in my ears, and sweat was cascading down my body worse than ever. I didn't feel like a hero... but I didn't feel like a murderer either. I felt empty.

I looked into the cell that was giving off the emanations. I didn't see the shadow that had been there earlier. "Give me the guard's keys."

Tyler looked to see what had my attention, and tossed them up to me. "Don't give my sis more reasons to yell at you."

"I won't. I think I found Margaret."

I had to try several keys, but finally found the one for the lock. Opening the door carefully, I poked my head in. Just as I whispered "Margaret, are you here?" a bedpan swung into full view.

Aunt Margaret couldn't stop her swing in time. She slammed me hard in the face with the metal dish, drenching me in warm, old-lady pee. As she realized who I was, she sputtered, "No, no, no, hon... you don't come into this room!"

I remember wanting to ask "Why not?", but failed to get it out before the energy of the room overwhelmed me.

CHAPTER TWENTY-THREE
1972 – THE FARM

I was looking into the side of the surgical bowl again. My mother had just barely mouthed, "Remember." Within a few seconds, the reason for her extra caution became obvious. The cell was filled with people. Doctors Tweedledipshit and Tweedledumbass were closest. Morpheus was there, as was a nurse. My mother's legs were up in a stirrup contraption, and her full abdomen was tight.

Oh hell no. I did not want to see my own birth. I felt myself instinctively retreating from the memory. Like she had before, my mother seemed to sense she was losing me. She said a little louder, "Please, remember."

"Remember what?" Tweedledumbass asked.

She looked to Morpheus and relaxed her mouth a bit so her speech would have a slight slur, "Remember what a good field agent I am. Please, don't do this."

Though months had to have passed, Morpheus still looked decrepit and broken. He glared at her coldly through his good eye. He then pointedly spoke to the doctor, "Do not address the subject again."

A wave of tightness and pain rolled over my mother's abdomen. For a moment she couldn't even breathe.

"Sir, the contractions are closer together."

"Then be sure you are ready. Remember my orders, doctor. And if you don't want her to turn your brain inside out and murder you with it, keep her drugged at all times."

They spent several more minutes ordering the harried nurse to monitor her pulse, prep the equipment, and administer another shot. When the nurse moved to insert the needle, I felt a brief release of my mother's dream energy. Out of the corner of her eye, I saw an illusory overlay of a hallucinatory arm a few inches from her real arm. Succumbing to the phantasm, the nurse professionally and methodically injected the drugs into the pillow. Waiting a few minutes to ensure her deception hadn't been detected, my mother slipped into the ocean on the border of her dreams. Young Aunt Margaret was here on her shore, waiting.

"It's almost time," my mother said.

Aunt Margaret nodded sadly. "I know you think you've figured this out, hon. But, are you really sure? Can't you convince them to keep you alive as breeding stock? It'd give you a chance to figure something out. Something that's not guaranteed to kill you."

My mother hugged her. "You know Bruadair is going to kill me as soon as the child is born. And I will not let my son live even one day in their lab."

"Don't do it, Janet. You're throwing away both your lives based on half a legend and a really well-told story. There has to be a better way."

I felt my mother's overwhelming sadness behind her determination. "There is no more time. My son is coming today. Can I count on you to do your part?"

Tears were forming in the corners of Aunt Margaret's heavily mascaraed eyes. "I will do everything in my power, and I will use every power at my disposal to help you both live through this."

"My son's life comes first, Auntie. Please, promise me."

She sobbed a little, but nodded. "I promise," she said faintly.

"Raise him well, and keep him hidden."

If Margaret replied, my mother never heard it. A contraction ripped her out of the dreamscape and back into her body with a wrench of pain. Her breath was coming in shorter gasps.

"It won't be long now," Tweedledipshit said knowingly. No shit, jackass. Even I could see that, and I work in Marketing.

Every sensory organ went into a strange overdrive. My mother could smell the doctor's cologne and hear the ticking of his wristwatch. The no-slip tip on Morpheus' cane made strange grinding rubber noises into the floor. The nurse had a healthy halo of dream energy. My mother could feel the current of slightly cooler air trickling from a grate in the ceiling.

It was time.

Television portrays labor kind of wrong. A sharp feeling like the soreness of a full-bodied workout was taking hold. Every muscle was pushing at once. Clenching against the pain, my mother breathed out deeply. She went into a lightly meditative state, similar in feel to when she was about to enter someone else's dreams.

The nurse noticed the change first, "Something's happening."

The Tweedledoctors immediately put up their masks and snapped on gloves. Morpheus ground his cane into the floor, but made no other movement. Through my mother's heightened awareness, I saw sharp lines of focused dream energy coalescing around his eyes. He was watching supernaturally.

The sharpest pain she'd felt yet was accompanied by a warm rush. "Did the table collect the amniotic fluid?" Morpheus immediately asked.

The nurse looked under the table, "Yes, Sir."

With the internal cushion gone, my mother's pain had escalated. Through sheer discipline, she held on to her meditative state. As she breathed, she was filling her pores with all of the dream energy she'd been accumulating. It was slowly balancing throughout her entire body instead of being concentrated in her hands.

Her mind was holding the image of her dream shore, not focused on it but aware of its presence, when another vibration convulsed through her body. Instead of contracting inward, it felt like her muscles were all pushing down. The feeling was a completely dichotomous combination of pain and feeling like she had to go to the bathroom

Her body wanted me out.

She wrestled to accept her body's physical demands while she maintained an awareness of the dream realm.

Another wave rolled through her body.

"She's nearly completely dilated," Tweedledipshit announced to the room.

"Follow the plan," Morpheus ordered.

Another wave. More downward convulsing. Something inside her shifted.

People in the room started moving and taking positions around her, but they no longer mattered.

They would never matter again.

All that mattered was the little boy inside her.

Her body convulsed. She pushed downward with her body and her mind. She focused all of her physical awareness and dream energy on the one point where my head would appear.

They would never matter again.

She guided the image of her dreamscape down from her mind through her core.

There was shouting outside of her body. I made out Morpheus screaming, "RIP IT OUT OF HER!"

They would never matter again.

A final contraction provided the spark that ignited all of her focus and energy. She felt a tearing in her uterus. Her corded muscles provided a conduit for her living energy. The collision of her body's stored dream energy into her bloodline's tie to the dreamscape ruptured reality itself within her birth canal.

She sacrificed her flesh to empower the binding of this world to the dream world for but a breath of a moment.

I felt an old lady's hands grab my body and rip me forever from my captor's grasp.

My mother pushed me through with a scream.

Her scream echoed across the barrier into every dimension.

Her scream was the first sound my baby ears knew.

Her scream will forever haunt my adult ears.

She screamed in my mind.

She screamed in my soul.

I joined her, screaming in my heart.

Chapter Twenty-Four
2012 – Providence, Rhode Island

"I told you not to go into that room."

I looked up into Aunt Margaret's face. Tears were streaming freely down her jowls. I was lying across the back seat of the SUV as we bounced down the road. I was still wet and smelled like pee.

"Was that?..."

"Yes, that was the room where you... where your mother had been... kept. Hush now, I'll tell you the rest later." She looked pointedly over the seat behind her.

I needed to know what happened next, but wasn't sure who was listening. I looked around. "Where are Tyler and Alan?" I asked suddenly worried.

Halldora was driving, Atli next to her. "They're with Tyler's car, calling in a hit-and-run," she said softly. "We have that old agent, Bruadair, tied up in the back behind you."

Ah. Questions would have to wait.

"My place ain't safe anymore, but I want a few things. Packed a bag when you showed up, I only need a minute to get it."

Halldora was pulling behind the diner a minute later.

Ida Lynn.

"Wait," I said. "Drive past!"

Halldora shot me a questioning look in the rearview mirror, but she steered back onto the highway.

"The woman in that diner, Ida Lynn, works for the Sandmen. If she's watching, she may report that we're on the loose."

"That saggy-titted bitch!" Margaret swore. "You just let me deal with Ida Lynn. Don't suppose you got any dream power left?"

I shook my head, "I'm sorry. I used it all to take Bruadair down."

She harrumphed, "Can't think of a better use. Atli, d'you still have that effing case that was in the back?"

He nodded, grinning slightly. He handed it over to her as Halldora was pulling into the front lot of the diner.

Holding the case like an old lady carries a purse into church, Aunt Margaret jumped out of the SUV before it was completely parked. She overplayed the doddering routine as she pushed through the diner's front door.

"I am not gonna miss this," I said as I hopped out behind her. Halldora and Atli were in agreement right behind me.

Every single person in the diner looked happy to see Aunt Margaret. And every single one of them froze in equal states of confusion and terror when she pulled the tranquilizer gun out of the case and loaded a cartridge.

"Ida Lynn, m'dear," she called a touch too sweetly. "Can you stand up so I can get a good look at you? I'd hate to have to shoot you through the bakery display. Nobody wants blood on their macaroons."

Hands above her head, Ida Lynn tried to stand with as many napkin dispensers and menus shielding her as she could. "Now Margie, you know I didn't do nothin' wrong. Them people made me…"

"Can it." The pop from the tranquilizer gun made a few people scream and everybody jump. The red flechette settled neatly into Ida Lynn's shoulder. Once people realized that nobody was going to die, a collective sigh washed over the diners.

"We're going to talk about what happens to women who hire thugs to scare me into selling my place. Everyone, your meal's on me tonight. Help yourself to drinks while we wait for the authorities to come git this woman. You two," she motioned to Atli and me, "help me take her in back and tie her up for the cops."

I was pretty sure she had made all that up on the spot for the benefit of gossipers seated in the restaurant. Far be it from me to disobey my aunt.

I had an aunt.

It was an entirely illogical moment to get hit with an emotional wave over knowing who my family was, but that never seemed to matter to emotions. Atli noticed my eyes getting a bit watery as we dragged Ida Lynn to the back, and he offered a smile of encouragement.

Halldora gave me a shove to keep me moving.

The noise in the dining room picked up as soon as the kitchen door stopped swinging.

"God bless them fuckers, I'm going to miss most everyone out there."

Aunt Margaret reached down and palmed Ida Lynn's forehead. I recognized the use of dream powers, but the way Margaret went about it was far too elusive for me to figure out what I was seeing. Seconds later she was pulling away. "I got what I need. Let's get my stuff and split."

Almost out the back door she paused, "We gonna take that big truck all the way to Canada?"

Halldora shook her head, "They've probably got it tracked somehow. We each have a car back at Tyler's house, including James's borrowed Jeep."

She put a hand on my forearm, "Be a dear and grab the Kitchenaid mixer, will you?" I nodded, and gathered up the heavy mixer and as many attachments as I could find near it. I initially went to put it in the back before I remembered Bruadair. I didn't want him turning it into a weapon. I was just setting it on the floor in the back seat when they walked around the corner of the diner. Aunt Margaret was pulling a lone wheeled suitcase. Halldora and Atli had been loaded down with what looked like random, unpacked stuff. I checked our prisoner as they crossed the lot. His breathing was shallow, wet and labored. He was alive, and I assumed the Reapers had a plan for him.

I never wanted to see him again.

TYLER'S HOUSE

My traveling gear was still packed in the Jeep. We added Aunt Margaret's pile of stuff to mine and decided she would ride with me so we could talk alone.

Halldora, Atli, Tyler, and Alan were ready in under a half hour. I wanted to ask if Outré life demanded the ability to uproot and flee quickly, but realized as I opened my mouth that it probably did. Mine certainly would for the foreseeable future. So instead of asking dumb questions, I opted for taking a shower to wash away the guard's blood and old lady pee. I asked Atli to burn my clothes.

Tyler had to leave his car behind, but he rode with Atli. I was to follow them. Halldora and Alan would drive the SUV west to a dumping point, hand Bruadair off to some names I didn't recognize, then fly ahead and meet us in Canada. Tyler made a smartass comment about warning Gestur we were coming, but Halldora shut him down with a sharp look.

When the highway had many miles behind us, I started the conversation. "Before we go into my real questions, why does Halldora hate gay guys?"

Margaret looked at me, "I suppose that's her story to share. I'm pretty sure you can figure it out."

I thought back over everything I'd witnessed. "Did Atli break up with her by coming out?"

"I'm not gonna be the one who spills those beans," she pursed her lips theatrically.

"Damn. How long had they been together?"

"They met as teenagers when some old biddy heroically managed to gather up all the local Reaper kids and hide them for a while."

"So how do I patch up my relationship with her?"

"Damned if I know. I've never made a relationship stick."

I tried to mentally imagine the many possible ways that talk with Halldora could go.

Aunt Margaret interrupted with the conversation I'd been avoiding. "You've probably got a load of actual questions for me."

"Even more now than when I first met you."

"Yep. For the record I'm still pissed that Halldora let you get anywhere near the Farm. You were supposed to be long gone by now."

"They like you too much to leave you to the Sandmen's clutches."

"She should've followed her orders."

"Things worked out."

She was quiet a moment. "They don't always."

I knew what she was referring to. "Can you tell me what happened?"

She examined my profile while I drove. "You saw it from her perspective, I should be asking you what happened."

"I… every…" I tried to order my thoughts. I could only hear her scream.

Aunt Margaret patted my shoulder, "It's ok. Give yourself time to process it. I know enough. When she created the tear between our world and the Dream, she birthed you through the rupture. In the real world she was glowing white-hot bright, blinding everyone in that room except that fucker Morpheus who wasn't watching with his physical eyes. He was wounded, though. I'd never seen him so weak. He tried to jump forward and grab you, but he fell or slipped or something. I could never quite shake the feeling that she kicked him in one final act of defiance. Anyway, I grabbed you with my dream hands before he got you and I pulled you to your mom's shore. I always liked her dream realm, it was so warm and sunny there. No matter what the world threw at her."

A moment of silence passed. The scene was still vivid in my mind, and I could see Aunt Margaret's tale unfold clearly.

"But I knew that as soon as she felt you slide from her body, she was going to explode and take them all with her. Ain't nobody's body built to force the dimensions to cross over each other like that, and she did it in her… her… you know… in her birthing parts."

I laughed a bit through new tears. Aunt Margaret normally cussed with the best of them, but hearing her stumble over anatomical names was truly endearing.

"So there you were, newborn and trapped in a dream world that was about to cease to exist. Fortunately my dream self is a helluva lot stronger than this old body. I got you up through the transition over to my dream realm fast enough." She sobbed a little, "I felt the explosion behind me. All of her memory, and dreams, and power went nova. It hurled me out of the dream world completely. I must've been knocked unconscious for a bit. When I came to, I had been blasted across my living room, landing ass over teakettle. Everything was covered in a layer of frost, and there was a screaming baby in the comfy chair where I'd been sitting."

We let a moment of silence pass between us.

"I called some people I knew who were good at this sort of thing, and I had had identity papers forged for you since you weren't born in no hospital anyway. I gave you the most popular, and therefore unnoticeable, boy names in use that year, but your mom's handle from her missions seemed like the right last name. I figured I owed her that. I then set about to get you adopted. I'm sorry that didn't work out, but the foster family seemed to take good care of you. I checked in on their dreams often to make sure they didn't mistreat you."

"I…thank you…"

"Don't thank me. If I'd been stronger or better…" her voice caught in her throat. "I can't help but think if I'd come out of hiding and stormed into the Farm like you did for me, maybe you'd have grown up with your mom."

"Maybe. I guess. But the Farm was a lot more dangerous back then than it was today. And you were doing everything she asked you to do. Plus you had a solid reason for staying hidden. And, well I'm old enough to have gotten over myself a little. At least, I stopped being mad about it all. And, I've learned that because you did as she asked I was never a lab rat. I owe you everything."

"Don't go getting all mushy. We got a long way to drive."

I chuckled at that.

"I should call my boss tomorrow."

"Don't."

"And I have friends at home who will wonder why I'm not answering my phone."

"Are they good friends?"

"The best."

"Then lie your ass off to them."

That shocked me.

"I ain't kidding. They're going to have Sandmen agents in their heads for a good long while. The best and surest way you can protect them is to give them a lie they'll believe. Just make sure that your lie also sends the Sandmen away. If they truly are the best of friends, they'll understand when you apologize later and fess up and show off your powers to prove you ain't a nutjob."

"What if I don't tell them anything about the powers?"

"You will. That's how it always goes."

I took my time digesting everything she had to tell me.

I was grateful for the long road to Canada.

Epilogue
2012 – Somewhere in Canada

"Hello again, Old Woman."

"Hello yourself, Old Man."

The younger generations had all been settled into rooms. Gestur and Margaret were seated on a porch beneath my open window. When I moved closer to listen, I saw they were watching the northern lights paint the sky. Yeah, okay. I was totally eavesdropping.

"Why did we never get married?"

Margaret snorted, "Because your brother's a creepy, lecherous old Viking and your wife would've killed me."

"They're both dead now."

"That only makes them creepier. That's also not what we should be talkin' about and you're stalling."

Gestur sighed heavily. "I'm not ready to lose people to a bloodline war."

"Well who is ever ready for any war? What a thing to say! But this one won't be fought on battlefields under the sun like the good old days. You know as well as I do that this war'll be fought in the shadows."

"And in the minds and dreams and even the graves of the Outré."

"Most likely. But it's the right thing to do. Morpheus has crossed the line."

"Yes. He has." Gestur motioned back at the house, "Does James know why Morpheus wants him?"

"Nope. Halldora thinks it's because he can use powers from both bloodlines. And I'm perfectly happy letting them all believe that."

"You know he needs to know. We need to know if he can repeat his mother's feat."

"Gestur, he has zero experience. My Janet was perhaps the most powerful and intuitive Sandman in a long time, and trying to cross a dimensional barrier ripped her apart. What do you think will happen to James if he tries?"

Icy realization shot down my spine.

Gestur brooded silently.

"Exactly," Margaret continued, "he'll die. He's the only person alive to have crossed over and back. Hell, I'd wager my feminine mystique that he's the only person to ever be born through another dimension. I don't deny that we're going to need him. But we're going to need him alive and fully trained in both bloodlines. And he's going to have to learn to work with the others."

Gestur was silent for a bit. The northern lights shifted in the sky. "You think they're ready?"

"They're gonna have to be."

Appendix

Auras

Everyone has an aura. Normal folks have weak, thin auras that are often only detectable when emotions run high. By contrast, Outré have very strong auras. Margaret, Janet, and James have the exceptionally rare ability to dampen their auras, allowing them to pass for a normal person. Margaret's the only one who can keep hers dampened while unconscious, though Janet was well on her way towards mastering that talent. James, unfortunately, has a long way to go.

Detection

In addition to seeing Auras, most Outré can see when other powers are in use nearby. Just as we normal people have varying levels of visual acuity, individual Outré vary in how sensitive they are when picking out powers.

What Are the Outré Bloodlines?

Outré bloodlines are extended families each of which is widely believed to be descended from a common ancestor.

Each bloodline is identified by its mystic tie to an aspect of reality. Because of their connection to these forces, Outré auras are significantly stronger than normal. So much so that most Outré also develop the ability to see auras in order to recognize one another. Most Outré practice their powers as extensions of their auras, trained to use the aura as the storage space for their particular flavor of energy.

KNOWN BLOODLINES

These are the bloodlines James met or learned about in his early adventure. Have no doubt he will meet others.

- **Sandmen, children of the dream:** Tied to the mystic powers of dreams, Sandmen are primarily a mental bloodline with very little physical power. Sandmen who develop powers start with the ability to observe the dreams of someone sleeping near them. As they explore that further, they learn to force dream-like hallucinations upon waking individuals. A very strong-willed Sandman can force a waking individual to fall asleep, but that's generally the only physical power a Sandman can develop. Unlike most bloodlines who remain fractured, the Sandmen were able to find each other through a shared dream realm. This allowed them to come together in the late 1960s organizing into an Agency-like structure and secretly selling their espionage services.

- **Oracles, children of insight:** Another bloodline renown for mental powers, Oracles have visions. Some are more adept at seeing the present at far distances, others can at predicting the future or read the past of an object. Oracles are by far the most perceptive when it comes to detecting nearby Outré abilities in use.

- **Temptresses, children of emotion:** An unfortunate moniker they cannot shake, Temptresses bridge the gap between mental and physical abilities. They have the ability to enhance and manipulate emotions at close range, but it always seems tied to their target's bodily reactions. Most Temptresses are strongest with one emotion over all others, and in certain regions they may be known exclusively for that emotion. Wrath and Lust vie for the most common. Males are called Tempters.

- **Reapers, children of death:** Tied to the powers of death, a Reaper's first ability flares to life when someone nearby dies. If the young Reaper is fairly strong, he or she may see death creep up on the person before it happens. Even if they cannot presage the death, the core Reaper ability allows them to see the spirit of the deceased separate from the body. Some Reapers choose to help the spirit pass on, others may be paralyzed by fear or dread, still others may try to assert command over the spirit. Regardless, they cannot deny what they've seen. Aside from the ability to see death, most of the rest of a Reaper's powers will be very physical. Because death carries so many negative connotations, Reapers are a very fractured and secretive bloodline. The way they develop and use their powers remains highly regional.

- **Sirens, children of music:** One of the most physical bloodlines, Sirens are all very musical. They are the only bloodline with individuals who might not "see" auras, instead hearing short informative medleys for people they meet. Young Sirens usually realize they're different when their body generates a destructive noise in defense against some threat. For some, it's a concussive drumbeat. For others, it's an ear-shattering screech. Sirens tend to develop either fine control, such as the ability to whistle a seven-part symphony or throw their voice across the room, or they develop raw, cacophonous blasts of powerful sound. The elders who can do both are old and dangerous, able to enrapture and mesmerize audiences while literally bringing down the building around them.

- **Myrmidons, children of battle:** Last of the major bloodlines, the Myrmidons are entirely physical. Theirs are the powers of combat. Each starts with uncanny battle reflexes, but it quickly grows into supernatural mastery of one aspect of combat. Some become blademasters, others gunslinging legends. The rarest are those who master strategy and wield battalions and armies with godlike precision.

A NOTE ON OUTRÉ POWERS -OR- WHY DON'T ALL SANDMEN HAVE THE SAME POWERS

Think about guitar players. Sure, really good guitarists are probably gifted with some natural talent that's just in their blood, but most of it comes down to training. A cowboy who picks up an acoustic guitar and is trained as a country musician is a very different artist than a band leader with an electric guitar trained as a rock-n-roll player. They are vastly different guitar players, but they're still lumped together under the aegis of "guitar."

How does this relate to the Outré?

Historically, people lived close together and learned from each other. It makes a lot of sense that Reapers in the Carpathian region, possibly even living under Prince Vlad Tepes himself, might have all learned the same blood-based death powers thanks to their shared cultural heritage. They might even consider themselves a whole separate bloodline. They are going to be very different from the Reapers of Egypt, who in turn are vastly different from the Valkyrie of the north.

In this current generation where information is suddenly so accessible, Outré powers are starting to diversify widely based on desires, wishes, training, and changing global identities. Having more access to information previous generations could not have ever imagined has given young Outré innumerable ideas for developing their powers.

ACKNOWLEDGMENTS

Wow. We made a novel! To quote my great-grandmother, "How d'ya like them apples?"

It's not that I didn't believe this novel could happen. I just owe a great debt of thanks (and cookies) to an awful lot of people. If I forget anyone, please accept it as the error of a chaotic mind and not an intentional slight. Here goes.

Bonnie, Leigh, Katie, Derrick and Roger. Tony, Nick, Akira, Ryan and Lisa. Rebecca, Josh, Dan, Kyle, Kurt, and Akira. Becky, J-Fo, Matty P, Navik and Dan. Bryan, Grant, Ed, Chris and Ross. Hayden (virtually). I've rolled dice with each of you, and in turn you've each played a role in helping me level up as a storyteller.

My four amazing beta readers. None of you asked for credit, and each of you deserves it in spades.

Diane, Elizabeth, Colleen, Halley, Carrie, Ted and everyone on the Fourth Floor. Thank you for the support and encouragement I needed while I learned how books actually came together.

Cloo. Your artwork is amazing. I'm so proud to display it on this novel.

Jane. Your support, wisdom, guidance, knowledge and friendship were integral to this story. I hope I've gotten it right.

Lexi. There's so much to thank you for. Meow, Miss Kitty!

Mom, Dad, Matt, Josh & Keenan. Thank you for always making me feel loved no matter what has happened. And thank you for encouraging me to chase my dreams.

FROM THE AUTHOR

What do I want to say in my first letter to you?

"Support your favorite artists?" You already know how important that is. In these days of MORE and FASTER, the craftsman is devalued by the very people who desire his/her art. But I'm preaching to the choir.

"Be nice to one another?" Again, you know that's important as well. Sure, the world knocks us around and tramples over us and sometimes we forget... but only momentarily. And then we try to do better. I love us when we're doing better.

"Go to my website for more?" I'd be a fool of an author if I didn't offer you a treat as my way of saying thanks. So I'm honored to share a few more. Check http://www.vancebastian.com/outre-tales/ if you'd like to read a few stories about some of the characters who've helped James along his way. I'm not going to put that web address in my site's navigation, so it's our secret.

"Thank you?" YES! That's what I want to say in my first letter to you. Your support will allow me to keep writing for you, and I'm grateful.

From the bottom of my heart, thank you.

-     Vance Bastian

CPSIA information can be obtained at www.ICGtesting.com
Printed in the USA
BVOW04*2303210416

445086BV00037B/205/P